THE TIME TRAIN

THE TIME TRAIN

ERIC M.
BOSARGE

Medallion Press, Inc.
Printed in USA

Published 2016 by Medallion Press, Inc.,
4222 Meridian Pkwy, Suite 110, Aurora, IL 60504

Cover design by Arturo Delgado

Cataloging-in-Publication Data is on file with the Library of Congress

Typeset in Adobe Garamond Pro
Printed in the United States of America
ISBN # 978-1-94254611-5

10 9 8 7 6 5 4 3 2 1
First Edition

For Megan

The past is never dead. It's not even past.

William Faulkner,
Requiem for a Nun

Chapter 1

Amos

I couldn't outrun the shadow of Christ no matter how many trains I jumped on. I baptized myself in the wind of freedom every ride, holding my arms up like a saint atop the car, but he was everywhere I looked, everywhere I stopped, condemning me.

In the jungles, what they call *tent cities* made in copses a mile or so from any train station, someone would always mutter a prayer of thanks for beans or the chicken they stole from the local farmer, or beg forgiveness for having stolen it. Every town had a church, every street corner a preacher talking about the wiles of the devil. It got so that even I thought I knew what evil was.

Back home, Christ had been nailed to the wall: my father's crowning achievement. Some kind of artist, Ma said he was, creating the Lord out of soft pine like that, even taking the consideration to carve the folds of his loincloth. They pinned him to the plaster behind the radio, and he sat there, his idiot-crude face listening to every word and every song, and when we were at church, I could picture his little wooden body jumping and twitching every time Reverend Simmons pounded his fist off the pulpit or shook the Bible above his head, threatening brimstone.

It wasn't the only one my father carved. There was plenty of firewood. Before long, there was one hanging in every window, and when we bowed our heads to pray in the evening, the sun cast the long shadow of the crucifix across the table, blessing what little we had. Tough to live like that, in someone else's shadow, never able to be proud of what you did, or take responsibility for nothing. The cow had a new calf, it was because of Him; we had a good crop, it was because of Him; and when the bad stuff happened—like the time I had to stay home from school because Minnie bucked and my father fell off, hurting his shoulder so bad he couldn't lift it to plow, or when a storm came through and ripped half the shingles off the house—it was all because Jesus willed it and worked in mysterious ways. It didn't make any difference what anyone did because they felt like it; it was either divine inspiration or the devil made him do it.

I didn't want to live like that. I wanted to make my own choices and be responsible for what I did. I took the carving from above the radio and dropped it into the stove, just when there weren't any more flames but still a decent bed of coal, so that when he burned up, if there weren't any wind in the flue and if Ma were real keen when she opened the stove to stoke it, she'd look in and see the stillborn Christ turned to a pillar of ash, thin as a Bible page and twice as fragile. I don't know if they saw it or not, but I knew when I jumped my first train that I couldn't go back home.

The rush of it was something I didn't expect, seeing the countryside move past at a rate your mind could hardly keep up with. The stack of smoke pouring out of the engine was thick and dark and snakelike. I thought of the fire and the coal shovel and thc ashen Jesus I left behind and thought, This machine might carry me straight to hell.

When I arrived in New York City, I knew if there was a hell, I might have found it. Dirty and noisy; people moving everywhere; the air was filled with the sounds of people trying to sell newspapers, clanging carriage bells, the clomping of hooves, motorcars passing, dogs barking, and the constant hum of conversation. It all made my head feel like I'd been kicked by a mule.

It wasn't like the other stops, the ones in the country, where everyone who'd hopped a train would jump off as it crawled into the station, walk into a shanty, share what they had, and talk about which cities might have work and how much money they needed to earn before they could return home. If they were going to return home at all.

After stealing a few apples and failing to get a job shining boots, I decided it was time to leave, but I barely knew how. The tracks at the station were a tangled mess, rail ties all woven like a basket, bulls roaming in tight-fitting uniforms. They weren't like other bulls I'd seen, a pocket watch hanging from a sweat-stained shirt and leather vest, the worry lines of a father etched into their faces. These were young men, hard and clearly well fed, wearing blue uniforms. They carried batons and chased after even the oldest men trying to hop a train.

I jumped on the first one I could find leaving the station, but I could tell by the speed and direction that it wasn't going to leave the city, only go to a different station. Before long we were crawling over a long bridge and heading to what looked like more of New York.

Sitting inside the open boxcar on hay and what was probably goat shit on the floor was the first time I wanted to return home; the first time I thought that maybe I'd made a mistake. I started thinking about my future, or what there was left of it. I didn't want to work inside a factory with one of those long, black snake spires of smoke rising into the air. I didn't want to be a farmer, like my father, always depending on providence and hoping for something to work out.

I heard a voice comment on my shoes, and I faced the shadows. I'd thought I was alone.

A Negro leaned forward and smiled. He was missing a front tooth, and his upper lip was twisted on one side and a little bloody, like someone had just roughed him up good. "I said, nice shoes."

I didn't say anything for a moment, remembering

all the nasty things my father had said about Negroes, even though he never had any dealings with them beyond harvest time when he was selling the crop, and then he complained about everyone short-shifting him, so I figured they were no worse than anyone else. I hadn't met a bad person on a train yet. They were all together like in the same car, usually all looking for work, and didn't nobody need to be beat down more than they already was.

He took out a small red bottle of something, removed the cork, and gingerly took a sip. He offered it to me. "Sharing is fair," he said.

I took a sip. I shouldn't have. It wasn't shine. It was something else, the thickness of molasses with the bitterness of blood. It didn't burn on the way down so much as make my throat turn cold.

I gave the bottle back and looked at his shoes. The toe was blown out of one and had a floppy sole great for tripping. "Yours ain't so nice." I backed away from the door. The train was over the bridge. Brick buildings rushed by even though we weren't traveling very fast.

"Well, how 'bout a trade?" the Negro said.

"No, thanks."

He reached into his pocket, took out a knife in a leather sheath, set it on the floor of the car next to him, and patted it gently to make sure I seen it, then opened his palm to me. "How 'bout this ticket? It's good for a first-class ride. I got it off one of them *gentlemen* with a stovepipe hat and them spat-on shoes. Says it's good for today, Brooklyn station. That's where we're headed."

"You can't read." I could hardly read and didn't see why he should be any different.

"Sure can. Look." He held it out to me. It looked like a ticket. Had large, block letters and numbers printed on it. I'd never seen one before.

"Where's it going?" I said, even though I meant to say that I didn't have a ticket for this train. That you didn't need a ticket to move from one station to the next, so long as you was clever, but that wasn't what came out.

"Does it matter?"

I wanted to ask him about his face but didn't want to be rude. The car was small enough.

The smell of baking bread rushed into the car, leaving an empty hole in my stomach. I thought I was hungry back on the farm, but you don't really know hunger until you wonder when your next meal will be.

"It's a passenger train," he said. "Inside they feed ya. From one stop to the next. It's all you can eat."

"How come you don't want it?"

"Look at my skin." He touched his shoulders as if it was something he could pull off. "It look like they'll let me on a white car?"

I leaned my head back and looked out the door. The car was slowing down, buildings moving by at a horse's trot. Carriages with drivers in suits waited for the train to pass across a road behind a motorcar, the driver wearing round goggles. The scene slowed down, then my eyes couldn't keep up with it. I wondered at what was in the red bottle.

"Don't you want it?" His hand was on his knife, and he wore half a desperate smile.

"Sure, I want it. You want my shoes for it, is that it?"

"Yessir, I want the shoes. These have taken me far enough."

I stood, took the ticket slowly, then lunged for the door. You could get hurt flopping from a train, but it probably wouldn't be as ugly as getting stabbed inside one.

He was on me quick, had me spun around and my face pressed to the side of the car with his blade prickling my back before I could do anything. The darkness of the car spun to keep up.

"You wasn't thinking of skinning old Charlie, was you?" He took the ticket from my hand and kicked me in the back of my knees so I went down. "Shoes. Now."

The brakes squealed and the whistle blew. I figured I might be able to get out of the car but not while he was standing in the doorway. It felt like I'd been hit on the head, like either I or the world was about to fall over.

I started to unlace my shoes.

"Dishonest," he said, the knife low next to his side.

"I'll be honest that I'm keeping the laces," I said.

He laughed and kicked his way out of his shoes. "Fair is fair, and I guess that's fair enough."

I didn't have any choice to put them on. They weren't like any shoes I'd seen before. They were made out of a soft, spongy material and cheap, thin leather. They were too big, and I could feel where the pads of his feet wore into the soles. I slid mine toward him, careful to make sure they stopped before the door. I didn't want to get stabbed.

I put the laces through the first two holes and then looped them around the toe, keeping the sole up because I didn't want to trip when catching the next train and land headfirst on the tracks. I thought: He may have just killed me even without using the knife. It's a good thing I kept the laces or they'd never fit.

"That's pretty clever," he said, pointing at the laces as he twisted his ankle back and forth, trying to force his feet into my shoes. Brick buildings slid by behind him. The light spilling in made him look even darker than he was.

"You gonna keep the ticket, too?"

He put the second shoe on as the train braked hard. He had to take a step to the side to keep from falling. He put the knife away. "I may deal with dishonest people, but I'm no cheat." He held out the ticket to me.

I reached for it, and he let it go. It caught the air and was out of the car in seconds.

"Best go get it," he said.

And I did, right after I punched where he was missing a tooth. He grabbed for me as he stumbled back. I stuck my foot behind his ankle and pushed.

He stumbled, arms pinwheeling, and caught the door handle. A train roared past behind him, flashing so bright I squinted and held my arm up to shield my face from the fury. Something pulled at Charlie's feet, lifted them up like they was tugging on him, and he screamed as his body stretched like a candle flame straight out behind him, then his lower half disappeared. He shot into the car and rolled onto his back, his legs and hips gone. I knelt next to him and held his hand. The blood didn't flow from him so much as it rose out of the floor. His eyes found me. I'm certain I was the last thing he saw.

I felt bad for going through his pockets but knew he'd have done the same to me.

I jumped out of the car, rolled onto my side, and scrambled between the tracks as another train, not as loud or fast as the one that got Charlie, plunged past. I looked down and there was the ticket, sitting on the edge of a puddle, the water holding it for me. I picked it up and left a thumbprint of blood on its face. I shoved the ticket in my pocket and rinsed my hands in the puddle. I looked up when the train passed.

I was right in front of the platform, muddy water dripping from my hands. I thought of a baptism in a mudhole I'd once seen where the man in the white robe came up dirtier than he went in, and I almost threw up. People stared down at me. I felt like they'd seen me through the cracks in the cars, pushing Charlie out of the car.

A few of the people on the platform laughed at me; others turned away in disgust. That's when I knew they hadn't seen a thing.

A bull started to yell. I scurried down the track toward

the far end of the platform, hoisted myself up, and came face-to-face with the prettiest girl I'd ever seen. She had hair black as coal and just as shiny, a smile white as piano keys, and her features were delicate as silence.

I felt my face turn red, so I looked down and noticed she clasped a ticket like mine in her gloved hand.

"You'll be on the train," I said.

She opened her mouth to say something but managed only a gasp as I was jerked off my feet.

The bulls took me to an office at one side of the long building behind the platform and I shuffled in, my feet feeling like they were stuffed full of lead.

The men searched me and found my father's silver pocket watch, the matches and twine I used to start fires, a drawing of my mother one of her friends had done—it was nice but didn't look much like her—and Charlie's red stuff and his knife. They didn't feel the paper ticket flat in my back pocket.

A man with a black mustache and all the stiffness of someone in charge sat down in a wooden chair in front of the small desk facing me. He unclasped the gold buttons of his jacket, spread it to either side of his waist, and set his hat on his knee. Two of his cronies stood to either side of me, their hands on my shoulders. One of them had long, girlish nails.

"You're too young to be a hobo," the man in the chair said, his voice surprisingly girlish.

I didn't say anything.

He sniffled hard and picked up the red bottle off the desk. “Smallest bottle of shine I’ve ever seen.”

The men behind him chuckled. They didn’t sound like girls.

“It ain’t shine,” I said.

He clasped it in his hand, and it nearly disappeared. His hands were big, soft. Like he’d never really worked. “Well, what is it?”

“Don’t know. Makes things different, though.”

“Different how?” he said, almost snarling.

I looked at the ceiling for a moment. There was half a footprint along one of the boards. It took me a moment of puzzling to realize the board was probably walked on before it was ever nailed to the roof.

He asked the question again.

“Can’t rightly say.” I knew I should be worried they were going to hurt me. I wasn’t. “Are you fellas going to rough me up or cut me loose?”

The man in charge unstoppered the bottle. “Depends. Got anything else of value hidden on that skinny frame of yours?” He took a sniff, and his eyes got real wide before he blinked. “What is this stuff?”

I cranked my head to the side and bit down on one of his men’s knuckles, taking a chunk out. I stood and kicked the chair into the other man’s knees and stole his baton as he went down, cracked him on the back of the head, wheeled, and grabbed the knife off the desk. The man in charge had eyes wide as Jesus’s when he’s appalled at a sinner, and I knew then that all I had in mind about the train being a machine of the devil and carrying me straight to hell was probably true and there was no use trying to fight it. What happened to Charlie didn't make sense, but murder never did.

I hit his wrist with the baton, and he dropped the red bottle into my hand. The other man, whose hand I bit, was backed into a corner. I wondered if I looked as different as I felt, if skinny old me had changed somehow and people just sensed I was dangerous, like a hound knows a wolf is nearby in the woods. A boy with a stick and knife wasn't scary. Or was I?

I stoppered the bottle as I stepped outside and stuffed it into my pocket. I plunged into the crowd, knowing that if I could get low, I could get away; and if a train passed, they'd stop looking for me altogether.

People cleared out of my way. I reckoned it was because they were all well dressed and smelled good. I had the stink of a cattle car on me, and it had been several days since I'd looked at water, let alone bathed.

After pushing through the crowd for a few moments, I ran out of people and stopped at the edge of the platform. The girl with the black hair was up the platform apiece and staring at me, smiling almost.

I winked at her. She broke into a full smile. Behind her, I could hear the bulls I roughed up shouting. People struggled to get out of their way. It didn't make any sense what happened next. One moment there was the sound of a rushing train and flashing like the center of a lightning storm, just as it had on the car with Charlie; then there was a train car in the station, all silver with clear glass windows and electricity snapping from wires on top like I'd seen the time I snuck into a circus. I thought it was just the red stuff, but everyone on the platform gasped and tripped over each other, trying to get away. Everyone except the black-haired girl. She covered her mouth as a door slid open like a fish gill and a fat man with round goggles stepped out very slowly toward her. I could tell she was too afraid to move, that everyone was.

"Rosaline!" a woman called.

It was too late. The fat man grabbed the girl's arm and yanked her back into the train. The door slid closed, and the train started to pull away from the station.

I was moving before I made the decision to take a step. Had I stopped to think about it, I probably wouldn't have moved at all, or I'd have turned and walked the other way, using the distraction to disappear. Instead, I ran toward the train, jumped off the platform, and landed on the rounded lip of its bumper.

People on the platform pointed at me. The woman who'd shouted, Rosaline's mother, had some strange kind of mixture of emotion reserved for wonder filling her eyes.

The train had a full head of steam in seconds, and it was a good thing I was holding onto the front of it because I would've fallen off the back, and it would have been a sight worse than when I'd fled from Charlie's funeral car.

If I hadn't tied the toes of my shoes up like I had, there was no way I'd have been able to keep my footing, either. The rounded toes clung to the bumper.

I looked ahead and will admit what I saw turned me yellow. A train with its cattle pusher was headed straight for us. I thought about jumping, but we were already on the bridge and I would have been filleted by the iron girders, so I clung all the tighter and shut my eyes. A fierce clap of thunder turned me deaf. I saw the red flashing of daylight behind my closed eyes. I didn't open them. I was too scared to face it. If I had, I'm sure I would've known what hell looked like.

After what seemed like hours, the sound stopped and the light returned. I opened my eyes and found the engine rushing through a meadow, a bowl of green bordered by mountains with long blades of grass bending in waves like the sea. The sun was bright, and after squinting at it for a moment, I realized how goddamn beautiful it was. If there was a paradise, this was it, and I didn't deserve to be there. If I'd died and this was heaven, I didn't expect to stay there very long. As if in answer, my hand slipped; if I hadn't been quick, I would have been plowed six feet under. The train was mirror slick. I'd never seen metal so shiny. Not even in church.

The train stopped and let out a long bellow. I jumped off, not sure which side of the train to hide on. If it hadn't been for the wide-open meadow, I would've run for the first cover I seen. I completely forgot there was a reason

I jumped on the train, even if it wasn't a good one. I hid beside the wheels, which were grimy and didn't have the long drive rod on the outside like most steam engines.

The mountains had to be miles away. Anyone on those ridges would've been able to see the train stopped and easy pickings for bandits. I couldn't imagine why they stopped here.

The door slid open, and I crouched low enough to still see who spilled out. It was the fat man, the one who'd grabbed Rosaline. Little metal steps unfolded from the undercarriage of the train and nearly touched the ground under the fat man's full weight. The train rocked on its springs when his bulk was on solid ground. He was of unfortunate geometry, as my father would say about any fat pompous person, made out of a series of triangles. He had a beard on his chin like a billy goat's and a cone of curly, wiry graying hair on his head. His driving glasses looked twice too big for his face. He turned around in the meadow, raised his arms in a stretch—he carried a crooked brass staff in one hand—turned around and laughed. I crouched lower. If it weren't for the tall grass, he would have seen me.

Rosaline popped out of the train as if pushed and fell wrist-deep in her petticoats onto her hands and knees.

A Negro came out of the train next. He extended a hand to Rosaline, and she spat on it.

He slapped her hard across the face, and the fat man didn't even hit him with the staff. I never saw a darkie treat a white woman that way, and there was no hell below or above that would make me allow it. I got to my feet but was stopped short by a better look at the Negro.

It was Charlie. His face wasn't messed up, and I'd have bet he still had his tooth, but it was him all right. There was no mistake.

"Well, hello there, young man," the fat man called out. I couldn't get over how big his fish eyes looked in those goggles of his. I'd heard some people call eyeglasses cheaters. If that's what they were, this man was seriously breaking the rules of the game.

"Charlie, retrieve him," the fat man muttered.

Maybe I was still under the influence of the red stuff, but Charlie was just as fast as he had been. He sprinted after me and halved the distance before I could even slip on the crushed stone near the tracks. He grabbed me by the scruff of the neck and my pants so that only my toes dragged on the way back to the fat man. It pinched my nuts, and the seams of my shirt ripped and snapped like a fire. He dropped me right next to Rosaline, and I couldn't meet her eyes.

I was hotter than a cat that Charlie had touched me, beat me again, and even worse, in front of Rosaline.

"Tell me, boy, how did you arrive at this particular junction?" the fat man said.

I didn't say anything. Doing nothing earned me a whack from Charlie so hard in my lower back that I dropped to my knees and gasped like a fish.

"Let's be polite, Charles," the fat man said. "Perhaps he's hard of hearing or slow to think up an answer. We can't go being uncivilized. That is, after all, what led us to such unfortunate times."

Charlie stood back. The man in the goggles eyed me. There was no confusing if he was looking at you. In those ridiculous goggles, his eyes were as big and round as a cow's and twice as dumb. If it weren't for the way he spoke and the fact that it was his train—if that's what it was—I would have guessed he was the dumbest person I'd ever laid eyes on.

"So," the fat man said, "how did you come to be here?"

I still didn't say anything. My head was spinning. Moments ago I was on a train with Charlie, watching his life spill into the floor.

"You're from the station," Rosaline said, sitting up and clasping her hands at me as if praying. "Help me," she whispered.

The fat man laughed. "Clearly *that's* going to happen." He leaned to one side, and his staff clicked and dripped like a candle toward the ground. Its head became flat and fanned out into a snail-shell wheel as it grew three legs to become a stool.

The fat man crossed his arms over his belly and sat on the stool as Rosaline and I looked on in utter disbelief.

"Perhaps we should start again," the fat man said. "I'm Sir Reginald of Raleigh, descendant of President Walter Hindsley and currently the only emissary to *The*

Kind. Please, sit and introduce yourselves."

Rosaline huffed. Despite the trick stool, she wasn't impressed. She straightened her skirts and sat, then motioned for me to do the same. I could tell whatever she asked me to do, I was going to do it.

I got to a sitting position, wasn't comfortable. There was no way to sit on the ground that allowed you to be ready for a fight.

Charles sat near the fat man like a dog, and I relaxed until I saw the handle of his knife poking out of his back pocket. I felt for his knife, where I'd tucked it into my pants at the small of my back. It was still there. I wanted to compare the two to see if they were the same but didn't want to show my hand. I wondered again about how he could be here, alive, and blamed it on whatever drug he'd given me. There was no other way. Then again, with staffs that turned into stools, it could have been some kind of elaborate theater.

"Now please," Reginald said, acknowledging my stare at Charlie. "Whatever preconceived notions you hold about African Americans have long been dispelled. Relieve yourself of them this instant."

"What?" I said.

Charles leaned forward. "I'm not dumb." His voice was different. There was no country to it, just a queer accent that smoothed out the words and made him sound like he should be wearing spectacles, nice clothes, and have his chin tilted back in an uppity way.

"There," Reginald said, "now that's out the way, let's have a moment to talk. Introduce yourself, please."

I wanted to lie but didn't see the sense in it. "My name is Amos. I'm not sure how I got here. I tripped in front of your train and held on."

Reginald leaned forward onto his haunches. "Held onto the outside?"

"That's impossible," Charles said.

"Nothing's impossible," Reginald muttered. "There are simply things that haven't been proven yet."

"While we're all being polite," Rosaline said, shifting enough so that her petticoats rustled and you couldn't help but pay attention to her, "would you mind telling me what I'm doing here?"

Reginald turned to Rosaline, and his magnified eyes blinked to show he'd forgotten about her. I couldn't believe he sounded so smart with those damn eyes of his. All I could think was cow.

"Your great-great-great-grandchild was the cause of all this." He waved a ham-hock arm at the countryside.

"My—?" Rosaline stammered. "I'm not even . . ."

"Are we just going to look at them?" Charles asked the fat man.

Reginald took a deep breath and sighed, seeming to sink into his fat rolls like risen dough that's been punched. "No, there should have been changes by now, so we've either failed now or in the future." His gaze roamed over the pasture.

"I'm not even married," Rosaline said.

Reginald tsked and shook his head, the folds of his neck moving like a gullet. "It's always so sad to meet someone like you, eyes blinded to the future."

"I suppose I'll need some of this," Charles said. He stood, unfolding his long, lean frame. He reached into his pocket and produced the small red bottle. He unstoppered it and tipped it up. I could see the outline of the same bottle there in my pants. I knew it was there, had to reach for it so I could feel it, and took it out so I could believe it.

I held the bottle before my face, and as he drank, the level of the bloodred liquid lowered as if he was draining it out of my hand.

"Charles," Reginald said, slapping Charlie on the thigh.

Charlie stopped drinking and the level steadied.

"I think we have a problem," Reginald said, pointing at the bottle in my hand.

"Get in the train," I whispered, and thankfully Rosaline was quicker than I hoped she'd be.

She flew up the steps. I was right behind her and got the most unsensible notion that I could smell her, some kind of flower I couldn't name. It made me want to catch her.

Charles caught me by the scruff of the neck, and rather than fight it, I stepped back on his foot and threw my head back. I connected with his face good, but it didn't stop his blade from sinking into my shoulder, which made me drop the knife I'd stolen from him. It felt like a hot brand, and the scream that came out of me was higher than the hiss and moan of a cattle brand.

Charles let go and left the blade in my shoulder.

Rosaline waved me toward the car. I tumbled toward it as Reginald shouted behind me, "Get your asses off my train!"

There was a clicking sound as I stumbled up the steps and into the train. The door slid closed behind us.

There were so many flashing lights inside that I almost heard the noise of them, yelling at me, begging me to pay attention.

"What is this place?" I said.

Charles or Reginald banged at the door. Rosaline ran to it. She flicked a lever, and a bolt threw itself across the inside of the door.

"I think it's a time machine," Rosaline said. She went to the conductor's seat and sat, fluffing her petticoats automatically. "He did something with this lever and hit a bunch of these keys." She looked at a bright, fishbowl window with words inside it.

I stood, attempting to reach toward the nearest thing to haul myself up on, and cried out in pain. The knife was still in my shoulder. My breath came in quick spurts. I'd never felt anything like that.

"I've no idea what to do with this," Rosaline said, looking down at a blackboard with a bunch of minuscule buttons on it. "Every letter and all the numbers." She shook her head.

Reginald pounded on the door. "Come on out!

There's no use trying to escape!"

I looked out the front windows of the train and saw Charlie standing there. His face was bloodied up good, and strings were floating from the toe of his shoe where I'd stepped on it.

"It was me," I said.

"What?" Rosaline said, grabbing for my hand.

There was something I was supposed to say, standing there, her touching my hand and looking up at me. I was the hero in this story, like David and Moses. I was the one who did the impossible, and somehow I'd already done it and had to make sure I did it again.

It almost made me believe in Jesus, except my head spun even more with the notion that this was all divine intervention. That me, standing there with Rosaline, this was the real kind of thing God intended, what they only grasped at when they said God willed it.

She ripped the knife out of me, and I knew it was all horseshit.

"We have to get off the train," I said, and even that didn't make sense.

Rosaline knew it. She let go of my hand and went back to the strange buttons in front of that glowing window. "Now, if I just remember what he pushed. Something up here, then here," she said, and I grabbed her.

"No," I said. I opened the red bottle and took a good draft.

As the liquid sucked all the heat out of my breath, I

thought that hell wasn't, in fact, hot. It was the coldest, numbest thing you could ever imagine. Heaven was a warm meadow with endless waves of grass and a pretty girl. Hell was that same meadow frozen over, not a single drop of water, not a single kernel of food, blue fingers and failing wits. Except all you can do is stand up to the cold. If you let it stop you, it's already won.

"We need to open the door," I said, and Reginald pounded on it as if to make it so.

"He's crazy," Rosaline said, grabbing my hand once again. "And maybe so am I."

I turned the lever with whatever courage the red stuff gave me, but I knew it wasn't courage. It was something else. It was a bottle of evil. It allowed you to do stuff, to feel less and react more, because when Charles came on board the train and dragged me off, I knew that I would see him again and that when he met me, I'd still kill him. It didn't make sense, not a bit of it made sense, but when he threw me into the grass and kicked me in the ribs I just took it, despite the fact I stupidly stuck my arm out to steady myself, and the pain made me see red and yellow dots dancing over everything.

He went to kick me again, and I grabbed his leg and stood. His other leg came out from underneath him easy enough, and I drove my elbow straight into his nuts. I straddled him, started working on his face. Something hit me hard on the back of the head.

I knew when I woke up that it was Reginald who hit

me with his staff. The smell of the meadow, sweet and pure, and the endless blue sky above me helped me forget how terrible it was.

I sat up slowly and saw the train chugging off into the distance, lightning sparkling above it like it was trying to set the meadow on fire. The car flickered a few times, then disappeared altogether.

I shook my head and laughed. It didn't make any sense, me being in a meadow alone. I thought for a moment that this was all just a dream and that I'd wake up in my bed or a jungle and it would be like a big warning, a sign I was about to make a bad decision. I actually looked around for the bearded man cloaked in white somewhere on the gray-and-white speckled peaks of the mountains, or on the back of the only cloud in the sky. He wasn't there. Tiny yellow flowers gave the green of the grass in the distance an almost shiny look. I leaned over and picked a buttercup with three golden blossoms on it. It was spring. I tried to remember what season it was and thought maybe I had just fallen off a train somewhere. I left New York and someone, maybe Charlie, had given me something that made me gassed, and I'd toppled off and landed in a soft meadow. I stood up, looked over at the tracks, saw they weren't normal. The rails were shiny, and there was hard, smooth cement underneath.

I heard the thunder and lightning, and the train reappeared, coming from the other direction, dragging the thunderstorm above it like it was in a foul mood.

There was a red smear of something on the front where I'd held on before, and I thought I figured out what kind of train killed Charlie.

It stopped in front of me, and the door slid open. Reginald spilled out, shielding his head with his hand as Rosaline whacked at him with his own staff.

"Get off me, you unreasonable woman," Reginald shouted as he tumbled out.

Rosaline was hot on his heels. She must have hit whatever mechanism turned the device into a stool, because it fairly exploded in her hands and stuck in the doorway, barring her exit. She pulled the stool back into the train, and the door slammed closed.

Reginald straightened his vest and drew a long breath. "Well, that certainly didn't go as planned."

He glanced at me. "And I suppose I won't be picking Charlie up anytime soon. What did you do with him?"

I pointed at the front of the train. "I think there's some of him on the front."

He arched an eyebrow and inhaled deeply, causing his nostrils to suck in a little bit. As he exhaled, all the stress left his body. He scratched his neck and head, causing the triangle of curly hair to wiggle back and forth. Red dots climbed his neck like a rash, and there were scratch marks where he'd repeatedly drawn his nails across the skin. "I make it a rule not to reappear in the same spot in the same time, thereby duplicating myself and the train. Perhaps that's a rule best broken in this particular instance."

The door of the train slid open. Rosaline had managed to turn the stool back into a staff and held it like a club. "I assume some of this interior is delicate," she shouted. "I'm fixing to molest it if you don't return me to my rightful place!"

Reginald laughed. "Destroying that mobile would only ensure I've achieved my purpose."

Rosaline's fingers fanned on the staff, relaxing a bit. The fire in her eyes didn't die.

I thought about her place, felt inside my pocket for the ticket. It was crumpled but still there, bloody thumbprint and all.

The door to the car slid shut. Reginald grunted. "Blast it all to hell," he said and scratched at his neck.

"What's beyond the mountains? Why do you need her grandchild?" I said.

Reginald's large eyes squinted at me for the first time. "The wasteland." He pointed at the car. "And it's her fault! Well, her grandson's fault, but nevertheless, we wouldn't be here if it weren't for her. And you."

"Me?"

"By the way, how's that shoulder?" He stuck his thumb right in the wound.

I did a fair bit more than wince in pain, and that was all I could do. Reginald was on top of me, both big hands wrapped around my neck, his weight pressing me down. We fell backward into the grass. Even if his hands weren't on my neck, I wouldn't have been able to breathe with that elephant of a man crushing me.

The blue sky was strangled by black at the edges. Swirls of dark, angry clouds spiraled about Reginald's head like some sort of celestial crown of agony, and for the second time that day, I passed out.

I woke to rain. The sky was blanketed by dark, angry clouds. At least I hadn't imagined those. Reginald was in the grass beside me, his big eyes staring unblinkingly at a blade of wet grass. A trickle of blood ran half a finger-length down his forehead. A drop of rain hit it, and the rivulet vanished into the skin.

Rosaline dropped the metal stool and helped me to my feet. She pointed to her right at a spiraling tower made of dark metal. It hadn't been there before. That didn't surprise me any more than the fact that the disc at the top was changing shape and something like a long spiral staircase was descending toward the ground.

"You know what that is?" I tried to wipe the rain off my face with the bad arm and ended up supporting it and ignoring the rain. My sleeve was soaked sticky with blood.

"No, and I don't want to find out. Come on." She led me toward the train. "I think I figured this thing out."

Inside she bolted the door and took a seat in the front, where the fishbowl windows were. My head hurt, and it was almost too bright to look at. I peered out the window at the tower. Something was moving on the spiraling staircase, tumbling over itself with long, flailing arms. I was relieved to see Reginald still in the grass, passed out.

"Must have hit him pretty hard," I said.

"Hard as I could," Rosaline said. She pecked at some of the numbers, and they appeared in the window as if she'd written them perfectly on paper.

"It's a paper window."

The corners of her lips turned up. "Why'd you jump on the train?"

I swallowed hard because my first response was to say that's what I do, jump on trains, and it was no good.

"Were you trying to save me?"

My mouth was dry. Looking at her made my whole body seem heavy and light at the same time. I managed a nod.

"Thank you." She pressed a final button. The paper window said *7 June 1933, 11:00.*

I thought about all the sadness we left behind and wondered if maybe we should go someplace else, but everything on the front wall of the train buzzed to life. Lights ignited inside every corner of every gauge. I was sure it was going to blow up, until the car began to trudge forward.

"Hold on." She took my hand as the train picked up speed.

I looked out the window. Reginald was no longer in the grass. We were moving so fast I didn't think much of it.

I kept my eyes open this time; it made me glad I had shut them before. I thought I would go crazy seeing all those lights, with more color and streaks than any sunset and far more brilliant. It was laced with lightning that flashed so brightly my head felt like a spike had been driven straight through the back of it. Then all of a sudden it stopped and we were back on regular tracks with wooden crossties and New York rising off the horizon in the distance.

Rosaline still held my hand. I rubbed the back of it with my thumb, and she smiled. She hugged me, and even though her squeeze hurt my shoulder something awful, I didn't want her to let go. She smelled like flowers after a fresh rain, and her shoulders were smooth. She fit in my arms perfectly.

"Thank you," she said.

"For what?"

"Saving me."

"But you saved me," I said and caught movement in the corner of my eye. The growing smoke plume of a charging freight train was headed straight for us, its menacing grill seeming to smile at the thought of our destruction even as the shrill whistle pierced the air in warning.

I pulled Rosaline toward the door, pushed her out first, and jumped after her. She tumbled down a dusty hill. Thankfully, it was just soft dirt. I kind of stumbled after her as the whistle of the train bore down.

She stopped behind a tree and pointed at the car.

"It's Reginald," she shouted.

I looked back in time to see the humongous shape of Reginald disappear inside the train. I couldn't picture him clinging to the front of it as it jumped through time, but I knew that's what he'd done, that he'd gotten the idea from me. I wish I'd lied then. Damn my soul, I wish I'd lied.

The car started moving away from the oncoming train almost instantly, the lightning crackling atop it. It accelerated to breakneck speed, easily outrunning the steam engine before sparkling and disappearing.

"He's gone," I said, although I had a feeling we hadn't seen the last of him.

Rosaline took my hand again and raised her voice enough to be heard over the passing steam engine. "Any idea where we are?"

We stood on the edge of a farm with a chicken coop. I didn't want to stay at another farm any more than I had in the past. There was still no going home.

I took out the ticket and showed it to her. "No, but I know where we're going."

She placed her hand on the ticket, covering it up. "My parents were sending me to my aunt's house in the country. They're broke like everyone else." She lifted her chin at the rails and the passing train. "And besides, Reginald knows where the ticket goes, and he's still out there, someplace."

"Sometime," I mumbled.

She didn't hear it over the sound of the train.

The caboose thundered by, and the following silence was so complete I could hear the throbbing in my head. In the tree above, a bird called. A curious jay looked down at us, his head cocked. I remembered something my mother said about birds: they were the eyes of God, always watching, always near. I felt maybe she was right, and for the first time I thought maybe God was pleased I knew how to hop a train. I crumpled the ticket in my hand and led Rosaline away from the tracks.

"You ever hop a train?" I said.

Chapter 2

Amos

The church was beautiful with half the roof missing, stars showing where wooden rafters once allowed the faithful to hide from God. The ominous sound of artillery cannonaded over the countryside; flowers of light flickered on the horizon. Each frosted breath hung before my face, clouding my vision. I massaged the smooth surface of the photo with my thumb, and the outline of Rosaline's face appeared with each artillery flash.

I was alone with all of this. I shouldn't have been.

They say everyone finds God on the battlefield. That's true; I had talked to him plenty with my chin in the mud, crouching in bushes, behind trees, stalking the rear of a creaky Sherman tank that had no business going up against Tigers, but I'd never prayed like I did when Lieutenant Spinelli's head erupted in a geyser of blood in the noontime sun. Fifty-caliber machine guns twisted everyone else around like puppets whose masters were having a seizure.

After that, the church just kind of drew me in. I curled up in the bottom of the rubble, in the crevices between the hunks of granite that used to be walls, and waited. In the daytime, I could move around; I could keep my head low. I wasn't going far from God at night.

In the meantime, all I had to do was sit with the memories of Rosaline and wait for the sun, shivering at the thought of the artillery shells pounding the nearby town to rubble.

"Is this where you've been hiding?" a voice called.

I didn't move. I didn't breathe. I squeezed the photograph so tight I thought my thumb would go through it.

"I can see the heat signature of your body," the voice said.

It wasn't German. It didn't make sense.

The sound of someone walking through the rubble, pebbles skittering with every step, grew closer and closer as I pretended not to be there.

"Amos, I know you're there. It's your old friend, Reginald."

The name broke whatever ice had frozen me. I stood with my gun pointed in the direction of his voice. I wasn't a great shot, but even I couldn't miss a silhouette as obese as Reginald's. The edges of his nose and most of his cheeks glowed ghastly red from light cast within his spectacles. He leaned on his cane. The outline of his waving hand flashed jerkily in the light from the artillery shells.

"Move and I'll shoot you," I said.

"Oh, I know," Reginald said. "I'd rather not be on the

other end of one of those rounds. Those guns last forever, no matter how high the body count. Quite valuable in the future, actually."

I hadn't realized it, but the face of Rosaline was pressed to the stock of the rifle. I felt her breath as she whispered in my ear, "Kill him," and my finger itched on the trigger. Then I remembered the first time we talked. *Really* talked.

I figure Rosaline fell in love with me when I asked her if she wanted to talk about it, because that was the thing; we couldn't stop talking about the first time we met Reginald. Not that first day when we walked away from the train tracks and not for years afterward. We talked about the lightning that sparkled over the train when it picked up speed, and I told her what it was like to ride on the front of it. She asked whatever possessed me to hop on, not knowing where it would go and how far and how fast it would travel. I mumbled something about wanting to see her again. She kissed me. Her lips were soft, and I wondered if she'd marry me.

When all the dream from the kiss had left her eyes, she said, "Maybe we should have kept the train."

Her words echoed in my head.

"Where is the train?" I asked Reginald.

He laughed quite loudly. I wondered if his goal was to get me killed. Everyone's head was down tonight. Laughing like that, making noise, was a great way to get shot or, worse, captured.

"On the tracks, right down there," Reginald said, pointing at the half wall of the church.

I stood on my tiptoes and couldn't see over it.

"You probably didn't hear the train because of the artillery." Reginald tapped his cane lightly, and the red light on his face dimmed. That cane was magic; I remembered that. If he lifted that cane in my direction, I'd shoot him.

Reginald tapped the cane again, and it became a stool. He sat on it, and his girth spilled over the sides.

"Why are you here?" I said.

Reginald touched his spectacles again, and a pale green light spilled onto his face that made the folds of his jowls glow emerald.

I wondered if he was an apparition, if I was already dead and he was here to take me to hell.

"If you ask me that five minutes from now, I'd say to kill you," Reginald said, shaking his head slowly. "But it turns out that was a really bad idea, so I'm not here to do anything."

It didn't make any sense.

My memory swirled with Reginald's talk about the wasteland and that thing called *The Kind* tumbling down the side of the tower, rolling over and over itself like some kind of tumbleweed from hell. There was an urgency to its movements, an animalistic hunger. I knew if Rosaline and I had stayed there long enough, it would come for me. For us.

Maybe even Reginald.

After our last encounter, Rosaline and I had settled in a place called Advance, Indiana, where I worked for a decent farmer who was a lot like my father. He didn't make me attend Sunday service, and I had Rosaline, so it was okay. We kept a carpetbag with fresh clothes, some money, and our marriage certificate under the floorboards so that we could move quickly if we had to. We didn't have to. We changed our last names when we got married. We never saw Reginald again and almost allowed ourselves to forget about him in the way that a nightmare fades after waking up. In the army, I hadn't honestly thought much about him at all. I had all I could do to keep everything in front of me, to stay alert enough to know who and when to shoot.

A white light blazed and fizzled, just on the other side of the church wall.

"Ah, right on time." Reginald rose from the stool and walked away. At the corner of the church, he looked back. "Would you like to see something you may never see again?"

I hesitated. The allure was irresistible, and I reasoned if Reginald wanted to kill me, he could probably destroy me without calling me first.

I climbed down the slope of granite, tumbling stones preceding me.

"Yes, he's here," Reginald said, touching his ear.

I stopped, raised my rifle.

Reginald waved at me to put it down. “Really, simpleton, I’d have had you dead to rights if I wanted. Put the safety on.”

I lowered the gun to my hip, kept my finger on the trigger.

Reginald waved me closer as he took off his cheaters, pulled the front of his shirt out of his pants and used it to clean the lenses. “I wanted to show you I was breaking my rules, our rules, for you.”

Beyond him sat the shiny steel engine from the distant dream that was my memory and, behind it, another one just like it.

“Two of you?” I said.

Reginald held up his hands and walked toward the second car as the door slid open. A fat man tumbled out. It was Reginald. It had to be. No one was that heavy.

“I take it this isn’t such a good plan?” said the Reginald who’d just arrived.

He peered beyond his fat self and looked at me. I waved. Even in the darkness, I could see the traces of anger etched on his face.

“We can’t kill him,” Reginald said to himself.

“Why not?”

They both gave me the same look, their magnified eyeballs glaring as if I was stupid. I wasn’t from the future, but I wasn’t entirely incompetent. I had snatched Rosaline from Reginald’s clutches once before, after all.

The first Reginald pointed at the horizon. Detonations

played on the underbellies of clouds like sunlight on the surface of a rippling brook.

"Because if we kill you, there will be no one to stop them."

"The Nazis?" I said.

"The Nazis," the first Reginald said at the same time, although with completely different intonations.

The first Reginald turned to the other. "If you thought the world was a police state before the collapse, wait till you see the future if he's dead, and that's saying nothing of *The Kind*."

Reginald's large eyes blinked slowly at the future version of himself. "The tide of fascism hangs on this man's actions?"

"Yes, well, they don't call it a Medal of Honor for nothing."

Reginald's lips folded into themselves. He pushed the tip of his crooked cane into the dirt.

"Well, it's not easy to kill a legend, is it?"

"Actually"—the first Reginald laughed—"he's incredibly easy to kill. I snuck up on him using these." He touched his spectacles. The red glow returned to his face.

"You killed me?" I said.

"With your own gun. Begged for your life, too."

I shot him. Before I even realized what I'd done, I shot Reginald in the gut. He fell to the ground, clasping his enormous midriff.

The second Reginald raised his cane, about to strike me, then stopped as a hail of gunfire erupted from the tree line.

"The train," Reginald said and ran toward his silver chassis.

The Reginald I had shot lay on the ground, reaching for his fleeing self. Germans hollered in the night as I ran back into the church and dove into the granite rubble.

Lightning flashed. The quiet mechanical sounds of Reginald's time train boiled into the atmosphere. Since the war had started, I'd missed those days when there was no Reginald and no God and no Rosaline—dare I say it—more and more. If it weren't for her, I never would have been conscripted. I never would have been fighting in the war.

If it weren't for her, I'd never receive the Medal of Honor and the flood of Germans would continue across the Atlantic.

My heart sounded like the artillery burst and beat so hard in my throat that it was hard to breathe as I peeked over the top of the granite mound. At least a dozen German soldiers stood over Reginald. One of them poked him with the barrel of a rifle, another pushed the butt of a rifle into the hole below his ribs where I'd shot him. Others were slowly approaching the time train. I heard Rosaline's voice in my head, clear as if she'd spoken: "We should have stolen it."

An officer approached the door to the train, pointing his soldiers at the interior like a hunter directing hounds.

I checked my Garand, sighted the soldier walking into the train, and fired.

The interior of the train exploded in a red haze. The lights flickered.

The officer swept his finger in my direction, and gunfire erupted. I dropped back behind the granite, scrambled alongside the wall, and found myself standing at the base of a spiral stairwell. The wall stretched on to the back of the church, which was a dead end. I cursed myself for not doing a better recon before choosing a place to hide. I should have known the church like the back of my hand. Knowing no one could sneak up on me had felt like a bonus, but in fact I'd only laid the trap.

Always have an exit, I reminded myself, and darted up the stairs. The spark of a ricochet bounced in front of me, and something hot stung my cheek.

At the top of the stairs, the bell met me with a gong. I hit the ground as more bullets bounced off its metal surface, the staccato tattoo like coins hitting a tin collection plate, only louder.

I took one of my grenades, pulled the pin, lobbed it down the stairs.

The bell chimed as the grenade exploded. A geyser of dust rose up the stairs and choked me.

Bullets continued to bounce around the bell tower. I knew the longer I stayed down, the higher the soldiers would climb on the spiral staircase.

There were too many of them, and even Reginald's words about me being a hero, about receiving the Medal of Honor, didn't matter. I was going to die there. That didn't mean I had to like it.

I got to my knees and fired twice down the stairwell, saw the muzzle flash, felt the kick of the M1. I didn't hear it. I'd spent what felt like an hour in the shallow depression of an artillery explosion a few nights before. I was glad rain had filled up the bottom of the muddy hole, because I'd added a little to it. I'd never been so scared in all my life, the explosions detonating all around me so loud I could feel the empty space within my chest, the savage beating of my heart pulsing black at the edges of my vision. Without sound, battle was nothing. Shadows fell with each squeeze of the trigger as I aimed down from the bell tower before I clicked empty.

Behind the wall of the bell tower, I took my final grenade and pulled the pin, then launched it over the edge, close as I could get it to the train. The motion somehow put me at ease, like I was back home throwing stones into the cow pond out back, trying to hit the dragonflies.

I had pretty decent aim, though. This time was no exception. The grenade landed at the side of the train, rolled underneath it. The explosion was far greater than anything I'd ever seen before.

It felt like all the air had been sucked out of the atmosphere. My stomach clenched, and I had the sensation of swaying before I even realized I'd closed my eyes.

For some reason, I crawled toward the bell and stood up inside it.

The tower swayed to one side, and I flexed my

shoulders against the pitted copper surface and pulled my knees inside.

We fell forever, that old bell and I. And then we rolled. I was tight inside it and just went along for the ride until it settled, when I fell into darkness.

"*Aufstehen*," a voice said.

I blinked, unaware that I'd been knocked unconscious.

"*Aufstehen*," came the voice again. I stretched out my legs slowly and kind of wiggled out of the bell.

A German NCO stood over me, silver *litzen* decorating his shoulders. He shoved a Mauser pistol in my face, grabbed my collar, and pulled me to my feet. I remember thinking how small the barrel of the Mauser was compared to what I'd done: three walls of the church had crumbled. I was fairly certain there weren't many Germans left alive.

"*Gehen*." He pushed me on the shoulder.

I took a few steps, then stopped. Reginald's body was slumped behind a chunk of granite. Of course he'd survive. He always would. He knew everything that was coming. I changed direction and the German yelled new orders. I didn't really care if he shot me.

I crouched beside Reginald.

"Are you really dying?" I said, helping him sit up. His arms were massive, bigger than my legs. I couldn't get him up. His head ended up resting on the back of my hand.

"Yes, I'm really dying, you buffoon. You shot me."

"What about the other you?" I said.

The German was chattering on, his anger clear though the words were unintelligible. I figured I was safe as long as I didn't look at him.

Reginald smiled. Blood stained his teeth. "I suspect he'll be changing his mind about returning. I suspect," Reginald said, and his head began to feel lighter. "You're going to like what happens next. Act. Quickly."

His skin turned white, the kind of translucence reserved for the fairest newborns, and fireflies swirled beneath his skin, deep within the soul of his eyes. I stood. The German fell silent as Reginald exploded in a thousand points of light that arced into the sky and drizzled like shooting stars.

The German muttered what could only have been prayers, and I felt the weight of my rifle strap on my shoulder, saw the grenades tugging at my chest. The bell tower cut a sudden silhouette into the sky. I knelt and spun the rifle off my shoulder.

The German officer raised the Mauser, barrel pointed at the sky in surrender, and faded from existence.

The night was hauntingly still. My heart pounded at the edges of my throat as my mind raced.

The artillery shelling had stopped and Reginald the First had obviously never been here. Or the Second. The soldiers had probably never come to investigate the light thrown into the sky by the arrival of Reginald's train, but they were probably still coming. I turned and knelt, pointing my rifle at the darkness of the tree line.

Shadows moved within.

I backed up quietly, crouched beside a hunk of granite, and prayed as phantom German soldiers emerged from the wilderness. They paid no attention to the church, moving silently past, at least twenty of them. I guessed they were all that was left of a platoon that had been fighting in the village. At the rear was the same NCO who'd coaxed me out of the bell.

I waited to exhale until the officer's back was to me. That's when I remembered Reginald's words about a Nazi world in the future if he'd killed me, and I cursed God.

Doing nothing was just like being dead. If it hadn't been for Reginald, I probably wouldn't have known what the stakes were; they were just one small platoon moving across the countryside at night.

I got to my feet and fell in line behind them, trying not to walk so quickly that the sound of my footsteps would alert them.

Light spilled over the horizon, and the stars were fading into the cool blue of morning. The platoon was marching toward American lines, probably to attack at dawn. My rifle had only five shots. Even if I did hit five of them, which I wouldn't—I'd be lucky to hit two—there were still at least fifteen left to deal with.

Then the absurdity of my position hit me: I was following, in step, a German platoon. All they had to do was look over their shoulders to see me and I'd be captured.

I slowed down, considering whether or not to run back to the church, when the officer turned and saw me.

"*Gehen*," I said, remembering the German pushing my shoulder, driving me forward, and quickly stepped up to him. He opened his mouth to say something to his troops, and I shoved the muzzle of my M1 into his mouth and grabbed his sidearm before he thought to. I spun him around by his shoulder, put my arm across his throat, holding the Mauser to his head.

"*Gehen*," I whispered.

That's when the gunfire erupted. Three German soldiers twitched midstep before falling. Others hit the ground on their own. I fell on top of the officer.

I pushed the pistol into his temple. "Surrender," I commanded. "Surrender!"

"*Wir kapitulieren*," he shouted.

"Surrender," I said again, and this time he shouted his surrender over and over until the gunfire stopped.

Hearing his order, his troops got to their feet with their hands in the air and repeated his call. Nearly all of them had heavy packs, all but two, who pointed their rifles at me.

I killed a lot of men in the war. Those two are the ones I feel the worst about. The quizzical way they looked at me and their commander didn't register until after I'd shot them and they were on the ground. I can't help but think if I'd waited two more seconds, they'd still be alive. But I'm not Reginald. I can't go back in time to change anything.

I stood over the German officer and whispered, "*Aufstehen*."

His eyes widened. He got to his feet.

I was credited with single-handedly capturing an entire platoon. It didn't hurt that the German officer, eager to save face in the prison camps, said I was like a commando, that I moved like a ghost, that he was certain they had fought one man, valiantly sneaking through the shadows, throughout the night. I've never benefited so much from another man's lie.

The story spread: *Separated private takes full platoon captive and marches them back to the line at first light.* The platoon was full of demolitions experts—the men with heavy packs—and their target had been a bridge that would have sealed off American forces, halting their advance for at least the winter. I was a hero, and it felt only a little like cheating. I kept telling myself that even if Reginald hadn't shown up and told me, I'd still be a hero, I'd still have done something, because he knew from the future that I'd done something miraculous in that church, the details of which I was sure to mention in my report, just in case something else changed. But I still hated him. It felt like he'd robbed me of something.

After that, Reginald's future began to haunt me, because even Reginald, with all his tricks, was afraid of it.

The boat ride back to the States was awful. The whole time, everyone was talking about U-boats and the violence of the Pacific theater.

I arrived at Grand Central Station, for once riding inside a passenger car rather than a stock car, and was greeted by all the swirling chaos that I remembered from the first time I met Rosaline and Reginald. I hated the city with all its foul smells, all its sounds, the constant shuffle of indifferent people.

After finding the schedule for the train to Pittsburgh, I bought a sandwich from a street-side vendor who refused my money.

"You're a hero," he said with a thick European accent.

I sat on the first park bench I found and started picking the onions out of the sandwich. It felt like years since I'd eaten fresh bread, but onions still turned my stomach.

"I killed your son," a voice said.

I picked the final onion from my sandwich and wiped my hands on the outside of my duffel bag. I didn't want to turn. I didn't want to see Reginald again.

"Several times." Reginald sat next to me. The wooden boards of the bench bent a little under his weight.

"If it makes you feel any better, I killed you, too," I said. It was a shame there were so many people around and I couldn't kill him again. I didn't know much about the future, just that my great-great-great-grandson did something he shouldn't. That was more than I should have known.

"I'm sure." Reginald laid his crooked golden cane across his lap and leaned back with a sigh. "It doesn't make a difference, I'm afraid."

I took a bite of my sandwich.

"Killing your grandson didn't work. Killing you didn't work, except maybe to relieve some tension." Reginald shook his head slowly, glancing over the busy park.

A squirrel ran out between my feet and snatched a piece of onion in his paws. I hadn't known squirrels to eat onions before.

"Cute little tree rats, aren't they?" Reginald said.

"What now?" I said.

Reginald looked at me, and one corner of his mouth perked up in a smile. "I love this decade, you know? The fifties are interminable, but this period, right now, before the end of the war when everything falls to shit internationally, it's really not quite bad."

"Are you going to continue killing my family?"

Reginald shook his head. "I don't know." He inhaled slowly and sighed. "No matter what I've done, *The Kind* still come. Quite frankly, the only place to live is here, before they arrive and sully everything. Or perhaps I should say before they come and clean up everyone who's sullied everything." He laughed at his own joke. It just made him seem more defeated, more pathetic.

"So you're simply going to live here now?"

"Oh, gracious, no. Nothing is that simple. But there are a lot of people I care about in the future. A lot of people I've lost to *The Kind* and their ilk. They really do need a place to live . . ." He turned to me, placed his fat, hairy hand on my knee the way a grandfather might.

"You know I haven't been causing you headaches for no reason, right?"

"You call murder a headache?"

"In the big scheme of things." He leaned in and whispered, "We're talking centuries, Amos. Centuries of growth and change, the likes of which you can only imagine. Humans set foot on the moon in a matter of decades."

I had to look at him to know he was serious.

"All of humanity, everything I've ever known, is gone. You can't blame me for trying to save it. I assure you, none of it was personal."

It was his fault that I hated him a little less. I hated him all the more for it. "You're a monster."

He smiled, knowing I couldn't have really meant it. I'd kill every German in the world if it meant keeping Rosaline safe.

He leaned back, blinking at the bright sun. "Things are going to change."

"How?"

"We'll be careful, but things will change. Inevitably." He used his cane to help him to his feet.

"Take care of little Walter," Reginald said. "You might start him speaking French a little sooner. It will serve him well at CERN. Give Rosaline my condolences about her father. I'll see you in a few minutes. Oh"—he snapped his fingers as if he'd forgotten something—"sometime after the war is over."

Reginald hobbled off, and I ate my sandwich. I

should have left the onions in. The meat tasted sour. I fed most of it to the squirrels. Not in a hurry to go anywhere, I listened to the sounds of the city, watched the birds moving in the trees, the people passing through the park, all with someplace to go.

I felt a tap on my shoulder and turned to find Rosaline.

I practically jumped into her arms and was pleased to find the way she smelled and tasted hadn't changed a bit.

Walter was in the carriage beside her. I scooped him into my arms. "Why are you here? How did you know I'd be back?"

I'd planned to take a train and surprise her.

"Reginald said you'd be home today."

My knees weakened. The rush of the city grew louder. "What do you mean Reginald?"

"He said he couldn't kill me. Couldn't kill you, either."

Reginald had been right. Things were going to change.

Chapter 3

Reginald

Four of us sat around the fire. Our bellies weren't full, though we'd eaten a dinner of pheasant boiled in water with canned blueberries. The berries made the meat bitter, and the bird was barely big enough for one, but it was better than nothing.

I poked a stick into the fire, and sparks drifted into the sky, mingling with the stars. We started the fire as soon as The Wedge had followed the sun below the horizon. I'd never get used to sitting around a fire each night. It made men talk. Made them say stupid things because there was nothing else to do.

"What are you going to do with your share?" Wayne said. The fire played on his face, drawing shadows behind every whisker, making him look rough as he'd like to be. Wayne used to be the kind of bouncer who wore a tuxedo. I got the impression he was more comfortable without it.

I didn't say anything. The truth was we were each richer than we'd ever been, but it wasn't like we could walk into a bank and make a deposit or stop by a dealership and drive away with a new Rolls. We couldn't even enroll at a college; there weren't any. *The Kind* had destroyed all of that.

The cash didn't even make a good pillow.

Martin was reclined, worn running shoes close enough to the fire to melt the soles, head resting on his share. He had always had the sinewy body of a runner. Now that food was scarce, his cheekbones were even more pronounced. "You're asking the wrong question, Wayne. The question is, do you think there's anyone, anywhere, that will give us anything for American greenbacks?"

"Seeds," I said, poking the fire again. "Seeds are worth more than what we have. You can't eat paper."

If we'd had the money four months before *The Kind* showed up, two months even, I could have built a fortune, could have amassed something worthwhile. Had I known they were coming, I would have placed special emphasis on resources; a hamlet in Vietnam, perhaps, or a farm in the jungles of Costa Rica where there was a triple canopy The Wedge's surveillance couldn't penetrate. There was no telling how far *The Kind's* reach had spread, but I'd lay a safe bet that the United States of America, joke that they were, had fallen.

"When there's no more food left, I'm going to take a run at them," August said. He looked ridiculous in his Russian fur hat with the flaps down over his ears. It wasn't warm by any means, even though it was May. He'd picked it up off the street in Nashua and hadn't let it go.

He knew the cold was coming. We were somewhere in New Hampshire's White Mountains, traveling toward Mount Washington. There was a communications center there, and we figured it might still be standing. When the threat was coming from above, no one would think to go up. There was a good shot that we could receive an uninterrupted signal from Europe, although the thought of climbing more than a mile straight up made my feet hurt worse than they already did. My father had been there, in the end, hiding. Even though I didn't have any desire to see him again, there was nothing to do but search for him.

"You think this is a war?" Martin said. "Everyone is excited when there's a war, like when we invaded North Korea. Everyone acts like the gunfire is no big deal, until the rockets are aimed at you." Martin shook his head with a laugh. "Just you and God and a ball of fire."

"I don't believe *The Kind* uses rockets," I said. "I believe they are far more fond of taking prisoners, actually."

And they were. I'd seen their tentacles wrap around a man's midriff so tight vomit dribbled from his mouth as he was lifted back toward the ship. All the people who disappeared had been taken inside. No one knew what *The Kind* really was—mechanical drones or flesh. I suspected they were mechanical, but who would get close enough to find out?

"Why'd you have to go and bring that up?" Wayne said, leaning forward.

"I didn't bring it up," I responded.

"Fuck you, Reggie," Wayne spat.

"I prefer Reginald and demand a certain modicum of respect."

"You and your big words," Wayne said, getting to his feet. He had a revolver at his side with two bullets in it. I was quite certain he didn't want to use either round but wouldn't hesitate to waste one on me.

"My words found three million dollars in currency," I said.

"And we used a thousand of that to start a fire."

"An offense I've always wanted to commit. Just like using it for a pillow, and I'd roll a cigar with a hundred if I had any tobacco."

"Yeah, all right, Reggie," Wayne said.

My mother demanded everyone call me Reginald, and I intended to honor her wishes, even if she had turned into a horrible woman at the end. I stood quickly, and Wayne mirrored me, the fire separating us.

"It's not time for a pissing contest," August said.

"It's precisely time for a pissing contest," I said. "We have three million, and there are four of us. I can't imagine a better time for a pissing contest."

That did it. Wayne drew the pistol, and I struck his wrist with the burning end of my stick. He pulled his hand back quickly and the gun fell into the fire.

I leapt over the fire and the gun went off as I drove Wayne to the ground, the end of the firebrand under his chin. The weight of the fall crushed his windpipe. The flicker of the fire danced in his eyes as the light of his life went out.

I didn't feel anything, and I was sorry that part of me had already died. Wayne was a muscle, a man who could move things, but muscle had counted for nothing since the arrival of *The Kind*. His mouth made him more annoying than useful and my belly would've been fuller if he hadn't been there to feed.

I felt August's and Martin's eyes on me as I dusted off my trousers. None of us were friends; we'd met on the run and had no association prior to the collapse. It was the first violence between members of our group.

"Let's none of us go pulling guns on each other again," I said.

August nodded as Martin stared at me. Martin was the one to watch, then.

I picked up the firebrand and used the tip to fish for the gun. If it had been a semiautomatic model with a clip, it would be useless. Since it was a revolver, there was a good chance it could still fire if rescued quickly.

I moved a log, saw something smooth and red glowing in the middle of the fire. "Wayne, you stupid son of a hog. What did you build this over?"

The gun went off, and we all dove to the ground.

Our faces lifted from the dirt, we all started laughing.

"Was that all he had?" Martin said.

"I believe so," I said.

August and Martin stood, peering into the fire, and I knew if I acted quickly I'd be able to kill them both. I saved the thought for later and used the tip of the firebrand to poke at the glowing red iron handle in the center of the fire.

"Is that a door of some kind?" August said.

"Water," I said. "Go get some."

I pushed the gun out of the fire with the tip of the stick and waited as August ran away, his clumsy feet breaking every stick in the forest. There was as good a chance of him falling prey to a bear as to *The Kind*. Luckily for him, we'd only camped a few hundred feet from the stream.

"I'm not afraid of you." The muscles of Martin's jaw rippled in the firelight, and his cheeks became even more hollow.

"The feeling is mutual," I said, taking off my spectacles to clean them. I'd found many times that the ability to be casually concerned with the trivial while facing great danger infuriates most men.

"But I don't want trouble," Martin said. "How can I trust you?"

"You can't. Simple as that. And you shouldn't. Not me or anyone else, unless they are as stupid as our dear friend Wayne over there, and if that's the case, I wouldn't think it too bright an idea to place my life in their hands."

Martin said nothing. I made a mental note that he either wasn't quick with words or didn't feel the need to spar verbally.

"I served—"

"I know. You were conscripted. That's why you're here, remember? I recruited you. Now please, don't act like I killed him out of anything but self-defense."

"You goaded him."

"I drew a line in the dirt."

"You implied you were going to kill him."

"And I did. But I didn't lift a hand until he raised a lethal weapon in my direction. And the implication was that his motives were suspect, not mine. We took the money because it was easy, and some people may still value the face of a dead president. Apparently, Wayne thought three-quarters of a million was worth my life. His was far less than that to me."

"You think you're pretty clever, don't you?" Martin said.

August tumbled back into camp holding a bucket. I assumed we weren't as remote as we'd once thought. We'd have to do better reconnaissance in the future before setting up camp.

"You're clever. I'm far beyond that," I said.

August dumped the water on the fire. It sizzled and released a plume of smoke and steam.

Martin and I coughed and ducked away.

"No more fighting tonight," August said. He unzipped his fly and proceeded to urinate on what was left of the coals.

"I agree," I said. "You clearly win the pissing match."

We spent the next few minutes in the dark, waiting

for the handle to cool as the moon crested the mountains in the east, chasing The Wedge. Without even a breeze to stir the leaves, the silence was almost maddening. It never ceased to amaze me how quiet the world could be without automobiles prowling the roads every second.

"What should we do with the body?" August said.

"Bury him if you want," I said.

August didn't move, so I assumed he didn't wish to dig a hole.

"We should dump him in the river," Martin said.

"How very 1900s. Wash the pollution downstream," I said.

"Anyone Christian?" August said.

The silence stretched on like the mute shadow of a cross.

"Well, I don't think he was Christian either, so he probably doesn't need a burial," August said.

"That's probably the smartest thing you've said all night," I said. "Who can I dare to touch the handle?"

August got to his knees. "I'll do it." He shimmied toward the fire pit, reached forward, and tapped the handle a few times. "It's barely warm."

"Good. Let's see if we can open it."

It wasn't nearly as hard to open as I thought it would be. A thin layer of earth had covered the door itself and kept most of the metal insulated from the fire. I half-expected there to be a 1950s bomb shelter under the door. But something about the setting, on the side of a mountain road, not in the suburbs outside of DC or behind some suburban house oozing paranoia, had me thinking it could be more.

Martin eagerly jumped in to help August with the heavy door, and I recognized another way I could kill him if I needed to. Just ask him for help. He had served, after all. Probably felt a sense of comradely duty. I had served as well—those of means had a mandate to serve as officers—but felt it in no way to my advantage to disclose my training to anyone, least of all Martin. And if they recognized me beneath my beard and the dirt, they hid it better than I could have imagined.

The door opened with a tired breath and fell heavily back on its hinges. It looked like a well. I nudged some dirt forward with my shoe, and the sound of dust showering on tin rose to our ears.

"It's like a submerged submarine," August said.

Martin didn't say anything, just stared into the hole. I could tell what he was thinking.

"Spent some time in a hole?" I said.

Martin looked up quickly as if shaken from memory. There had been bunkers in North Korea. Nothing good happened in them.

"Who is going first?" Martin said, and again my suspicions were confirmed. The heavy metal door and a light rock would quite easily trap anyone who went down there.

"August?" I said.

"I got the water," August said.

"I found it," I said, looking back at Martin.

Martin's head tipped to the side in metronomic consideration. "I'm claustrophobic."

I placed my hand on his shoulder, gave him a little squeeze. "We'll be right behind you."

He didn't say anything. At least he could hold his tongue.

Martin stretched an arm into the hole, and I had the peculiar impression he was reaching into the dark side of the moon, across continents, his hand perhaps surfacing somewhere in the middle of the Indian Ocean. I swept away the notion of the way *The Kind* traveled.

I returned Martin's smile when his wedding ring clinked against what I assumed was the top rung of a ladder. "Imagine that. A ladder," I said, dashing Martin's smile.

August held his hand as he lowered himself into the abyss. Before his head disappeared, I produced a small penlight from my pocket.

"Just now you give this to me?" Martin said.

"Just thought of it."

He flashed the penlight in my eyes on purpose. It was all I could do not to kick him down the hole.

The small circle of light crawled across the metal floor below, and Martin stepped down. "It's like aircraft steel."

Fluorescent light flickered and Martin's shoulders jumped. His hair was thinning on the top of his head.

"I guess it's safe to go down," August said.

"Someone needs to stand guard," I said.

August's mouth crinkled.

I climbed down the ladder. Martin stood before a fire door with a ten-digit security panel to the right. An antechamber, then. I inspected the interior. The construction was solid—steel, not aluminum—and they had used rivets, not bolts. No amateurs here. The floor was a metal grate, which eliminated footprints, and there was very little dust on the metal beneath, despite the grate being bolted down.

The best secrets are seldom used.

"What now?" Martin said, and I almost commended him for not pushing random buttons, which would've most likely permanently engaged the lock if it wasn't done already.

"In or out?" I said.

Martin faced me. "What?"

"The purpose of this construction. Is it to keep something in or out?"

"Out," Martin said.

"Then it must be worthwhile to enter." I motioned for Martin to step aside, which he did but not before letting loose a begrudging sigh. "I'll need the penlight back," I said as I inspected the security panel. "Do you have a knife?"

Martin reluctantly handed me a small blade.

I held the penlight in my mouth as I took the small tactical knife and slid it into the only crack between the plastic frame and the calculator-like buttons of the security panel. I lightly tapped the hilt of the blade. The plastic casing cracked.

"You seem to know what you're doing," Martin said.

"Educated guesses, I'm afraid."

I picked at the edges of the plastic, careful not to disturb the interior, until the wiring harness was exposed. All rainbow colors. I motioned for Martin to step forward and pointed at a wire. "This is green, right?"

He took a second too long to answer, and I knew he was trying to think of a way to exploit my weakness. Yes, pretend to be a tree at some point, I thought.

"It is."

"This one right here. It's green? You're positive."

"God, yes, it is."

"Good." I scratched the surface of another wire with the knife until the copper was exposed. I took the battery out of the penlight, took off my glasses, touched the positive side of the battery with one end of the frame, and placed the other on the wire. I placed the negative end of the battery against the wire, and there was a small spark.

The lights went out, and I must admit I cursed but not as loudly as Martin did.

"You all right down there?" August yelled.

I wished him quiet as I yanked out the first wire my fingers found and touched both it and the green wire to opposite sides of the battery.

The lights returned, and the mechanics of the door whirred to life like a giant clock.

I replaced my glasses and peered at the door, praying it would open onto something useful.

The door slid open. Two banks of computer screens flashed to life on either side of the room at the same time as fluorescent lights.

Useful, I thought, recognizing the excessive depth of the monitors, as they used to call them, nearly a quarter-inch thick.

Martin stepped forward. I placed a hand on his chest. "Do you hear anything?"

He listened obediently. "No."

"Then it's likely battery-powered. Keep track of where you are in case the lights die."

His gaze roamed my face. "Thanks," he said, and we stepped inside.

"What's down there? Want me to wait?" August called.

"No," I called back and told him to come down and shut the hatch gently.

Martin was looking at one of the computers. "This is ancient. I don't even recognize the operating system." He touched the screen. Predictably, nothing happened.

"Keys and mice," I said, pointing him toward the desktop in front of him.

The walls were plain except for a corkboard in the far corner. Detailed elevation maps of towns with names like Manchester were pinned to its surface, rail lines highlighted, and in the corner was a map that was far more geometric, like flow lines around an oval with various offshoots, marked with digits that resembled times and dates—no years, only days and months.

"I think we've uncovered something of great significance in the early 2000s," I said.

Martin humphed. He appeared to be confounded by a password prompt.

A door at the far end of the chamber had the kind of metal wheel usually reserved for ships. I felt a little sick at the prospect of opening it. This wasn't a secret underground lair reserved for a president; it was a command center, a backup for something that was probably quite mundane.

"Open that door," I said, pointing Martin in that direction.

"Why?"

"I opened the last one."

Martin's lips scrunched on one side, and he walked over to the door.

"I was hoping there would be some food," August said.

Martin grabbed the wheel on the door and strained against it. The muscles in his back and neck were impressive.

"Should I help him?" August said.

"Only if you wish to eat more," I said.

August helped Martin with the locking mechanism, and the wheel surrendered. A foul, steamy breath slipped through the door. August pinched his nose. "That's not edible."

I approached the open door and listened. The sound of a giant seashell met my ears. The penlight cast a feeble beam on train tracks.

"It's a subway system of sorts," I said.

August's face slackened and his mouth fell open, hurt as much as disappointed. "So all this was useless?"

"Not exactly," I said. "The ground is flat and easy to travel."

The maps on the wall made sense. With any luck, we could find a route directly to Mount Washington and travel well out of view of *The Kind* and any other bandits we may encounter over land. "And if we can find out where we are . . ." I crossed back to the corkboard.

"We won't get lost," Martin said.

I removed the map from the wall and studied it on the nearest table, with August and Martin peering over my shoulders. "Are any of you going to check what's in that locker?" I pointed across the room.

Martin turned as though he hadn't even seen the locker in his first perusal of the room. He might have been in North Korea, but he clearly wasn't fit for more than general infantry.

August went.

I placed my finger on the map. "Here. Control room twelve. Look right to you?" I turned the map toward him. It was best to make him feel included.

His gaze roamed the map. He nodded slowly. "Or this one, here," he said, pointing at four.

"These mountains are aligned much the same as the ones outside the entry hatch. Would you agree?"

Martin studied both maps.

"I got flashlights, an oxygen tank, a gas mask, and

some walkies," August said, returning to the table with all of it. "And these." He smiled as he held up some sort of snack bar.

"Check the date," I warned him.

"I have no idea," Martin said, finally.

"Well, you'll just have to trust me. Because Mount Washington was north and that's this beast on the map, here. I suggest we take this route." I traced my finger along the straightest line.

"I can't say you're wrong," Martin said.

"Also," I said, pointing at the gas mask that August set on the counter, "that says twelve."

On the center of the gas mask, *12* was written in black marker.

Martin smiled. "More than clever. What about the train lines? Didn't *The Kind* destroy the tunnels in New York?"

I remembered the plumes of choking dust and Evelyn's screams as chunks of concrete building the size of boulders fell between us. I forced the rage into my stomach, balled it up tighter so that someday it could explode.

"That was the rumor, yes," I said. "But I'm fairly certain that was less tactical decision than incidental damage."

"What if we walk for miles and then have to turn around?" August said.

"Then we turn around," Martin said.

"Yes," I said. I took off my glasses and rubbed my nose, contemplating how it was that none of us had ever heard of subterranean rail lines in New Hampshire. It seemed impractical, moving that many tons of earth for such a diluted population.

"About thirty miles," August said. "Some people could do that in a few hours."

"No one could do it in a few hours in the dark, with that air quality."

Everything had changed since *The Kind*. It used to be that you hopped on a train, went to work, went out to eat, and came home. If for some reason you were hurt or ill, you would go to the hospital or a doctor. If one of us were to break an ankle in the tunnels, it'd be far more likely a death sentence.

"I'll leave the decision to you," I said. "We'll travel far faster during the day if we don't have to remain hidden from The Wedge, but it is not without peril."

"Flashlights could die," August said.

"There could be wolves in the tunnels. Or bears," Martin said.

"Or other humans," I said.

"Well," August said, picking up the food bar and breaking the seal. He sniffed the chocolate surface and took a bite. It made my stomach rumble. "I'm all for whatever," he said while fighting caramel.

He handed each of us a bar. I ate mine greedily.

It was slower going in the tunnel than I would have liked. The rocks slid into each other and the ties constantly snagged my toes. We decided to use one flashlight at a time, but the semidark only made it worse.

Without the moon, stars, or any landmarks to gauge our progress, it was impossible to tell how far we'd gone. The utter darkness and thickness of the air made everything swirl with patterns fabricated by the mind. Slung over my shoulder, the heavy duffel bag kept slapping my legs. Eventually, I decided I'd had enough.

"Does anyone want my share?" I said, setting the bag on the ground.

A flashlight hit me in the eyes. "You don't want it?" August said.

"Not enough to carry it." I motioned toward the bag. The beam of the flashlight jumped to my knees and the bag on the ground.

"Easiest money I've ever made," August said and grabbed the bag.

"Congratulations," I said, "You're worth two million. Now you just have to live with it."

August grunted. As we kept walking, the sound of his shuffling feet became more erratic.

Best money I ever spent.

I uncharacteristically took the reins off my mind and let it wander, gnawing on the fact that we were rats on our planet. I despaired at how few generations may pass before all the progress our society had made would be for naught. *The Kind* didn't have to eradicate humanity, just break it. Take down the Internet, the wikis, and most people wouldn't know how to do anything. A life of salvage awaited us all while *The Kind* prowled above the world, using our own against us.

Lost in reverie, I bumped into Martin, who led the way.

"Did you hear something?" Martin said. His beam swept the cold, gray corridor and the ridges in the concrete grew ribbed shadows. It felt like we had taken refuge inside the skeleton of a snake.

"I didn't hear anything," August said.

The sudden stillness was broken by the sound of dripping water echoing through the recesses of the man-made cave.

Martin's flashlight clicked on, painting a circle of light on his trousers. The toes of a pair of work boots faced him.

"Jesus, why are you standing so close to me?" Martin said. The flashlight bounced up and illuminated the barrel of a rifle, inches from his nose, held by a snarling man.

"Nobody move!"

Martin stumbled back and dropped the flashlight. Pale blue LED light flooded the tunnel, myriad diodes blinding us.

"What do you want?" they demanded.

"Safe passage," I called.

Murmurs. There were more of them.

"To where?"

"We're headed to Mount Washington. To use the communications center."

Sporadic laughter, like the first sprinkle of rain, fell around us. We were quite well surrounded.

"How'd you find this place?"

My eyes adjusted and made out his ghostly pale face. He had a beard made patchy by scars. "We tripped over an escape hatch," I said. "Had I known it was the entrance to a lair, I would have left it be."

"What monitoring station was it?"

"Twelve," I said.

Someone grabbed at the bags on August's shoulder.

"Hey," August said, reaching for his millions.

They put him on the ground and jammed the barrel of a rifle on the back of his neck as they unzipped the bag.

Martin put his bag on the ground without prompting.

The money looked almost blue in the LED light.

"Turn around. Walk."

With their lights behind us, we went back the way we'd come. It was peaceful; the going was easier with more flashlights illuminating the path. Knowing that we weren't accidentally going to get stuck down there was actually a great relief.

"My name is Reginald," I said to no one in particular.

"We heard that," someone replied.

"Not in the mood for talking?" I said.

"There will be time for that."

Ah, I thought, no one here is the leader.

"You can have the money. You don't need to kill us," Martin said.

I laughed a little at that.

"What are you going to do with us?" August said.

No one answered August's stupid question, and in the darkness my mind had time to drift back to all the times I drove the Cadillac through the tunnels, carting the carcass of some poor has-been behind me and watching people on the street and in other cars going their ways, doing their simple things, worried about who liked whom, when it was all very fleeting.

I used to think that someone should teach them all a lesson, and now that something had, I was all the more unhappy for it, still in the tunnels, surrounded by more has-beens—only they were still kicking. I was told once that the best medicine for depression is to delight in other people. I thought it trite but sapient at the same time. It was a shame there were so few delightful people in the world.

I found myself missing the most curious of things—like rain tapping the windshield at a red light, the water splitting colors before being wiped away by the blade, the interior glow of the cabin at night, the steady illumination of the alarm clock in the darkened bedroom, the syncopated rhythm of Evelyn's breathing marking the passing of hours, the insubstantial feel of a strand of hair as I brushed it away from her face.

I forced my mind to focus. I counted six people. Outnumbered two to one. It was a little insulting.

As they marched us up concrete stairs onto a small platform, something else occurred to me I was ashamed to admit; there was only one set of tracks. There was no return, and despite what my legs were telling me was an hour's worth of walking, we hadn't passed a single station. We'd been traversing a circle. The maps, they were either plans or completely unfounded in reality.

The man with the patchy beard marched us up a few steps and stopped before a door built like a hatch on a submarine, which belied the expansive cavern it opened to. There wasn't much left of the world, and in my mind eternal flames towered into the sky over the major cities. The interior of the cavernous space reminded me of the greatness of what had once been. Nearly as long as a football stadium—and the ceiling just as high—the cavern was lined by smooth concrete. It could have been an aircraft hangar. I almost mistook the pale light at the end of the cavern for artificial illumination, until I saw that the smoothness of the walls gave way to natural stone. There had been an original cave, a sinkhole, perhaps, that was expanded.

"Incredible," I whispered, wondering for what purpose such a huge endeavor was constructed. It wasn't mass transit. This was something else entirely.

The design of the dome was unique and consisted of shafts of concrete meeting in the middle of a hexagon, which acted as a keystone, bearing the brunt of the weight. I was overcome with the desire to shout and hear my voice echo and reverberate in the chamber.

Beneath the grandeur of our past civilizations' architectural might was the new reality of our world: a tent city populated by the winking eyes of fires, bedrolls, and tarps.

A woman nursing a baby looked up at me warily from her camp chair. Stringy brown hair covered her breasts. She stood and ducked inside a ragged-looking tent.

A woman holding an AR-style rifle cleared her throat. Her hair was held back in a ponytail, cheeks angular, dark eyes. She stared at me, unafraid to make eye contact, a poker face that didn't hide anger very well.

"I'm Reginald," I said, extending a hand.

She turned away.

"This way," said the man with the spotty beard.

On our left, our shrunken and distorted bodies slipped across the surface of a shiny railcar. It looked like an Airstream trailer with iron train wheels. It sat atop a turntable aimed at massive steel doors heading back into the track we'd just left. I had a feeling it was the only train to ever travel on them.

All this for that one piece of locomotive, I thought, wondering who might be living in it, if the leader of this new underground society had claimed it for his own.

"How many are you?" August asked no one in particular.

"Several hundred," the man with the spotty beard said, waving us toward a metal fire-escape-like staircase at the edge of the cave.

A few of the others who had herded us through the tunnel laughed, hoisted the bags full of cash onto their shoulders, and followed the woman with the AR up the metal steps.

We followed them into what must have been a control room, lined with computer workstations. A holo-table stood at the center of the room displaying mountains, the opening of the cavern at the center. There were no satellites left, so they had surveillance equipment somewhere on the slopes. They had probably known we were camping in their neighborhood.

At the back of the room, a tall man wearing earphones hovered over a ham radio. The man with the beard set one of the bags down next to him, and removed his earphones. He stooped and looked into the bag for a long moment, glanced at us, then asked a question in a tone too quiet to hear. He had playing cards tattooed on his neck. Three of them, all aces. He wore a black coat with a name tag over the front pocket that said YUDA. Another ex-military, I thought, and we're surrounded by his security force.

"Where'd you get the money?" Yuda said.

"They stole it," I said.

"What the hell, Reginald?" Martin took a step toward me. It earned him a rifle butt in the stomach. He dropped to his knees.

Yuda looked at one of his guards. "He wasn't carrying a bag."

"I didn't know what they were carrying," I said. "Nor do I think it's worth hauling around."

The muscles of August's clenched jaw rippled beneath

the surface of his skin. He stepped forward, and two men grabbed his arms.

"Bring them out back for now," Yuda said.

"Fuck you, Reginald! Fuck you," Martin shouted as they hauled him away.

August at least had the presence of mind to go quietly.

I turned and faced the window that looked over the cavernous space. If I acted comfortable, perhaps they would, too.

Yuda approached and stood next to me, silently staring out.

"Thank you for your hospitality," I said.

"We haven't given you any."

"Well, then, thank you for not killing me. Or them."

Yuda grunted. "Would you care if I killed them?"

I took measure of him. Everyone had lost weight, had grown more lean, and the herd had certainly been thinned since the collapse, but even before their arrival he would've been a formidable man—hawk-like eyes and the clear disposition to call someone out on their lies.

I smiled sadly. "What's a few more?" I motioned to the window and the refugees below. "Did you find them, or did they find you?" At a distance, moving around in the expansive cave, they looked like insects.

We looked like insects, I reminded myself. Just because I had superior elevation didn't mean I was any better than them. I was, of course, but still.

"We found them, brought them in," he said.

"Are we the first to have found you?"

Yuda nodded.

"Then others will, too. And as big as this place is, you can't afford to have it overpopulated. How are you feeding them?"

Yuda's lips bunched. "You act like you're staying."

"Is that an offer?" I extended a hand. "My name is Reginald."

We shook, and I heard a collective sigh escape behind me.

"How did you find us?" Yuda said.

"We were on our way to Mount Washington."

Yuda faced me. "Why?"

"To use the communications center."

"You can't do that," Yuda said. "Communications were the first thing they compromised, likely from light-years away."

"How do you know?" I said, my gaze slipping to the radio operator.

"Because every strike we planned they attacked before it ever mobilized." Yuda let that sink in.

"You were military?" I said.

Yuda nodded. His thumb scratched his index finger. "Air Force."

I resisted the temptation to ask what his MOS was. The Air Force performed a lot of private-sector duty those days.

I made a sad face. It didn't fit. "If they took out our communications, why are you using that?" I nodded toward the radio.

"They haven't picked up on analogue. Yet."

"Interesting. What is this place?"

Yuda's eyes turned to slits. "Our home."

"That's not what I meant."

"I know what you meant. Are they dangerous?" Yuda said, indicating August and Martin with a toss of his head.

"Probably."

"And you?"

I hesitated long enough to show sincerity. "Yes."

He fixed me with a hard stare. "At least you're honest when it suits you. The money?"

"I told them where it was. I had to do something to ingratiate myself with them. It's not safe to travel alone."

Yuda nodded and turned away. "You can stay until nightfall. We don't need people like you and, as you've already pointed out, we don't have the space. Alicia, Saul, show him out."

The girl with the ponytail and the man with the patchy beard stepped forward to show me out as Yuda walked back to wherever they had stashed August and Martin.

Alicia stopped before me, and I replayed what had been happening before she cleared her throat earlier. I was staring at a mother—innocently, I might add—and then she—

"I hadn't intended to stare," I said to her.

She squinted.

"Earlier. I was just—" I sighed. Fumbling for words had its merit, mostly because it appeared sincere and made other people experience sympathy. I've bonded over many bumbling words with women before. "I'm sorry," I said finally, trying to impart deeper meaning to the words with my eyes.

Judging by her quizzical look and the way Saul stepped in and turned my shoulder, saying, "All right, come on, get out," my actions had the desired effect.

I wandered through the refugee camp toward the far end of the cavern where a patch of sunlight fell through the opening of the cave. I felt like a taxonomist cataloguing a new species of subterranean human. Such squalor—the pop-up mansions available at hardware stores meant for weekend escapes being used as permanent shelter, and the dirt on everyone's faces—made me feel sick.

I was just as dirty, and there was no River Jordan or Ganges to wash our sins away.

The opening of the cave was enormous. It was easy to imagine helicopters descending into it. The morning sun shone through the opening, and golden drops of water fell into a pool stirred by fish. A boy stood at the far edge of the pool, dragging a net through the water. I watched him for a few moments, enjoying the way the amber light flashed on the surface of the subterranean pond, obscuring the rust-red rocks worn smooth from millions of years of water beneath the surface, as he pulled out writhing white fish.

I looked back over the cave and felt certain a bigger secret had yet to be uncovered.

A black man appeared at my side. "The fish are blind," he said. "They feed off the microorganisms and any insects that disturb the tension of the water surface. The microorganisms metabolize sulfur and other metals. Too many fish, the water would not be safe to drink. Without the fish, people would starve."

"So you're saying it's hopeless."

He indicated the boy with a jut of his chin.

The boy took the fish from the net and dropped them into a wheelbarrow—where they continued to swim inside an aquarium.

"We've started a breeding program. He is transporting some of the fish away to another, more isolated body of water. Water that is not safe to drink. It is part breeding program, part—"

"Water purification project, as I assume the water introduces the microorganisms," I said. "I stand impressed. Are you a naturalist?"

The man shook his head. "Science teacher. Middle school."

"Reginald," I said.

"Charles."

We shook.

We watched the boy continue his chore, chasing fish around beneath the surface of the water. If it had been a mountain brook, perhaps in Alaska, and he was scooping salmon, it would have been idyllic, but it was tough to forget where we were, how perilous our circumstances were.

I was staring up at the mouth of the cave when Charles said, “Did you ever hear about the wolves in Yellowstone?”

I shook my head.

“In the late 1900s, they reintroduced wolves to trim the elk population. That in turn allowed other species to thrive. Through a long and cascading series of events, the return of the apex predators returned a balance to the ecosystem that had been missing for nearly a hundred years. Even the paths of the rivers were stabilized, because there were fewer first-order consumers eating seeds.”

Sometimes I hated my ability to grasp the abstract. The world above was burning, humans huddling in basements and places like this, and he was talking about the pending ecological changes as though they were a good thing.

“Are you always this depressing?” I said.

Charles laughed. “Some things are hard to unsee.”

We started walking back toward the end of the cavern. “Tell me, what do you know about the construction?” I said.

“Clearly government sponsored,” he said. “There are aluminum labels riveted to the sides of computers, the train. ‘Property US Government.’”

“Any idea what they were doing?” I said.

“My first guess was some sort of particle acceleration, but it only has train tracks and the one car. No stops.”

“Have you inspected the train?”

“Just the exterior. Yuda says it’s off-limits. Whatever technology they were testing, it’s clearly outdated and probably was never successful."

"Clearly," I said, trying to imagine myself letting go of the mystery. It wasn't in my nature to let go.

At the edge of the cavern, Alicia shadowed us, her face popping up in gaps between tents and tarps. I could only imagine what Martin and Yuda were discussing. I hoped he was begging for his life, but Yuda didn't seem the type to put down a stray dog.

"Should you be telling me all this?" I said. "Yuda is going to throw us out at the end of the day, if he lets me leave with my life . . ."

"Yuda thinks he is in charge of all this," Charles said, "and for some people, he is. For others, he's just a figurehead, a smaller representation of an organization already toppled by a new regime."

"Ah," I said. "*The Kind.*"

"They change our DNA, you know?" Charles said.

I clenched my teeth and, despite the poor light, Charles must have seen, because he apologized.

"It's okay," I said as we approached the train. There was a large steel door on the side. I imagined a hundred armed soldiers guarding men in lab coats as the train pulled out into the long, circular track many years ago. "So much money spent building this, they must have been working on something big."

"Or something they thought was big," Charles said. "My guess is it goes back to the second Cold War, before it was revealed that the major governments were sponsoring terrorist cells."

“Such a dark period in history.” I placed my hand on the train. The surface was cold and smooth. Foggy condensation formed between my fingers. “A train, though.”

“Would you like to see the inside?” Charles said.

I nodded quickly. “Very much. I thought you said it was off-limits?”

“I was never much of a conformist.”

I followed Charles to the other side of the train, dragging my hand along the smooth surface. It wasn’t really made for speed. Fast, yes, but land speed record, no. The rivets were countersunk, and the surface wasn’t made out of the kind of material that would absorb radio waves, rendering it technologically invisible, so that wasn’t the purpose. In fact, the silver would have made it stand out like the sun. And the fact that it used rails, not mag-lift. I shook my head.

On the other side of the train, I slipped my fingers into a slit on the surface and pulled. The door swung open. The interior was completely dark, and I no longer had my flashlight. I wondered if Charles was a strategic plant to get me talking. I stepped onto the train, deciding I didn’t care. If he was, at least he was interesting.

“Sorry to break up this field trip, Professor, but he needs to come with us,” Alicia said.

So close.

Alicia was accompanied by two men. I smiled at her. She didn’t return the gesture.

“Professor?” I said to Charles.

The corners of Charles's mouth turned down in a sheepish grin. "I left the university to teach middle school. I preferred teaching to publishing."

"Now," Alicia demanded.

"Another time," I said to Charles and left with my escort.

Charles nodded gravely. "I hope we will have the opportunity."

Yuda struck me in the cheek as soon as I stepped through the door. "I knew I recognized you."

On my knees, I placed a hand on my jaw, working the pain into something manageable and using the gesture to buy time to survey the room. It was much as it was before, only no one was openly armed.

That hardly made it fair, though.

Martin and August stood near the back of the room, looking exceedingly pleased to see me on my knees. Perhaps they'd been closer to Wayne than I thought.

"You lied to me," Yuda said.

I got to my feet and looked him square in the eye. There was a fire burning there, something I could feed.

"I don't like to be called a liar."

That earned me a good blow to the stomach. I wished I'd been full so I could have vomited on his shoes. It felt like something had ruptured.

"Whose body was outside station twelve?" Yuda said.

"Wayne," I gasped. "He pulled a gun on me."

"And you sold us out," Martin said. He had a black eye. He would have sold me out if he hadn't seen any other way. In fact, he probably just had.

I got to my feet, faced Yuda.

"Take him out of here," Yuda said.

"Why me? Why not them?" I said.

"Because there's something too easy about you. The lying, the way you assume you know things—"

"I knew three million things," I said. "Imagine what I could do for you."

Yuda laughed. "Just like your father."

"I'm nothing like my father," I growled.

Yuda crossed the room and grabbed one of the duffel bags. "Here. Don't forget your cut." Yuda shoved the bag into my chest. It fell at my feet.

"I didn't want it in the tunnel, either," I said and turned to let myself out, leaving the bag in the middle of the room.

The radio operator turned. "Sir, we're receiving a distress call."

The operator flipped a switch, and a voice emanated from an intercom somewhere in the room. "Yuda, it's Saul. Don't let Reginald take us on the train!"

I stopped. Saul looked at me. Yuda looked at Saul.

"What are your coordinates?" the radio operator said.

"Who are you?" Yuda said.

"They're coming, so get out of there. And don't let Reginald take us on the train!"

Yuda grabbed the microphone. "How many are you?"

No one answered Yuda, and the sound of gunfire and

screams was slowly replaced with static.

Yuda grabbed my shoulder, spun me around, and pinned me against the glass overlooking the refugees. "Who was that?" he demanded, nose inches from mine, so close I was going cross-eyed trying to fix him.

I could kill him. I knew I could kill him, and I wanted to, but as the stranger in this town I'd rather take a beating in front of everyone than give one.

"How should I know?" I said.

He pushed me against the glass and let me go.

"Don't look at me," Saul said. "I'm standing right here."

Alicia's chin was held high.

Yuda huffed. "Get him out of here."

My glossy reflection slid across the surface of the train the same way it went out.

I took one final look at the cavern. A triangle of golden sun stung one wall and radiated warmth over the people. Charles waved at me from the center of the tents and started over.

"Come on," Alicia said. "Get out of here."

"At least let me say good-bye," I said.

She huffed. "You knew him for two minutes."

"And we're already fast friends."

"You're leaving?" Charles called when he was closer.

"Being pushed out of the nest," I explained. We shook again.

"Be careful out there," Charles said.

"Come with me," I said.

Charles arched an eyebrow.

"This is a great hiding place, but it will make an even better tomb for whoever stays. Come with me."

Charles looked back at the cavern. "I've thought that many times. It's the first time I've heard someone say it aloud."

"That's why they built it here," I said. "If something went wrong, the contingency plan was to pull the plug, bury everything. I wouldn't be surprised if there are charges placed somewhere," I said, pointing as the sun spilling in the cave was eclipsed. Bits of dirt and pine needles rode a wave of air across the mouth of the cave and floated down. It sounded like we were standing inside a telephone booth during a hurricane.

The people in the tents looked up at the darkened fury, a kind of sleepy disbelief on their faces.

Alicia caught her breath, and I thought of a mother I once saw playing with her baby in a public pool. It looked like she was waterboarding the poor thing, dunking the infant over and over again, until someone explained that she was blowing in the baby's face, making it take a breath of air before dunking it. I thought, we should all take a deep, deep breath. We're going under.

The door to the control room burst open. "Everyone! In the tunnel! Now!" Yuda shouted, his voice echoing through the cavern.

He might as well have been yelling at cattle.

"Move," Yuda shouted, and they finally heard his voice.

Everyone moved at the same time, flowing toward

the tracks, a tsunami of people.

A sound like high-tension ropes snapping echoed throughout the cavern, and the sunlight flickered on the walls as the first of *The Kind* descended into the pit. One of them, long arms flailing, rolled down the wall like a squid, tumbling over itself faster than a man could fall.

Men appeared on the stairs beside Yuda, and the crackle of rifle fire reverberated throughout the cavern as the refugees in the center began to scream.

Charles grabbed my arm.

"Ready to leave with me now?"

"Now," he said.

Alicia raised her rifle to her shoulder.

"You'll hit only people from this distance," I said.

She lowered the rifle.

Martin and August were hustling down the stairs, running toward me, bags of money bouncing off their thighs with each step.

"The doors in front of the train," I said to Alicia. "Do they open?"

She nodded quickly.

"Open them."

She ran to a control panel beside the doors, and I made the mistake of looking back. My father decided he was going to run for public office long before I ever knew his mind, but I marked the occasion by our sudden arrival in the Church of Christ, a nondenominational cesspool of Christian thought that was haven to three hundred of the local poor. We helped with potluck in the basement and, in our suits, were completely out of place. The first sermon I ever heard was on Gomorrah. And I knew why Lot's wife had been turned into a pillar of salt. It wasn't because she was sad to leave all that wretched sin behind; it was because she was only too ready to watch it burn.

At the back of the refugee camp, the first screams of people molested by *The Kind* boiled the air, cannonading off the walls as tentacles seared flesh.

A man with a boy in tow crashed through a tent, like a skydiver tangled in his chute, and the black whip of a tentacle coiled around his ankle. He was pulled back so quickly that the image tricked my inner ear into the sensation of falling and I almost lost my footing.

The boy's arms flew to his neck before I even saw the coil around it, and he was yanked off his feet, a ripple of disturbance in the flutter of tarps and tent.

A current of people washed by me, and still I didn't move.

Water and fish from the pool hit the far walls of the cave as *The Kind* rolled through it. I caught sight of a woman high in the air, a tentacle coiled tightly around her waist. Something flew from her hands. It was the nursing mother from before. The baby never hit the ground, though. Another tentacle caught it, and I remembered the baby in the community pool. I took a breath.

"Here," August tossed the bag of money at my feet on his way by.

"I said I didn't want it," I called as he slipped into the crowd of people pushing toward the small door into the tunnel.

More of *The Kind* rolled down the walls of the cave. I didn't want to watch anything burn. I'd already seen enough. I ran for the train.

Knobs and buttons glowed on a control panel in front of Alicia. I shouted at Alicia to hurry. There was no way she could have heard my voice over the screams.

A rocket fired from the catwalk of the control room screeched overhead, arced over the pool, and connected with the far wall of the cavern.

The earth shook. Rocks fells from the ceiling.

A tentacle whipped the landing of the stairs in half, and the man holding the RPG threw his arms up as he fell to the ground some twenty feet below. One of *The Kind* was on top of him instantly, and even as it smothered him its tentacles flapped and flayed at everyone near enough to reach.

The train doors opened with the sound of a castle drawbridge, a steady clanking as the gears turned.

I looked for Alicia and Saul, to tell them to hurry, and saw Charles shuffling behind me, carrying the bag of money in front of him, knee knocking it with every step.

"You never know!" Charles shouted.

Inside the train, I looked over the controls for an ignition button. I touched the main monitor, ran my hand around the frame, and found a small button recessed into the back surface.

The cabin lights flickered on at the same time as the computer screen. People streamed through the doors in front of the train, disappearing into the darkness, and the light in the cavern dimmed. The computer screen asked for credentials.

The train rocked as Charles and Alicia got on board. Saul was right behind her.

Charles said, "Do you know how—?"

I felt the cold barrel of Saul's rifle on my neck. "Get out of the fucking train."

"Saul," Alicia said.

Rocks pelted the roof of the train like hail.

"I can't let you take the train," Saul said. "That was my voice. I know what I sound like."

"That was probably a trap," I said. "*The Kind* stopped our communications. You don't think they could mimic our voices?"

Something flew over the train, and for the briefest of moments, my mind struggled to reconcile the perception of a swooping bird with crumpled wings and the young man's contorted face as he barrel-rolled through the air. We were the last thing he saw as he disappeared into the darkness.

"Let's not stick around and find out," I said.

Saul removed the rifle, his resolve visibly weakened. If it weren't for our present circumstances, I'd have taken the rifle from him and smashed his skull. I pointed Charles at the sun visor affixed to the roof. He folded it down and something fell into his lap.

Charles held a name badge out to me. It said Silverman.

"Saul," I said, and he glanced at me the way a defeated mongrel stares at its superior. "Point your resolve somewhere more useful," I said and shot the door with my index finger like a gun.

Saul grunted and headed for the door of the train.

I took the name badge from Charles and flipped it over. It had a series of numbers on it. I typed the name Silverman, followed by the numbers.

"That can't be the password," Alicia said.

Something hit the top of the train, making the sound of a dull, startled gong, and she screamed as a body tumbled down beside the driver's side window. Behind us, *The Kind* would run out of distractions if we didn't move it.

The screen flashed to a set of buttons very similar to a rudimentary calculator, except without any of the usual symbols for addition, multiplication, etc. It had a comma, a colon, and a forward slash.

Saul opened the door and said something very macho as he switched his rifle to auto. The muzzle flash strobed in the cabin, and a solid ringing replaced the report long after he ceased firing. His call for us to hurry came through a muted fog, and I wondered if he actually thought he was keeping them at bay.

A calendar was taped to the dash. A date was circled in red ink. *July 21, 2041.*

"That's impossible," I said.

"What?" Charles had a finger in his ear, and his face was bunched up.

I punched yesterday's date, *6/24/2080, 13:00*, and a new prompt appeared. *Confirm date?*

"It's a damn time machine," I muttered.

"Maybe it was supposed to be?" Charles said.

"As long as it moves." I pushed *Confirm*.

The train lurched forward as Saul loosed an awkward volley before his rifle clicked empty.

Headlights illuminated people diving out of the way as we left the turnstile and angled into the tunnel. People streaked by, disappearing into whatever darkness we were leaving behind as the train accelerated. Some waved for help, most just kept running.

I made out the shape of August and Martin running, the bags of cash swinging against their legs, and it gave me no pleasure to see them jump off the tracks.

"We'll see you in a moment," I whispered.

The support columns built into the walls became a blur, and the sound returned as Saul slammed the door closed.

"What?" Alicia said.

"When the circular track comes back around," I said. "We'll see them again. Hopefully we can run over some of *The Kind* when we do."

Alicia grabbed my shoulder. "Make it stop."

"Why would I do that? So we can be the first of the

last to die?"

"It's a dead end," she screeched.

"*What?*" Charles shouted.

"It's a dead end. We were going to expand it—"

"Stop," I commanded the train. I pushed the button on the side of the monitor that started the whole thing, and if anything, the train increased velocity.

"That's station eleven!" Saul reached across my field of vision to point at a blur of steps.

"How many are there?" I said.

"Thirteen," Alicia said.

"Thirteen? Who makes thirteen anything?"

"There goes twelve," Charles said.

"Do something," Alicia screamed.

I got to my knees, peered under the dash, removed a brushed-metal panel. I grabbed a handful of wires, and a shock ran through my hand so strong that I couldn't let go. I heard more than saw the sparks fly, and a new sound, something like a turbine spinning up, flooded the cabin.

Charles helped me up as Alicia screamed.

Squirming snakes of electricity pressed at the corners of the windshield as if forming a web around the car itself, like we were inside a pupil succumbing to an electrical cataract and looking out. The last thing I saw behind the webbing was a cinder-block wall rushing toward us. I closed my eyes and prayed to a God that, if pressed on any day before or after, I would swear doesn't exist and, through the tsunami of sound, I doubted would be able to hear me.

My prayers were met with silence and a knotty feeling of weightlessness in my stomach, tight as an electromagnetic coil.

We emerged to gray daylight, drumming along on a raised track, hurtling toward the remains of a bridge whose rails ended in a twisted, vinous mass, bent and tangled from the heat of a searing explosion.

I pushed back to the controls, looked under the dash, and saw a pedal I'd missed in the darkness.

"Of course," I said. My father had a car without auto-drive once. He said the secret was in the sole—of his foot—a remark he'd found funny despite being a pun, the absolute lowest form of humor, which he knew I despised.

I stomped on the pedal. Immediately we pitched forward and the brakes made a shrill, grinding sound, as if they hadn't been used in centuries, which was nearly true.

Alicia tumbled against my back. I barred her falling any farther with my arm. Her brown eyes found mine, and she looked from eyes to lips as the train stopped, a safe hundred yards from the end of the bridge.

I wish I'd kissed her, even though I don't think she had the slightest feelings for me. The moment was akin to a New Year's Eve with a stranger, and she was beautiful. If I'd known what would happen to her, I would've kissed her; it might have given me reason enough to care about what would befall her. If the pain of Evelyn's death hadn't been so fresh . . . I gently pushed her to her feet.

"It's daytime," Saul said.

Outside, the earth was scorched. Devils of dust swirled over stumps and rocks dotting the landscape. Thick black smoke scraped the sky, and the gray clouds looked like the belly of a rotten fish.

"It's *daytime*," Saul said again, and this time we took his meaning. It wasn't safe to travel in the daytime, especially in a moving mirror that broadcast our position.

Charles pressed his face to the glass, peering at the sky. "There." He pointed.

A ship cut a dovetail hole in a tower of smoke and cloud. The sound of thrusters was like the hum of a thousand blow dryers, the insatiable appetite of locusts.

"What do we do?" Alicia said.

I knew then, beyond any doubt, that I'd made the right decision in not kissing her. Evelyn never would have had to ask. She would have elbowed me out of the way to get to the controls. Neither of us backed down. Ever.

"We haven't gone back far enough." I turned to the controls, punched in a new date, the same day, five years earlier. That would give us plenty of time, and we had money. We could change things, maybe not stop *The Kind* but investigate with the knowledge that they were coming. Rewire the past to change the future.

"There's not enough space." Alicia gripped my arm, fingernails digging so deep that I winced. I grabbed her hand and twisted it off.

I must have hurt her, because she pulled away and looked at me. I was almost sorry.

The plume of smoke slowly moved against the mural of gray sky. The twisted rails, bent like elephant tusks, grew larger as the train hurtled toward the remains of the bridge. A river coated with brown foam curdled beneath the bridge, several hundred feet below. Its surface became corrugated as the wind from the thrusters of the spacecraft struck its surface. It hovered at the end of the bridge, twisting metal tentacles hanging like tendrils of a jellyfish, windshield eyes black and emotionless, waiting for the hurtling train to fall into its grasp.

Lightning curled at the periphery of the windshield, crawling closer to the center and obscuring our vision of the spacecraft until it was replaced with a tunnel of swirling lights so dazzling I felt as though I was witnessing the very glory of the creation of the universe, the fury of a screaming God, and I despaired.

I'd kill everyone in the train if I could, deliver them all into an eternal fiery pit if it meant I could take down a single spacecraft with us, to replace a single solitary night of drinking with the presence of Evelyn, even if she was mad at me.

We emerged senselessly screaming at the blue sky of a summer day. I've never been so thankful to see rippling leaves responding to a breeze, each rustle a reassuring note that I'd have that chance. The bridge was complete.

We cruised to a stop at the other end around a half mile from a station in an area populated by middle-income housing, apartment buildings with porches built into the architecture, climbing the side like rungs on a ladder. On the second floor, a man in a tank top stood up from a patio chair and pointed a cigarette at us. It was people like him that made me hate my old life by forcing me to witness the moments they squandered while the notion of how to make my own life mean something eluded me.

"Where are we?" Alicia said.

"Five years in the past," I said quietly. I could think of only Evelyn, how even if I raced off to see her today, she may not be happy to see me, how even if I did re-earn her love, it might not make my life mean anything.

"So they haven't come yet?" Saul said, smiling.

"What about the others?" Alicia said.

"They haven't even found the cavern yet," Charles said. "Technically, they're all still alive."

The thought of them, still in the cavern, frozen as they fled, a muzzle flash casting light on the facial features of those brave enough to stay and fight, made my hands tremble. I gripped my thighs and squeezed, trying to send the tremors deeper.

Charles went to the back of the train, pushed the door open, and stepped out. A gust of warm, humid air entered the cabin.

Outside, Charles fell to his knees and kissed the concrete the tracks were built on. Alicia and Saul followed, Saul carrying the bag of cash. Apparently it was communal now.

Birds chirped. The sound of traffic filled the cabin.

It was oneiric, being back in a world that all of us had consigned to the recesses of our memory, and disgusting to watch Alicia and Saul tumble out of the train, hold hands, and jump up and down like school children, their glee rising to the heavens.

In a way, I envied that they could show their happiness. I wanted so much to hurt them that it pains me to even admit it.

A young couple walking a Dalmatian on a purple leash stopped. The man reached into a pocket and placed a cell phone against his ear. It occurred to me that with the train, I could do anything I wanted. It was the ultimate escape vehicle.

I didn't step off the train.

More people appeared on the porches of the apartment building, pointing down at us. Sirens rose in the air.

"We shouldn't stay here long," I said to Charles.

He was stoic, wearing a very dour expression as he realized he was the center of hundreds of people's attention. "No, we should leave," he said, raising his voice for Alicia and Saul, who didn't hear us.

Saul lifted Alicia up in his arms and spun her around, dancing farther and farther away from the train in a fit of giggles across the plateau of a road. I surmised Saul had been harboring feelings for her for quite some time. We were a catalyst for their happiness and they were indulging, and meanwhile, Godel's theory about the absence of time had become real. All those people in the tunnel were still there, fighting, just like I was still in my mother's womb, waiting to be born, walking through the refugee tent city with Charles, and standing in the train. Time was not linear; it was all at once. I couldn't decide if that meant they had time to celebrate or not.

The whine of a dump truck's electric engine approached, mingling with sirens. They were coming for us. One of the people in the apartment building had called the police. They were going to come and if we let them detain us, we'd be stuck in an interrogation room, where the passage of time would once again be very, very real.

Saul set Alicia down in the middle of the road. Breathless, she looked at me and pushed her hair behind her ear.

Horns blared.

They stepped back as the curtain of the dump truck swept past. It was like they didn't want to come back to the train and the future it represented.

Several of the people on the balconies were aiming cell phones at us, recording the spectacle.

The whine of a train whistle blasted, and I hung out the door to look back. The sneering grill of a train hurtled down the track. It would obliterate us if we didn't move.

Across the street, Alicia looked from the train to us. Her mouth hung open as she shook her head, a caravan of vehicles swimming up the road.

"We have to move," I said.

"What about them?" Charles said.

"We'll come back for them. We can't lose the train." I

extended my hand to Charles and helped him in.

Alicia shook her head. Saul waved as though we were on a plane and he on a deserted island, except he wasn't. He had Alicia, and they had their happiness, and without the train we would all be doomed. I closed the door as they jumped. As if their protestations would change my mind.

The whistle of the train bore down on us as I sat at the control panel and punched in a new date, fifty years prior. The whine of the engine spooled up as police cars pulled to a stop in front of Alicia and Saul. As the first officer made contact, her head shook like a tree branch struck by a rock, then disappeared behind a cruiser.

The train whistle reached its crescendo and held its high pitch for several seconds before we attained speeds it couldn't match, and the sound fell away behind us. The lightning and the swirls of color seemed tainted and blemished, their beauty stained. The fury of God was no longer a mystery. I feared him no more than any man.

"We won't be able to get them back," Charles said. His lips were slightly parted, as though he had more to say but wasn't sure he could commit to forming the words.

"No," I agreed.

"They'll be fine, though," Charles said.

I nodded solemnly. "They'll be fine."

Alicia and Saul would be fine. For at least four years.

For the first time in two months, I ate a full meal. Hamburger, fries, and two large milkshakes. I'd forgotten how tender meat that wasn't grown in a laboratory could be. And the people were so clean, even those covered in fat-fryer grease. It was before unemployment passed 30 percent, before America invaded North Korea. The Second Cold War hadn't started. The implications were mind-boggling, and I wished I'd spent my life studying history rather than biological weapons.

Despite all the possibilities, Charles and I chewed with bovine solemnity as the swirls of people who had no idea the world would end in a few short decades buzzed around us. There were so many things that we could go back and change, so many events that we could stop from happening, but nothing that could change the inevitability of *The Kind* arriving on our doorstep with the intention of complete domination.

I hit the bottom of the second shake with a bubbling slurp, and Charles stirred from his revelry. "What do we do?" he said.

I took a deep breath before speaking. My stomach was beyond full. Painful indigestion pressed at the upper corners of my rib cage. Somnolence dulled my senses but not to the point that I could ignore the fact that my father had seen how he wanted his life to look and made choices to create that reality. Despite how much I hated him for paying more attention to his dangerous political aspirations than to me, I'd always admired him for that. And I had more than he did. I actually knew what was coming. There really was no choice.

"We go back," I said.

Charles finished chewing before he spoke, a gesture that reassured me I'd chosen the right traveling companion. "We can live out our lives here, grow old, and never see the day."

"And you could pass another, what, fifty years with the medicine available today, knowing what will befall everyone you meet?" I said. "And what happens when one of us falls in love? You can't deny it'll happen and when it does, there will be children. And those children—"

"Will inherit our fate," Charles said.

That was to say nothing of the implications, the tangled web of time in which our actions might eventually affect our birth.

I pushed the shake away. The food had soured in my stomach.

We returned to the train and sat pensively, bathed in the glow of electronics, bouncing ideas off each other until we arrived at a conclusion. We couldn't circumvent their arrival—manipulating the government to develop a space defense system did not seem feasible—even if my father was in charge. I knew him all too well, and he thought the money spent on SETI was better spent on new and improved carbon sequestration techniques. We need to fix our home before we destroy another, he was fond of saying.

The only option was to go far into the future to see what *The Kind*'s plan was. Knowing their plan, we could gain an advantage, or we would turn tail and run, something I've never been too ashamed to do, even if it did mean leaving people behind.

A hundred years past the first invasion, the swirling spectral lights of time travel dissipated to reveal an emerald-green bowl of grass, a valley so breathtaking that Charles and I started laughing.

The future was a beautiful place.

I stopped the train, got out, and ran my hand through the supple grass to make sure it wasn't an illusion.

Charles squatted, took a handful of earth, and let it fall like the sands of time from his clenched fist. "They're dead now?"

We climbed back into the train and drove to the precipitous edge of the valley, where I stood on the brakes. The tracks vanished abruptly.

An expanse of scorched earth stretched in all directions. There was no smoke, no tree stumps or exposed roots, only dust and rocks and the swirl of the former combined with ash. In the distance, sheets of rain fell from opalescent clouds flickering with electricity.

"Do you think we did this?" I said.

Charles nodded. "Win at all costs."

I squinted at the landscape, hoping to find something, some sign of life, alien or otherwise. Only rocks, sand and shadow, and a huge mountain I took to be Washington until Charles muttered, "Is that The Wedge?"

"No," I whispered.

On closer inspection, I was wrong.

"We did win," Charles said. "Look—that's The Wedge!"

He covered his eyes to scan the sky, then ran to the door and jumped out to get a more complete view. He turned on his axis like a planet, head tilted back in exaltation, and I thought of Alicia and Saul, celebrating as they drifted into the open street.

"It's gone!" Charles shouted.

At his feet, I noticed the sprouts of small plants, and I had an overwhelming sensation that they were fighting. Fighting to regain an earth taken from them.

A spacecraft drilled a hole in a cloud as it emerged, its retrorockets firing with a throaty breath. The ship was oblong, more football than saucer, the surface a dull gray that matched the clouds. Thunder rolled in the distance.

I don't think either of us had the strength to run.

A spire spouted from the ground, twisting tendrils rising like thorny rose stems to form a platform that cradled the spaceship.

"They are in the earth," Charles said.

The ship changed shape, and one of *The Kind* tumbled down from inside it onto the tower, rolling over and over itself toward the ground, coming for us.

"I'm tired of running," I said. I wasn't going to let them win. Not anymore. Not again. Or maybe I was just tired from not having slept in two days. I stepped in front of Charles. "Go back to the train. Save it."

The Kind reached the base of the tower and tore

through the field, sending stalks of grass and debris high into the air. It was like a tire with strips of flailing rubber attached to its surface. I held up my hands and yelled at Charles to run. I'd lived my whole life running from my legacy, doing terrible things to people in the name of an army that had no conscience, returning from duty to become an undertaker to spite my father, and finally someone, some thing, was ready to put me down.

It stopped a few feet from me. Pieces of dirt and grass were stuck to its smooth ebony surface, which didn't fluctuate. Didn't breathe. A nictitating eyelid rolled away from its hundred soulless eyes. Rows of square teeth were barely hidden by a flap of black skin.

"Reginald," Charles whispered.

The Kind struck as I looked back at him. It rolled over me, its enormous weight flattening me, the smooth, slimy surface suffocating as its girth pushed the last trace of air from my lungs. Then its plastic skin was unrolling itself inside my throat, pushing into my sinuses, my ears, wrapping itself around my eyes and sending flashes of memory into my mind even as it stole them.

I floated with Evelyn. She was standing in line at the grocery store, buying sandwich meat, and I remembered how I'd stopped at the bar the night before with the cadaver still in the back of the Cadillac, only left because I saw my father on television, giving a speech about some new air strike operation in Columbia. She was waiting for me when I got home, not even upset, just worried.

I felt stirring cotton sheets over us, exhaling a summer breath as they floated down on top of us like a parachute and the kiss of hope. Yet I couldn't help but feel as though I'd been cheated.

I woke to starlight and a glowing belt of rocks that used to be the moon.

A hazy, dark figure sat beside me, the dull lump of a stone in his raised hand.

"Are you you?" Charles said.

I sat up slowly, rubbing at the pressure in my temples. My whole body ached, yet something warm filled the spaces between muscle and ligaments in my limbs, something crackling with purpose, something on fire.

"Reginald?"

"Yes, it's me." I stood, the fatigue and pain in my body already fading, the muscles recoiling as springs. The twisted tower was still there, waiting.

"It left me here, and you didn't kill me?" I said.

"What did it do to you?" Charles hadn't lowered his arm yet but clearly wasn't going to use the stone.

"I'm not sure," I said, and I wasn't. The sky fascinated me, darkness more beautiful than the sun of any summer day, and it felt as though any warmth left in my soul had been snuffed out.

Something erupted from the surface of the spaceship, and the grass was knocked flat beside us. Charles jumped. Neither of us said anything.

He stepped back as I walked the short distance to

where the grass was disturbed, following the path the projectile had burrowed through the brush as it rolled to a stop, and stood over a small black sack made of wet, leathery skin, like an embryo. Its surface felt like *The Kind*, part submerged wetsuit, part dolphin skin. I found a perforation on its surface and drove my thumb in the same way a desperate warrior would gouge an eye. Charles didn't ask what it was or what I was doing to it, and I liked him all the more for it. Warm liquid spilled out, and I forced my hand in. I felt around inside, grasped what felt like a wedge of stone, and pulled. The surface of the sack stretched and ripped until I had it free.

I stood, turned so Charles could see. He raised the stone high, ready to attack. There was no need.

I wanted the stone to be useful, to mean something, and it shifted its mass, dribbling toward the ground until it looked like a stalagmite of unpolished gold.

"There's something for you in there as well," I said. "Take it. We need to go back."

Images were surfacing in my mind, ideas of an entire race that was once not unlike us, fleeing a dying planet. Darkness pressed at the corners of my vision, and I clenched my jaw, furiously focusing on the nearest blade of grass until it receded, and I felt the darkness take its place, waiting for when I stumbled.

"I am an emissary," I said, more to myself than to Charles.

Charles approached the sack, nudged it with his toe.

"It stinks. Why'd you reach your hand in there?"

"You'll want the smell on you where we're going."

He gasped and complained as he reached inside, dry heaved but didn't retch.

In the train, Charles shook one of the two small bottles of red liquid that were inside. "What is it?"

"For use in cases of extreme moral ambiguity," I said.

His jaw flexed. "Reginald, how do you know these things? How do I know you're you? How do I know you're not one of them?"

I punched the date on which we'd first met into the control panel. "Because," I said as the train began to move, slowly at first, then faster and faster until the frizzy, yarn-like tangles of electricity appeared at the edges of the windshield. "It wants to live, so it will allow us to live, too. In a niche, mind you, but survival in a niche is better than annihilation—of both species."

Charles thought about this as the colors of time and space played on his face. "That was the last one."

"So are we," I said.

When the tears filled Charles's eyes, it was the first time I didn't think less of a man for crying.

"We made a truce," I said.

"How will it know? This is a hundred years in the future?"

I shook my head. "I can't explain it." There were no images to go with the knowledge. No memory of studying a text, of listening to a lecture, or figuring out a mechanical problem for myself. I thought, maybe this is what it's like to be a computer, to have information magically installed, crackling in your synapses.

The colors painting us disappeared, and we were plunged into darkness.

"We could win after all," Charles said.

"No, we can't," I said. The darkness of the tunnel from which the train was born appeared before us, lit by the headlights of the train.

People ran toward us on the sides of the track, facial features nothing more than speckles on eggs, tiny toy soldiers with painted-on panic. They were insectile, and I wondered if I was viewing them through the eyes of *The Kind* or if it was just me and all my cynicism. Sparks of light flashed in the darkness as the last of Yuda's forces fired in volleys, falling back in shifts, as one of *The Kind* quickly advanced, tumbling to a stop in front of the train.

Charles yelled as we collided with it. It was like running into a gel-filled balloon, like being inside a bullet striking a mound of dirt.

The surface of *The Kind* gave, and the train pitched forward. The rubbery surface of *The Kind* split and burst, showering the train and everyone in the tunnel with the thick, viscous yellow fluid of its entrails.

The train was blocking the doorway. I grabbed the golden metal cane *The Kind* had given me and jumped out with Charles fast behind. The ground was ice-slick, coated with the slimy entrails of *The Kind* that had exploded. Part of that was in me, and I could feel its terror as the train collided with it, its last thoughts amounting to nothing more than sound and fury.

Gunfire echoed through the tunnel.

"Get back!" I yelled to the gunmen.

The train rocked as one of *The Kind* pushed against it, trying to squeeze into the tunnel, and I thought the train was going to roll over on top of me. A paralyzing pang of panic shot through me at the thought of it being damaged, of losing the ability to slip through time. I'd never be able to see Evelyn again. I wasn't sure that I knew exactly what to do to prevent *The Kind* from annihilating us, or even if I could, but for the first time, I felt certain that if I tried, I could do something about it. *The Kind* was inside me. A part of it had touched my nervous system, infected my soul with knowledge I hadn't even accessed yet.

I wondered if Evelyn would recoil at my touch, if pieces of her would cleave and fall away like a sand castle meeting the tide.

The train rocked back and the front wheels jumped the tracks, but it didn't fall over. I ran to the end of the train and was almost knocked down by a man fleeing from one of *The Kind*, unfolding itself into the space between wall and train as it had done to gain access to me, its skin stretching and contorting as it pushed itself further through the crack. I held the cane like a javelin and charged. The back of the cane bounced into my chest as it connected with *The Kind*, and if it were not for the way it was contorting itself to fit through the small space, I would've gone flying, but its skin gave. The staff plunged through its skin like a needle slipping into a vein.

The surface tension was too much. The thing hemorrhaged and a wave of thick fluid washed over me, bowling me over. There was pain inside it, and I knew that all of its watery insides would conduct electricity, that its centralized nervous system was at the core of its advantages over us.

Charles took my arm and pulled me to my feet.

The whites of his eyes were red. "Get up."

"You drank some," I said.

"I wanted to run," he said. "Of course I drank some."

What little light there was in the cavern dimmed as one of *The Kind* rolled into view, its skin the color of midnight with a dark, oily sheen. Its tentacles tapped the ground pensively.

I held up the staff and stepped forward.

The thing shrank back, rolling over.

There were hundreds of them in the darkness, the small patches of light reflected on their skin belying their mass.

Their tentacles began writhing, beating the ground, creating a thunderous sound like a stampede that shook my senses and made me want to cower. I didn't.

"They are mine," I shouted, and my words drove them to silence.

I stared out at them, their black masses like swollen tombstones, and fought to control my bladder.

A single tentacle stretched forward, moving across the dirty concrete floor of the cavern like a slithering proboscis, a tongue. I thought to stab it with the golden cane. It was moving so slowly, so tentatively stretching toward me that I had the curious idea that it wanted just a taste, to feel what I was made of. It touched my shoe as if blind, and climbed over my sock to feel my ankle.

As soon as it touched me I could hear their thoughts—not understand them, mind you, but feel their intentions, like one shared deliberation among legion, and I knew that she was here. The one who had pinned me down in the future. She was here, in this cavern, smelling herself on my skin, receiving whatever thought forms I was sending without meaning to, and then she was gone and something far darker, the black point of a needle, took her place.

I stabbed the tentacle with the staff and it writhed, splitting itself down the center to pull away from me.

Charles appeared at my side. "What do we do now?"

I sensed the movement of others behind me, Yuda's men filing into the space between train and doors.

I thought of Thermopylae.

The tentacle retreated into the darkness, leaving a cold spot on my leg where it had touched me.

We could defend the tunnel.

The Kind began to retreat, one by one their greasy shapes rolling up the walls in procession, out of the cavern into the night.

"We won," Charles said.

"No." I faced the crowd of people that had gathered behind me. "We won the way a mouse wins when it reaches its hole before the talons of an owl crush its spine. It's their world now. But if we stay belowground, they'll let us live. As a species."

There was crying. At first I thought it was because of my words; then I realized not all of *The Kind* had gone. The smallest of them were still here, the shadows of their bodies glistening in the light, twitching as though trying to move.

Someone shone a light on one of them, and I realized I was wrong. They were humans, or at least they had been. What appeared to be a woman was covered with layers of black, slimy skin, something foreign, and half her skin was necrotic, as though it had come in contact with some toxic agent. Her nose twitched to one side with new musculature; her eyes were black as charcoal.

I stepped closer and she tried to move away, shimmying like a seal caught on a beach, arms limp as if the bones were broken. Charles approached, stood over her, and looked back over his shoulder at me. His eyes glowed red in the darkness. He brought the rock from the future down onto her soft skull.

He put them all down, and when the light of the devil faded from his eyes, he cried inconsolably in the darkest corner of the cave.

The Kind left us alone after that. We were part of the landscape. An animal that knew its place in the food chain, kept in check by natural predators.

But we were alive.

Chapter 4

Alicia

The only thing worse than living through the invasion of *The Kind* was knowing I'd have to live through it again.

"What day are they going to invade?" Dr. Allman said, his clipboard and pen at the ready as if he hadn't written the date every day since my return from the future.

"March 18, 2080," I whispered, too quietly for him to hear.

His pen scratched the paper. Every other doctor in the last century used a recording application to take notes. I couldn't decide if that made him more or less likely to survive the collapse. Judging from his slender, muscular build, he exercised, but that didn't mean anything.

Dr. Allman took off his glasses, set them on the table, and sighed. "I've become somewhat of a pioneer since we began our time together." He looked out the window at the busy metropolis below West Forest Psychiatric Hospital. From our vantage point on the seventeenth floor, we could see the roofs where pine trees, maples, and ornamentals grew. From space, the city looked like a network of roads built around endless squares of forest. On foot, it was just another rat-infested city, the rich living in lush gardens above the rest.

"Shared delusions are rather uncommon," Dr. Allman said, "and thanks to my work with you, I've become somewhat of an expert."

"Using the word *somewhat* twice doesn't make you sound modest," I said.

Dr. Allman smiled patiently. "Yes, that's somewhat true." He laughed at his own joke. "I've been working with you and Saul for almost four years now, and I think the strength of your delusions has diminished. Would you agree?"

My knees were very interesting.

He waited, perfectly comfortable in the silence, as always. Once, I sat across from him for an hour without saying a word. Our sessions went on like that for a week until I started talking about what I was probably doing; the other me, the one from the past, living a perfectly comfortable life, wasting time pursuing a degree in English and dating Andre, a bookish type with a dry sense of humor and a penchant for quickies.

I called her once—the other me—from the nurses' station. I'd promised Haley my dessert if she would keep the staff busy. I told the other me that *The Kind* was coming. She laughed and hung up, and the memory of adding the contact CRAZY DO NOT ANSWER into my phone became crystal clear.

I told Dr. Allman about her, that I could prove it. That there was someone out there with the same name and I could tell him things about her that no one else would know and if we were just introduced, if we just had a few minutes to talk and share secrets, she would realize that I was her.

Dr. Allman said my name wasn't that unique. I told him her birthday, address, and international identification number; he showed me the police forms from when I was arrested with all of Reginald's money. Same as mine, Dr. Allman pointed out.

There was a word for what I was, depending on who you asked. Dr. Allman said the word was *dissociative.* I said the word was *screwed.*

"What's for lunch?" I said. "It's Wednesday, so it'll probably be some sort of fish. I was hoping for steak on the last day. When the food is gone . . ."

The thing was, I wanted to believe him. I wanted to believe I was crazy. I wanted there to never be any *Kind* but knew they were coming. I never would have had the money and never would have been hiding in the damn hole with everyone else. And the train. And Reginald.

It was exhausting, the circles that everything went in. The past was the future and the future was now, and it was all very Benjamin Compson.

"What concerns me most, Alicia, is the consistency of it," Dr. Allman said. "In most cases, after at least a few years, there's a split that occurs."

"Do you think I could request something else?" I said, still talking about lunch. "I'd like to do some carb loading. Maybe macaroni. Except we had that yesterday and I don't want leftovers. We'll have enough of those in the coming days."

"Usually," Dr. Allman said, ignoring me, "the patient begins to make the fantasy their own after prolonged periods of separation."

I saw Saul out the window yesterday, smoking a cigarette, gazing at the sky as if longing for *The Kind* to come. Besides that, I hadn't seen him in a year and a half, and that was at the final hearing before both of us were declared criminally insane, and it's a good thing. No one who just shows up with a duffel bag full of cash on the street is innocent, and we knew from our time waiting for a grand jury that jail sucked. It was better not to change our story. Doctors and meds were awful, mind-numbing in the worst sense. If we just held on long enough, we would emerge well fed and probably able to flee, whereas in a jail, escape would be . . . unlikely.

"Saul hasn't changed his story, huh?" I said.

Dr. Allman looked like he was explaining something to a child. "Alicia, you're the one who hasn't changed her story. Saul came to grips with his delusions months ago."

My mouth went dry. I swallowed hard, got up, and went to the window, peered up at the sky: the sun was high, the clouds were bright cottony things. Just like I remembered it.

"Alicia, we need to develop a plan."

"My plan?" I said, not turning around. "My plan is to get the hell out of here and head north. I'm not waiting until the stampedes this time. No way. I'll be leading the way. This time it will be easier to run, too. I quit smoking five years ago—well, I ran out of smokes, and the whole time I thought how much of a moron I was, smoking every new artificial I could get my hands on just to look chic."

"Alicia."

"No," I shouted. "You don't get to tell me what to do, or how I should think, anymore. Today. Is. The. Day."

Dr. Allman stared at me, face passive, until I turned away in a huff. I placed my forehead on the cool glass, looking down, wishing I could jump. Foggy breath obscured the view.

"There's someone here who would like to see you." Dr. Allman waved at a face in the small window of the door. A tech in white scrubs named Derek, who had weight-lifter arms sleeved in tattoos, opened the door and Saul walked in slowly. His face was wider; he'd gained weight. Probably been taking his meds. Derek quietly left and closed the door.

"Forgot already?" I said.

"Alicia," Saul said, holding up his hands.

I had to inhale slowly, completely, to avoid blowing up. I couldn't do anything that would allow the good Dr. Allman to give me a PRN agitol or something worse. I had to stay sharp. There were only a few hours left.

Saul stood by the door, watching me. "Remember

when we were in New Hampshire? That night we were on guard duty?"

Dr. Allman's head snapped in Saul's direction.

"We said we'd do things differently," Saul said.

Dr. Allman pressed a button on the side of his chair, and a little red light flashed above the door frame like a blinking eye.

"Let's do those things differently," Saul said.

The door opened. Derek and Nurse Eileen, who'd been pretty until one of the patients had broken her nose, and a tech with spiky hair came through the door.

Saul held his hands up. "Wait—there's no problem."

"Take him out of here," Dr. Allman said. "This was just a ploy to gain access to her."

"Check your news feed, Doctor," Saul said.

Derek grabbed Saul's right arm. Spiky grabbed the other.

"Check your news feed," Saul yelled.

They had him out the door in seconds. Saul wasn't very big compared to most men, although he was great with a rifle and had taught everyone how to hunt.

Those days were back. They were coming.

The door slammed closed. Dr. Allman scratched something on his pad and looked up at me.

"I apologize for that. We'll just have to wait until tomorrow. I thought for certain we could move to avoid an incident beforehand. Well, best-laid plans."

"Are you going to check your news feed?" I said.

He sighed, clipped his pen to his pad. "Am I?"

I sat across from him. "Doctor, I'm ready to move on. I've been living with this idea of a nightmare, in fear of it, for four years. I'm ready to be proven wrong. I'm so, so ready to forget what's coming."

"Alicia, what happens when I check my news feed and nothing is there? You tell me to refresh it? To wait five minutes and try again?"

"There's a man," I said. "His name is Dr. Morris Spinner, and he works at Spectral Labs in New Mexico. At around 12:30, he's going to author a press release that causes a media frenzy that lasts for approximately six hours before all communications stop. Everyone will say he's crazy; then the other observatories will point their giant telescopes as night falls, and the panic will start. At sunrise the following morning, The Wedge blocks the sun, and all holy hell breaks loose. It's 12:33. You have fifteen hours to get your family somewhere safe." I pointed at his cell phone where it rested on the desk. "Check your news feed."

Dr. Allman cleared his throat. "If I check my phone, I'm empowering your delusions."

"No—"

"And I'm afraid I've done that enough for one day."

"No," I shouted.

He pressed the button on the side of his chair. The red light went on.

I dashed to his desk and grabbed his phone.

"Put it down," Dr. Allman growled.

I hit the activation button, and a password prompt came up. "What's the password?"

The door opened. Derek and company were back.

"Six of agitol and two of lorazepam," Dr. Allman said.

One of the nurses ran away to get the drugs.

Derek and Spiky grabbed me by the arms. I thrashed, I screamed. My legs flailed. I caught Eileen in the chin. I think her tooth sliced my big toe. I still had Dr. Allman's phone, and they were trying to pry it from my hands one finger at a time.

"Hold her, would you?" Dr. Allman's hand was around my wrist.

I kicked him in the chest. My toe left a smear of blood.

His face turned red as he dove in again, pushing my legs to the side. His fingers bent my thumb back until I screamed and let go.

Dr. Allman stood in the doorway of his office, shaking his head and shrinking as they dragged me to my room.

I felt something like a pinch on my neck, the mosquito bite of a needle, and the color started to drain out of the ceiling tiles, a clever side effect of agitol designed to surprise and disorient the patient while the second effect, a creeping darkness at the periphery that seeps into your vision until there is just a pinhole of sight left, takes over. Through the pinhole, I saw Dr. Allman looking down at his phone and then, nothing.

I sit in the quad, birds chirping and the whisper of chestnut leaves above me as morning sun bathes my skin. A book of poems by Alistair Murphy rests on my lap, the simple lines exploiting the beauty of a dandelion flowing across the page. The click of a ten-speed bicycle whizzes by. I lean my head back and think how perfect it is, how I'm going to graduate in a few months, how lucky I am to have been impregnated by a selfish man courageous enough to admit he wants nothing to do with the baby in my stomach. It will be a boy. It will be named Alexander, and when it's born, he will have rosy cheeks and tiny pink lips and the sweet smell that all babies have, and even the dandelions in the poetry and their ubiquitous nature are beautiful. I don't care if I'm not married—my mother always said people don't have to be married to be good parents—even though that's what I always wanted, because I will be a good mother. Having a baby is not just the start of the baby's life; it will be the start of mine, because I'm graduating and everything is starting over. No more going to parties and getting wasted on haze because this is me. I'm new. I've been reborn.

A shadow crosses the surface of the sun, and at first I think it's a cloud, more like an eclipse; then the light itself turns a kind of sickly red, like the sky has gotten scarlet fever, and I'm scared. I'm scared for my baby. Screams break the relative silence of the campus as what sound like jets streak overhead. They're not jets. They are long, teardrop-shaped ships. Hundreds of them, pouring out from the massive ship blocking the sun. I'm on my feet, peering at the sky, and I can't breathe because my heart is hammering at the inside of my chest. I feel the queasiness coming on that I felt this morning when I vomited, and then it was good; it was like I was making room for the life growing inside me. Now it's different; it's like there's no room left, no chance for me, no life left for anyone.

A sound like a teakettle of boiling water rises. Something strikes the ground in front of Bonney Hall. A geyser of dirt and steam, then another and another, and shards of glass fall to earth in place of the dirt. I'm running back toward the dorm, showers of hot rocks and glass stinging my face and hands, and I left the book by the tree and it wasn't mine and everything is dark.

I'm sitting in the basement of the dorm. The muffled screams of people outside occasionally filter through the mattresses pushed up against the window. Someone sits in the corner with headphones, turning a knob, scanning the waves for signals. There aren't any. There may never be again. Heidi, my roommate, holds my hand. I can still smell the haze on her from last night. She's probably hungover. It doesn't matter what time of day it is. I feel nauseous, though, so I think it's morning.

There aren't any more sirens. Throughout the day they played on repeat, changing direction, calling to each other, and there was gunfire. We stayed indoors, out of sight, barricading ourselves in.

There's nothing but mini-fridge leftovers. I know that we can't last long, maybe another twelve hours. The water they were getting from the spigot has dried up and that's city water, which means this is serious. Infrastructure has fallen.

The lights blink and people scream. Heidi squeezes my hand.

"We have to leave," I say.

She's a poli-sci major and is great at telling everyone why they are wrong. She's doesn't tell me I'm wrong, which just makes me more scared.

"What's your plan?" she asks.

"Let's go get Roman's keys."

Heidi nods.

Two seniors stop us at the foot of the stairs, stubble on their faces.

"You can't go up there," John says. He's an RA, premed, totally full of himself. Probably happy that he's playing savior already. He is short, has a low voice, a beard to prove he's a man, and by the sound of it, I'd say there is something wrong with him.

"I'm diabetic," I lie. "I need insulin. It's in my room."

"Well, you just can't go up there. I mean those things," John says, as if that's enough.

Heidi huffs and pushes him aside, outweighing him twice over.

"Don't try to run," John calls. "You won't get very far."

And even though he's right, I can almost see Heidi bristle.

We walk up the stairs and someone slides a mattress

to one side and the door swings open. Daylight blinds us, drives daggers so deep in our skulls I feel nauseous again. I think maybe that's hunger. Maybe I just need to eat something.

The last thing I ate was some chips and ginger ale the night before. It doesn't occur to me until much later that if I'd known, I would have had duck and chocolate mousse pie and mashed potatoes with gravy and cranberry sauce and everything we used to make at Thanksgiving. There's nothing like that anymore.

I called my mother once from the hospital. She answered with a cough. I could almost smell the cocoa e-cigarette through the line. She asked me how college was.

"It's fine," I said, trying to recall the last time we'd spoken. I remember fog hanging under halogen lights. We were outside the mall. It was Christmastime. It hadn't snowed yet, despite there being a chill in the air. She had on long, red leggings and gold pumps and her hair was frizzy. She hadn't changed it since she was my age. We'd eaten at a pizza joint, and during the meal I left to go to the bathroom, and when I came back I could smell the haze, skulking around the booth, overpowering the smell of garlic pizza. Whatever stress she'd had about Christmas presents and money was clearly gone.

She reached across the table with greasy fingers and touched my face. "You're so beautiful."

I dabbed a napkin at my face and tried to remember why I should tell her I was pregnant. Tried to imagine my child not being let down by her when she forgot birthdays.

I told her college was good and that I wasn't dating or getting into trouble, even though I had been doing both of those things.

I know I'm stuck in the nightmare that will keep me awake for the rest of my life. I can't wake up because they pumped me full of agitol that pushes you so far under you sit on the shores of your subconscious, facing the demons in waves, getting to know them while holding an eternal breath, so I'm standing in the window of Roman's room, holding his keys, looking out the window at what's left of the campus. Heidi and I are still holding hands, and she's making a hiccup-like crying sound. I tell her to stop; she just doesn't.

The parking lot is cratered. Pits of glass so smooth it almost looks wet. I pick at the scabs on my face from the shards, almost as fine as pimples. It's strange to know that when I finally lay my head down in the back of Roman's Camaro, I'll feel the slivers in my cheek and that a month later I'll carelessly scratch at my face and a little piece of glass will fall into my palm. I'll roll it between my fingers and start crying, remembering how Heidi turned to me, her face in the reflection of the window sincere, and said, "We need to leave. Now."

And if we'd waited, or if we'd gone sooner, or if we'd changed direction, things would be different.

The shadow of the spacecraft darts across the pavement in front of us like a giant bird, and I know how mice feel when a hawk descends. I know how fast they run with the adrenaline pumping through their legs, driving them on.

One of *The Kind* is on the ground behind us. I click the unlock button on Roman's Camaro and the lights turn on and the engine starts and I know it will be me driving, not the auto-drive, and I'm glad that my mother was poor and I had to learn how to drive, because there is no way the passive auto-drive will outrun these things. And my mother—it's a good thing she's already dead to me.

I think of her as I leave Heidi screaming in the rearview, arms waving as that black mass of alien flesh rolled toward her. She is lifted off the ground by something like a swaying branch and then she is gone and the whine of the electric engine is so loud with my foot on the accelerator, you would almost think it was running on petroleum.

I slept under a bridge in the tiny backseat, woke to someone tapping on the glass.

He wore black fatigues and had a rifle and three stripes on his shoulder. "Whatever you do, do not bump the horn when you climb into the front seat," he said.

Dr. Allman liked his name when I told him the story. Yuda. He said it was an original creation. I often wondered if I was crazy. I used to write stories and poetry, and if it weren't for Saul, if it weren't for him being there to validate my story, I would've believed I was crazy three years ago.

Even if I had bumped the horn, nothing would have happened. The charge was spent. Without plugging in or paying at a meter, I might as well have been sleeping in a turtle shell with leather seats.

That was when I met Saul. He was already with Yuda, had joined the merry men, ready to follow anyone with a plan to fight back. He was standing near the edge of the bridge's shadow, head tilted back, staring at The Wedge, holding a rifle across his chest, even though it was only a twenty-two. When he turned around, it was one of those moments where you know someone will be important to you, that they will push your life in a certain direction and that you were supposed to meet. I didn't think that was possible, not after *The Kind.* All the bullshit about an afterlife and the constant search for meaning that echoed through the canonical texts in all my English and philosophy classes had already flown out the window. I think; therefore, I am something, but amoebas and phytoplankton are God's creatures, too. And he doesn't answer their prayers, either. Yet I had that moment with Saul when he turned and smiled at me and his hand almost left the trigger guard to wave.

I was surfacing. I could feel the color of my thoughts starting to return even as I first felt my eyelids twitching.

I should have paid more attention to the news when I was in college. I remembered things happening, grand things, like when Huxley ran for office, and I would predict things like the government bailing out Google.

But the little things, the kind of things that would be impossible to predict, always eluded me. I had been too busy with my nose in a book or dating Andre to really pay attention. I'd say things like there will be a plane crash in the Indian Ocean, and they are going to think no one survived. They'll find one, floating on the evacuation slide and it will look like a jellyfish from space, and Dr. Allman would look at me. Three months later it would happen, and he'd smile patiently and say, "What's going to happen tomorrow?"

Sometimes I'd have a smart-ass answer, tell him he'd wake up and kiss his wife and then die in a car crash. He didn't like that. I told him once he'd stop wearing ties, and then I choked him with it. I don't think he liked my predictions after that.

It was easier to hurt people, having lived through the first invasion of *The Kind*.

Yuda said he had a place in mind. He said he knew the coordinates, because he'd been a helicopter pilot and he'd flown important people to it once, and he laughed. I wasn't sure if he was joking or not, but the story made sense when we finally got there.

We traveled at night, when *The Kind* didn't seem to patrol as much. The last place we slept was an old diner that still had a propane stove. We scrambled a dozen eggs that were a week past expiration, ate all the artificial bacon, drank a six-pack of nonalcoholic beer, and talked by the light of the propane burner on the stove. Saul sat next to me and talked about how he missed his family.

He wasn't going to try and cross the country to the West Coast until the skies cleared. He figured that would be soon enough. Someone would discover their weakness. There had to be one. In all the movies there was one. He was a dramaturge at heart.

I asked him if he had a girlfriend. I held him when he cried.

I could feel my toes. They were cold, and there was a haze of red behind my eyelids. Color was returning. I still couldn't move. This was the half-life, the moment when things changed, the moment the company who had designed agitol called the reclamation, where the patient gets a pleasant sense of euphoria and becomes grounded while still in a dream state.

Once you're strapped in, you can only go along for the ride, said the person in the noose.

We walked for days. Always tripping along at night, always biting back the rage. Always trying to keep silent and duck for cover whenever one of their ships crossed overhead.

The Wedge was always there when we hunkered down, its leading edge catching the light of the sun at night just like the moon as it went through its phases. When it passed over, if you looked up at the right moment you'd see things spark against its surface.

"Those are satellites," Yuda said. "None of them will survive with that thing in orbit."

We sat on the roof of an Agway, our bags freighted

with seeds. Yuda swore it was better than food. Saul said the same thing, but my stomach didn't agree. It showed optimism, and I liked them for it. My stomach was swelling. The baby kicked. I crossed my arms, feeling the need to keep it warm.

"How big do you think it is?"

I thought Saul was talking to me. I thought that he saw, that he knew I was pregnant. I'd thought about telling them both, then I thought of Heidi in the rearview and the way her stomach rumbled, how I knew even if she did make it to the car—which she wouldn't have—that she probably was a burden in the making. The kind of person who got other people killed.

I didn't want to be like her. Yuda had a coldness about him. The way he moved. A week before this, we were holed up in an abandoned motel room and heard someone screaming outside. Yuda wouldn't let me open the door, and Saul motioned for me to get back.

It was daytime and I was tired and at first I thought I was dreaming. Then I saw her. She was young, maybe as old as I was, a little heavier, wearing just a bra and jeans, her brown hair blazing in the sun. I pushed past Saul, back to the door, and Yuda clamped his hand over my mouth. "Wait," he said, and pointed a finger out the window.

The Kind had already had their way with her and she was starting to turn. She had red marks all over her torso, ribbed lines like something had coiled around her tight.

Her hands were stretched out like she was afraid to run into something, her footsteps tentative and small, and her back had something massive and black on it, holding tight to her body like it was trying to seep into her skin.

"They're fishing with her," Yuda whispered, and pointed farther down the street. A shadow behind a truck watched and a black, rubbery tentacle twitched back and forth by the rear tire like a cat's tail.

The woman in the street turned and looked straight at us, her eyes pure black like a snake, and Yuda dropped the curtain.

I stepped back and waited, our guns pointed at the door, and I was back on the roof of the Agway.

"It's massive, but it's closer than the moon so it's hard to tell," Yuda said. "I'm a pilot, not Copernicus."

"You think they will leave?" a woman named Bea said. We'd picked her up the day before, just outside Manchester. She'd been taking care of her father and when he saw what was coming down from the sky he keeled over, grabbing his chest. We saw smoke coming from her chimney and let ourselves in through a basement window, found her sitting on the side of his bed, a damp washcloth on his forehead. She didn't even know me, yet sobbed into my arms. Her father's skin was the color of rotten corn, folded fingers on his chest mottled and gray. There was a pen and a pad of paper beside the desk. The words *To Whom It May Concern:* were smudged with tearstains. If it hadn't been for the white flag smoke climbing out of the chimney, all we would have heard was a shot.

Yuda didn't say anything, just stared up at The Wedge slowly slipping across the sky above the Agway.

"I don't think they're going anywhere," Saul said. "Not unless we give them a reason."

We waited inside the motel for the girl in the street to go away. She just kept stumbling around, like she was looking for something. She knocked a side-view mirror off a car, left streaky red footprints on the hood as she climbed on top of it and loosed a scream. From where I sat next to the bed, it sounded like someone was burning alive.

She pulled at her hair. It came away in clumps, revealing a soft, black skull.

"Someone should put her out of her misery," Saul said, but we didn't.

I felt the darkness more than saw it. That's where it always dumps me. The pharmaceutical company that produces agitol designed it to attack neurosis. Francine, one of the other patients who has bright red hair and a Boston accent, said it's like being held underwater and watching your death over and over. She's right.

A succession of lights darted across the ceiling and the tops of the walls, over and over again, chasing its own tail. The memory of the woman on top of the car, pulling gobs of hair off her skull, was still fresh in my mind, and I sat with it, letting it wash over me, pull me along, until a finger of panic traced over my chest, like a sewing needle pulling a thread of fear through each one of my ribs, constricting it until I was short of breath.

Maybe I was wrong. Maybe I was crazy. I prayed that I was absolutely schizo and the world inside my mind was as deep and vast as the universe.

I sat up. The moon shone through the window, a big, pathetic-looking thing, paler than any I'd seen before, thanks to the agitol. In the street below, strobe lights danced atop abandoned police vehicles, their armored sides rhino-thick. Several of the buildings had jagged rooflines and the white, foggy glow of fires flickered inside their broken shells.

It was night. Things were burning. The moon was cut cleanly in half by The Wedge.

The Kind had come.

The world spun. I slipped to my knees and cried.

Several minutes later, the door to my room opened.

"We should get going," Saul said.

The color was starting to return. The fires out the window were taking on a yellow tint, the strobe lights a purplish-white. "I didn't want it to be real," I said.

Saul stepped into the room, touched my shoulder. "Neither did I."

"When are we leaving?" someone said. I turned quickly. Shadows of other patients hung in the doorway.

"Always knew you were right. Always knew you were from the future," Jazz said.

Saul went to the door and yanked off a sticky note and handed it to me. "It's from Allman," he said.

The note had two hastily scrawled words. *I'm sorry.*

"They didn't stick around once they saw The Wedge," Jazz said, hiking up a makeshift pack on his shoulders; a twisted bedsheet, sagging with the bulky shapes of canned goods. "All of 'em up and left. Soon as the reports came in, they just ran home to their families."

"We should go," Saul said.

I went to the window, looked over the city, the lazy columns of smoke. There would be pits with bottoms of smooth glass, melted sand, the acne scars of alien invasion.

"Do you think we could have done something? Something more?" I said.

Saul shook his head slowly. The shadows of people behind Jazz swayed impatiently.

"We really need to go," Saul said.

"What if I don't want to?" I said. "What if I don't want to live through this again? What if I just . . . ?"

"What, you want to die? Is that what you want to do? Because if it is, I got twenty people who want to live, and at least we know what the hell we're dealing with. If we don't help them, no one will."

I took Saul's hand and pulled him back toward the window, whispered to him so they couldn't hear me. "But Saul, they're crazy."

He pulled his hand away. "So were you until a few hours ago."

He walked to the door, the others shuffling back out of his way. "Get dressed. You can thank me later."

They had raided the kitchen for canned goods and broken into med carts. They all had their medication—what happened when that ran out, or did it matter?—and enough antibiotics to stave off infection through the winter. In a way, we were better off than we were the last time.

Saul stopped at the edge of the awning and looked up at the sky, the silver line of light that was The Wedge blocking out most of the stars we could wish on. The sweetness of ocean, mixed with the stench of burning building material and the suffering smell of singed hair hung in the air.

"Where do we go first?" a woman with stringy gray hair said. I'd never met her before, but had seen her in the cafeteria.

It was cold. Shards of glass sparkled on the ground like frost, puddled around the abandoned cars in the street. "A shoe store," I said. "I always wish I'd done that."

Saul looked down at my feet. Slipper socks.

"That's a good call," he said.

A man named Sally with shoulder-length hair fanned over his shoulders and wearing a woman's sun hat picked the lock of the first shoe store we found. "I can pick that door. Can pick. Let me. I'm going," he said, so fast it was almost mumbling, and I thought, Yuda is never going to let any of these people join him.

Sally pushed the door open. Bells jingled and a dot of green light appeared on his white scrub top. The light flicked to his head and someone called out, "Get out of here!"

Everyone turned and ran, but Saul grabbed my arm.

The light bounced on Sally's forehead, and he stood still like it was a bee.

"We just want some shoes. We know a place that's safe," Saul shouted into the dark store.

"But," I said, remembering how *The Kind* had come there, too, how we had been overrun.

Saul squeezed my hand, telling me to shut up.

The other patients were at the edge of the building, waiting.

"Please light, don't blow. Up, Sally didn't want to hurt just pick the lock it's useful a skill. If you. Please light. Sally. Don't blow up," Sally said.

The light flickered. "Damn it," someone said inside.

I gently pulled Sally out of the way. A flashlight hit me in the eyes. I covered my face. The circle of light crawled down to my feet.

"What size are you?" the voice called.

We ended up taking him with us. His name was Bernie, and he had a laser pointer and a piss stain between his legs. He was a good guy.

We moved at night. During the day we hid in basements, under bridges, or any dark place we could find, the lower and more soundproof the better as we made our way north.

There were screams, almost constantly at first, then people began to figure it out, that they had to keep their heads down when The Wedge was in the sky.

Something pushed on the corner of the bed, climbing quickly toward my face. For a second, my heart froze, then took off like a rocket, ricocheting against my chest even as I saw the whiskers, the pointy face.

Gray, black, and white tiger stripes nudged my chin and began to purr.

"Hi, kitty," I said. "Where did you come from?"

Pale pink afternoon light pushed through the blinds. I was in a bed with Snoopy sheets. Pictures of cats hung on the wall next to pin-ups, and the faint smell of urine hung in the air.

I looked around the room. "Oh, right."

Last night I'd given up on the basement. Even from Snoopy's bed I could hear the snoring. It was Moncrief—certainly not his given name—he had a penchant for earth-rumbling snoring. Saul was going to smother him with a pillow some day. I just knew it. A ceramic kangaroo stared at me. It had a silver wristwatch hanging on its neck like a laurel. I peeled it off. Four o'clock.

"You need to keep your head down during the day. This is too early," I said, and sat up. My pink running shoes were beside the bed.

I took the cat and found the kitchen. The entire house smelled like rotting food, but it had a gas stove. "Huh," I said to the kitty, who meowed. The stove clicked and the burner lit.

"Let's see if they were coffee drinkers," I said. I found a pot, some water in a filter pitcher inside the fridge, and a handful of coffee in teabags. The water had some mold on the surface. I didn't care. I was going to boil it.

There were pictures of a wedding in the living room, a typical couple smilingly happily, surrounded by everyone they loved. The cat dug at my ribs a little, and I put it down. He scurried behind a couch, appeared at the other end and ran down the hall.

I'd slept in the kid's bed, I thought.

The cat stopped at the end of the hall and looked back for my help. I followed. The sound of the water boiling on the stove faded behind me as my soft-soled shoes kissed the floor with each step.

I pushed the door open. Green walls. A dresser, a king-size bed. The cat stood on a lump in the center. There were three shapes under the covers, a blackened, oxygen-deprived hand peeking out from under the comforter. Six legs. I grabbed the cat off the bed.

I looked. I shouldn't have looked, but I did. It was like a tableau from one of those old Christian horror books, the family hiding from the glory of God, cowering together, the man with all he holds dear in his arms, faces shying away from whatever was about to befall them, and I wished I had done things differently. I wished it had been me, not Heidi that had been taken by *The Kind*. I wished I hadn't had it growing inside me, forcing me to fight so hard.

Because I wouldn't have. I was supposed to teach kids how to read and make Shakespeare fun and write more papers and then, five years ago or two months now, whichever it was, I was supposed to die. I wasn't supposed to live through this. Maybe Saul was, Saul who could sleep in the basement with Moncrief's snoring, but not me.

I would have named him Alexander. Today might have been the day that I was screaming and shouting and going through a birth without anesthetic in a basement lined with mattresses. I gave birth to a six-pound silent fetus, blood, and tears.

They set it on my stomach, said I was begging for it. That I needed it. And when I saw it wasn't breathing, I wasn't sure which of my prayers God had answered.

I poured the water over a filter bag. Found a bag of sugar and dumped some in. Opened the slider and stepped outside. Just the smell of fresh air, coffee, and sunshine made me remember why life used to be worth living. Before, there had always been promise. If I worked hard enough or, hell, if I just got lucky, things would explode into heaven. It never happened, not for most people, but it was always near. You could always smell it, taste it in the air. Feel it incubating.

The coffee was bitter, burned my tongue, and was clearly synthetic. It was better than no coffee at all. I sat with the kitty coiling about my ankles like a snake, and watched the sun slip behind the trees. I had no idea where I was, and for the moment, it didn't matter. It felt like old times. I didn't even care that the sun was up. I imagined that *The Kind* had never come and this was all just a dream and maybe I was crazy and was still in the hospital and when I woke, I'd be pleasantly aware of the fact that I'd been the victim of the longest nightmare in history, in my sweaty cotton sheets.

I drank the entire cup and decided on more coffee. When I got to my feet, the world spun. I tripped over the kitty. He squealed and darted back into the house, down the hall toward his late family.

The Wedge appeared to grow out of the roof, the gray shingles boiling as heat waves streamed off it. I looked at the coffee cup like a lover that had just insulted me.

The family. All of them. No bullet holes. All huddled together.

The water pitcher. They poisoned the water.

I dropped the mug. The tea bag spit out and lay on the deck like the carcass of a drowned mouse. The wood grain around it began to swim like rivers over-running their banks, veins flowing in contradictory north and south. The trees bent and shrugged as the colors of the sunset dripped. Oily clouds slid on top of each other like grease on a pane of glass.

I remembered thinking that I might as well climb into bed with them. I might as well have snuggled up and blown my brains out.

Something cut a swath through the sky, erupting through the cloudburst and swirling the colors of the sunset. It sounded like the icy breath of a jetliner at low altitude, growing closer, rumbling.

For one second I looked back at the house, the siding bent and warping, shingles flapping like thousands of mouths. My pie-eyed reflection surfaced on the sliding glass door. I came closer, realized I was looking at my soul, the part of me that existed before whatever poison I'd ingested had stripped it from my body and imprisoned it in the house.

My reflection cupped her hand, and her lips formed wide shapes long before I heard the sound of her voice.

Run.

I didn't need to be told twice.

With each step, the ground felt farther from my feet and spongy, like running on a trampoline. The houses in the subdivision had eyes, and I saw myself in all of them as I passed. Blue and red dots danced at the corners of my vision, and they turned into words. The blue said *breathe,* the red said *faster.*

As the ship flew over me I felt the warm breath of a hurricane, pressing my clothes flat against my skin and making them heavy. The air turned sour. Then there was pressure around my waist, and the ground tumbled onto the sky as I was pried from my feet. I squirmed and I kicked my feet and I hit at the metallic tentacle that clasped my waist and wrist. Nothing I did stopped me from rising into the black hole on the underside of the ship. My tangled hair didn't hide the tentacles.

Red and blue lights danced before my eyes and the world spun as it does in the moments before waking with an unquenchable thirst and a desire to vomit, with an impossible desire to sink lower into sleep and never drink again.

Black lines darted over the lights, the tentacles of *The Kind* pushing buttons and changing screens as universes slipped past the ship. I could see the moon, the cratered surface of it impossibly close, and beneath, the earth, flat and small as a silver dollar.

I dreamed of Saul and the others, holed up in the tiny basement, and hoped they wouldn't drink out of the pitcher. I hoped they would drain the hot water tank, or maybe just leave. I wondered if Saul knew when he gave the all clear that the family had killed themselves, was shrouded under the sheets.

I wondered if he put them there, like that, holding each other.

For one sick moment I thought maybe he had. Then I realized that I was floating and spectral light was passing before my eyes, and my mother, sitting at the kitchen table with a *real* cigarette hanging out of her mouth, was staring at me as she exhaled smoke.

"A friend gave it to me," she said.

Real tobacco cigarettes were expensive. Nearly fifty bucks.

"Where did they get it?" I said.

She looked down and closed the billing app. "Don't know where they got it, but it sure. Is. Good," she said, and coughed.

I knew she was lying when John came in and she

stubbed it out. Flecks of ash littered the table and she wiped them away quickly.

John turned around and closed the door slowly when he saw us sitting at the table. Work gloves hung out of his back pocket. He held onto the doorknob a moment too long, looking down at it as if unsure if he was going to rush back out. He opted for the bedroom instead.

"John," my mother called as he swept past. "John, I'm sorry."

She chased after him, her robe fluttering.

"Leave me alone!" John yelled, and she stumbled back into the kitchen, eyes glazed, one red cheek covered by her hand.

What was left of the cigarette was in the ashtray. She fished it out, fought the pocket of her robe for her lighter, and lit up.

I spent the evening reading under the expansive branches of a willow tree, watching their tendrils stir the air like lazy horsetails, listening to the sounds of my mom's and John's muted screams rolling through the fog.

A mountain rose up before me, a black mass like cancer, its surface shivering like a child as people walked toward it. Rings of a nearby planet caught the sunset and someone knelt next to me and took my hands. I didn't have any breasts. My clothes were streamlined, simple, and I had to pee.

A woman with blazing eyes the color of lava peered into my face and said something I didn't understand. She squeezed my hand and her warmth seeped into my skin. I still held the book in my hands, the one I was reading underneath the willow tree. She folded it shut, tucked it under my arms.

She wanted me to trust her, to believe that everything would be okay. Then she led me forward, or tried to. My toes dug into the gray dirt, kicking up dust.

The Kind's air ships breathed tornado fire as they lifted off to our right. I tried to scream and run as they streaked across the sun, a pale orb the color of sunflowers; black blemishes constantly blooming and fading on its surface.

The woman with the fiery eyes bent down and she was speaking, vowels tumbling out of her mouth in a language so foreign I couldn't even place it, and the sound was overwhelming, so loud and so many voices within her mouth that I had to shut my eyes.

When I opened them, children surrounded me, poking me with sticks and chanting something, teasing me, pulling my hair. A woman with a thick braid of hair down to her middle back stood at the front of the class. Her dress was loose silk, only hinting at the ample hips and breasts beneath, a black collar making her neck appear more slender and a large horizontal stripe at the waist. She was beautiful with sharp cheekbones, severe. She pointed a laser at the children and one by one they jumped back as if bitten. She scolded them. I didn't understand. Beside her something had been peeled apart, flayed, and hung in front of the class on thin metal posts for observation. A pale yellow membrane clung to the inside of black skin.

The children sat down and the woman approached the thing. She touched it with her laser implement and sparks of electricity danced under the surface of its lemon innards as its limbs, still nailed to the posts, thrashed.

There were words, and a voice, loud and in my head, begging, pleading for it to stop, and all the children covered their heads with their arms, cowering because they felt it. Because they knew.

It was just like us.

And I was just like them. The woman with the braid was explaining it to us. I didn't believe it. Didn't want to acknowledge that maybe, somewhere deep inside as the woman with the lava red eyes of a demon who dragged me forward, that I had already been touched, that I already had the thing that was flayed in the classroom deep within my veins.

A pall settled over my eyes, transparent like sunglasses, but much, much darker, and I slipped back into the sleep of the soon-to-be hungover.

My feet were heavy; the sun was bright. We watched the rockets, that's what they called all the ships, lift off, their thrusters struggling to leave *Inmo*, and wondered why they'd want to make us heavier, more dense. They said it was to travel. Only something as soft as darkness could move at the speed of light.

It was propaganda, but it worked.

There are moments of déjà vu where you're not sure

if time is running backward or forward, or all at once. Everything is scrambled and floating, each moment you've ever thought you'd lived. It's magical.

Glass fractured beneath my feet, and I stared up at myself in the broken reflection. Dreadlocks had grown off my arms and legs. My face. My chin. I was melting. Dripping flesh, chunks of hair clinging to my hands. I shook it free like strands of gooey yarn.

Black flesh bulged where my skin used to be, rubbery and stretchy, the surface of a thick balloon, and I became interested in shadows. In the way they moved, the dance of daylight under trees. I was fascinated by the things hiding in them.

I was hunting.

The sign said *Vacancy*. The *V* was cracked. Beneath the sign grasshoppers danced in the grass. A seagull stood on top of a minivan, turning his head back and forth. He flew at me, scuttled along the ground and scooped up a piece of the flesh that had fallen away.

A curtain shook behind a thin windowpane as though a breath had stirred it. I saw myself, standing between the back of the curtain and the surface of the glass, looking back. Some time ago, maybe now, I was on the floor next to a bed that hundreds of people had screwed on, waiting for what used to be a human to go away.

My skin was black. My nose twitched, the muscles inside my face rearranged to pull it to one side and I was rounder, thick in the middle like. My eyes. No longer the rich honey brown, were as cold and black as a lizard's, betraying nothing of thought, of fear, of trepidation, of personality.

I sat beside the bed in the motel room, holding my breath as the woman outside approached the window, footsteps crunching glass. Her head moved like a bird next to a mirror, inspecting itself, trying to decide what to do. I was afraid she was going to attack the window, break it down and find us. I was afraid one of us would sneeze. I was afraid something would happen that would let it know that we were inside, hiding, waiting until the evening.

In the reflection of the glass, the smooth black skin on my forehead refused to furrow. My round black eyes refused to squint. I wondered how I would cry. I wondered how anyone would know me. I wondered what they had done to me. I needed someone, something, to hold me.

I began to run, not really feeling the bouncing sensation of being in control, of pushing off with each step, lumbering, feeling as if the ground was the belt of a treadmill beneath me, and then I tripped and the earth and the sky tumbled and mixed together and The Wedge overhead, it was beautiful, in some way, like the straight edge of a canyon that we lived in. It was like a shelter.

They told us not to be afraid in so many vowels. They told us not to worry, that it wouldn't hurt.

The first injection was like sludge, with bubbles that wouldn't rise to the surface, and they held me down and put it in my veins and the surface of my clear, almost translucent skin began to darken to a shade of purple like the *alircon* nebula at the edge of the galaxy. They said that would happen, that our skin would look like the dust of stars, that because of the change we could travel to them. We could answer the call.

That didn't stop me from screaming until I was hoarse, didn't stop me from thrashing and rolling and kicking. And when the change came over my eyes, the keenness to see in the dark that they promised, what they hadn't predicted happened; in the daytime, it was impossible to focus on anything but shadow.

We were made of stars and we were meant to travel to them, to be able to see them.

I needed to be touched, to be held. I needed Saul to face me and look at me and tell me that I wasn't a monster.

I needed to get my soul back from where it had been trapped in the house. I needed to move faster. The world tumbled, and I sank deeper.

I was sitting in an art class before a charcoal-blackened piece of paper, using an eraser to resurrect a saucer and teacup out of the jet-black darkness when I stopped, took up a piece of charcoal and filled in the curves, the movement of light on the edge of the saucer. The instructor, Mr. Katz, came around and peered over my shoulder, wondering what I would do next. I scratched the effigy of a cross down the middle of the paper with the eraser, a dirty, dusty thing, and Mr. Katz moved on without a word. I was going crazy. I just felt, I just needed to see it, emblazoned on the paper. To think for a second that something bigger than me was out there, and that it gave a shit.

My mother disappeared into the fog of the parking lot and I never saw her again. She was on a trip with some of her friends to New York and got hit by a car as she crossed the street. The report said she had been drinking, that it was most likely her fault, and it hinted that there was more in the toxicology report. I stood over the stainless steel slab in the morgue, looking down at her. Her hair was flat. It was probably because she'd spent time in a body bag. I hoped it had been white, so that she didn't have to be afraid of the darkness.

I remembered the family, all wrapped up together under the blankets, and wished that I had just crawled onto the slab with my mother, slid myself into the freezer and gone to sleep. But I hadn't. The earth still tumbled, and the sky was still appearing and reappearing and my limbs, they were gone.

I knew where I was going. I needed to warn Saul.

The clapboards on the house still danced and the eye-like windows still glared gloomily out at the street, reflecting the lifeless bodies inside. I knew they would open the fridge. That some of them would drink. One, maybe more of them, would die. I had to stop them.

The teacup was still on the deck, the half-dried tea bag drained of color in spots. I pounded on the sliding glass door, my limbs flailing against my naked reflection, trying to drive it away, to get my soul back.

When it shattered, I heard the screams of children. I heard the sound of jets. Saul was inside on the radio saying, "Please, help us."

Muzzle flashes danced in the dark edges of the room and grabbed my attention, held it like movement in the dirt holds the attention of a hawk. I drove toward them, trying to take their weapons, trying to take.

They screamed as I touched them. The howling of *The Kind's* ships descending all around the house drove all of them to the ground, everyone retreating into the basement.

I tumbled down the steps and saw Saul, his eyes wide, the radio hovering before his lips. "Yuda," he said. "It's Saul. Don't let Reginald take us on the train."

Yuda's crackly voice came back. "*What?*"

"Don't let Reginald take us on the train!"

I touched Saul, and he squirmed. I tried to hold his arms as he stabbed at me with a knife. I almost didn't feel it. Didn't care that my memories, in all their fleeting electrical impulses, were slipping out into the world, puddling on the floor.

I used to dream of someone whispering they loved me as they drove deeper and deeper, my hips rising to theirs, giving myself to them. I was giving myself to Saul.

All of me.

Chapter 5

Amos

Even an atheist would admit that if God had a plan, Reginald was part of it, and I hated him for it. I could feel it in every corner of my soul, each digit and joint of my feet. It was easy enough to write him off after the first encounter, despite having Rosaline to confirm that I wasn't crazy. The second time I saw him in France, it was clear he'd become something more than a man, maybe even more than a prophet; he was a God. He had sat down next to me on a bench in the park yesterday and gave me a gold Victory Knox watch—a hunk of gold I had first thought was a part of his cane—and promised his intentions were good, and that he could prove it.

I decided to go to the bank earlier than Reginald had suggested, my little act of defiance. Reginald was more monster than God, more Bacchus than Jesus, and I refused to submit to him for any reason. Or trust him. But he had piqued my interest.

I stopped at the doors to the bank and smoothed my

hair in the reflection of the glass. Gray hair was starting to show.

The door swung open and a nice-looking redhead with a child, all done up in lederhosen and suspenders, strode out, and I shoved my hands in my pockets quickly.

"They make something for that," she said about my hair with a knowing smile as they brushed past.

I was twenty-seven, and no matter how far I'd gotten from my father, I was still destined to have his gray hair.

The inside of the bank was busy, a line six people deep, and the snapping sound of typewriters and ringing phones echoed off the marble floors. I waited in line anxiously, the thick pile of money Reginald had given me in my jacket pocket like a brick against my chest. I should have taken the money and run away with Rosaline, but I knew Reginald would just show up again later, making sure that everything happened as it should, or didn't.

God worked in mysterious ways.

I approached the teller, a man with spectacles about to fall off his nose, deeply etched lines in his face, and a gray moustache, and he waited for me to speak.

"I'd like to make a deposit."

"How much?" he said.

"Fifteen hundred," I said.

He whistled long and slow, tilting his head back to see through his glasses. Hair from his nose grew into his moustache.

"Another deposit? You must be raking it in." He

leaned across the counter. "You a gambler? Card shark?"

I didn't say anything as I passed him the stack of bills.

"Not interested in my staking you, huh?"

"That sounds violent," I said.

He scrunched up his face, wrinkles deepening. "That's what you said yesterday."

"Yesterday?" I said. "I was here yesterday?"

The teller touched the ends of his moustache in consideration. "I thought I could smell the booze on you. That's why I thought you was a gambler." A key on his adding machine snapped once before he started counting. He stopped when the twenties were gone. "Most people don't come in smelling that way at this time a day, unless they're taking money out."

"It was an interesting day," I said.

He laughed as the stack of bills in his hand got shorter and the one on the counter grew taller. "Well, you were right. Fifteen hundred."

"Could I make a balance inquiry?" I said. "Just want to make sure I know how much the house has."

"I knew you was a gambler. Usually I need a day to check the books, but I know from yesterday, counting today's deposit, you've got twelve large. Most people would keep some in their mattress."

"Really?" I said, looking over my shoulder for Reginald. I didn't see him, just a series of impatient-looking gentlemen in suits and women who were all too happy to be waiting in line to pick up some of their husband's money to spend.

"Well, not all of them. If they did we'd be out of business."

"Listen," I said, turning back to the teller, "Do I ever come in here with someone else? A fat man?"

"You best lay off the sauce," he said. He punched a few more keys into the adding machine and ripped off my receipt. He wrote a few words on it and signed it before he handed it to me.

"So, what's your secret?"

I tapped the receipt on the counter. "I'll tell you when I know."

He laughed, but I could tell he was disappointed.

Outside, the sun had been blocked by dark clouds. "Really, Amos?" a voice that sounded far too familiar said.

I turned and saw him standing there, casually leaning against the edge of the brick window frame. "Five minutes early? Did you have to?"

"You figured it out."

"And what would you do if I wasn't here?" he said.

"I'd walk away, happy to know I have the account number and hoping I'd never see you again."

"Exactly," he said. "So I had to walk back to the train, then reset and walk back here, over an hour's travel, just for five little minutes and your stupidity."

"You've lost weight," I said, winding the watch behind my back. "Lean times in the future?"

He spread his arms and looked down, as if surprised.

I tossed the watch to him.

"Your watch is fast," I said as he caught it.

He flipped open the face, brought a monocle to his eye and looked down at it. "I see," he said.

"You got me running numbers for you? Are you a bookie now?"

Reginald rolled his eyes. "I assure you, it's nothing as pedestrian as all that."

I hated that I didn't have any reason to doubt him. Despite his attempt to kill me, twice—sort of—he'd never lied to me, even when he intended to murder my unborn offspring.

"Then what is it?" I said.

The corners of his mouth pulled back in a wicked grin. "I thought you'd never ask," he said, placing a hand on my shoulder and guiding me back toward the park.

"How would you like to help me shape the future?" he said.

"I thought that was already done?" I said.

"Well, it's not as rosy as I'd like," he said, still smiling that fox in the hen house smile.

"You're the prophet, fix it."

"I'd like to," he said. We stopped for a bus and some cars to glide through an intersection. "But there's a problem with that."

In the distance lightning danced in the sky. There was no thunder, no rain. The sun was at our backs. I thought somewhere there ought to be a rainbow.

"You see," he said as we stepped into the road, "there are certain strings that have to be pulled. People that need to be nudged in certain directions. What I'm proposing requires someone to maintain a diligent watch, here. In the past."

"In the present," I said.

"Is that what we're calling it?" He quickened his pace until we stopped at the edge of the park and looked in. A child laughed at his wind-up robot, clumsily walking itself toward him, and a couple lay on their stomachs on a colorful blanket, sharing a book as their radio blared some kind of music.

"What are you asking of me, Reginald?"

"That you make some strategic business moves. You will profit greatly. Your family will profit. You will gain money and influence, but you will be at my disposal."

"You want me to serve you?" I laughed. "There's no way I would ever, ever, serve a murderer like you."

"The money never gets you," he said, in a voice that was just loud enough for me to hear. "Listen," he said, brightening, "I understand your hesitation. I understand why you may not want to help me, but rest assured, even in our darkest encounters, my motives were only for the good of mankind."

More truth, I thought, remembering his words from our first encounter. Rosaline's future great-great-great-grandson somehow invited those things—I shuddered at the thought of the tower and what rolled down it—and his goal was to kill her. One thing we both wondered about, though, was how come he didn't kill her right then and there on the train platform. Maybe that was just more proof of his humanity.

"Prove it," I said.

Reginald bowed in a most graceful way, putting on airs. Upon rising, he said, "I'll show you just how much I'd like to save the world. If you believe me, you have to make a few stock trades and business purchases for me. Deal?"

"Maybe," I said, letting his hand linger in the air.

"You'll have to ride in the train again," he said.

"As long as it's not on the bumper," I said.

Reginald laughed so hard I looked at him funny. "Oh no," he said. "You definitely wouldn't want to do that," he said, wiping tears from his eyes.

We walked out of the city toward the train station, and stopped at a barren set of tracks.

"Will you hold this?" he said, extending his cane to me.

I took it from him. Despite being solid, and gold, it was light as a feather.

"Or sit on it, I don't care," Reginald said, walking toward the train tracks. He stopped abruptly, rubbed the bridge of his nose, and shook his head as he reached up and pulled on something, causing the very rail yard to wrinkle. "I'll never get used to that," he said, pulling at the fabric of the world.

I hefted the cane in my hands and considered hitting him, repaying the favor of our first visit wherein he must have struck me five times. All this could end, right here.

Then he began rolling up actual fabric—burlap, by the look of it—that hadn't been there moments before, revealing the wheels of the train, and the thought left me. Many times over, I wished I had struck him and beat him dead then.

"How are you doing that?" I gasped.

"This old thing?" he said, clearly enjoying my guffaw. "It's just a bit of camo, that's all. Here, take a look," he said, holding the bundle out to me. I switched it for the cane.

It was fabric with something shiny mixed in. "I'll explain it later," he said. "Come on in the train so I can tell you about one of the greatest disasters in history."

"Wait, what disaster?" I said, following him into the train.

It was strange being inside the train again, seeing the new technology. I asked him how it worked.

"Bloody hell if I know," he said.

The disappointment must have shown on my face as we started moving, placidly at first, away from the city, the Hudson River on our right, and started picking up speed after Reginald pushed a button.

"Okay, listen," Reginald said, turning to me as the train really began picking up speed. "Here's how it works. Basically, we're all energy condensed and when you reach a certain speed . . ."

The sound of the train rushing forward, and the fingers of electricity wriggling toward the center of the windscreen, drawing my eyes like a siren's call, made it impossible to follow him, although I doubted if I'd understand any of it anyway.

We emerged to a dark day. Snow covered the tracks. It didn't seem to bother the train. The crosshatched outlines of fallen trees were like ghosts beneath the snow.

"Where are we?" I said.

"Russia," he said, "2042. It was the Ukraine for a while, but it's really always been Russia. No one has been able to live in this area in over sixty years. In a week, this part of it will be deemed habitable again, although only poor people will move in at first. It's a shame, really."

"What happened?"

"Ah, the history of tomorrow," he said, stopping the train near a depression in the snow that could only be a body of water, several hundred acres in size. On the other side of the pond, long, crumbling six-story buildings rose out of the earth like jagged teeth, snarled metal crawling out of their ends like twisted hair. "We're in a place called Pripyat," he said. "You remember what the Americans dropped on Hiroshima and Nagasaki to end the war?" he said.

I nodded. I hadn't liked that it ended that way.

"It happens here, by accident . . . sort of," Reginald said. He went to the door and threw it open. A cold blast rushed in and I shivered. "Grab a coat out of the back, and let's go for a walk."

It was a woman's coat, lined with fur and still stinking of the smell of flowery perfume. I didn't have much of a choice. I contented myself with the fact that, as usual, if Reginald wanted to kill me, he could have done it by now.

He needn't have brought me to the future to do it.

Snow crunched under our feet as we walked across the frozen lake, which occasionally groaned, the sounds of cracking ice running away from us at an inescapable pace. "Are you sure the ice is safe?" I said.

"Of course not," Reginald said. "But we're in Russia and when in Rome, we do as the Russians."

I'd heard the expression, although not mangled to that extent.

When we reached the far side of the pond, the buildings rose like those in Brooklyn, rivaling some of the new apartment buildings, the concrete style of architecture vaguely familiar, as if something I'd seen in a dream. They had no windows, mostly, save a few broken pieces still clinging to the panes, and anything metal had long been salvaged. Standing still, the sound of the snow falling was like a gentle whisper, a sound that could have been warm and comforting.

Reginald covered his eyes and scanned the side of the building, looking up, waiting. On the top floor, a mitten-clad hand reached out and waved.

"There she is," Reginald said.

He walked toward the building.

"You're not going inside there, are you?" I called.

"Yes, *we* are," he said, not waiting to see if I'd actually accompany him.

The inside was full of rubble and refuse piled in corners; a shredded mattress, springs exposed, newspapers, rags that used to be clothes. Everything that was once wood had been torn out; doorframes, trim, and stair rails.

"She's very young, but quite nice," Reginald said, heading for the stairs.

"Who is?"

"A little girl who took refuge here some time in the last year. They find her, you know, and although she's quite something to look at, they don't find any trace of radiation in her."

Our footsteps and the striking of his staff on the floor were loud in the stairwell. Snowflakes rode a cold breeze in through a window before settling. I watched as Reginald's step left a perfect footprint in the thin patina of snow. I wondered why it was he that was able to leave footprints across time, across continents, and felt as though the universe was unjust.

A little girl appeared at the top of the stairs, smiling grotesquely with webbed lips. She was missing pieces of her face and half her lower jaw. I stopped, breath stalled in my chest. It reminded me of being in the Rine forest, of hearing explosions and knowing my buddies were now all around me, their shattered bodies scattered through the trees.

I almost fell backward down the stairs, catching myself and falling into the wall instead.

"Come now, don't be rude," Reginald said, barely looking back.

The little girl said something quiet and held out her

hands, ready to receive a gift. Her hair was long and black, what there was of it, at least. She'd been burned. She couldn't have been more than five feet tall and was clearly happy to see us.

I forced myself to take a step, and the next one was easier, and when I remembered to breathe, I knew I would make it.

Reginald stopped before her at the top of the stairs and reached into the pockets of his coat. "What do you say?" he said, touching her nose like a button.

I cannot tell you how disturbed I was to see him around a child. He was so assiduously evil that knowing he was in a position to influence a child, especially one so clearly starved for attention, was frightening.

"May I *pleave* have one treat," the little girl said, with considerable effort.

Reginald smiled and dropped something in her hand.

She stood on her tiptoes, and he bent to receive his treat: a kiss on the cheek.

"*Spasibo, dedushka*," she said, and turned and led us into an apartment with the only door I'd seen.

She dropped the wrapper for whatever Reginald had given her, something golden and plastic, in a bin and sat down on a couch with its stuffing showing. I sat on a stool that was uneven, and Reginald sat on a kind of red crate, and we watched as she ate her treat.

"Who is this, Reginald?" I said.

"She likes candy. Can't hurt her teeth much, wouldn't you say?"

I'd only spent two, maybe three hours around Reginald my entire life, but I knew that he'd only answer my question in his own time.

"She was caught in a fire," he said, his voice low. He blew on his hands as if to warm them. "Tried to slide down a laundry chute, got stuck, and then was lucky, or unlucky enough to have the fire extinguished. They found her, like a kitten stuck in a tree, at the age of three."

He reached into his pocket and tossed me something. A lighter with a clover on it.

"Open it, strike the flint," Reginald commanded.

I flipped open the lid and caught the little girl staring at me. I pushed my thumb on the wheel. She flinched as sparks flew. The wick didn't catch.

"It's okay, do it again," Reginald said.

I worked the wheel again, and this time the wick caught. The girl screamed and practically flew across the room into Reginald's arms, burying her face in his chest.

He nodded at me, and I closed the lid.

"*Eto Bezopasno*," Reginald said several times.

"Why are we here?" I said.

Reginald stroked the child's hair gently. "I told you," Reginald said. "History lesson."

Outside, Reginald squatted before the girl, a hand on her shoulders. "*Ne volnuytes'. My skoro vernemsya . . .*"

She nodded, dotting tears from her eyes.

"*Da*," Reginald said, placing another candy in her hands and pulling her chin up. He pointed at his cheek, and she kissed him again.

"*Do svidaniya*," Reginald said, and she watched us leave.

The sun grew low, setting before us as we walked across the frozen pond.

"Who was she?" I said.

Reginald didn't stop. His words blended into the wind and the endless gnawing of our footsteps on the snow, and I had to piece them together. "My great-granddaughter."

I didn't close my eyes when the train jumped again. The lightning formed a tight mesh like the gauze the medics used to press on gaping wounds in the war, obscuring a tunnel of color that was mesmerizing, and I remembered seeing God there for the first time. I felt certain, even more than I had with my head down in the mud during the war—I was only hopeful, desperate then—that God was real. There was no way he couldn't be. And it wasn't that Reginald was God—that was completely, wholly blasphemous. Reginald was just a man, but the fact that he could travel through time, that he could change things like we were going to do, that was proof enough.

Then I realized how many generations had lived and died around that town with Reginald's little granddaughter, and I knew why people lost faith.

When the train stopped and we got out, the weather was better. There were still no leaves on the trees, and the first bite of winter stung the air. I thought about the coat he'd let me wear, the one that smelled like perfume. It definitely wasn't Reginald's.

"Who wears the coat, Reginald?"

He tsked. "Surely you're bright enough to figure that out," he said. He stopped and turned to me, tucking the staff, which was a little bit shorter, into his coat. "Whatever you do, don't speak. Relations with Americans are not exactly pristine at this point."

A truck roared past hauling a load of lumber, and I realized that I wasn't just in a foreign country, I was in a foreign time, and both were hostile.

"You have a knack for finding trouble, don't you?"

Reginald produced an *ushanka* from under his coat and placed it on my head. The earmuffs were warm. It felt strange. "Trouble finds me," Reginald said. "Come on."

He led me toward the same apartment building I'd seen before, except this time there was a glass door with a lock on it barring our entrance. Reginald produced a key and let us in. A warm breeze flowed out of the building, and I walked up the steps behind him, watching his feet strike the floor, realizing how I had also been fortunate enough to walk across the same steps decades apart on the same day. In a way, we were immortal. Delusional, too, I thought, chuckling to myself.

Reginald stopped. "What's so funny?" he asked over his shoulder.

"You, taking the same flight of stairs, decades apart on the same day."

"You get used to it," he said, and resumed up the

stairs. His footsteps were heavier.

We stopped before a door and waited after Reginald knocked. On the stairwell, shouts in a language I didn't understand burst from above. I decided arguing sounded nearly the same in any language.

Reginald knocked again.

"What if she's—"

"*Ona zdes'. My budem zhdat',*" Reginald said, holding a finger to his lips for silence.

"*Da,*" I said, and smiled.

The door opened, and a woman with striking blue eyes stood there. I immediately noticed that her eyebrows were crooked, or that one grew pointedly down, toward her nose—which only made her more curious—and she threw her arms around Reginald's neck and kissed him.

She began talking quickly in Russian. Reginald nodded. It was very clear from the way she looked at him she was in love.

She led us inside the small apartment. The living room was open to the kitchen, the entire space hardly any bigger than the railcar we'd arrived on. After I closed the door, Reginald told me to sit next to him on a faded green couch, whose back was covered with a patchwork quilt. She set about making tea and chattering on in Russian. Her speech wasn't frantic, but there was an urgent quality to it. Or maybe it was just me, knowing that these people, who were our allies in the war, now hated us.

Reginald produced something small and round from

his pocket and pushed buttons on its surface, configuring it. I tried not to appear too curious. "Sometimes," Reginald said quietly, so as not to disturb the woman, "I like to just listen, to hear her speak in her native language."

"You mean you don't understand her?" I said.

"A little," he said. "But so much of communication is nonverbal."

She finished with the kettle and turned to face us, her hands on her hips. She was skinny, even under the loose clothing.

Reginald pushed another button and set the round device on the coffee table in front of us. "Okay," he said, and a voice just like his echoed the words in Russian.

I pointed at it. "How did you do that?" I said, and the echo of my voice became Russian as well.

Reginald pumped his eyebrows at me.

"Who is this man?" the echo of the woman's voice said.

"Svetlana, he is a friend," Reginald said.

I shuddered.

She licked her lips. "Where have you been?"

"Away, on business," Reginald explained.

"How long have you known each other?" I said.

Reginald touched and held a button on the translator device, at which the woman launched into a tirade. Reginald spoke over her. "Three months, of her life, but it's been longer than that for me."

"Three months, and you already have a grandchild?" I said.

"Well, time travel is not without its disadvantages," Reginald said.

He took his hand off the translator and the echo of her angry voice filled the room. "Three days, and I haven't seen you at all. You don't call, you don't write, and there's been no way to find out where you've been. What have you to say for yourself?"

Reginald paused. "I've been away on business. What do you expect me to say?"

"You should have called."

"I wish I had," Reginald said. "Normally, I would have made a special stop to call and tell you that I missed you."

"Our business was unavoidable," I said.

"Careful," Reginald warned.

"And what business is that? Drugs? Women? Or is it just one woman?" she said.

The teakettle began to whistle behind her. She huffed and took it off the stove. The spoon clinked angrily inside, and she served my tea in a chipped cup. I thanked her anyway.

Someone groaned elsewhere in the apartment.

Reginald covered the translator. "That's why we're here."

The woman yelled at him. I didn't need the translator to know why we were keeping secrets.

A young man emerged from the back rooms, mouth open in a yawn, stubble dotting his face, eyes at half-mast. He entered the kitchen without even seeing us sitting on the couch. He got a box of cereal from a cupboard, poured some in a bowl.

"If he only hadn't drank so much," Reginald said, hand still on the translator. "Nearly two thousand people would still be alive. Countless birth defects could have been avoided."

The woman came forward and pulled Reginald's hand off the translator. "What are you, spies?" she said.

Reginald stood, and as he did the young man in the kitchen, a boy, really, looked up and squinted at me. I held up a hand in acknowledgment, and he did the same, a little dribble of milk clinging to his bottom lip.

Reginald took her hands and held them close to his chest, looking deep into her eyes, which were filling with tears. I had to look away.

The rest of the apartment was cluttered, a basket of laundry sat on the kitchen table, which was a small metal thing, and the walls were bare. It really wasn't much better than what I'd seen before, in the future, when the place was completely uninhabitable.

Reginald held her in his arms, and her blue eyes stared dully at me over his shoulder. I thought, if he leaves today, as he undoubtedly will, she may never let him back in. Or if she does it will be a trap; she'll inform the authorities. He'll be imprisoned as a spy.

Maybe that's already happened, I thought, and he's correcting it.

"How long are you here for?" the boy said, the translator even echoing the way his mouth was full as he spoke. Fascinating technology. "Are you leaving again tonight? In five minutes?"

"Listen, *Iosif*," Reginald said to the boy. "You need to be sharp today at work."

Iosif set his cereal down on the counter. A little milk splashed over. "What did you say?"

"Reactor four needs to stay at thirty percent power," Reginald said.

"How do you know that?" Iosif said.

"Here. Have a cup of coffee," Reginald said, handing a bag of ground beans to him.

Iosif hit the bag with his hands, and some of the beans sprayed through the air in a long brown arc, landing on Iosif's mother's face. She gasped and closed her eyes.

"Get out of here!" Iosif pointed.

Svetlana was crying, hands over her face.

Iosif slapped Reginald and turned his shoulders, pushing him toward the door, speaking so quickly that the translator couldn't keep up. Or maybe it just knew better.

He chased us all the way down the stairs and yelled at us in the doorway. A group of men leaning against a small car took notice and stood up.

"Hurry," Reginald said, and we began to run. They didn't chase us.

Back on the train, I watched Reginald closely. He didn't look back. It was the last time he would see Svetlana, and he didn't even care. It didn't make any sense.

"She knew you for three months?" I said.

Reginald nodded as he pushed the buttons.

"Did you care about her?"

"Not enough," he said. The train began moving.

"What do you mean, not enough?"

The lightning played on his face, curling and writhing across his skin before boiling in color. He didn't explain.

We emerged on the other side in a crowded city. I could tell we were in the future, with the sleek vehicles and electric light. I should have been more excited. I should have cared. It didn't seem real.

"So, it worked?" I said. "And that was it? Throwing a bag of coffee at a young man made all this possible?"

"Yes," Reginald said. His eyebrows were low.

People on the sidewalks were pointing at the train.

He worked on the screen some more, and the train began to move.

"Time is a funny thing," Reginald said. He looked over at me. "I knew I wouldn't see her again if this worked, but . . ."

We emerged to a sunny pasture. One that looked all too familiar, the green bowl surrounded by mountains that he'd taken me to as a child.

His face fell and when the train stopped, he launched from his seat and out of the train.

I followed slowly, sensing a trap, and found him outside in the grass, on his knees, vomit on his chin. He wiped his chin and looked up. "I thought it would be easier," he said. He swallowed hard and stood up, and I could tell whatever emotion had broken free wouldn't show again.

The sound came over the horizon, and I shivered. There were two of them this time, of the same teardrop shape, and the same vinous towers climbed out of the earth to cradle them.

"We should go," I said.

Reginald watched the ships, eyes squinted against the sun. "Don't worry," he said. "They won't hurt us."

I expected them to tumble out of the spaceships like they did the last time. Maybe they weren't hungry. Maybe they were staring at us the same way, wondering what we were going to do.

"What else can we do?" I said.

Reginald turned on me suddenly. "What?"

"Are there other things, disasters, that we can stop?"

He struck me, open handed, across the face. "Do you even understand what we've done?" he said, and walked back to the train.

I climbed aboard, angry at him for hitting me, and even more angry at myself for not understanding. I thought about it as we traveled back, as I made the stock trade Reginald asked me to make, deposited the money in my account two days earlier, and as he took me across the city, crisscrossing the last two days, opening account after account at what had to be nearly every single bank, repeating the same trade until I had enough money to own several of the banks, and I still didn't understand until I lay my head on the pillow that night.

We'd fed the monsters.

Chapter 6

Angela

The world basically ended because of Dr. Morris Spinner. The first time I saw him was at the inaugural unveiling of the Phoenix Observatory, one of my father's philanthropic endeavors. In typical fashion, it was teeming with designer gowns, diamonds, sequins, and bowties. My father had spared no expense; a holographic projection of a deep space voyage swirled on the domed ceiling of the observatory, nebulae and stars and galaxies slowly spinning by like some sort of adult mobile. The motion made me sick, so I was pretending to study the toothpick in my martini when Morris appeared in the curved reflection of my silver bracelet, his shadowy face looming in front of the distorted galaxy like a God.

I shuddered. His fingers were warm, gentle as he took the toothpick from me. He turned, the muscles of his back perfectly visible beneath the tailored tuxedo jacket, and appraised the ice swan beside us. Its frozen skin was like a prism, reflecting and manipulating all the celestial bodies of the artificial sky above our heads.

He breathed on the end of the toothpick, the kind of slow breath someone would use to warm their hands, and stuck it into a spot on the side of the swan, just above its wing.

"That's the center," he said. "If you don't move."

He moved out of the way like a circus conductor stepping into the shadows, and I saw that he was right. The light of every star bloomed inside the ice swan and converged and twisted and morphed around the tiny toothpick like it was a North Star.

He smiled confidently, the kind of face a camera would love even if he had dimples. He wasn't wearing glasses. I imagined he'd look better with them, sandy hair and sharp features indicative of a strong work ethic and devotion to his physique; brawn, and brains enough to know he didn't have to use it.

Butterflies brushed the inside of my chest and heat rushed to my cheeks, but I kept my composure. "You look through the big lens thingy, don't you?" I said.

He nodded smugly. "I look through the big lens thingy," he conceded.

Outside, under more placid stars, we spent most of the evening talking as I used his words to paint the mental picture of a heroic doctor ready to track down interspace neutrino signals, the Morse code of aliens, using tiny subatomic particles to communicate. It had been hypothesized for years that faster-than-light neutrinos would be the best way to communicate across the vast distances of space as they could penetrate roughly fifty light-years of solid lead, and finally Dr. Spinner had developed a better way to detect them.

What made him even more irresistible was that my father had warned me about him before the party, vaguely referencing some kind of family disgrace *his* father endured, the kind of thing Dr. Spinner had to change his name to avoid being associated with. That, and the good Dr. Spinner had a reputation as a playboy.

He was a sure thing.

Morris occupied the curator's suite, designed to allow the senior scientist to maintain residence, and we slipped off to it before the party was over, carelessly crashing down the stairs, stopping on the landing to make out, me allowing him to slide my dress up to my hips and caress the outside of my thigh and bottom before pushing him away.

I made him open the skylights. We made love under the stars in a four-post bed, sharing the hot breath of champagne, and in between each feverish bout he would point out the constellations above.

"That one," he said, "is Perseus. He'll move by four, maybe seven, degrees by the time we're done," he said, and rolled on top of me again.

I'd never been so turned on and believed him when he said Perseus had actually moved by ten when we finished.

Slanted light the color of solar honey streamed through a window showcasing an expansive view of the Arizona mountain range with frosted peaks. The bed was empty. I inhaled deeply, hoping to smell breakfast, and was slightly disappointed that the smell of bacon did not meet my olfactory glands.

As with an air-conditioner droning on into the night, I didn't notice the sound until it stopped, and it returned almost immediately, an angry, staccato agitation like the MRI I'd had when I tore my MCL in eighth grade. I sat on the hospital gurney, lying perfectly still as the alien eye circled me, listening, waiting for some voice in my ear to tell me it was okay to move.

The sound began again and I jumped. I wondered if something was wrong, if maybe some of the machinery of the new neutrino telescope had broken and I needed to get out of there. I didn't know much about particle physics—I didn't need to know much about anything with my father's money—but it sounded like a great way to inadvertently set off a nuclear reaction or create a black hole.

As I looked around for my clothes, I realized there was a precision to the noise, something purposeful, and the brief unreasonable fear I felt subsided into a puddle of nothingness. I couldn't find my clothes, so I wrapped the beige comforter around me and went to investigate. The suite was large and the sound, much louder than an MRI, resonated throughout his living room, rattling glasses in the cupboards. It came from a door underneath the stairs. I placed my ear to it and it stopped abruptly, as if I'd inadvertently pressed a sensor.

I thought about going back upstairs, finding my clothes, and leaving. It would be a one-night stand, not my first, but that meant I wouldn't see him again and if I did, he would have the wrong opinion of me.

The sound began again. I opened the door.

The basement was surprisingly industrial. Metal support columns ran every which way in endless lattice formations like the underside of a bridge. The metal stairs were cold on my feet, and it smelled . . . clean.

A large metal tube, reminiscent of the pictures of the Large Hadron Collider I'd seen in history class as a student, ran the length of the corridor.

The sound was almost deafening. In my mind's eye I saw thousands of particles, their pulse as steady and strong as the beam of a laser, darting within the tube I walked beside.

I screamed as strong arms wrapped around my waist and dragged me back behind the stairs into a room with metal walls, pushing me to the floor.

Morris's brown eyes stared at me. I admit, in that moment, I wanted him to take me.

He didn't.

"There's radiation out there," he said. I noticed the straps of the heavy lead vest a radiologist would wear.

"What are you doing?" I said.

We got to our feet and he led me to an observation room—he was wearing only boxers, a T-shirt, and socks under the apron, so cute—where a series of computer screens diagrammed something far too complex for me to understand, with algorithms beyond anything I'd learned in algebra class. A scattered holographic dot plot slowly began to look like one of the constellations he had pointed out last night. "There," he said. "That's Procyon B. One of our closest neighbors. Imagine, all this time, it was right in our front yard."

"What am I looking at?" I said, suddenly feeling very naked and looking around the room to make sure no one else was going to come barging in.

"That's where the signal has been coming from," he said.

"What signal?" I said.

"From *them*. They answered," he said, as if I should have known. "Just this morning." He scratched at the stubble on his chin, ran a hand through his messed up hair. There was a black fondue chocolate handprint around the collar of his shirt from where he'd ripped it off last night. I remembered him feeding me the strawberry, his lips brushing mine as I sucked the succulent juice from it. I wondered if he'd even slept.

"What do you mean, from *them*?" I said.

He stopped, and I could tell he thought less of me. I was an annoyance, something he had to humor. He looked down at the blanket I'd wrapped myself in and took pity. "It's an alien signal," he said. "I started sending out neutrinos seven years ago. I got a message back last night. I've been replying, using pulses of neutrinos to communicate in binary code. Simple, plain language stuff a four-year-old programmer could use."

The MRI sound stopped. He punched a few buttons.

On one of the external views of the mountainside something twitched slightly to the side, like a mechanical snake, languidly taking in a new vibration, tasting the next smell on the air.

"You've found . . . life?" I gasped. It felt like the floor had fallen out beneath me. I was suddenly overly aware I was naked, and there was a slight breeze caressing my lower body. I felt like Eve on judgment day. There was nothing to hide. For the first time, the food shortages and all the pitiful little fund-raisers and philanthropic events I'd used my father's money to curate, *as was my charitable duty*, didn't matter anymore. So what if the rising carbon levels had made food less nutritious and everyone needed to take supplements—and my father benefited because he owned half the pharmaceutical companies? So what if people starved? It was the same thing as running over a squirrel or popping a frog on the highway. Everyone was a god to something else, a big, merciless, unfeeling angry god.

Morris was like that. A god. Something the rest of humanity could only hope to become. He'd literally reached out and touched the heavens.

Morris was talking and I hadn't heard a word of it. "We always knew the neutrinos were special. That with careful, refined techniques they could become something like interspace Wi-Fi. You remember Wi-Fi, don't you?"

I nodded. A few decades ago they had outlawed junk-band Wi-Fi for its cancer-causing properties. The reality of it, my father said, was that the Internet was designed to kill fascists and that everything else, all the other carcinogens, had been set up as a distraction so the fascists could take down the Internet. It had had devastating effects. For people like me, the kind rich enough to plug into their own servers or subscribe to super Wi-Fi, it didn't matter.

Morris tapped a finger on the screen showing Procyon B. "That's eleven light-years away. That means it will take a little less than eleven years for them to receive my signals. Don't you understand what this means?"

I nodded slowly. We weren't alone. Or at least, something out there was sending us signals, and it was smart enough to use binary code. A flash of hundreds of old movies I'd watched in our home theatre came rushing back.

"What if they're not friendly?" I said.

It stood to reason they wouldn't be. Automobiles and squirrels.

"What?" Morris's head wobbled at me. "You think that matters?"

"What if it's—?"

"What if they're malicious?" a thunderous voice called out.

In the doorway was a fat man dressed like an absolute fool, a leather vest, dirty cargo pants circa 2000, and the goggles people used to wear before automobiles had windshields. He held what looked like a golden staff. With a flick of his wrist the surface of it dripped like a taper candle and formed a three-legged stool with more mass than the staff had right to. "Forgive me," he said as he sat on it. "It's been a long journey, and my knees aren't what they used to be."

"Who are you?" Morris said. The muscles in his arms were clenched tightly, like he was ready to fight. I didn't think he'd have much trouble with the fat man, but I didn't know the fat man yet.

"Seems to me," the fat man said, stroking his curly, triangular goatee, "you're on a deep-sea fishing expedition, using bait that will attract something far too big for your boat."

"What do you—?"

"Beaming out these neutrinos," the fat man said, cutting Morris off, "in random pulses and bursts, using a language you can't understand, seems like pure madness." He laughed to himself. "But what do I know?" He coughed a little, and I got the feeling he was imbued with the type of madness necessary to dwell underground, like a dwarf from one of those epic fantasy movies. "You wouldn't happen to have any water around here, would you?"

Morris shook his head.

"Figures. Just so you're both well aware, harming either of you is not my intention." He leaned forward, pulled his heel up onto his other leg. "I'm actually here to protect you from an assassin from the future."

"Hasn't that been done before, like twenty times over, by Hollywood?"

"Not like this it hasn't. And besides, killing you won't do any good. They come anyway."

"Who comes?" I said.

"My lady," the fat man said, bowing his head. "Forgive me. It might be best if you left."

"She will do no such thing." Morris pulled me back.

"Indeed." He stood and the stool fairly jumped into his hand as it re-formed into a staff. "I have no idea what will become of you, but I do know that this is effectively ground zero."

The fat man twirled his staff expertly and suddenly swung it like a club at the instrument panel. A shower of sparks and smoke jumped into the air.

Morris ran at him, but the fat man was ready. He swung the staff like a sword and caught him in the side of the head. Morris's head snapped to one side, and he fell like a crumpling sheet free of the line.

A puddle of yellow spread between Morris's legs onto the floor, and the fat man stood over him, looking down with no small amount of dissatisfaction. I couldn't move as he bent down, fighting his girth, feeling for a pulse. He nodded quickly. "Good."

He straightened his leather vest and stopped suddenly when he realized I was staring at him. "What? I just saved his life."

Hot tears rolled down my cheeks.

The fat man didn't seem to like them.

Sparks sizzled, and the lights flickered. "I always hate it when the power goes out," he said.

The puddle of pee between Morris's legs had

expanded, and I could see his black socks and his hairy legs, and it all just looked so silly that the only sensible thing to do was cry. The sobs were out before I could even choke.

"Listen," the fat man said, "he's responsible. For all of it. You have a few more years before they arrive. Why don't you go home and spend the rest of the time with your family?"

I cried harder. My father was never home, and when he was, I didn't want to be around him. Not only was he a bore, but he had no sense of humor and had done his best to distance us from the rest of his family, who lived in Virginia in what was called a hollow. They weren't worth his time, never had been. My mother was on the island of Mustique in the West Indies, getting massages from tanned men half her age and living comfortably off alimony. She was queen bitch, a crown she'd earned by proclaiming to her lawyer, while the door to the parlor was half open, that she'd eat her young if it meant my father had to keep her on salary for the rest of his life.

I'd never hugged her since, and one time for Mother's Day, I gave her a roll of candies and said, "I got you these. I know you like them, and nothing else is good enough for you."

That was in sixth grade. The last point of contention in their divorce was who would take custody of the brat. Me. My father lost on that count, but it saved him fifty thousand dollars a month to keep me at his place. I'd had nannies ever since.

The fat man took out a pipe, the whole time shaking his head and muttering as if he were debating something. He lit the pipe with a strike-anywhere match and made soft popping sounds with his mouth as the first plumes of sweet cherry smoke escaped—real tobacco? Where had he gotten that?—and it was all so surreal.

There was something else, out there, communicating with us, waiting for us to answer, and the fat man had mentioned fish, and fish were Christian.

The fat man turned to me and blew out a plume of smoke. "You're hardly dressed for time travel, but that's an easy fix. I'm of the opinion that the only ones I should save are those who've had the misfortune to live through the actual invasion. You see, it hardens people. To see reality swept away. Makes them less superficial, binds them together."

Morris was beginning to wake up. He shook his head briefly, as if dusting cobwebs, and pushed himself up. His muscles failed him the first time, giving up like a cloud of dust, before making it to his knees.

"But bringing you with me before the invasion is just so counterintuitive," the fat man was saying. "And if I take you, is that just the beginning? Is there a reason everyone shouldn't be saved from yesterday? And you," he said to Morris, "it's all your fault and everyone knows it. Why should I save you? Your unfounded research and unscientific practices cause all of this."

"I . . ." Morris rubbed his jaw. "I think I have a concussion."

"Well, good," the fat man said. "You deserve to die, truth be told, in a horrible manner befitting the son of man. And now, if she wishes, I've decided the lady should fetch her clothes and accompany me to a safer locale."

"I'm not going anywhere with you," I said.

Except, I wasn't so sure about that. I certainly didn't want to stick around to see the end of the world, or the invasion, like he had said. Who was to say that would even happen?

A little knot in my stomach told me otherwise.

Morris got to his feet and charged at the fat man like a bull. The fat man nimbly stepped aside, and Morris's head collided with the control panel. Something loud whirred and clicked to life, a stuttering MRI, and then more sparks flew and the lights went out. Emergency lighting flickered to life immediately. The fat man pulled him out of the electrical equipment, which was sending up acrid black smoke signals.

"I'd kill him, but it doesn't do any good. They still come. Every damn one of those writhing things."

"You're not lying, are you?" I said.

"Why on earth would someone break into an observatory to lie about aliens?" he said. "They'd have to be crazy."

"Are you crazy?"

"Probably, yes. But I'm not delusional." A klaxon blared to life, making me jump to the point of almost dropping the comforter.

A hologram clock rose from the center of the floor. It counted down to sixty.

"We best get out of here," the fat man said. "Help me take him."

"I thought you were here to kill him."

"I was, but it never gives me as much pleasure as I'd like. Even when I use the clippers."

I paled, and he grinned.

"You're messing with me?" I gasped.

He bent over Morris and took his arm. "Help me, and mind the urine."

We dragged Morris up the stairs. I found my clothes, dressed, and as I stepped outside, the sprinkler system in the living quarters turned on. I looked back over the posh interior as a misty rain mixed with smoke, a tongue of flame lapped at the bottom of the basement door, and it occurred to me that my father's girlfriend had probably designed the interior. I hadn't noticed it before. The stark white with dark accents reminded me of a dress she'd worn to my graduation. She'd been young enough to be graduating herself, although my father refused to discuss her age.

Outside, we loaded Morris into the back of an old car, which he promptly slumped into, his forehead smushed up against the window.

I suddenly realized that this man, whoever he was or claimed to be, had promptly disabled my boyfriend and was going to take us in his strange little old car to some place that probably resembled the middle of nowhere.

"The invasion," I said. "What's it like?"

He exhaled slowly, the question obviously trying

his patience. "They take people, change their DNA by touching them, and if it weren't for the train that I found, nearly everyone would be dead."

I didn't actually think he was speaking English.

"I know this is very hard to understand, but if you come with me, I'll show you."

"How do I know you won't rape me?"

He straightened and cleared his throat. His mouth opened as he was about to speak; then he shook his head, reached inside his vest, and pulled out a revolver roughly the size of a cannon. He opened the cylinder, poured five rounds into his hand, making sure I saw their shiny brass jackets still full of deadly bullets, and replaced them. He handed the butt of the pistol to me.

"If I try to rape you, shoot me."

I reluctantly took the gun. It was much heavier than I thought it should be and appeared quite old despite its excellent condition.

"There's no safety, so don't point it at me unless I really deserve to be shot." He chuckled.

He walked around to the driver's side, and I realized the car didn't have auto-drive.

"I thought you said he wasn't worth saving," I said, intending to stall him.

He rolled down the window after he got in. "Are you coming or not? You can't stay here. Look behind you."

The entire complex had been engulfed in flame.

"I assume there's something radioactive in there," he

said, and I got in the car.

He left the windows down as we drove. The breeze coming through felt like a hair dryer. I laid the gun on my lap, the barrel pointed at him. With his big hands on the steering wheel, I could see heavy sweat stains under his arms, and beads of it had formed around the follicles of his pointy beard.

"What's your name?" I said.

"Sir Reginald of Raleigh. My father was Walter Hindsley."

I gasped. His father, Walter, was something of a legend. He'd single-handedly dissolved most of an incompetent government in favor of a far more powerful, centralized entity. If it hadn't been for him, North America never would've united against threats in the Far East. It was believed he was in exile in Cuba, chased out by his son—"Which makes you Reginald the brave," I said. "A war hero."

He laughed so hard he had to wipe spittle from his goatee. "Hero." He shook his head. "It's not nearly as impressive as all that, I can assure you," he said, knee-deep in the brakes to avoid careening off the switchbacks of the newly paved road. He seemed to be enjoying steering the car. I'd have felt so much better if it had auto-drive. The distant mountains and ridges slid by casually at a distance. The side of the mountain on my right was a blur. I closed my eyes trying to fight down the same sickness I felt last night before I met Morris.

"The invasion," I said, remembering again what this was all about. "Why waste your time with me? Shouldn't you be busy planning a resistance, following in the lineage of your grandfather?"

"Time," he muttered. "I've never had so much of it."

"What?" I said.

He shook his head and refused comment. The base of the mountain was approaching, and with it a long valley sprinkled with cacti and wind-eroded towers of rocks. I hadn't seen much of the scenery last night when I arrived in the dark. I felt the cool steel in my hand and wondered why I was so eager to believe this man.

Reginald pumped the brakes hard, and the golden staff on his lap slid forward. He grabbed it before it could fall toward the gas pedal with what appeared to be supernatural speed.

"What is that thing?" I said. "I've never seen anything change shape so easily."

His fingers wrapped and unwrapped about the knobby top of the staff, in a motion that made me think of a predator breathing, assessing the situation. "There are many things you can't understand, not by words alone. So pardon me for asking for your trust until more is revealed in time."

"What if I don't trust you? What if I want to get out of this car?"

He looked at me as he stood on the brakes.

I snapped forward, my head almost hitting the dash.

"Would you like to get out?" he said as the car was engulfed in a cloud of dust. "I've plenty of time but very little patience, and what remaining sum I have has come at an extremely high premium." He licked his lips and blinked, long and slow. "Try to understand, nearly everyone I care about has died. And those I've replaced them with are not long for this world, either. You can live out the next few years in pleasant ignorance, or I can save you from the pain of watching everyone you care about die. But rest assured, they will almost certainly all perish."

Tears sprang to my eyes unexpectedly. The dry desert air choked my throat.

"It's not easy to live after this. I thought I saw something in your eyes that indicated you'd welcome a challenge, even if it came at a cost."

The engine groaned, and we started to move again. It occurred to me we were driving a car that ran on petroleum.

"If I was wrong, it's best you tell me now," he said.

I wiped my eyes. There was something about his casual handling of the situation that made it believable. He was either a phenomenal liar, or he was telling the truth. He had honest eyes, even if he was a bit condescending, a little crazy. And it was clear he didn't care a shit about me. Patty, my therapist, said that falling for disinterested men was a weakness of mine.

The car abruptly sped through the desert beside a pair of railroad tracks, slinging gravel and dirt into the undercarriage. It sounded like a storm and reminded me of the day we spent at my grandmother's house outside Toledo. There was lightning and thunder and, in the distance, a funnel cloud touched down. We hid in the basement, and I remembered the flickering lights and my father began to sing a song called "Do a Diddy," which he claimed was nearly a hundred and fifty years old, just to drown it out. His awkward singing scared me more than the rain.

When we came up from the basement, sticks, shingles, and bits of wood were strewn across my grandmother's little yard. The swing under the oak tree was wrapped about the branches like a giant spiderweb, and an old porcelain tub had crashed through her wire fence. There was a frantic pounding on the door. My father opened it and revealed a man wrapped in a bedsheet, his eyes bulging, just absolutely wild, and it looked like he had a fake mustache that had fallen half off and streaked down his face. It took a moment before I realized it was dried blood. He just kept saying he needed help, over and over again. Apparently, the tornado had ripped the roof off his house while he was in the bathtub. The twister had picked him up and carried him for nearly a mile before depositing him in my grandmother's yard.

It felt like I was in the tub, like the roof had just been torn off and something implausibly safe and sturdy had come along and I didn't have a choice. I was just along for the ride.

Morris groaned in the backseat. Reginald smiled. I

pondered his strange sense of humor as the road we drove on fell away and the car dropped suddenly. Up ahead, something shimmered in the distance on the train tracks. The shadow of a tall black man shielded his eyes before it.

"Is that a subway car?" I said as we got closer.

"I found it in a subway, of sorts," Reginald said. "But no, it's not a subway car."

It was, in fact, a subway car, and I could see several modifications, which included an awkward metal pole construction on the top that resembled a lightning rod, and the rivets on the surface were countersunk as if speed were an issue. It was about the size of a retiree's motor home. I started to think that Reginald was truly crazy, and not in the amusing way, and I gripped the handle of the pistol.

A cloud of red dust overtook us as we pulled to a stop beside the train.

"End of the line," Reginald said as he opened his door. Because of his girth, he had to shimmy a little before he could stand up.

"He's in the back, Charles," Reginald called to the man standing beside the train.

Charles was long and lean, fingers dangling low at his thighs. He had a sharp look about him despite having a round face and soft, molded features. He wore a white T-shirt that had seen better days and jeans worn thin at the knees. He held up what looked like a small, red perfume bottle. "Will I need this?" he said.

Reginald waved him off. "Not likely. I imagine he's slightly concussed."

Charles went around the back of the car while Reginald popped open a door on the side of the train. It looked very much like a motor home inside, equipped with only an array of antiquated electronics.

"This is him—you're sure?" Charles said before opening the door.

"Positive," Reginald said.

There was a click before the scream. Morris jumped out of the car so fast that Charles didn't have a chance to defend himself.

Morris, in his white shirt and boxers and black socks, leapt and wrapped his legs around Charles's chest, and they toppled to the ground and stirred up clouds of dust as they struggled. It was clear Morris had the upper hand with his arms wrapped tight around Charles's neck in a sleeper hold.

Reginald bounded out of the train, moving surprisingly fast for a big man, and held his staff out as he charged like a boar.

He struck Morris on the back with his staff several times in a weird syncopation to Charles's frantic tapping-out on Morris's arm before I realized I still held the cannon.

I pointed it at the sun and fired, hoping it would pop like a balloon and plunge the whole world into darkness. The gun kicked so hard it might have snapped one of the small carpal bones in my wrist.

All three of the men stopped and stared at me.

Morris had sweat-caked mud all over his legs, as if some sort of demon had manhandled him. Reginald straightened, dusting off his leather vest even though he hadn't been rolling in the dirt.

"You're welcome to stay," said Reginald, "but he's coming with us."

I pointed the gun at him. "That's very rapey of you."

Reginald's mouth puckered like a sphincter, and the muscles of his jaws clenched visibly beneath the folds of his jowls.

Morris let Charles go and unfolded himself. Morris stood and scrambled back, like a dog who has escaped a beating.

"Very well," Reginald said. "You can stay. He can stay." He reached into his vest pocket, took out a jingling set of keys and dropped it onto the desert floor, creating a little puff of dust at his feet.

He sneered as he drove the end of his staff down into them. A static shock of electricity shot out from around the end of the staff, sending the dust in the air to the ground immediately. The sand turned lava red before Reginald removed the staff to reveal a molten pit of glass.

"I hope you very much enjoy your walk through the desert," Reginald said.

"Spectral Labs is nearly thirteen miles away, and it is early morning. The temperature will rise to over one hundred, and without water it is difficult to imagine a set of circumstances where heat stroke wouldn't set in before your arrival, which is to say nothing of Morris walking across hundred-degree sand in stocking feet."

"Wait," Morris said. "How . . . ?" He pointed at the car keys.

Reginald twirled the staff over his hand like a baton, and I got the strangest notion that the staff was clinging to him. "I have greater tricks," he said, "but we'll have to attend the train together if you wish to see them. I cannot stress enough that I mean you no harm."

I hated him in that moment. He was sweaty and gross and thought he was smarter than I was, and it infuriated me. My finger massaged the trigger.

Reginald saw the motion, raised his chin in defiance.

"We're being silly," Charles said. "This can all be explained."

"I'm listening," I said.

"We're building a world in the past, before the invasion," Charles said.

Reginald mumbled something.

The shadow of a vulture passed between us.

"Are you serious?" Morris said.

Charles and Reginald said yes without saying anything.

"Why do you want me?" Morris said.

Reginald pointed at the mountain with the observatory. "Your neutrino pulses were an invitation to *The Kind*, and according to history, they arrive in two days, descending over every major city and forcing humanity down into every crack and crevice until there's almost nothing left."

"In the future, we've struck a truce, but it's no way to live, scurrying from hole to hole," Charles said. "When Reginald and I found the train, we decided to go back, to start a new civilization outside history. A place where we can move forward without—"

"You're insane," I muttered.

"We're out of options," Reginald said. "Can't go forward, can't go back. Well, we can go back, but it's a temporary fix."

"You still never answered my question," Morris said.

Reginald fixed his gaze on Morris. "We need you to check for neutrinos, maybe decode their transmission and send back a warning rather than an invitation."

"What if I can't?"

Reginald tapped the tip of his cane on the edge of the rail. It gave a bright, copper-penny sound. "You'll have several hundred years to work on it."

"You have nothing to lose by coming with us," Charles said.

"You can keep the gun," Reginald said. "Shoot us any time you like."

"I'll go," Morris said.

"Well, that was easy," Reginald said.

Morris bent and slapped at some of the dirt on his legs, which didn't do any good. "Tell me you have some pants in there."

It must be a ruse, I thought. He wants to take the train and get away. That's why he's agreed. Morris stopped near the puddle of glass and carefully tapped the surface to see if it was cool. He used his finger to dig around, and produced a lumpy bowl of glass like a scorpion paperweight, only with the keys inside.

"That's some electrical pulse," he said.

Morris followed him onto the train and asked where they found it. Reginald answered, but I couldn't hear him.

Charles approached. "What do you do for work?"

I pointed the gun at his stomach. He didn't seem to mind.

"I give away money," I said.

"Must be nice. I was a science teacher before the collapse." He started for the train, grabbed hold of the door frame, and turned back to offer a hand. "You really don't need the gun."

Inside the train, Morris was exclaiming how incredible everything was. A headache courtesy of last night's consumption was starting to come on. If I had less of a moral compass, I'd have thought haze a better option; at least that left you with only a craving, not a hangover.

"Hey, um . . ." Morris snapped his fingers, searching for my name.

"Angela," I said, accepting Charles's hand to board the train. "My name is Angela."

"Right." Morris sat in the copilot's seat, an impressive, even if dated, computer array in front of him. "Sorry."

"I take it you're not really familiar with each other,"

Reginald said.

Morris flashed the sheepish smile of a frat boy.

Reginald appraised my body, to the point that my skin crawled. I sneered. "Seems to me it's your loss," Reginald said to Morris and faced the controls.

The train began to move, powered by the whine of an electric engine, and accelerated to easily over one hundred miles an hour. The body of the train began to shake, and I started to wonder if this was going to be like the games I used to play in grade school, where we would go into a closet and come out on the moon or Jupiter or as pirates in the early twentieth century off the coast of Kenya.

I could feel the windy vibrato in my chest as it shook the chair I sat in. A squiggly finger of electricity passed over the windshield. I gripped the arms of the chair, suddenly feeling very sick and ready to be off this horrible ride. The light grew semidark, illuminated by strobe-like flashes of light before being replaced by myriad greens, reds, and yellows dyeing my hands like the holographic representation of space on the domed ceiling of the observatory the night before, only much more frenetic. I wondered if I could go back to before last night and warn myself not to attend. If after all this was over I would want to trade several years of normalcy for whatever reality I was being sucked into, because it looked like we were traveling inside the belly of an agitated electric eel, the horizon an endless tunnel of swirling colors and lights which the best haze could only hope to emulate.

The momentum released abruptly, and I leaned back in my seat, afraid we were about to crash.

Charles winked at me as the snakes of electricity squirmed back to the corners of the windshield.

Reginald wriggled out of the driver's seat and opened the door. A blast of hot, humid air rolled in, and I could almost feel my hair curl. There was no way we were in Arizona. It felt like Florida. Or Baltimore in July.

Outside, a green pasture bordering the railroad tracks was surrounded by an old barbwire fence. The sun shone brightly around fluffy thunderheads.

Morris jumped out of the train and grabbed a few shoots of grass from one side of the tracks. He crumpled them, rolled them between his palms, and sniffed. "This is virtual reality, isn't it?"

Charles laughed.

Reginald touched his spectacles and they darkened, shielding his eyes as he looked out at the tree line. Cicadas buzzed. He waved an arm high over his head several times.

At the edge of the woods, a man dressed a bit like a Quaker stepped out.

"That's where we're going," Reginald said.

Morris's hands dropped away from his face. The grass fell crisscross on his stockinged feet. "Not until you tell me how this works."

Reginald swept a hand toward the train. "Quantum mechanics. Even Godel knew the right punch would drive a hole through the space-time continuum."

"Where did you . . . How does—?"

Charles placed a hand on Morris's shoulder. "None of it matters. What matters is we save the world."

Morris shook his head. "It matters very much. If we have this, and we can move from Arizona to here in the blink of an eye, we can travel anywhere. To the stars!" He flung an arm at the sky, and I remembered the neutrinos, how he was attempting to communicate with them.

Men streamed out of the woods.

"Did you find him?" the man leading the way called. He was dressed like an American farmer in denim overalls, a straw hat, and sweat-stained shirt, but as he grew nearer his complexion and eyes unmistakably indicated an Asian heritage.

Reginald didn't turn away to answer the question. "Morris, Dr. Spinner," he said formally. "Now is probably a good time to explain that I knew your father."

The elation drained out of Morris's face, and he swayed a little, as if pushed by a breeze. A fly crawled across his kneecap, coming terrifyingly closer to the leg of his boxer shorts.

"I saw him," Reginald said, stepping closer, deliberately taking his time as if navigating precariously placed rocks along a shoreline. "Right before he died, actually."

Morris's mouth hung open. The fly disappeared up the leg of his shorts, then crawled back down.

"He asked me to tell you something."

"You're a liar," Morris whispered.

Reginald stopped within reach of Morris. "He said, 'Tell my son, finish my work.' You were already performing your mandatory conscription, as was I."

The fly disappeared up Morris's leg, and his quadriceps shivered like the foreleg of a horse trying to dislodge it, only it wasn't the fly that caused the reaction. He curled his fists into hammers.

"You killed him," Morris said.

The Asian man and several others arrived, and their smell was rank, like field hands at lunchtime.

"He didn't commit suicide, as the authorities believed," Reginald said. "But that was the way he wanted it. The way he knew it had to be. I took him with me, into the future, showed him things that can't be unseen, things I perhaps should have let you live through before dragging you back. Problem was, you disappear in the future. Most of the rail lines are pounded to dust, and whatever hole you crawl into is just too deep to unearth. Either that or you die in the first wave. We didn't have a choice but to take you just now. Your father knew that, and everything he did, every choice he made, was designed to shape your life, to send it in this direction because he knew, when the time came, you would help save us all."

Morris leapt at Reginald, and his hands almost found his throat before Reginald sidestepped and swung the staff like a club into Morris's stomach. He went down hard.

Several flies darted through the air around Morris where he lay on the ground, and I thought about that old Charlie Brown cartoon with the character constantly trapped inside the lopsided, dirty rings of Saturn. My mother used to watch those every Halloween and Christmas because she said they reminded her of her grandmother. It occurred to me that right now, where we stood, my grandmother, maybe even my great-great-grandmother, was probably alive, carrying on unawares that her descendant was standing beside a time-traveling train.

The thought made my head spin like the flies swirling in the afternoon sun. I backed up and leaned against the train. Its hot surface burned my back. I turned to look at it and all I saw was my flat, distorted reflection trapped beneath its shiny surface. It reminded me of all the times I stared at myself in the mirror when I was a child, when I was in high school, when I was drunk, or high on haze, wondering who I would become, what I would do with my life. If there was ever going to be one big thing that I could hang my hat on to say to my grandkids, that was my moment, the one I was put on this earth for. If it wasn't soon, I'd be just like my reflection on the side of the train, inconsistent, mutable to the point of deafness, and insignificant.

I didn't want to be invisible to my grandchildren.

I went to Morris, stepped over him, and straddled his chest. He smiled up at me, blood on his teeth, and I pushed the barrel of the gun up under his chin. "Are you useless? Or deaf?"

His jaw hardened, and he cleared his throat. His eyes

roamed, accusing the people who were chuckling.

"These people need your help," I said, driving the barrel of the gun a little higher under his chin. "Are you going to help them or fight them?"

Morris coughed and blood and mucous splattered on my face. I squeezed the trigger, just not hard enough to make the gun go off.

Reginald pulled me off Morris. "As much as I'm enjoying this, I'm afraid coercion isn't the best means to achieve compliance." Reginald was smiling at me, except he wasn't. His eyes were full of delight, and his face was placid. He'd be a very handsome man if he lost some weight.

The Asian man offered Morris a hand. He refused and pushed himself to his feet.

"We'll show you how we live now or, as the case may be, how we live in the past," Reginald said. "After you see that, you're free to make your own decision, and I'll bring you to any time, any place you'd like to see."

Morris wiped his chin. It looked like the motion hurt him, because he immediately looked at his palm and wiped away some of the sand and grit that had stuck there.

As we walked through the trees, the men behind us threw a switch I hadn't noticed and gently guided the train onto a separate track into a copse of trees. I kept sneaking glances, watching how they worked in unison until they placed a large, black tarp of invisibility over the train. Then it flickered, and all I could see was countryside.

They had brought technology into the past. The

notion made my stomach unsettled, and I remembered the drinks and the hangover. I looked around at my traveling companions. None of them had canteens. For the first time in my life, I hoped they had clean water where we were going, and I smiled.

They led us through a deep hardwood forest with little undergrowth, and I kept thinking how the rustling leaves made it feel like we were inside a waterfall. We neared the edge of a field bordered by barbwire fence. Inside, cows lazed, chewing their cud and eyeing the woods with distrust. I kept looking under trees for hidden benches, in crooks of branches at each bird watching us, for hidden cameras. It didn't seem real.

The trail opened up, becoming more of a farm road than woodland path.

"This land was donated to us by a wealthy man," Reginald explained to Morris.

"Why would he do that?" Morris said. "Oh, wait, let me guess, you gave him a stock tip."

"How long have you been here?" I said.

We came to a small, still black stream crossed by a wooden bridge that might have been suitable for trail bikes.

"Three years," Reginald said, his voice trailing off.

The others began to walk single file across the bridge, and Reginald and Charles motioned for us to follow.

On the other side of the bridge, the Asian man raised his hand and knocked on something invisible, making a hollow, metallic sound. In front of him, a vertical slit in the countryside appeared, and the men stepped through it.

"You must understand," Charles said. "When we say the world ends in several years, we mean the world *ends.*"

"Our only hope, as far as we can see it, is to change history by either developing a means to stop the invasion from happening, or to harden our defenses before they arrive."

"You're accelerating the pace of change," Morris said.

Reginald scanned the countryside, apparently concerned we were being watched.

"But what if we change ourselves right out of existence?" Morris said.

Reginald sighed and looked at Charles. "Remind me that our theoretical conversations really were this tedious when we first started."

"Worse, I'm afraid," Charles said.

Reginald mopped his brow with a handkerchief I hadn't seem him produce. "Please, let us step inside before we expire. Yuda," he called, "open that door."

The Asian man appeared out of nowhere, standing in the darkened hole of whatever bunker we were supposed to enter.

I followed the men inside. A cool rush of air prickled my skin, and I became aware of how bad I smelled. I hadn't used deodorant since yesterday or—I let it go.

The interior of a small room flashed to life under low-hanging fluorescent tube lighting. It was like a retro club in New York I visited a few months ago with Carlie. I felt a pang of panic at the thought of never seeing her again before I realized that, in fact, she was still alive, in some time, in some way. Everything had crystallized, like the sand under Reginald's staff.

Morris held his head between his hands and squinted. "I think I should lie down. Last time I felt this way I—" He wobbled on his feet.

Charles caught him and, with Yuda, helped him down a long set of stairs that opened onto a vast, underground warehouse-like room filled with tents, yurts, and people of all ages. It must have stretched on for a mile.

In the far corner, the unmistakable swirling caution lights and sparks of steel-working builder bots carried on construction. A line of people formed at one side of the space, where long tables were set up with food. The ventilation must have been good, because I couldn't smell any of it.

I made out a conveyor belt in the back, where new earth was being moved.

Yuda, Charles, and a few others carried Morris toward one of the yurts.

Reginald stopped beside me. "We're nearly at capacity, but we expand every day. If there are people you wish to save, there's a bit of a waiting list, owing to the small wrinkles in the space-time continuum that are at our disposal, but there's really no rush."

"There's only my father," I said and realized he had basically asked me if I had a boyfriend.

He subtly grasped my hand in his, which was big and

soft, and said, “Come, there are people I want you to meet.”

As we turned, a man placed a hand on Reginald’s shoulder, stopping us. He had a strong jaw and sandy blond hair and appeared to be in his thirties. “Is he here?”

“Angela,” Reginald said, “this is my friend Amos. And yes, he’s here, but he has a concussion. I suggest we keep the surprises to a minimum.”

Amos’s tan face paled. He wore a dress shirt and suspenders, tan leather shoes, and had the lean stomach and shoulders of a working man.

“Does he know what all this is about?” Amos said.

“He knows enough, but I’m serious; he doesn’t need another surprise. Not until he’s recovered.”

Amos looked at me for the first time. He had blue eyes and was very handsome.

“He’s Morris’s great-great-great-something-or-other grandfather,” Reginald explained.

I gasped and suddenly felt very insecure. It was like I was meeting the parents. I extended a hand and introduced myself.

Amos kissed the back of my hand. “The pleasure’s all mine.”

“Amos is the farmer nice enough to let us use his land. I saved him from New York a while back, and as far as I know, he’s the only authentic to travel with us into the future.”

“I hitched a ride,” Amos said.

“Yuda put him in the sick bay,” Reginald said, tossing

his head in the direction Morris had been taken.

Amos nodded in thanks and backed away. "I got another shipment of steel coming tomorrow, nine o'clock. I'm running out of new companies to purchase from."

"Perhaps you should purchase your own, then," Reginald called.

Amos blinked, apparently considering the option for the first time, and turned on his heel like a soldier.

I let my hand slip from Reginald's grasp. "Explain this to me. How is it possible to make all these changes without ripple effects?"

Reginald smiled like a patient teacher. "It isn't. But like I said before, we're working toward a different future."

"If it all can be different, as you say, then why is it any of our concern? I mean, maybe Morris gets to become an astrophysicist only because that guy buys a steel company."

Reginald let his eyes wander over the expansive cavern. "We're still alive, and we can't go back to our own time. What else is there to do but try?" He led me toward the food tables. "Besides, we can always change it again if we get it wrong."

They were serving cornbread and a vegetarian chili. "You a new one?" said the chef, a white man with a grizzled gray beard.

I nodded.

"Twenty eighty-one. You?"

It took me a second to understand what he meant. "Seventy-four," I said. "Six years before the—"

Reginald's lips pursed tightly. "The collapse," he said.

The chef gasped. "Jesus, you got her before?"

"Collateral benefits. We'll see you later, Al," Reginald said, ushering me away. We sat down at one of the tables.

"The food here is organic," he said, holding the bowl of chili under his nose and inhaling deeply. "Not like the organic where we're from. It's really grown, really harvested. It's the best thing about being in the past. Real meat, real food."

The chili wasn't what my hungover stomach wanted, but the cornbread was good, and it mopped up some of the acid. Nearly every passerby waved or acknowledged Reginald in some fashion or another.

"You're pretty well liked, aren't you?" I said, breaking apart another piece of bread.

Reginald's chewing slowed and he looked over the cavern, full of people and activity. "I saved most of these people. One, two, and three at a time, bringing them back here."

"But you didn't invent the train?"

"No." He took another bite.

Charles sat down beside us at the table. "But he was the first one to make it work."

"How'd he do that?"

Charles laughed. "We think when he ripped some wires out of it, he changed the configuration to just the right settings."

"We went back," Reginald said, mouth half full, "out

of curiosity, and found someone involved in the project. He's around here somewhere. He said the government never got the thing to work."

"We needed someone who could help with maintenance, if need be," Charles explained. "Although we like this place—"

"It's idyllic and boring," Reginald said.

Charles nodded. "And no one wants to get stuck here."

"So what you're telling me is, this whole thing happened because you tried to hotwire a train?"

"All of it," Reginald said.

"That's the dumbest thing ever."

Charles and Reginald exchanged a serious look, and they both started laughing till tears rolled down Reginald's cheeks.

Charles stood, pointed at me, and took his food. "Have fun with this one, Reginald."

"So, you brought back all these people," I said. "Were any of them close to you before the—?"

"Collapse," Reginald offered. His spoon scraped the bottom of the bowl. "And no, none of them were close to me. I'm afraid I didn't have any friends until I found that train."

"No wife, no girlfriend?"

"I had a fiancée." He didn't offer more.

"What happened to her?"

"I tried to convince her the collapse was real, like I did with you." He looked around and rubbed at his neck as if the chili were too warm for him. "What jobs can you do? Everyone here has one."

"I . . . I don't know." I was good at helping people with their makeup, but no one was wearing any, and I was good at organizing parties and fund-raisers. That didn't matter at all.

Reginald spun the bowl in front of him, staring far beyond its depths. I wondered what he'd seen behind the controls of that train.

"Well, Conductor," I said, "tell me what I should do."

He gave me the kind of practiced smile that men reserve for babies so the world doesn't think them monsters.

"We'll need to have a word with Morris." He pushed himself up from the table.

I rose and gathered my things.

"I think it'd be best if I spoke to him alone," he said.

"But you said—"

"They always need help in the kitchen. I'll introduce you. They can find a more suitable role for you later, if need be."

"But I want to talk to him," I said, realizing that it was true. I did want to talk to Morris. Somehow, he was the key to all of this.

"Loraine," Reginald called, waving a hand.

A woman wearing a tank top approached. She had a lot of freckles, and her shoulders looked like they had too much skin, as if she'd lost a lot of weight recently. I looked around and realized that no one except Reginald was overweight. I wondered about that and didn't like the conclusion I reached.

"Loraine, this is Angela. Get her some decent clothes and show her around the kitchen, would you please?"

Loraine wiped her hands on a dishrag she'd been holding. "You just arrive?" she said, eyes narrowed. "Well, come on, then."

I turned to Reginald. He was already walking away.

They gave me a T-shirt advertising a 5K race and a pair of baggy jeans that needed a belt, and although it was more comfortable than the dress I had been wearing, it felt like part of me died when I cinched the belt tight to its final notch.

I washed dishes in a large laundry sink until my hands were pruned. Sweat formed on my spine, causing my thin shirt to cling to me. Something bright and pink floated in the water. I reached for it as the bubbles burst underneath it, and it swirled in the sink like a lure. I reached down deep, dredged it up with some cheap, thin silverware. It was one of my nails.

Tears sprang to my eyes. This was the future, a world without manicures and dresses and galas. I searched my memory for 1950s fashion and found it lacking, full of polka-dotted dresses and pie baking. No planned excursions to Africa or humanitarian missions to Belize. They probably didn't even have shopping malls, and if they did, what would I be able to buy there? I was no longer rich. The name Aldon Howell meant nothing here.

This was the age of the Cold War. This was before the Internet and cell phones. This was a nightmare.

I ran outside the confines of the kitchen and searched for the entrance to this subterranean world forged in a place outside of time. A family reading a book looked up at me tentatively, the kids annoyed and wondering why their father had stopped reading. The whir of concrete-mixing builder bots permeated the air.

I felt sick. I had to get out of there. I had to see the surface.

I needed to get back to the train.

I ran toward the tunnel that I thought was the exit, crashed through a wooden door, and ran down a series of creaky, wooden steps into the darkness. This wasn't the way out, but maybe this would be better. Maybe I could be alone down there. Maybe I could just pull the dirt over me and die.

At the bottom of the stairs was another wooden door, this one heavier than the first. It opened onto a dark tunnel. Men's voices called to each other, and the glowing outline of a man wielding an acetylene torch flickered in the distance. I could smell the fumes.

"Angela," a woman snapped behind me. "You can't be down here."

It was Loraine. Her wiry hands found my wrist and pulled me back up the stairs.

"I thought this was the way out. I felt very claustrophobic all of a sudden," I said. I let my voice fall.

"Fuck it, that's not true. I can't live underground."

"Poor thing. It'll be night topside," she said, leading me up the stairs to the exit.

"It was morning a few hours ago," I said.

"Maybe where you were. Time means nothing on the train. *Mutable*, as Reginald says." She pushed open the door.

The night sky sparkled, the loose band of Milky Way stars thick as cream.

"They turn off the generators at night," Loraine said, thumbing open a pack of cigarettes. She offered me one.

I shook my head.

She struck a match, and her face glowed orange. She watched the small fire burn before lighting her smoke. "Without the camo tent, it's easy to see the sky. Less light pollution, too."

I looked up, wondering if I could see any differences. I wanted to see New York, stuffed full of taxis and men like Don Draper and Bogart, maybe see Florida before it grew into an endless hedge maze of gated retirement communities.

"They let you leave the, uh . . ." I motioned toward the stairs.

"The Den? They're pretty strict, actually. Lots of talk about a singularity or something. Either way, it's better than what we were living in, right?" She laughed, coughing a little as she exhaled smoke. "Real tobacco, real food. Just that alone helped me lose weight." The cherry of her cigarette glowed as she took a drag. "You seem like you made it through okay. Not a scratch on you."

"Made it through what?"

Her cigarette hand dropped to her waist. "They got you pre-collapse, didn't they?"

"Um, yeah," I said, wishing I had a drink or some haze. I felt jet-lagged and needed something to chill me out.

"Goddamn it, I thought they didn't do that. You know, that really fries my ass." She turned away, kept talking in a sort of whisper. "And they brought him back, too. Probably gave him a blow job."

"What?"

"We're not talking to you," she said over her shoulder.

Ice formed around my bones. She kept mumbling.

"I think I'm going back inside now," I said.

"It's called the Den," she said and wheeled on me, steamy smoke pouring out her nostrils. "They could have saved Bobby, you know. I knew exactly where he was and when he was and Reginald said someday they would. But that was three months ago. I asked him yesterday, and Reginald said, if he had time to make a trip . . ." She gave a sick laugh. "He's always got time, and he said no. Had the balls to say it didn't matter. That Bobby was still there, still doing exactly what I pictured him doing in my mind. And you know what I said? I said, well, how 'bout getting picked over by *The Kind*, his goddamn face melting off as whatever they infected him with took over. Was he still doing *that*?" She dragged hard and exhaled. "He said, yeah, he's doing that, too. And then he turned away and mumbled about learning to walk and read and ride a bike . . ." Another drag. "You know what that means?"

Tears glistened in her eyes when the last of her cigarette glowed an inch from her lips. "That means I can't sleep. Because all I can think of is him, his insides turning to mush. Forever."

The cigarette dropped. She ground her toe on it.

She brushed past me to the door. I had to follow.

The lights were low when we went back in, and at the bottom of the stairs, a man holding a modern rifle guarded the entrance. "Probably shouldn't venture too far out until you've been oriented," he said. "Everyone needs a cover story."

There was a word for what the rifle was, something out of place because of the time. I couldn't remember what it was.

I walked back toward the kitchen and sat down at one of the tables.

A woman with dark skin and no hair joined me almost immediately. "You're just in today, aren't you?" Her voice was soft and reminded me of an Asian poet I'd heard read once, named Malara something.

"So?"

"Don't listen to Loraine. She wants too much. I told her she should let it go, forget about her husband because as long as we're here, there's a chance. Who do you miss?"

I gave her a stern look. "Everything." I hated that I was here, hated that I had all these wackos with battle scar

PTSD asking me questions, expecting me to act grateful. "They should have left me."

I felt her eyes on my back as I walked toward the yurt they'd taken Morris into. There was something feral about this place, just beneath the surface. I couldn't imagine hiding here, spending the rest of my life underground, under any circumstances. It didn't feel right.

Anachronistic. That was the word. It popped into my mind as I stopped near the yurt and listened to the low voices coming from inside.

Charles, in his slow, accented words, said, "How many months until it is completed?"

"Shouldn't be more than five weeks," another voice said.

"We should discuss this elsewhere," Reginald said.

I ducked and walked quickly to the back of the yurt, trying to look casual. I shouldn't have bothered. Everyone was gone, probably hunkered down for the night. It felt like there was a curfew. In the distance, a young couple swinging towels at each other raced toward shower stalls, their laughter disguised by the constant, droning sound of the builder bots.

I wouldn't have been surprised if I had died and this was hell. I started thinking about all the bad things I had done. I'd stolen pie, cheated on tests—a lot of tests, using a retinal camera my father had given me. I think he knew what I'd use it for. For him, school wasn't about learning the material. It was about learning how to get by. Learning the shortcuts other people weren't strong enough to take.

I used the retinal camera to catch him cheating and posted the pictures on the Internet. We didn't speak much after that.

Reginald, Charles, and a tall, thin man with a shiny bald head walked silently away from the yurt.

I came around the front and found a guard sitting on a stool, quietly shuffling a deck of playing cards. He was in his twenties and his forehead was large, accented by a receding hairline. He looked up sheepishly, showing me the queen of hearts, a woman clad in white lace, her skin softened by an artist's airbrush.

"Do you believe these? Amos gave them to me. Said he used them in World War II." He laughed and shook his head. "There's not even any wear on them. I mean, look at this," he said, pushing the near naked woman toward me.

I nodded dutifully.

"Except for this one card," he continued, shuffling through until he found a joker. "This one's got a spot on it. Either wine or . . . it's not wine." He scratched at it with his thumb, sniffed it. "I like to think that it's a German's. I guess Amos was a bit of a hero. You know how much these would be worth before the collapse? I could take like seven years off my school debt. You know, that's the best thing about being back here. There's none of that hanging over my head, worrying about how many meals I can eat and still not run credit."

I'd never had credit like most people my age. "You know," I said, "one of those women could probably be your grandma."

His shoulders slumped, and he spoke to his palm, "There goes date night."

I laughed despite myself.

"So, what's your plan?" he said.

"What do you mean?"

"Well, my plan is to work with radio waves and telecommunications. I mean, I wasn't an engineer before the collapse—point of fact, I was a tower monkey—but there are a lot of little things I know that could really speed things up. I mean, what we're really talking about is the technological evolution, in a way. Ideas feed off each other exponentially and such. You know, I didn't catch your name. I'm Jeff."

"Angela. I'm going to work with neutrinos."

He looked around. "You know, we got this guy, just in, supposed to be some kind of neutrino ninja."

"I know. Actually, I'm here to"—not *see* him, I thought quickly; I'm more important than that—"*question* him."

My father would be proud.

Jeff stood. "Listen, he's not too sharp right now." He rapped a knuckle off the side of his dome. "Got his bell rung. And I heard he's on the dangerous side."

"I can handle myself."

I walked through the flap as if it were my business, turned back, and faced him. "What exactly do you hope to do with your genius?"

"Well, like, fiber optics. I know that doesn't get us to

super-Wi-Fi. There's a big jump between the junk bands and that. Have to walk before you can run."

"Good luck with that."

The inside was dark and smelled of sweat, like a boys' dorm room in the winter when it was too cold to open the windows. I sat on the cot, and he inhaled sharply.

"Hey, Mr. Neutrino," I said.

He grabbed my wrist, hard. "Angela."

His hand followed my arm, groping for my face in the darkness.

I turned my face away until he stopped reaching. "They didn't touch me."

"This is like some kind of twisted acid trip. They must have drugged us last night."

I helped him sit up. He groaned and grabbed his head.

"It's your fault. You're the one who attacked him."

"Oh my God, what did they . . . they gave me."

He didn't make any sense. "Your concussion set in. Trust me, my ex used to play football. That feeling that you get when you try to think is like a warning sign. It never went on for him."

"What?"

"We need to get out of here. Can you walk?"

"Yeah."

I pulled him up.

He tottered, then fell back on the cot.

"Seriously, if you're too much of a pussy to help me out, I'm going to blitzkrieg your ass."

"What?"

"Fucking Ivy League schools." I knew more than most people forgot. Maybe that was what my father was trying to tell me with the retinal camera.

"You're"—I pulled Morris up—"different," he said.

"Tell me about it." I wanted to hit him on the head. "Let's go."

"Where are we going?"

I told him to shut up.

Outside, Jeff stood, half barring my way. "Where are you going?"

"I'm taking him to sick bay. He has a concussion."

"The doctor has already seen him."

"You're an electrician, telephone line worker, right?" I said.

"Yeah, sort of."

"Then do you know how many times someone with a head injury should have their blood pressure taken after head trauma?"

"Vital signs," Morris offered. His stomach rumbled and he clutched it, which only helped our cause.

"Well, no," Jeff said. He had the deck of cards in his hand.

"When he's cleared, I'll take the next shift, okay?" I said and kicked myself for not thinking of that sooner. I could have gotten rid of him from the start.

Jeff was shaking his head slowly. Morris straightened up and lunged. He connected like he never could with Reginald, making a deafening pop, and they both went down.

Jeff was out cold. I helped Morris to his feet.

"Got him," he said. "I was golden. Semifinals golden. Boxing."

Christ, he needed several weeks, maybe longer, to just lie low.

It was harder to find the train than I thought. In the darkness, it was tough to see the trail, and it didn't make it any easier with Morris cupping my breasts.

"Look at all the fields," he kept mumbling. "We could lie down for a while. I'm not even tired, but you—you look sleepy."

"Jet lag from a train," I grumbled. I hated babysitting. Especially boys that couldn't take care of themselves. The football player, Mack, had been one of those guys whose mating call was to wrap his arm around my neck, white-knuckling a bottle that repeatedly bounced off my collarbone, and tell me how much he loved me over and over. It ended in sympathy sex, in leave-me-alone sex, and that was the way Morris was hanging off me, talking about rolling in the bushes.

"I just need to stop for a second." He threw his head back—I caught him before he fell—and stared at the stars. "By degrees," he said.

"What?"

"They retrograded. By degrees. We really are in the past. The"—he inhaled deeply—"constellations are tight."

I followed his gaze to the sky, a view that most of the pastoral getaways my father had taken us to—a camp in Maine, a private island off the Keys—failed to compare to. There were so many, so close and so bright. It was like there was no light pollution at all. The croak of a bullfrog punctuated the silence.

Morris reached up, trying to shrink the sky between his fingers like a photo on a touch screen.

Even I knew that the universe was expanding, that what he was talking about was the stars getting closer together. They looked just the same to me.

I reminded myself that he wasn't drunk, that although it was stupid to attack Reginald, in retrospect it was courageous.

"Discretion is the better part of valor," I said, pulling him along. "We need to beat feet."

He touched his head as if the motion hurt him. "Brain slosh. If I'm not bleeding, then I should just need . . . rest. I need rest."

"No time for that."

His hand on the small of my back made me recall some of last night, the way we'd rolled across the bed, taking turns being in charge. It hadn't been like that with most men who wanted to spread my legs and then bend me over to finish. It was a your-turn, my-turn kind of thing. We climaxed at the same time.

We tripped up the small incline the tracks were built on. I looked around at the darkened countryside, trying to determine where the train might have been stashed.

Morris sat on the tracks.

I made my way toward a mounded copse of trees

protruding from the otherwise flat fields on either side of the tracks, kicking small stones ahead of me. As I walked, I looked at the stars and felt a level of curiosity I'd never experienced before. Something was up there, watching us. Or maybe looking down on us. I shuddered at the thought of every science-fiction alien invasion film I'd ever seen, including the old ones like *Independence Day.* In all of them, someone organized a revolt, humanity found a way to overcome or endure long enough to find a weakness, or they were eventually annihilated. I laughed at the thought of the *Planet of the Apes* and realized even that old thing might be possible with time travel. Take a smart chimpanzee back ten thousand years, set him loose to compete with Neanderthals . . .

And what would I change? It stood to reason from Reginald's comments that almost anything was changeable.

I reached the copse of trees and stumbled through the tall grass, trying to put the thought of snakes and biting spiders out of mind.

"Angela!" Morris called.

I wheeled and hissed at him to shut up and when I did, the back of my wrist brushed the cloth they had covered the train with. I ran my hand along it and felt my heart flutter. It was possible to go back. I could live in my college days again. Take shots of tequila until I puked, or maybe stay in a loop, maybe in that time Father took us to Prince Edward Island. I was young, but Father would still recognize me. And I could spend his money. In gobs and gobs, buying whatever I wanted, even bankrupt him if I needed to.

I wondered why I hadn't done that before. If we were normal, if we had struggled like everyone else, maybe we would have mattered to each other.

I felt the door latch and pulled it open.

On the tracks, Morris was up, the shadow of his body swaying and tripping toward me.

Lights flickered to life when I opened the door, illuminating the old-style computer screens. *Monitors*, they used to call them. So archaic.

Near the back, a shelf was crowded with books secured by a Velcro strap. I inspected them. History books. I undid the Velcro—it sounded like firecrackers in the silent interior—and flipped open one on the history of America. Passages were highlighted. Maryland, 1963: three fuel tanks exploded. Gas explosion in Quebec in 1965. A nightclub fire in Cincinnati in 1977. I flipped forward to a dog-eared page about 9/11. Another about the Boston Marathon bombing.

A sick feeling formed in my stomach as I slid the book back.

I sat at the controls and looked over the screen. Ran my fingers along the edge and found a power button. The screen flashed to a log-in prompt. Of course.

I leaned my head back and sighed. There was no way I could steal the train. It was naive to even want to. A sun visor caught my eye, with a small, leather-bound book tucked above it.

I took it down, flipped it open. Handwritten notes.

March 7, 2070, 6:30, sister's birthday party.

May 11, 9:00 a.m., she goes to father's brunch alone.

June 4, all day. At beach house. You get drunk and wander off.

I flipped forward a few pages to more of the same.

December 25, 2072. Christmas morning, asshole. Christmas morning.

The train rocked as someone boarded.

"Morris—" The name stalled on my lips.

Reginald stood in the doorway. He saw the book in my hand, and his lips curled inward. He sat heavily in one of the captain's seats and laid his staff across his lap. "Those are my private crosses to bear."

I closed the book. "You're trying to change the past."

Reginald's shoulders rose in a guilty shrug. "What can I say? I love her. Still to this day."

Morris climbed onto the train. Yuda followed, carrying a bolt-action rifle.

"They got me," Morris said, squinting at the lights. He sat down quickly, put his head between his legs and breathed deeply.

"You shouldn't be moving," Reginald said.

"Take me to see my father," Morris said. He looked up at Reginald, his confused eyes straining to focus.

"The train is not for personal use," Yuda said.

"Oh?" I directed a hard gaze at Reginald and held the book up for Yuda to see.

Reginald took a moment to answer, the hurt evident in every fold of his face. "It is only for personal use. And the invasion of *The Kind* is personal." He jabbed the staff onto the floor and got to his feet. "Everyone should get one."

"Reginald," Yuda said.

I moved so Reginald could slide into the pilot's seat. He punched in a rather lengthy code and looked up at me. "When to?"

"Twenty seventy-four," I said. "New Haven, Connecticut."

Reginald turned back to the controls. He turned wheels to select dates and searched through railroad maps.

"Reginald," Yuda said. He was behind the captain's seat.

"It's fine," Reginald said sternly. He faced me. "Better strap in."

"You're not following protocol," Yuda said.

Reginald placed a hand on Yuda's arm. "Stay behind, Yuda. We'll be back before you know we've left."

"Well, what the hell is the point of protocol if we don't follow it?"

Reginald didn't respond, and after a moment Yuda stormed off the train.

I strapped in and waited while the train lumbered onto the tracks. When we accelerated, I closed my eyes and prayed. Prayed that at the end of it all I would wake up in my bed and it would all be a dream. There would be no—what was the word?—*Kind.* No Reginald. I'd be happy if there were no Morris, too.

The lights swirled behind my eyelids, flashing blood; then we were slowing down. I knew something was wrong immediately. It was dark. No city lights shone on the skyline.

I left my seat and peered at the controls, thinking Reginald had pulled a fast one. He hadn't. It was 2074, two days after we had left.

The train came to a stop, and Reginald pushed open the side door. "There you are," he said, motioning for me to get out.

I did and slowly shook my head.

"You wanted 2074. Here you are. Next stop, 2075. We'll pick you up right here on the same day."

"No, that's not right. Look."

The stars were bright, glittering on the surface of the Hudson, brighter than they should've been.

Morris got to his feet, bracing himself against the inside wall of the train.

"Where's the city?" Reginald mumbled. He touched the spectacles on his face, and the lenses glowed red. "It's working," he whispered.

"What's working?"

He removed his glasses, climbed out of the train, and held them out to me. "Take a look. It will take a moment to track down what's actually happened, but I suspect this is a good sign."

The red light in the lenses faded but returned when I

put them on my face. At first, the grainy view of the city skyline was washed out in red, the cold Hudson a river of blood; then the lenses autocorrected and the image sharpened. I wish it hadn't. The spires of the buildings were broken and rose out of the earth like hollow, rotted fangs.

I covered my mouth and cried out.

"What is it?" Morris said.

"There should be lights. There should be people." I looked up the river, trying to recognize something. The skyline was warped and twisted in a way that made it impossible to even gauge where we were.

Reginald's jaw slid to one side, as though he was about to spit out something distasteful.

I slapped him, hard, across the face. "What have you done?" I struck at him again.

He caught my arm and squeezed my wrist. His fingers dug between the two long bones in my forearm, and I cried out in pain.

"I don't like being struck." Reginald's eyes were wide and round, as if an evil inside him was forcing its way out.

Something snapped and shifted in my arm. I screamed.

"Let her go," Morris said and cocked the revolver. I had no idea where he'd gotten it.

Reginald didn't let go, although for half a second his grip loosened.

"Let her go—"

"Or else what?"

I leaned back and raised my leg, intending to kick him in the balls. He twisted my forearm, and my knees buckled.

A warm, sour wind began to blow, flattening the hair on Reginald's head. He looked up suddenly, his eyes wild. "In the train, quickly," he said, dragging me.

Morris stepped forward. The gun went off in a brilliant, blinding flash.

Reginald let go of my hand and clutched his chest as he staggered backward, shot.

There was a light in the world now, shining down on us, hot and red and glowing bitterly like an oven or the inside of a hair dryer, the underbelly of an aircraft.

Morris shot at it. Three rounds before clicking empty. He threw the hand cannon down. "Get in."

I scurried inside the train.

Reginald lay on the ground, his golden staff next to him, the hair on his chin and clothing twitching from the downdraft. A red stain had spread across his chest.

Morris yelled for me to close the door, and I did.

I couldn't tell if Reginald was breathing.

The train began to move, and still he lay there.

The aircraft hung over him as we pulled away and the air turned sweet, like the smell of the river, and cool. I closed the door and fell into a chair as the train accelerated sharply, spiderwebs of electricity building in the corners of the windscreen.

"Where are we going?" I called.

He didn't hear me. It didn't matter. I already knew.

Morris's father, Alex, was shorter than he was and had darker hair and less of it. We met him at his home outside of Boston. He didn't look at all surprised to see us, simply threw open the door and turned around. He led us into a parlor populated with leather furniture. Above the mantel was a lovely realist painting of an urban subway station, in which the breeze of a passing train tugged at the long gray overcoats, hats, and scarves of commuters. Alex motioned for us to sit. The leather squeaked. He wore glasses and a vest designed to assure anyone who came near that he was intellectually superior.

It occurred to me that Reginald had worn a vest.

We'd killed him. Or left him for dead, or *The Kind.*

I didn't want to think of it. I'd always told myself I could do it, under almost any circumstances. It wouldn't be any different, really, than my father firing six million people with the stroke of a pen, but here it was where I hadn't even fired a round and I still felt guilty. That ship, whatever it was, was going to have him. And it was our fault. My fault for wanting to go there. His fault, maybe, for changing the future.

"What brings you here, Son?" Alex said. He didn't look happy to see his son, or even curious about his sudden aging. I could tell by the size of the holoscreen that we'd traveled back to at least the days of my youth.

"I need answers," Morris said, squinting through the concussion.

Alex packed a small pipe of haze and set it on the coffee table in front of us.

"Still on with that?" Morris said.

"Still?" Alex laughed. "I've only been unemployed for three weeks. I'm still in the pity party phase." He motioned to a china cabinet that held a decanter of whiskey. "There's something more acceptable over there, if you prefer."

"You know why we're here?"

"Something must have gone wrong," Alex said. "You're thirty years older. Or did you think I hadn't noticed?"

Alex pressed a button on the side of the pipe, and the haze glowed orange as he inhaled. If what Reginald said was true, he was still there, underneath the blazing lights of the ship. Just like he was still alive, back in the past, and in the future? Though I didn't like him, didn't even enjoy his company, the thought gave me a distant hope.

Morris laughed. "You know, it never occurred to me I could warn you. About the haze. How it would destroy your life."

"Is that so?" Alex said, a halo of smoke coiling above him.

Morris stood, dragged his hand alongside the back of the couch as he made his way to a corner filled with pictures. He took a frame off the wall and stroked it with the back of his hand. "She leaves, you know."

I didn't need to see the photo to know who was in it. "Can we please leave?"

"No," Alex said. "Stay. At least a little longer. I haven't finished hearing how my life ends up. Or yours. Cut short, I understand. Is that it? Or is it that there's something you think you want? Like a wormhole to another star. It's not like that kind of calculation is akin to hitting a moving bullet with another bullet at least, what, six million light-years away? Eleven? Which is to say nothing of the fact that alien conditions would be unknowable. You could die of radiation or the vacuum of space in seconds. Without advance knowledge, it's completely unfeasible."

"He's been here already, hasn't he?" Morris said.

"Been? He's in the other room, for God's sake."

Morris's face went pale.

"We just killed him," I blurted.

The door to the kitchen opened slowly, and the shadow of Reginald stepped forward. He was thinner, without a beard, and his staff struck the floor heavily with each step. He didn't have the vest either, and I snuck a glance at Alex's vest. They might have been the same, given some age and wear.

"It's not nice to kill people," Reginald said. "But I'd be willing to bet I deserved it."

Morris turned to the cabinet with the alcohol.

Reginald moved quickly and had him by the arm. "Are you convinced yet? Or is this whole thing a waste of time?"

"Remember your first grade science project?" Alex said. "Mapping the collision of protons? In first grade? I'm really sorry that your teacher made you change it to something more likely to have been your own work, but I nudged and pushed and prompted you to enter science at every turn."

"Well, thanks for that," Morris said, pulling his arm out of Reginald's grip. He opened the cabinet, and it bumped Reginald's shoulder.

Reginald waited a moment before stepping back so Morris could reach in and grab the bottle.

Alcohol danced into a glass. Morris took a long sip and stared at his father. "Don't destroy your life."

"He doesn't, you little shit," Reginald said. "He spends every spare second of his life on the train, coming to help you build a masterpiece in the past."

Morris dropped his glass. Glass shards sparkled. Amber liquid globs settled on the hardwood.

"All this time you thought he'd given up and left you," Reginald said. "Turns out, he was saving his life for when you really needed it . . . for when you really need him. And how does that feel?"

Morris stepped to the side, caught himself on the back of the couch, and breathed his next words carefully. "Why couldn't you just stop me from drawing them here?"

"That's exactly what I'm trying to do," Reginald said. "Now, go save me before I die."

Morris took a step toward Reginald, and Reginald matched it, pressing his forehead against Morris's. They looked like two heavyweight fighters without the gloves.

"Go ahead and kill me again," Reginald said. "If you'd paid attention, you'd see there were only four locations programmed into the train's computer. All of them lead to me, and I'm always five steps ahead of you."

"Stop it," I said.

Neither of them looked at me for a second, their eyes locked.

"Lamest pissing contest ever," Alex said and lit the pipe again.

Morris backed down. There was a red mark on his forehead.

He stormed out, and I followed because I didn't have a choice. I felt helpless and didn't like it. If there was a chance to make choices on my own, I decided I wasn't going to miss it. Like I had before. Choosing to sit by the pool drinking mimosas all morning instead of going to graduation. Missing my freshman language arts teacher Mrs. Adams's funeral and choosing instead to play racquetball and snort coke.

Those were the wrong decisions. They eroded something in my soul and were just things I had to push deeper and deeper to avoid feeling.

The stars made me sick. I remembered that. The sky swirling over my head like an involuntary space voyage. All of it was programmed by Morris, and then he came along and made some twisted sense of it. I thought maybe I should cling to him. But we were off the rails. It felt like no matter where we went, I would never fit again.

Maybe I never had a place to begin with. Maybe I was too stupid to see that this was my place.

Reginald lay curled in a fetal position next to the tracks when we returned, his curved shape visible in steady bursts of lightning. Morris brought the train to a stop and leaned toward the dash, peering at the sky. No, it wasn't lightning. The sky was blocked by a ship so big the edges of its triangular shape vanished into the clouds of the night sky. Lights flashed on its surface, pulsing like a lighthouse, illuminating the scorched surface of the earth and all its broken buildings with a bloody red light.

For some reason, I felt like it was my fault. Like I should have done more.

After pushing open the door, Morris leaned out and looked down at Reginald. His back was soaked in blood and bits of dirt, and sand clung to the wrinkled surface of the vest. "Jesus," Morris said.

He jumped out of the train and bent over Reginald as I scanned the sky. In the distance, what I thought were smaller ships hovered on the horizon, their red propulsion systems glowing like red stove burners, devils' halos. The line of them stretched one hundred and eighty degrees, as far as I could see.

They were all around us, waiting.

I jumped out of the train, grabbed Morris's arm,

and pulled him back. In the flashing light, it felt like a nightmare. One second Morris was bent over Reginald, feeling for a pulse; the next I had him, standing up, a small cloud of dirt hanging in the air, each second crystallized before I could even process it all.

Morris shoved me back, and I watched as he turned Reginald over, inspecting the wound.

On the ground, Reginald's hand rose off his chest, growing closer with each flash of light.

"There's too many of them," Morris said.

I thought, this is it. This is the moment when I need to stand up and act, to stop sitting around waiting for someone to do something.

I bent over Reginald, took his arm, and pulled. It was so slick with blood I almost fell. As I reached for a better grip near Reginald's shoulder, a kind of afterglow of electricity flickered across the surface of his insides. I stopped helping him, and his hand clenched my upper arm, hard.

His eyes were fixed on me, wide and angry in the flashing light.

Morris grabbed my other arm, and in the next flash, Reginald's eyes were closed and he was asleep. I let go and stood there as Morris dragged Reginald back toward the train, in each successive flashing of light growing farther and farther away.

The glowing circles of red light lining the horizon were gone. I was alone in the barren wasteland. The shadows were closer, slippery, like the night might take me away.

"Come on," Morris yelled, one foot on the first step of the train as he struggled with the body. The entire side of the train lit up when the light flashed overhead. A humming noise began to fill the air. Like locusts. Like hungry insects ready to feast on a body.

Because that's what Reginald was. A body.

A vessel.

"Get over here! Help me so we can go!" Morris tugged lamely on Reginald's vest, the one his father had probably given him even though he still wore it.

The light pulsed faster.

"Help me or I'm leaving you both!"

I knew he was a bastard and he meant it, so I ran to the side of the train, leaving behind the humming and the ships that besieged us.

I grabbed Reginald's fat ankles and lifted enough so that Morris could shift his weight up. He scrunched his face with the strain, closing his eyes, and I know he didn't see Reginald's shoulder, how the flesh inside was white, how flashes of cortical electricity shimmered in its transparency, or the hand that reached up and held the vest closed.

Morris looked at me as he started the train moving, squinting as if looking into a bright light, and asked why I looked so calm.

He must have been confused because I was terrified. We'd brought something back with us.

Chapter 7

Amos

Bells jingled overhead when I entered the diner. It was 1957. I hadn't slept—really slept—in days. Once Reginald came back into my life, his dust of prophecy had changed everything, and the very real obligations of success were trying during the best days—managing the farm and the two businesses I bought as "covers" to hide the fact that I was managing a secret underground facility for time-traveling refugees—and daunting during the worst.

And whenever I spoke to Reginald about it, he laughed and assured me that I couldn't make a mistake. He wouldn't allow it.

The worst part about my newfound success was that I hadn't told Rosaline. She still had nightmares about Reginald, still worried that he was out there, somewhere, tracking our movements, plotting to kill our son, Walter. I'd meant to tell her, eventually, but how do you tell your wife you've made a bed for the monster from her nightmares below the back forty? If I had told her in the beginning, right away . . . It had been too long. There had been so many nights when I woke to find her sitting next to Walter's crib or his bed, just warding the darkness, that I couldn't bear to tell her I'd conspired with the very man she so deeply feared.

From behind the counter, a black man with a stained apron nodded at me. "You can sit anywhere you like, sir."

The place was mostly empty. "Thanks."

Reginald was sitting at a booth by himself, glowering at me. He was thinner than he looked the first time I saw him but not by much. He'd been slowly gaining weight. Something about that bothered me.

The sound of my feet on the tile floor was like the strike of a clock, counting down as I walked toward him. I hated that I was afraid of him.

Reginald leaned back in the booth, inhaling deeply. "What are you doing here, Amos?"

I sat down across from him on the red leather seat. "I came to save you."

He laughed. Some of the other patrons eyed him askance, a woman with white hair and her balding husband, a white housewife in a polka-dotted dress with a child eating an ice cream sundae on the stool beside her.

"Save me from what?"

I reached into my pocket and pulled out a twisted chunk of metal—it couldn't have weighed more than a nickel—and set it on the table in front of Reginald. There was still dried blood in the accordion-like folds of the bullet.

Reginald stared at it. "What's that supposed to be?"

The cook came around the counter and set a plate with a burger and a mound of fries on top of the bullet, as if he hadn't seen it, and pulled a menu from his apron. He placed it in front of me and said, "Would you like something to drink?"

The bubbles in Reginald's Coke fizzed, dewdrops on the inside of his clear straw.

"I'll have what he's having."

"A Coke? Sure thing."

"No, all of it."

"One Coke, burger, and fries coming up."

Reginald smiled, his long moustache nearly covering his whole upper lip.

"Does he come here often?" I asked the cook.

The cook looked suddenly uncomfortable. "Reginald here is a good customer," he said, tucking the menu in his apron, and walked away.

Reginald picked up the burger, opened it, and squirted ketchup inside. "Did I deserve it?"

"Maybe." I grabbed the silver napkin holder and slowly turned it around and around, watching as my bent image passed on its surface. "I don't know yet."

Reginald glanced up as he put the burger back together. "And you took the train by yourself?"

"Yuda is here. We didn't want to risk it."

"Ah," he said, squeezing the bun together and holding it before his face. It was like some kind of macabre smile, ketchup blood dripping from gray teeth. "And how did you find me?"

"You had a receipt in your pocket."

Reginald tsked and took a huge bite of the burger.

A few hours ago, I watched as the doctor, a man called Barry who couldn't have been more than five feet tall, used forceps to pull the bullet out and sewed him up with a needle and thread while an IV, hung on a tent pole, dripped steadily. It was hard to believe that he was still there, clinging to life as I sat with him, that I knew the future before he did.

Maybe anyone could play God. Maybe becoming God was more about luck than anything else.

I began to explain. "They bring you—"

"Don't," Reginald said, holding up a hand. "I don't want to know. It'd be nice to be surprised for a change."

"What if you don't live?"

"Do I?"

It hadn't even occurred to me to check.

"It's not easy, is it?"

He was right. It wasn't easy. It never would be, and I felt like a sham. Like I was always a step behind everyone. I told myself that I was actually better off than all my contemporaries—all the other stock traders and businessmen. Reginald kept me aware of just about everything that could bankrupt me and fed me a steady supply of tips from the history books. I didn't want to use them all, liked to think I could handle the little stuff, but the truth was, I was nothing without him. Everything I'd become I'd owed to him—so why did it surprise me that the first time I'd traveled to the future was to save him?

"Being omniscient, taking time out of the equation as

the theoretical physicists always insisted"—Reginald shook his head—"and I still feel like I'm making a mess of it."

The cook came back with a Coke. "Burger be right out."

"I ever tell you," Reginald said, "in the future, they grow this, the meat, in a laboratory?"

"You've mentioned it."

He mentioned that he liked the food of the past quite a lot, actually. Everyone did to some extent. He took a small bite. Slowly, as he chewed, his eyes narrowed. "You really don't know, do you?"

"Know what?"

"If I live?"

I didn't think to look but didn't see reason to tell him that. I leaned forward. "Reginald, what do you do with your time?"

"Whatever I please," he said, stabbing a fry into ketchup.

"I mean, the woman in Pripyat, your granddaughter, this place. They said that *The Kind* arrived early, that we were changing things, but it hadn't pushed their arrival back. It made it move forward."

The cook was coming back with my burger. It smelled good, even to me.

Reginald dipped another fry, popped it into his mouth, and stared at me as he chewed. It was unsettling and he knew it.

"Fine," he said. "I'll show you what I do with my time. Finish your burger."

He watched me eat as I thought about Morris and Angela carrying his body back into the complex on a makeshift stretcher. Angela's hair had been messed up, her eyes were red, and smears of makeup ran down her cheeks. The soles of her bare feet looked like bruised plums coated in black dirt. She had a vacant look in her eyes and was waiting outside the medical yurt when Barry came out, white apron covered in blood. It was like being in the war all over again, when the surgeons came out with the blood of twenty men stuck to their hands and mixed in the sweat on their foreheads.

Angela watched him, her mouth open as if waiting for something.

"He'll live," Barry said, and she turned away, a knuckle to her mouth.

Later, her hands shook as she drank water from a tin mug. "Nobody saw it," she said.

"Saw what?" I said.

"On the inside of him. No one saw it, did they?"

"There was a lot of blood," I said. I'd never forget Barry's hands, in the plastic second skin, coated in darkness and how my stomach knotted, contracting so hard it nearly folded over itself like when I'd just finished doing sit-ups in boot camp.

"Oh, God," she said, tilting her head back and staring at the roof. "And I can't even go back."

"There's over a hundred years of future," I said.

"No, there isn't," she'd said and turned away. "I need

to find Morris."

When the straw hit the bottom of the glass, I asked Reginald the question. "How do you explain the years that were missing?"

Even over the beard and the folds of his chin, I saw Reginald swallow hard.

"They're still there." He leaned onto the table, and I thought for sure the empty plates would slide toward him as though affected by gravity. "Listen, if things are different in the future, things would have to be different now, wouldn't they? I'd have different memories. The circumstances that led me to finding the train, those would be different, perhaps not have occurred at all. We might not be having this conversation, right here."

The cook came back, piled up our dishes, and asked if we would have anything else.

"Brownie sundaes," Reginald said.

My eyebrows rose.

"In the future—no matter when the collapse occurs—food is scarce. Something I can't seem to forget."

"I understand."

"Do you? Because I'm not sure if you're really catching my drift."

"Your what?"

"Getting my point." He huffed, adjusted himself, the leather seat crackling beneath him. He leaned in to whisper, "*The Kind*, they can't be stopped. And while it's true that perhaps something changed on that one fork in the road where I brought in Angela, it really doesn't change anything."

"How did you know about that?"

Reginald's mouth snapped closed, the muscles in his jaw clenching.

"How did you know?" I said again.

"I think it's safe to say I survive whatever injury I've sustained."

"You talk to yourself?" I gasped.

The leather breathed a sigh of relief as Reginald stood. "Come on."

"What about the ice cream?"

Reginald rolled his eyes. "It will be here when we return."

"We'll be right back, Frank," Reginald called to the cook, who was holding two sundaes.

"Want me to put these in the icebox?"

"No, it'll only take a minute."

"No problem, Reggie."

Outside, I looked up, squinting through the heat lines rising off the street, and saw a familiar shape coming toward us on the far sidewalk. It was Reginald—and someone else.

I had no idea I looked like that. I mean, not really. There was a sort of weight in my movements, and I could almost tell from my gait that I still didn't know, that despite whatever Reginald was going to show me, I'd still be ignorant. A child following his father, for better or worse, toward the ice cream stand.

Across the street, I made a little wave, the kind I used to use when I was overseas; two fingers and thumb.

We'd been marching along a road that followed a river in Belgium when I saw troops returning. It took forever for their column to meet us. The day was cool, winter was coming, most of the trees were bare, and a single red leaf managed to float down the river in time with our march, like it was going to war too or had already been killed. It disappeared behind the returning column, and I made that little wave to a corporal whose arm was in a sling, mimicking his motion.

It felt like he was saying, I'm still alive but everything is not okay. "Careful out there, boys," he shouted. "Those Krauts bite!"

When the column had continued past, the leaf was gone.

I wondered why I didn't just cross the street and talk to myself but knew the answer. If I did that, I wouldn't have the answers, because I wouldn't go.

"Keep moving, nothing to see," Reginald said.

That's when it hit me: I was his prisoner. Despite all the money and land and holdings I'd accumulated, I was trapped.

The wind was at our backs as we walked along the tracks. Silken spirals of dust kicked up by our feet flowed out ahead of us like endless ribbon.

On the train, the light still made me wonder about God, a fusion of color streaks far more vivid than even the best impressionists could conjure. I wondered if maybe

Reginald was friends with one of the artists. I knew from our previous conversations that, obviously, time travel was limited to when train tracks existed, that it couldn't go any further back than that, and that the designers had programmed everything into the computer, the position of the earth around the sun and the earth's rotation, by some kind of math-magical algorithm even Reginald didn't understand. We were, as he said, standing on the shoulders of giants. Generations and generations of them.

We ended our journey on a side street in Brooklyn, and despite being a country boy, I kind of felt at home. All of this had begun there—except, I realized, that really wasn't true. It all began when I decided to burn the little effigy of Christ my father had carved. That moment when I put it inside the stove on top of the coals was the instant I decided to never be welcome in my home again.

I wondered if my parents still thought of me or if they were even still alive.

To think that I could change it, go back and warn myself, made my bowels weak. My back hurt at the thought of bending over endless fields of okra and cauliflower. I'd probably still hate them. And their God, who constantly plagued my thoughts.

The stone buildings lining the street all looked the same, despite the sleek automobiles and black taxis. Everyone walked around with portable computers and telephones, and the women were barely dressed. One, a teenager with long, slender black legs, was wearing jean shorts so cropped I could see the insides of her pockets and part of her bottom as she passed. Homeless people sat in every nook and cranny along the sidewalk. A woman wearing a bra made out of tin foil and cardboard walked past, her smile impossibly wide.

"Don't stare," Reginald said.

The sidewalks were dirty. Trash was piled outside every building, and as we walked over a grate, the subway roared and pushed a hot breath of foul, urine-laced air up our nostrils.

It wasn't the city I remembered. It was still just as busy, with people endlessly moving, but had never been this dirty. Like it was rotting. Like people were the flies feasting off the corpse of a dog.

We stopped before a brown brick building. Concrete statues of elephants decorated the pillars beside the stairs leading to the door. One's trunk was broken off midtrumpet.

Reginald produced a portable telephone from his pocket and held it to his ear. "Yes, I'm currently just outside 1146 Bridgewater Street in Brooklyn. I smell gas . . . Yes, it's a sort of rotten egg smell. Very foul. I'm afraid there still are people inside. My name is Chet Ashby. You can reach me at this number. Thank you."

Reginald set the phone in the crook of the elephant's trunk and began to walk away. I hurried to catch up with him.

"What was that about?"

He glanced at me without stopping, reached inside

his vest, and handed me a small, leather-bound notebook with a cloth bookmark in the middle. I opened it, found hundreds of handwritten entries crossed out, the first of which read, *1146 Bridgewater St., Brooklyn, July 7, 2076, Gas. 34.*

The crossed-out entries were similar, and I didn't have to look back to know that Pripyat would be there. They went back nearly forty years. I shuddered, thinking about spaceships in the field, two of them the last time.

"What about *The Kind*?" I said.

I didn't remember when Reginald produced the staff; he hadn't had it when we got off the train. It struck the sidewalk heavily with each step. "What about them?" He stepped to the edge of the sidewalk between two vehicles and hailed a cab. That action certainly hadn't changed over the years.

A black sedan pulled dutifully out of the line of traffic, its engine nearly silent among the noises of the city.

"I thought that saving people was sort of helping them," I said.

Reginald spun. "Do you think that's reason enough to stand by and watch people die?"

"No, I—"

"With power comes responsibility," he said, pulling open the door to the taxi. "Get in."

We exited the cab sometime later and emerged on another city street, this one far more rundown than Brooklyn's, with decaying apartment buildings all around. In the alleys, laundry lines crisscrossed like spiderwebs, sheets hanging like shrouds of insects. Reginald led me up a stairway into one of the buildings. Bottles and cans were scattered under the stairwell, along with other detritus, and I heard the scurry of cockroaches in the walls. The fetid odor of rotten trash was overwhelming.

I almost asked Reginald why we were here but decided not to, knowing that eventually we'd be heading back for ice cream, only a minute after we left.

We stopped before a door labeled 5D. Reginald pounded on it. He took off his spectacles, and the staff shrank into a solid brick about the size of a baseball. He tucked it into his vest.

"Who is it?" a woman's voice called from within.

I suddenly felt nervous. The light was dim, and we were in the kind of place that only criminals and the impoverished inhabit. I had a substantial sum of money on my person. Nearly a hundred dollars.

"Don't recognize your own brother?" Reginald said, smiling wide.

There was a long pause before the chain rattled and the door opened.

"Reginald?" A woman emerged from the shadows. She was pale white, like Reginald, but of slight build. Purple veins coursed down the sides of her freckled face and forearms. She scratched the inside of her elbow. "What happened to you?" Then she looked at me and shrank back inside. "Who's the Bible salesman?"

"This is my friend Amos. He's mute, actually. Never

says a word." Reginald smiled at me.

I nodded. I'd play it his way.

"And what do you mean, what happened to me? What happened to you? I thought you were in Hollywood, gone to make it on the silver screen."

She bit her lip. Strands of greasy, reddish-brown hair hung beside her face. She would have been pretty if not for the anemic look of despair, the dark circles under her eyes.

"Well, are you going to invite us in?"

"Reginald," she said, looking at me as if ashamed to say it in front of me. "What's with the weight? And the beard?"

"You know," Reginald said, laying a hand on her shoulder, "you're not the only one who can let themselves go."

Her chest jumped as she made a small hiccup sound; then she collapsed into Reginald, crying.

The inside of her apartment smelled like urine and a pall hung in the air. Old cigarettes filled every ashtray and empty bottle in the place. On the counter, spread neatly on a newspaper, was a set of syringes. Reginald picked up a spoon, the handle bent like the ring of the candleholder my mother used to use at night.

She rushed over, wadded up the newspaper, and ran it to the trash can.

"Jess, I've already seen it," Reginald said.

She came back, snatched the spoon from his hand. "I'm sorry this place is such a mess."

"Jess," Reginald said as bottles clattered together in her hands. He chased her down, held her wrists together.

"It's okay. I don't care."

There was a knock.

Jess looked at the door, then looked back at Reginald. "No."

Reginald let go of her hands. "It's not my doing."

Jess backed away, set down the bottles, and went to the door. She looked through the peephole and turned back. "Really, Reggie?"

She opened the door. "Hi, come on in. Let's have a family reunion."

Reginald sucked in his gut. A distinguished-looking, gray-haired man in a black suit and a woman in jeans and a red blouse entered. She was very pretty, her pointy chin and pert nose framed by wavy brown hair.

"Reginald," the pretty woman gasped.

"Evelyn?" Reginald said, and then, "Father?"

"What's happened to you?" Evelyn crossed the room to Reginald and looked up at him.

"I'm afraid I have a condition. I'll explain later," Reginald said.

"I didn't even know you were home."

"Just got back."

"Who is this?" Reginald's father, Walter, asked of me.

"It's nice to see you too, Father. He's mute. Don't expect a response."

The man's eyebrows rose. He held himself in a composed, dignified manner, bowing slightly and smiling at me. His hair didn't move, and he had a high forehead.

At least he didn't speak slow and loud to me. "Jess, do you know what it took for me to get here?" he said.

"I'm sure the building is the safest it's ever been," Jess said.

"Jess, we're worried about you," Walter said. "It's time for you to come home."

"All of you?" Jess said, looking around the room.

"They didn't even know I'd returned from service yet," Reginald said. "I got back yesterday. I knew I had to help you."

"I wrote him while he was away," Walter explained.

"Why didn't you visit?" Tears streamed down Jess's face.

"With the campaign . . ." Walter paused. "I've been busy. It's true. I didn't think you were ready to listen. I thought you'd think it was a calculated move, to gain sympathy with voters. I didn't want to appear callous."

"As opposed to being callous." She turned to Reginald. "You just got home?"

"I thought the surprise would keep," Reginald said, looking at Evelyn. "I knew you needed my help."

Walter put his arm around Jess. "Come on. Let's go home."

"You're not taking me to rehab?"

"Is that where you want to go?"

She shook her head.

"Then that's not where we're taking you. Tomorrow we can talk about what needs to be done. I just want to know you're safe." He stepped forward, but her feet didn't move.

"If you want to return tomorrow, that's fine. Come

with me to Camp David for the night, and in the morning you can return if that's what you wish. I only want to spend time with my daughter. I can't stay here much longer."

Walter led her to the door.

Reginald called, "Jess, is there anything you're going to need to . . . to get through the night?"

Jess hesitated, then went into the bedroom and came back with a small clutch bag with a broken zipper.

"God, I was hoping it would be clothes." It was clear from Walter's smile it was meant as a joke.

On the street, Evelyn hugged Reginald. "I'm glad you're home safe, but I don't like this look. What's going on?"

"It's not permanent. I'll be good as new in no time."

She smiled weakly at me. "Why is he dressed that way?"

I maintained my vow of silence.

"It's a long story. He was with me in Korea."

"Things got pretty hairy over there, didn't they?"

"You have no idea."

She kissed him quickly on the cheek and started for the limo.

Reginald pulled her back. "Evelyn, I love you."

She touched his nose. "I know," she said, and pulled away.

We watched them go, the taillights of the limo flashing before accelerating around a corner.

"Can I talk now?" I said.

"You wanted to see what I've been doing," Reginald

said. "Well, this is it."

"You're trying to save people?"

"Not all of them. I hate the Venezuelans."

"Ah," I said.

"I lost her once, you know."

"Evelyn?"

"Jess dies in two weeks if I'm not here today. And I wasn't. At least, not until now." Reginald let out a big sigh and stopped holding his gut in.

"Were you already home from some war in Korea?"

"Yeah. Right now I'm in a bar, lost in haze and drinking some concoction made to look like absinthe."

"Why don't you go get yourself?"

He shook his head. "I'm afraid. I'm afraid if I don't lose her, I'll never know what I had. And without going through what I go through, the opportunity to live again won't create such an imperative for greatness."

"What was she doing with your father?"

"She was his campaign manager. I introduced them."

"What is she now?"

Reginald's fingers curled and uncurled around his cane, the knuckles flashing white. "Someone contacts them early. We can fix that." He set off at nearly a run.

Despite his bulk, I struggled to keep up as he darted around cyclists and pedestrians on the sidewalk on his way back to the train. I felt sad for Reginald. Here he was, a master of time and space, and all he could do was save a few lives here and there as he attempted to salvage his own.

On the train, I plopped down in the seat next to him. "What's the hurry?" I said.

"I've been keeping tabs on someone. Their work dovetailed with Morris's."

The train started moving. Far in the distance the needle-shaped nose of a train grew bigger and bigger as we accelerated. I leaned back in the seat and pressed my feet against the dash.

"Hang on a bit," Reginald said.

I closed my eyes as the electricity began to form at the edges of the windshield, and I prayed that a Reginald from another time would come and warn us if we didn't survive.

We emerged to an open desert in the center of a valley with high walls. It had a disturbing likeness to the green valley he'd taken me to so many years ago, and I was again shaken to realize that, if we chose, that day could be today.

We left the train and traveled by foot to the nearest road, a dirty trek in sand so hot it felt like my soles were on fire, and even though there was virtually no humidity, the air was superheated, making it tough to breathe.

"In case you're wondering, this is an abandoned line," he said. "I try to stick to those while traveling in unfamiliar places." He held a device like the translator to his ear and ordered a car.

We stopped before a road black as coal, hot as fire. It took only a short while for a very shiny small car, without a driver, to pick us up.

It was night by the time we reached Garret Tremblay's house, which was perched on the side of a steep slope, guarded by a retaining wall that set it above the street.

I knew better than to ask questions.

A young woman with smooth, darkly tanned skin flickered into existence on a screen next to the door and asked if she could help us. The sounds of children playing inside Garrett's house echoed from within the screen. Behind her, I saw their movements, like running shadows, and the smooth lines of the interior, the glass forming a railing alongside the stairs, sleek white walls with elegantly placed rectangles of art.

"We need to speak with Garrett," Reginald said. "It's an emergency."

She hesitated; then the screen went black.

The city was quiet, despite its size. Nestled like a glowing jewel in the desert, Garrett's home had a phenomenal view. A large vehicle drove by, and it didn't make a sound.

I looked at Reginald, the question on my lips.

"Noise-canceling frequencies," he said, as if that explained anything.

He must have seen my puzzlement. "The device works because each frequency, even the sound of my voice, has an opposite wavelength. It's a luxury for the rich, originally developed as sensory deprivation therapy for insane asylums. If you walked to the side of the road, you'd hear everything. It's concentrated on Garrett's home." He looked up, inspecting the house, which rose to three stories. I assumed some of its geometry allowed for balconies.

The screen flickered back to life. This time it was a man. Wearing a white dress shirt, the cuffs of his sleeves rolled up, he unbuttoned his collar as he asked if he could help us.

"I need to speak with you immediately," Reginald said.

"What is this about?" Garrett said.

"It's about the neutrino signal you've been receiving at the observatory and the signal you're about to send back."

Garrett paused. His hand fell away from his collar. There was a buzzing sound, a click, and the door of his home opened a hair.

Reginald wasted no time pushing the door open, and the click of his staff accompanied him inside, biting at the black tile floor.

A little girl with dark skin and straight brown hair was turned around on the couch, facing us. Behind her the largest, clearest color television I'd ever seen hung on the wall, playing a cartoon of sorts.

Garrett's dark hair was slicked back, and his eyes squinted with suspicion as Reginald approached.

"How long have you known about the neutrinos?" Reginald demanded.

Garrett said nothing.

It was the wrong answer.

Reginald rammed him in the stomach with the end

of the staff. He doubled, placing a hand on Reginald's shoulder for support. He looked up at Reginald, eyes wide.

There was a loud click, and someone cleared her throat. The woman from the small monitor stood at the top of the glass-lined staircase holding a handgun with an exceptionally large barrel.

Reginald helped Garrett stand and smiled at the woman.

"Don't do it," she said, and in those three words I knew she'd shoot him, and me, and bury us in the desert somewhere and still sleep fine. She looked dainty—sexy, even—in the thin white evening gown that clung to her hips, but a dark, serpentine tattoo curled around her ankle. It reminded me of Reginald's staff, his cane, which he held only when the worst of his personality came to the fore.

Reginald was whispering something to Garrett.

"What?" Garrett's eyes widened. "That's incredible. How do you know?"

Reginald continued to whisper.

"You can't be serious."

Reginald wrapped his fingers in Garrett's shirt. "How long has it been since you answered the signal?"

"Let him go," the woman called from the top of the stairs.

"Daddy, what do they want?" the little girl said.

I went to the little girl.

"Don't touch her," the woman yelled.

I held my hands out at my sides. I didn't surrender

to Germans; now I was surrendering to a woman with a handgun at a range that made accuracy more chance than certainty.

"Forty-eight days?" Reginald said, his voice rising, echoing off the expansive space.

"Daddy," the little girl said.

I went to her.

At the top of the stairs, tears shone on the woman's face.

Reginald looked up and around at the ceiling. "The noise canceling—turn it off."

"What does that have to—?"

"Turn it off!" Reginald shoved Garrett.

Garrett flew backward, feet pedaling to keep up until he stumbled into a bookshelf. Several volumes fell. Garrett eyed Reginald, and I knew what he was thinking. How did that fat slob do that? How is he so powerful? I couldn't imagine the man it would take to best him in a fight.

Reginald pointed the staff at the woman, in a motion so sudden I didn't even see his arm move, and the glass railing exploded, shards of glass becoming ice, then snow. Some stung my face. I grabbed the little girl and held her. She fought me, and for a moment all sound was gone. Reginald's mouth was moving. Something dripped down my cheeks.

The woman had fallen on the stairs. Her body lay crumpled, one arm bent behind her back, legs splayed, white dress polka-dotted with red and hitched up around her waist. The little girl's arms stretched out, reaching for her mother, and she slipped from my grasp to the floor and ran to her mother, her bare feet leaving larger and larger smears of blood as she got closer to the stairs.

Garrett was on the ground and Reginald was over him, clearly yelling even though I couldn't hear him.

The little girl clung to her mother.

"Are you going to get the gun?" Reginald said, the sound suddenly returning.

He pointed the end of his staff at the wall below the stairs, where the gun had toppled.

The mother was alive, moaning, one hand lifting a strand of hair off her face even though the other was twisted behind her back, shoulder bulging oddly. Her daughter was whimpering.

I picked up the gun and dusted the crystals of glass away. It was heavy, silver. Full of bullets.

"Go to the control panel by the door and press the button for noise canceling," Reginald commanded.

"Which one is it?"

"The one that looks like a teacup on its side with an *X* over it."

I found the button and pressed it.

There was a low groan, the crackle of fire. Slowly Reginald, Garrett, and I turned toward the valley where the city lay. It was consumed by tongues of flame.

"Jesus Christ," Garrett said.

Reginald touched the end of his staff to Garrett's head. He twitched as if shocked and fell to the floor, limp and still.

"That's for bringing them here early," Reginald said and stepped over the corpse.

The little girl began to scream. Reginald pointed his staff at her. A bolt of lightning streaked across the room and cut her off midsyllable. She leaned back against the wall and turned her head to one side, eyes fixed on me, and I thought of the time we found that family hiding from the Germans in a bunker dugout below a barn, in earth made of years of horseshit. Only this time it felt like rather than reaching in and helping them, we'd stuck the barrel of a potato digger in the hole and burned a belt until there was nothing left but blood and dust.

Reginald pushed me, bumping into me almost, trying to get me to move, and I hit his chin with the butt of the gun.

He dropped, and suddenly I knew what kind of man it would take to beat him in a fight—one who wasn't afraid to do everything Reginald would do.

I walked to the far end of the living room area, up three small steps, past a dining room table, to a large glass door. I found a latch and slid it open, trying not to think how easy it would splinter, how quickly Reginald could shatter something so nice, and stepped out.

The smell of smoke was heavy in the air. Screams echoed through the valley. Fires flickered on the sides of the tall buildings, and the sound of automatic weapons peppered the night. In the sky, the burning eyes of spaceships hung on the horizon, occasionally darting toward the city, swooping low like birds of prey, and lifting off with God knows what in their long talons.

This was the end that Reginald had spoken of. The collapse, as he called it, of civilization The one I'd seen after all the dust had settled. When there were only two warriors left. Reginald, who had all of history behind him, and the ship that sat on the throne of vines—two ships now, I supposed, because Reginald had fed them. I'd even helped.

I wondered if there were three now, after he'd stopped the gas from exploding inside the building earlier. I wondered if that made any difference at all to anything besides Reginald's conscience.

The fires in the city grew darker, and I looked up. A huge black hunk of alien planet crossed the zenith, edging out the moon. Its underside briefly lit, hundreds of crimson cigarette holes flaring, and a wave of ships took wing to the night.

"They hunt at night the first few months," Reginald said behind me.

I still held the revolver in my hand. I didn't turn. If he wanted to kill me, he'd have done it.

"Then the truce takes over, and they leave us the night, knowing it will be harder."

"Why'd you kill them?" I said, angling my feet so I could see him in my periphery.

"You're right. I shouldn't have," Reginald said. He was

looking back at them with a curious eye, inspecting what he'd done not with shame or guilt but the fascination of a gallows man. "I had no idea they would be up to it so quickly. Now I've got to do it again, forty-eight days earlier . . ." I heard his fingernails scratching his head. "Best do forty-nine."

I wheeled on him. "You're going to do it again?"

"Of course. I thought it was clear why we were here."

He stepped forward, with that uncanny speed of his, and grabbed me by the chin, pointing my face toward the sky. "That's what they did. That's what Morris did. That's what I'm trying to stop. That family doesn't matter. I'd kill them a thousand times over in far less humane ways if it meant avoiding this."

"Not with me you won't."

"No. You're going to have ice cream."

I had the barrel of the gun against his belly, and even though I wanted to pull the trigger, I knew I wouldn't. I'd seen him in the future without the gut shot. I'd already made up my mind and was only playing with the idea. I hated him. Not just because he was callous and cold but because he could be that way and I couldn't.

The light of a new flame in the city burst on his face, and our tall shadows burned immortal on the wall of the house.

I was so angry all the muscles in my body flexed at once, creating a kind of paralysis. My finger curled around the trigger. I felt the hammer lift, and he let me go.

His boots crunched on the glass as he walked to

the front door. "Are you coming? Or would you like to live through this particular nightmare in some sort of penance?"

I never had a choice.

Driving at night was more than uncomfortable. Reginald stole one of the sound-canceling devices and quickly mounted it to the top of the car and wired it into the ignition harness, so there was virtually no sound as we drove. I could hear my breathing, my heartbeat, not the engine or the bumps we rode over while forging aimlessly into the dark. I was going to ask if the car had headlights when I saw Reginald's glasses, clouded with red fog that dyed his cheeks sanguine, and knew he could see fine. I was the blind one, alone with my memory, pondering the contradiction of Reginald appearing to grow as a human, getting it right this time around by helping to save his sister from whatever the haze was, and Reginald the murderer, killing an entire family without remorse.

The night was black. We held our breaths when spaceships passed low. I wondered what the inside of the giant, wedge-like spaceship was like as it continuously devoured the night sky, stealing the stars, so low it eclipsed the clouds.

I'd never been so happy to see the train in all my life.

When I passed myself again on the street and gave that little three-finger wave I had seen the corporal use before, I wasn't sure which of us was going to the front.

My ice cream was far sweeter than I deserved. It

didn't seem to bother Reginald as he shoveled spoonful after spoonful into his mouth. He stopped, just about to take another bite, after noticing I was making mine into an icky brown paste.

He set his spoon down rather abruptly and rubbed the bridge of his nose. "What's wrong?" he said, sounding very much like the words were painful.

"Nothing."

He exhaled very slowly.

I remembered the first day I met him, when he turned to me and dug his hand into my shoulder so abruptly.

"I have no desire to ask that question again. Or to waste time prying the truth from you."

"What did you do in the war?" I needed to make sense of what he was.

"Really?" Reginald said, eyes suddenly sad.

A farm truck rumbled past the diner, the pink-white skin of pigs visible through the high-fenced back.

"Horrible things, Amos. Horrible things," he said quietly, eyes distant. "I was responsible for extracting information. That's a euphemism, for being the man in a dark room, holding any number of bloody surgical instruments, making men scream words you wish they wouldn't say for a long time."

"How long was your tour?"

"Three years. And it was a very bloody war. After the north's first push south on the Korean peninsula, America decided it best to respond with mech soldiers, similar to the builder bots in our little lair. They'd been criticized in the past for using a take-no-prisoners approach, so they set each of their weapons to stun and incapacitated every combatant.

"I'd be willing to bet there's an entire city, big as New York, full of men I mutilated." He cleared his throat. "The wife of the prime minister of Britain was kidnapped on a humanitarian aid mission in southern China, and it was rumored she was held in Tongsin. It became the mantra, and in our downtime we joked that the only bit of English the Koreans would ever learn was 'Where is Madam Rider?'"

Reginald twirled his spoon in the ice cream dish, like a ballet figurine inside a music box, dancing on a muddy mirror pond.

"Are you going to eat that?" he said, pointing with the spoon.

I pushed mine toward him, and as he stabbed the spoon into the trough, I realized it was for him like drink for other men.

"I've done horrible things, Amos. And I'm not afraid to do them again. But I need you. I need you to go back and fight for me. There's going to be a very large conversation, and I won't be there to defend myself." He set down his spoon suddenly. "Do you realize you've known me longer than almost any other human being still alive? And it's a near certainty you know me better than anyone else. I need you. Always have. Who better to help shape the future than the man who sired the men who destroy it? Don't worry. I'm not a Luddite. I blame scientific inquiry more than their actions. Amos, can I count on you?"

I stared at him for a long time before speaking, and if I'd not fought in the war I'd almost certainly have never come to the conclusion that the world was a mess, and it required someone who was able to do things that were unspeakable.

"You can," I said. If we somehow emerged in onc piece after all this, people would have to get in line behind me to kill Reginald. He had no place in a civilized society.

"Good," he said, reaching across the table and taking my hand in his big, fat, soft palms in a fatherly gesture. "Then go back with Yuda and fight for me. Go back and make people understand that I've only ever wanted to help."

It didn't make any sense, going to fight for a man who had tried to kill me, but that's exactly what I did. It was what needed to be done.

Chapter 8

Angela

We stood in the cooling night, the tops of the rail line catching silver flakes of the rising moon, waiting. I hated that they left and that they would return mere moments later, not even giving us time to think when they could have been gone for years, or gone anywhere, maybe even stumbled onto whatever had taken hold of Reginald. Someone coughed and the sound quickly disappeared, dulled by a ghostly breath of fog beginning to rise from the earth and collecting in the low spots, hiding in the grass.

I wanted him dead. I wanted him killed, brought back to life, and killed again. There was evil in him. I'd seen it crackling beneath the too-white surface of his skin and was glad Morris had shot him. If he hadn't, no one would know that he had something inside him that wasn't human.

Far down the tracks, a flash cloud of lightning exploded into the thunderous roar of the speeding train. They rushed to a stop in front of us. Inside the train,

Amos looked jaundiced, sickly. I wondered if everyone who rode in it looked that way.

Later, I watched Barry walk out of the yurt Reginald lay inside, letting the flap fall behind him, and face Yuda and Amos.

I was against the wall, pressing my body inside one of the large steel I beams that supported the underground structure, hiding, listening.

"He's recovering well enough for any man," Barry said, "but for a bariatric patient with his blood pressure, it's extraordinary."

I felt the metal handle of the steak knife in my back pocket.

"Of course he is," Amos said.

I'd begged him to drop Reginald off somewhere in the West, sometime in the 1800s, on a desolate stretch of desert, but he wouldn't listen.

"We'll let everyone else decide what to do with him," Amos said.

Barry cleared his throat and cast a suspicious glance at a passing builder bot pulling a load of sod and stone. "Is it true what they said, about *The Kind* coming sooner than before?"

Amos gave an almost imperceptible nod to Jeff, who was sitting on a stool outside the tent, guarding it.

Yuda and Amos walked toward the door I'd followed them to before. Echoes of blue light bloomed and died on the walls inside before they shut the door behind them. I walked over and pressed my ear to it. Muffled voices and the sounds of construction met my ear.

At the back of the yurt, I sank the knife into the canvas side and quietly opened a hole to squeeze through.

Inside, the darkness was complete, save a needle of light from the flap Jeff was guarding. Reginald breathed gently, the lump on the cot barely moving. I hefted the knife and stepped forward quickly, too quickly, as the needle of light turned into a dagger.

"Did you see it?"

I turned and tucked the knife behind me.

Jeff waited, arms crossed. "Did you see *The Kind*, before they were supposed to be there?"

"I did," I said.

"So it's true what everyone's saying. He's working for them." He waved his arm for someone to come forward into the yurt.

A lantern flared as a black man stuck his head inside. He was young, probably my age, dressed in a red visor and a tank top that flaunted his arms.

"She was going to kill him," Jeff said.

The man with the visor scratched his forehead and sighed. "He said he was going to rescue my mom."

Reginald's breathing changed, like a hiccup, and Jeff grabbed my arm and led me out of the yurt.

The man with the visor held up his lantern, waved it back and forth and whistled. The night came alive with the sounds of tents unzipping, of people stumbling out of their fabric. A few lanterns flashed to life, then more, until there were at least twenty, and all of them, the entire camp, walked toward the yurt.

"You were watching me," I said to Jeff.

"We were waiting. That's one thing we've learned," Jeff said. "We have time. No need to rush anything." Jeff motioned to Visor. "Deon, get them in a circle." He turned to me. "Morris is concussed." Morris hadn't been right since we got back. He'd pause in the middle of a sentence, staring at the wall, and kind of shake his head as he winced. "Everyone knows it," Jeff continued, "but no one really liked you. A lot of us worked for your father, indirectly."

My hand flew to my mouth. "You knew who I was?" It made sense, although I never wanted to believe it. My father was always tabloid fodder, and after a while it had just become a game, posting pictures of this car or that view or the private jet. We were *celebribrats* and needed to be thinner and prettier and richer than everyone, even movie stars.

"Everyone knew who you were. You were the elite." He took my hand, held it gently in both of his. "You want to change that perception? Do it now. This is your shot."

A half circle had formed around the yurt, and everyone was staring at Jeff and me, waiting. "I don't know any of them," I whispered.

"That should make it easier," Jeff said.

"But . . ." I stalled.

"I told everyone we could trust you, despite

everything," Jeff said.

"How do you know?"

"Because deep down you're just like the rest of us. You don't want to be here."

I reached behind my back and pushed the knife deeper into my back pocket. If I was just like the rest of them, then they all wanted Reginald dead.

The door swung open behind us, and Amos and Yuda came out. The sounds of construction, of builder bots, sirens, hammering and welding, fell to silence when the door closed.

"What is all this?" Yuda said.

"They've come for Reginald," Amos said, and he walked to the center of the crowd.

People whispered at first, then Deon stepped forward. "Is it true?"

"Is what true?" Amos said.

"Did he bring *The Kind* down on us sooner?" Jeff said, forcing Amos to turn around.

"It is true," Amos said.

The crowd broke into whispers.

"He's not like us," I said, stepping forward. "There's something wrong with Reginald. After he was shot, I saw something in him. Something . . . not human."

Charles stepped out of the crowd, the light of the lanterns flickering on his black skin. "Reginald is not a monster. I saw him when *The Kind* attacked. You all did. He saved all of you."

"Under somewhat dubious circumstances," Yuda said.

"Where'd he get the cane?" someone shouted, and almost at the same time, from another place in the crowd, "Why did *The Kind* listen to him? Why did they just stop attacking?"

"It was a gift. From *The Kind*," Charles said. "A peace offering."

"You mean it was a bribe," Yuda said.

Amos snapped, "Whose side are you on?"

"I've never trusted Reginald," Yuda said. "You know that."

"And why is that? Because he saved you? I've heard the story a hundred times, from each of you. How he charged in on the train and lanced one of *The Kind*, then stood up to them. And what did he shout? 'These people are mine,'" Amos growled. "You, all of you, owe your lives to him. He could have run—"

"What's he doing in the future?" Yuda said. "Or, maybe, someone should tell you what he did while he was in the service."

"We should discuss that in private," Amos said.

"He's evil," I said.

"No," Amos said, coming toward me quickly, "he's not evil. He's helping people. He's trying to avert catastrophes and pull strings and change the future. What he's doing, none of you have the heart to do."

"Heart?" Yuda said. "Is that what they called it when he tortured half the people of Tongsin? They called him the Asian butcher, Amos. Doesn't that bother you?"

Amos faltered, shakily scanning the ground. "Haven't you noticed how much he's aged? He's literally giving his life for you. For all of you. Taking all of your—"

"How do we know *what* he's doing in the future?" Yuda interrupted. "You've seen only what he wants you to see. And if it's Evelyn he's trying to woo back—"

"It's true." Reginald stood inside the doorway of the yurt, a figure sealed in shadow. He stepped forward, and the ghostly lantern light played on his skin, making him pale as a martyr. "I have been trying to woo Evelyn back," he said, his voice feeble. He stepped forward, the cane at his side, and it was the first time I believed that he actually needed it.

"What's inside you, Reginald?" I said.

His sharp eyes fixed on me. "Coal. Heaps and lumps of it and other black and evil stuff."

"Reginald, you need to be clear with us," Yuda said. "What are you doing in the future, and why are *The Kind* early?"

"*The Kind* are early because there was another scientist, another—Morris," Amos said, looking at me. "I will take care of it."

Yuda crossed his arms, looking at the wall, head shaking slightly. "Reginald, we all owe you a debt of gratitude, and your idea of advancing technology is a good one, but it's messy. We need to diversify our efforts. The first new train will be done tomorrow. After that, you can do whatever you like, but I'll be handling my end differently." He turned on his heel and walked toward the exit. Some of the crowd followed him, and some of them waited to see what would happen.

"There's another train?" someone said behind my shoulder.

It was Morris. I hugged him.

"Did I—did I hear that right? There's another train?"

"It's down there," I said, pointing to where Yuda and Amos had come from.

Morris didn't say anything, but from the way he scrunched up his face, I could tell he was thinking.

The crowd dispersed in a receding tide of whispers.

"What about what I saw?" I said. "What about what I saw?"

Visor said, "No one believes you," as he swept past.

I was dumbstruck.

"No one wants more blood," Morris said.

"But he's evil," I said.

Morris shrugged.

Beside the yurt, Reginald and Amos whispered, like they were arguing. "Why?" I kept hearing Amos say. Eventually, Reginald shook his head and went back inside the yurt, leaving Amos to turn away, angry.

"Let's go see the train," Morris said, and we started toward the door, going deeper into the earth.

Chapter 9

Yuda

I was born to a single mother in a small outlet town, what used to be a suburb of Boston that had grown up like a cancer. It had been designed by city planners to house the squalor away from the gentrified city in a way that looked more rarified and felt more expansive than it was. Tall, sixteen-story buildings with concrete balcony cubicles rose up, and each villa—why they called it that I'd never know—had a view of the colossal side of another building. Any one of them built by the sea would have fetched five thousand chips a month to lease, but sandwiched in the way they were made it nearly impossible to ignore the neighbors a mere thirty feet away—the size of the road that divided them. There were thirty-seven buildings in the outlet, and each day they would empty in a flood of people going into the city, sliding and bumping and jostling each other as they got on the subway, and at night they would return, filthy and stinking of whatever work they'd done.

One of my earliest memories was on the balcony of our sixteenth-floor efficiency playing with colorful magnet letters on a board. I looked up and saw the other building, where a man was standing on the outside of the guardrail, directly across from me. He was watching me, a curious, sickly half smile on his face.

I held up the board, on which I'd spelled my name: Y-U-D-A.

The man's smile intensified, and he held his hands up to amplify his words as he stepped off the ledge. "Study hard," he called. He seemed to float there a moment. The next he was on the ground, body contorted as if holding a strange robotic dance pose.

I didn't tell my mother I saw him. She was more agitated than usual when she got home. That night when we went out to market, I saw a picture of the man on the ledge, just his face taken from a driver's license, on a screen beside the checkout line.

"Building twelve," a big man with olive skin said to his wife, who held a baby. "Couldn't make his due, so he took a coward's leap."

The wife saw me looking and shushed her husband. "Can't you find something more cheery?" she asked the cashier bot.

The screen switched to a music station where a ballerina in tattered, neon clothes twisted her body.

I had only the vaguest concept of dues and cowards at that age. I somehow got it in my head that he'd jumped just for me, because he had to tell me something that was so important it was worth dying for.

I wasn't incredibly bright, but I worked hard, steadily maintaining a satisfactory rating at school, high enough so that when I graduated I was placed in a technical college and taught how to manipulate data mines, place sales e-mails, and evaluate traffic reports for recommending advertising currency to local businesses. I was a glorified secretary. Even as I concluded my studies, people in the largest data firms were being laid off in droves, displaced by the latest algorithms and bots that could work around the clock. I couldn't find work, because I'd been only satisfactory in my studies, even in college; I had to pay for my education with credit.

I tried working. I got a night job posting lewd subject matter to websites, trolling for *hazmats* who were addicted to online prostitution and might confuse a link deceptively selling a *holowhore* for the real thing. What I was doing was slightly illegal, the sites I interacted with definitely were, but there wasn't much else I could find for work.

I had a girlfriend. Her name was Mica, and she introduced me to a few people. Before long I was posting content to message boards all across the nylon road, smothering the fact that I was probably helping perpetuate the sex trade in Mica's breasts and her secondhand haze. She had a beautiful, supple body. She managed to maintain an appetite unlike most *hazmats*, and the only thing that marked her as one were the dark circles beneath her eyes and the occasional crusty chapped lips. Her hair was always a different color, always a fruit; brown and yellow like a pineapple, tangerine, deep purple, pink and honey like a plum. She spent a lot of money on herself besides the haze, and part of me wondered where she got it. Part of me didn't care. The sex was good enough, or the haze made me think it was good enough, that whatever worries I had I successfully snuffed out when she was around. There were other women, but none of them had her tits, and I doubted any of them could Kegel like she could, making it feel like she was pulling me deeper, forcing me to be larger, inside her.

Even the money I was making wasn't enough to offset the credit I'd accumulated, so Mica got me started processing counterfeit chips and fumigating for certain DJs that frequented the cities. They'd set up their impressive sound systems at these posh places in the city, usually some nightly rental that was quietly renowned for being airtight. I'd set up the foggers about the third song after the doors were locked and security was set up. The haze rolled in like pesticide. Everyone it touched started moving in slow motion, snapshot still in strobe lights. Each night it was the same thing; people got gassed, the initial hit knocked them into slow motion, then the second wave came on and it became an orgy.

The night I saw green-apple hair, polka-dotted with yellow, I took off my gas mask and walked into the haze with the crowd, because I had to see. The haze made me slow, and it felt like it took forever to cross the twenty feet that separated us. As I circled, Mica hung in the air, her back arched, her breasts high in the air, riding a man covered in tattoos like she was a trophy. Then she was bouncing, taking him inside her in a way I thought only I had known.

I took her by the hair, turned her eyes to me. She lashed out like a giant sucker, placing her lips on mine, one hand finding my cock through my pants, the other working the zipper. I hated that I stayed, hated that I didn't outlast the man beneath her legs when I took her from behind.

The next morning a man in a suit knocked on my door and presented me with a video clipping of a party. I watched, surprised as all hell at my bald head bobbing, face partially obscured by the gas mask as bodies danced and writhed around me. There was a moment when the music stopped. I heard a faint rush of wind. I'd been whistling inside the mask as I set up the foggers. They'd had a microphone pointed at me.

They took me to an offsite location, sat me down in a chair, and directed my attention to a camera in the corner, making sure to tell me that I wasn't arrested, so I didn't need a lawyer. We're just talking, they said.

They talked. I listened. I understood. Mica had been running the underground parties. That's where she got all the money from, all the connections. They laughed when

I said I didn't know. It was tough not to feel stupid.

All they wanted was my cooperation. They sympathized with my position, my credit, said they knew a way to make it all go away and would make it happen after I gave a signed affidavit and recorded my answers to the prosecutor's questions. I'd never have to see Mica again, they assured me.

They didn't ask if I wanted to or not.

A month later I was in basic training, sweating it out at Tullahoma, Tennessee, enlisted in the Air Force. They paid off my credit and taught me the finer things about the *aerial view*, as they described it. I was intelligence, monitoring citizens' activities for potential threats and, as an added bonus, entering their psych profiles and preferences into a paid subscription data-mine service used by the largest corporations to enhance advertising efficacy. It was hell. I'd traded one indentured servitude for another. It felt like I was one step, a few words, away from falling off the ledge as my neighbor had so long ago. I didn't even have that option.

One night I brought six beers back to my apartment off base. When I went to open my fifth, an alarm sounded, complete with flashing red lights. It stopped when I put the beer back. I experimented, holding an electrical cord too close to water, taking the razor out of my shaver and getting it closer to my wrist. All of it triggered the alarm. When I came home the next night, every dangerous thing had been cleaned out of my apartment. All part of the contract. They owned me. I couldn't destroy or pollute my body.

On some level, I welcomed the invasion of *The Kind*. It destroyed all of it, broke every strand of every web that had me trapped. Once Tullahoma was overrun, which didn't take long, I put as much distance as I could between that past and what lay ahead. My training, creating composite psychological profiles, proved useful when it became clear I needed to team up with people to survive. I knew how to choose the right ones, the strong ones, the ones who would never be shown advertisements for levity or grief counselors or self-help books. After a while, it didn't matter. *The Kind* weeded out the weak anyway.

If I'd been giving everyone the questionnaire, using the logarithm they'd trained me to use on everyone, no one ever would have scored as high as Reginald. I'd been telling people that I was special forces, that I was more than a numbers cruncher—I could be anyone I wanted in this new world—but Reginald was legit. Everyone knew who he was because of his father. He had a reputation; the kind of hushed conversation that was meant to be mocking came off more reverential than anything. They said he was fighting the war by himself, and "Should I get Reggie?" was slang for *Tell me the truth or I'll kill you.*

I hated him the moment I saw him. Not because of who he was or his crook father but because it was only a matter of time before he knew exactly what I was, before he took over. I never expected it to take only a few hours.

When he came back on the train and stood up to *The Kind*, killing some even, I didn't have any choice but to go along. It felt just like being in that sham they called the Air Force, taking orders, waiting to see what would happen, hoping the alarm wouldn't go off when I reached into the fridge or picked my nose.

It was my idea to build another train. Reginald wasn't at all for it. He said there were too many threads, too many strands to keep track of as it was.

Maybe that's because he was trying to change everything, to rescue the world from itself as much as save it from *The Kind*.

Reginald was obsessed with the past, building this place, working out some kind of deal with Amos, who was supposedly at the heart of it all, creating rules for himself. He didn't think anyone knew, but we pieced it together. After every trip, he met himself again, sharing notes with the version yet to do what he'd already done. He had a system. It was brilliant—and self-indulgent. He'd obviously gotten used to taking the long way to the truth in his torture room.

When I first told him the plan to destroy *The Kind*, he didn't blink, just placed the staff on the table between us and twirled it by the ends, like he was rolling a cigarette. We were in his diner. I was watching him get fat. I supposed it was better than drink or haze because it didn't dull his intellect, but it did make him more disgusting to look at, the way he shoveled in burgers and ice cream.

"But it's already been done," he said calmly.

I leaned forward. "And who do you think does it?" I said. I sawed a tomato in half and popped it in my mouth. No one knew how to make a salad in the fifties. Damn if vegetables didn't taste good though, even without decent dressing.

The comprehension dawned like morning. "It's you," he gasped. "Don't say anything. Take this." He passed me the staff.

I eyed it.

He forced it into my hand. "Be quick about it." He stood to leave.

I stopped him with the tip of his staff against his fat stomach, barring his passage. "You're supposed to help me." Like it or not, I needed him. He was the only one who had ever killed one of *The Kind*.

"I can't," Reginald said through clenched teeth, his face turning red. "Don't you understand that?"

"No, I don't understand. This plan doesn't work without you."

"I can't know anything about your plan!" He shoved the staff out of his way. It clinked against the back of the booth with an iron thud, and I was momentarily distracted by how light it was. Gold or brass—or whatever it was—was supposed to be heavy.

Reginald exhaled heavily, then sat back down. "They were. They . . ." His jaw clenched. I guess he was having trouble saying the truth. Probably because he wasn't used to telling it.

My hand was on my pistol. I didn't remember moving it. "Reginald, you need to be very clear right now." I was thinking about Angela, about all the people who were gathered around, waiting to see what would happen to him, what would happen to our little group, the time refugees.

Reginald shook his head as though something escaped him.

"Are you working for them?"

"No. No, of course not. I'd saw my own head off if there were a single reason to think that my actions would endanger anyone."

I squinted.

"That may be hyperbole." He took a bite of the burger on his plate. "I assure you," he said through a full mouth, "my actions are my own. But I can't help feeling like I'm being . . . surveilled. Take this," he said, forcing my hand onto the staff where I'd left it on the table and closing my fingers around it.

"Why do I need your stool?" I said.

He cocked his head, staring at me like a bird of prey. "I can't speak to you anymore." He stood quickly.

"Reginald," I called as he pushed the door open. The bells jingled over it, and he swayed as he looked back at me.

"Tell me why I shouldn't shoot you," I said.

"You wouldn't be any better off without me." He left.

To me, the White Mountains had always had a mysterious quality to them. My grandfather lived in Berlin, and I went to see him once when my mother was away. By away, I mean she was serving thirty days for a minor felony of some kind on a plea deal. My grandfather was crotchety at times, ignoring my suggestions to cook anything other than what he intended to eat, which was usually some sort of Crock-Pot stew, bologna sandwiches during the day. He had no problem taking me out into the woods to blow off steam. He taught me how to fish against the backdrop of smoky peaks, how to read the moss on the sides of the trees as a compass, and how to start a campfire. There were still bears in the forest, he told me one night while we camped in the state park. Not many, but it only takes one. Apparently, skunks don't like it when you whistle, and chipmunks could carry rabies, as could bats. Timber rattlers were most likely under every rock. The fish—several brook trout the size of fish sticks and a rainbow that had to be a foot long—tasted great. He claimed they were stocked. Stuffed full of chemicals. GMOs. He knew the difference.

It was the best part of my childhood, sitting there, listening to him complain how everything had changed. I wasn't surprised to find myself, for whatever reason, heading north after the collapse, as everything was falling down around me, on a sort of subliminal track toward the White Mountains. There were cracks there, crevices that weren't man-made, places to hide that wouldn't show up from a satellite because they were buried in pine forest.

During the day, it wasn't smart to move if The Wedge was overhead. I did it once, walking along a road mostly covered by thick oak and maple branches, wishing I didn't know better than to fire my rifle at The Wedge. I stopped before nightfall and spent the next twenty minutes inside a culvert running under the road. My feet were soaked, and spiderwebs were everywhere, sticking in my hair, itching the backs of my hands. I went all the way through and made a beeline for a small house, a shack really, that had been on the opposite side of the road.

The interior was dusty and had been nothing more than a three-season camp. Skull-mounted antlers hung on the wall. Gas lamps, with filaments like the lanterns my grandfather had used when we were camping, hung from the ceiling.

I heard them before I saw them, the heavy, breathless exhale of their ships' propulsion followed by bending branches set upon by invisible wind. They hovered over the far side of the road where I'd entered the culvert and hid for a long time.

That's when I knew they'd been watching me. That they were hunting me, not just in the way a man would sit in a tree stand and wait for a deer to pass by but as bloodhounds stalk a raccoon and force them into a tree. I slunk below the edge of the window frame and felt something skitter over my foot—a rat, a mouse, something that decided my pant leg would be a good place to hide. I staggered back, grabbed at my knee to keep its sharp claws from digging any further up my leg, and kicked. It more fell out than anything, and without thinking I stomped and then stomped again in anger.

Sparks flew from the small body. The stain on the floor was of smashed circuits, not blood. I touched the small camera eyes, wondered at the hypodermic teeth, scanned the walls in wonder at who would wish to protect such a shack, and decided to be wary of booby traps.

When I remembered myself, my heart stalled. I couldn't hear the spaceship over my breathing; that didn't mean it wasn't there.

I got to my feet and peered out the window. Pitch darkness had taken over. The moon had yet to pierce cloud cover, and the thick trees of the New Hampshire wilderness shielded all starlight. I looked around, suddenly feeling constrained, as though I was being watched. I bolted through the door and around the back into the woods. I went fifty, maybe a hundred paces before falling to the ground in a pile of leaves, covering my head with my arms. The spaceship was there, floating over the road in front of the camp I'd been in, in a position that probably would have been just out of sight from inside. I noticed a giant white hole had materialized in its side, and panic set in. *The Kind* were on the ground.

As the first reports of the invasion came in, before the television signals and electricity were lost, reporters were always at a loss for words. Some kind of aliens, some kind of animal from another planet. Some kind of species, some kind of living, black ball-like creatures with some kind of tentacles. As the reports got worse and worse, capital city after capital city falling to ruin, they became known simply as *The Kind*. Maybe the misnomer was a joke produced by some intern sweating it out in a basement, a teleprompter miscue for talent that couldn't think, only read cue cards, or maybe everyone had only that one channel at that point—most people clung to TV like someone with emphysema to oxygen—but it stuck and it was easier to say than *the aliens* or *extraterrestrials* and didn't conjure the image of a big-headed teddy bear the way *E.T.* did.

One thing was certain: *The Kind* hunted.

I rose from the leaves, darted through heavy woods, bounding over stones as small branches slashed my face and hands. The moon broke through the cloud cover, and as I looked up to mouth a thank-you, the ground fell away from my steps. I tumbled forward and fell forever, the sky becoming a hole in a black sky farther and farther away with each revolution.

Cool water took my breath, so cold that I had to open my eyes, follow the silver bubbles to the surface. As I kicked frantically, unsure of how deep I'd gone, I saw the red eyes of *The Kind's* ship appear on the surface of the water, mere feet away, dimpled.

I waited, hands pushing water upward to stay submerged, until my lungs burned, until stars dancing at the corners of my vision were replaced with creeping darkness, until I felt certain the horrors above could be no more fatal than staying under a moment longer. I kicked and burst through the surface, coughing and hacking, to the sound of roaring water tumbling off to my left. The cavern behind me was huge, expansive, and quiet. The ship had gone.

As I explored the cavern, I began to realize what I'd stumbled onto. The guard post disguised as a camp with the mechanical rat still patrolling, the underground rail, the command center. The fact that *The Kind* had waited only seconds before leaving, deciding that, perhaps, a human couldn't live in such a place, meant it was perfect. I felt tiny inside the expanse, sitting beside the water. Even in the moonlight, I could see the fish below the surface. I knew I could survive down there, alone, like a Gollum, or I could do something better. I could tell people about it.

The cool underground river and the steel-edged darkness forged a new narrative. I wasn't a numbers cruncher, a government-owned corporate tool.

I'd fallen into darkness and emerged a different man.

The first man I tried to help was Jeff. I stumbled upon an A-frame chalet rising up in the middle of the forest with a huge window on the front climbing to the top of the dormer. I thought if anyone was smart, they'd choose this place because it had perfect views of the sky. You wouldn't have to stick your head up to see if The Wedge was there, waiting.

I pushed open the door and looked over the interior. There was a loft and what I guessed was a bathroom or utility room off the kitchen. Other than that, it was wide open. I smelled food. Bacon, maybe. I swept the house. Clean dishes in the strainer. Brown hair in the tub drain. The bed in the loft was made, covered in six or eight layers of thick blankets. I lowered my rifle. He stood in the kitchen as I came down the stairs, statue still, shotgun aimed at my chest. He had a thick, wiry beard with traces of gray mixed into it. Stockinged feet. Thick work boots sat unlaced by the door.

"You're quiet," I said.

"Are you trouble?" he said, his voice gravelly. His jaw slid back and forth. Something of the motion reminded me of a cat's tail as it played with its food, pondering the kill.

I shook my head. "I'm looking for survivors."

"And by that you mean you're after my supplies."

I set my rifle down against the couch. It was a worthless gesture because I'm sure he assumed I had a smaller weapon on me, which I did.

Jeff looked at a pink watch on his wrist. "Step this way."

"Why?"

He pointed at the tall windows behind me, where the shadow of The Wedge crossed over.

I followed his command, for the first time thinking that he might not need saving.

"Two and six. They change it every third day twice, then once every two days, down to once a day for three days, then start over."

I instinctively peered up at it, and Jeff pulled me back by my collar.

"Looks just the same as the last time you saw it. Die at your own place, not mine."

He pulled the Smith & Wesson out from where it was hidden in the small of my back, and I whirled on him. He held it out to the side, barrel pointed at the ceiling, and slowly lowered it to the kitchen table.

"Step closer," he said, motioning to my feet. The sun slipped from behind a cloud and a square of sunlight formed behind me, my heels perilously close to it.

I stepped forward quickly and grabbed the gun. I tucked it back into my pants. "Don't ever touch that again."

"Just thought you might want to have a civilized conversation."

"There's no such thing." I turned to grab my rifle. It was in the sunlight against the couch.

"You can leave it," Jeff said. "Or maybe you won't be going anywhere for a while anyway, so we might as well try to at least play nice." He set his rifle on the table. "You can keep that. It's fair. I have one, too." He pulled out a wooden chair.

He sat down easily and pulled a silver cylinder out of his fleece that might have been a flashlight. He unscrewed the top and pulled out two sticks of jerky. He offered one to me.

It was plain and tough to chew, but I was hungry.

"Deer. There's not a lot of time to hunt," Jeff said.

I looked back at the window. "We're not the only one's hunting, either."

"That's true. I don't like being lower on the food chain."

I took another bite and shook my head. It seemed only logical that, eventually, we would be. We never walked with dinosaurs, because we got lucky.

"You're a bit of a loner," I said.

"Got no one needs to borrow me."

"How'd you figure out their schedule?" I said. Most people's phones had died a long time ago and few people wore watches.

"How do you think?"

"Seen anyone else around here?" I said. "People that maybe aren't as well prepared as you, that may need a hand?"

He squinted at me, jaw working on the jerky. I wondered if he'd been chewing when he walked in; then I realized how closely he'd timed his return to the arrival of The Wedge. Despite his Northern accent, he wasn't stupid by any means.

"I found a cave just south of here," I said. "It used to be a secret government installation of some kind. There's still power and surveillance equipment that could give everyone warning. It's a safe place."

"And you need people to fill it."

"I need to do something." I pointed at the window. "That thing can't win."

He nodded slowly, pointed at a cupboard. "There's a bottle and some glasses in there. Pack of cards and a cribbage board, too."

The bottle was Blue vodka, apple pie flavored, sweet enough to attract hummingbirds. "This matches your watch," I said through the burn.

He smiled, showing surprisingly white teeth. "There's a family up the river a bit. I've checked in on them a few times. They could use a better place." He poured another shot for each of us. "To starting over."

Glasses clinked.

With his schedule, it was easier to travel.

A few weeks later we were in an abandoned showroom, the smell of salvaged White Owls filling in for the exhaust of lawn mowers that never ran, their shiny skin dulled by a patina of dust.

"I used to like riding these things. And snowmobiles," Jeff said, running his hand along the fender of a riding mower, wiping off streaks of dust. He threw a leg over, pretended to giddyup. Dust swirled around him, making everything seem slow.

I stood at the window, staring out at an approaching sheet of rain. The Wedge was blocking a light storm. The water pooled on its surface, creating a waterfall all around it. The sound, the droning of it, made my heart beat faster. It sounded like the air was being vacuumed out of the world.

"I used to need a beer for anything bigger than half an acre," Jeff was saying, his voice seeming to get quieter as the rain got louder. "Now I'd just be happy . . ."

The rain washed across the parking lot, rivers forming at the edges of the concrete as it swept toward us. The top of a convertible caved in and was filled instantly.

Jeff appeared beside me. "Here we go."

As it got closer, I saw chunks of pavement being blasted out of the parking lot.

"We should stand in a doorway," I said, tugging him away.

"Yeah," he said.

I looked back as the water hit the overhang. Two-by-fours and black shingles tore free.

It was like a giant pressure washer. A sandblaster.

The showroom windows shattered. Walking mowers twisted, driven by phantom eddies. We huddled in a doorway. A golden sign on the door said Management, and mold sprouted from a doughnut on a desk. The ceiling began to darken in spots like condensation. My toes were suddenly cold. An inch of water was on the floor. I thought about all the people who were huddled in basements with no power for sump pumps and realized there were so many ways to die. A piece of Sheetrock gave way from the ceiling, and a flood of water rushed toward us. I stepped into the office and hauled myself up on a file cabinet as the water roared past. Jeff lost his feet and was swept into the desk; then the water was swirling inside, filling the office. The file cabinet toppled. I fell. Something sharp poked my side, and I swear I could feel the hot blood pouring out of me as I floated toward the shattered front windows. I felt like I was being dragged out to sea in a riptide, and once I was out there *The Kind* would have me, would take me up to their ship and do whatever with me.

Maybe that was better. Maybe that was better than starving or worrying constantly. My foot caught in the spokes of a steering wheel, and I twisted to one side, grabbed the front bumper, held my breath as the water roared over me.

I woke up coughing, strung up by my foot like a cowboy that's fallen off. I unfolded and tried standing on my ankle. It wasn't broken but I wouldn't be running very far on it. I lifted my shirt, wiggled my finger through a hole over my ribs. A slim ribbon of blood flowed down my side from a hole that looked like someone had torn off a large freckle. Maybe it was a pen, I thought. I'd heard stories of straw being driven into telephone poles during tornadoes.

Jeff was on his stomach outside, lying in a slowly flowing mud puddle, chunks of asphalt pushing up beneath the surface. His hands sank up to the wrists as he pushed himself to his knees. The sun was shining through the clouds. Water drops falling off his clothes were celestite blue and shimmering. The sun split the clouds, and the arch of a rainbow appeared behind him, as if the heavens were cradling him.

"You all right?" he said.

I nodded.

His eyes grew wide, and I thought I must look worse than I felt, until I noticed the surface of the water around his ankles go gunmetal gray, dimpling.

"Yuda. Run," he said and was lifted off his feet, a splash of water following him into the air as he left the earth.

My first step sent me sprawling to the ground. Warm air rushed from the craft above, threading its way through the open, skeletal steel ribs of the building. I began to slide myself toward the back. My knee scraped on the concrete and the warm air grew heavy as water began to steam, curling in the corners of the ceilings in swirling downdrafts.

A tentacle wrapped around the wheel of a riding mower and tossed it aside.

I crawled faster and crashed through a door into the service bay, where crates of mowers were stacked in the far corner. The roof had held; the only evidence of the earth's recent baptismal scourge was a lumpy crescent-shaped pool of standing water that had leaked in under the rolling garage doors. A white pickup sat in front of the door. I got to my feet and hobbled toward the truck, pulled open the door, and was pleased to see the dome light come to life. A key fell from the visor. I stuck it in the ignition.

"Don't do that," someone called.

I turned, saw mowers in cardboard crates, a workbench covered in tools, the coil of an air wrench, and in the corner, a man with a white beard wearing a cap with an American flag stitched to the bill held a metal plate up with one hand, and waved me toward him.

The truck chimed its warning—the key still in the

ignition—as I hobbled.

I fell into the hole, missing the first rung of the ladder he was standing on and falling for what felt like an eternity. He was on top of me before I knew it, hand covering my mouth. My mind populated the darkness with the still image of the old man, a finger to his lips. I tapped the back of his hand lightly, and he removed it. He took my hand, pulled me to my feet. We listened.

The darkness was complete and smelled like gas and oil. I began to count my breaths to keep time, remembering back to some anti-interrogation techniques the Air Force had taught me, and got to eleven before the faint white outline of the steel plate covering the hole appeared above me.

He was lucky the ceiling held. He would have drowned down here, and no one would have known he was locked in an aquatic tomb. I felt the ladder, pulled myself up a rung, froze as the sudden crying baby sound of metal being twisted like Play-Doh echoed in the space above.

I heard the unmistakable click of a round being chambered, the frantic beeping of the key alarm of the truck, and waited.

More sounds of destruction came six breaths later, silencing the truck. I felt a hand on my shoulder, forcing me off the ladder. I sat down on the floor, waiting like a fool for death to come.

"This way," the old man said.

I followed by feeling my way through the darkness,

scurrying over steel barriers that rose a foot off the floor, carefully moving my weight over wiry obstacles.

Light bloomed behind us, followed by the sound of a giant tin can rattling as the metal plank covering the opening went flying. With the light, I could see the underbelly of the automotive service bay, each workstation separated by steel support beams, which I'd been crawling over. Old oil drums, red metal tool racks, air wrenches, and compressors crowded every corner.

Something warm slithered past my face. An air wrench flew off the shelf and smashed against the support column as it disappeared back the way we'd come. I jumped forward and scrambled toward the old man, who stood next to a ladder.

"Wait," the old man said as I placed a hand on the rung.

I screamed, "Wait? Are you fucking kidding me?"

He slapped me across the face. When I turned back, the lights were dimming as one of *The Kind* attempted to squeeze itself through the hole we'd come down. My ears popped as the pressure increased.

"Now," he said. "Climb."

I climbed with three limbs and was pleased to find the exit hatch had a working hydraulic assist.

The old man flicked a lighter and mumbled something as the first tentacles of *The Kind* reached him. He looked up at me, face creased deep with age and stained orange from the flame, and smiled.

I made it to the garage doors before the explosion. It

threw me into the soft, pliable metal. I woke long after the dust had settled, lying on a crack in the concrete floor an inch wide that ran back toward a crater where the service bay had been. I hobbled to its edge. There was nothing to see in its depths. No old man, no *Kind*, just dust and twisted metal.

I disengaged the chain garage door opener and pushed it open. My curved, insectile reflection was frozen in the red eyes of a spaceship. I was too terrified to move. The eyes, the red twin windshields with their swept-back, almond shape, reminded me of the gas mask I used to wear when pumping haze into the parties. I wondered if that's how they saw us, as though we were crazed on drugs, or if they were. I closed my eyes and prayed, expecting a steel-articulated tentacle to snatch me up like Achilles by my ankle. I waited.

Nothing happened. The cold, infrared eyes didn't blink, and the ship just hovered there a foot off the ground.

I circled slowly. A long, thin line made the ship look like the helmet of some sort of steel robot, except it wasn't steel. The sides were mirror smooth where heat hadn't seared it black like the surface of a grill. I wondered how far they'd traveled, how close they'd come to other planets, other suns.

A panel slid open on the ship. An array of glowing green electronics was visible within. I stopped, feeling as though I were standing in the shadow of something much larger than I and slapped at an insect on my neck.

A horsefly fell at my feet, twitching on an upturned slab of blacktop until it rolled and fell into the cracks and disappeared. The Wedge was hovering over the mountains in the distance, slowly pulling away.

Something snapped behind me. Startled like a deer, I was off, running toward the woods. I thought later that I flinched, fled, and failed.

I had training in electronics. There were moments when I was positively brilliant, when it felt like the haze was long gone and all the traces of its effects had left me. I didn't trust myself to climb aboard and stare at those foreign electronics.

I should have.

I came back later, my arms scratched white in places from snagging branches as I ran toward nothing until my hands shook and my lungs heaved for breath. I was a coward. The craft was gone. I should have gone on board; in that thought came strength.

Chapter 10

Amos

"You look like the devil had his way with you last night," Rosaline said.

I sat at the table, attempting to rub the sleep out of my eyes.

Behind Rosaline, evening light fell on the fields. I knew just over the rise Reginald and Yuda and everyone else were sleeping.

Rosaline didn't know anything about it. Every time I tried to tell her, she refused to talk about Reginald.

"Are we broke?"

I laughed. We weren't even close to broke.

"Then why the long face?"

"I was thinking about Reginald," I said.

She touched my hand. "He's gone. You know he's gone. We don't have to worry."

I'd been stopping by churches lately, the big, Catholic ones. I lit candles, sat in pews. Prayed. When I looked up and saw Him nailed to the cross, it hit me: Rosaline and I were still on that first train with Reginald. If I wanted to, I could go back and stop my involvement from the very beginning, but the train tracks didn't go back far enough, long enough, to see if Jesus was still hanging on that cross like he was in every single Catholic church, the same way everyone in the future was still being slaughtered by *The Kind*, in a sort of eternal suffering.

Rosaline brought the back of my hand to her lips and kissed it, held it against her face. "You need to let go. You can't change it. He's not coming back."

Maybe this was the moment I told her the truth. Maybe if I told her now, even if it didn't work out, I could go back and change it.

"You know how he traveled through time, right? We agree on that," I said.

Her posture became rigid as she looked at the stairs. Walter was still asleep.

"Then the future, that's happening now. And so is the past because, in a way, we're still kids on that train, at least to Reginald."

"You know I don't like to talk about this, Amos."

"My point is, if those things are true, and I can't explain it but I think they are, then isn't Jesus, in some way, still nailed to the cross? Like, now?"

The corners of her mouth fell to a frown. "You poor thing," she said, hugging me like a child. "I wish you'd had different parents."

I pushed her away, held her at arm's length. "If it

weren't for my parents, I never would have left. I never would have met you."

She hugged me. I thought of that little statuette nailed to the wall, the curvature of his wooden skin seeming to quiver in the flickering firelight. Maybe he was still turning to ash in my parents' stove. That made it an even bigger sacrifice. When I set Him, when I set God in that stove, that was the first time I wasn't afraid of the future.

Maybe it was a test, waiting for one person with the key to time travel to come back and take a claw hammer to those nails and pry him off the cross.

I had to talk to Reginald, to Yuda, and all of the people out there under the sod doing their best to move society into the future at a faster pace so when *The Kind* came, they'd be ready.

The acetylene torch cast sparks and shadows high on the walls of the underground. It reminded me of being on the train when the electric lace crisscrossed the windshield.

"Where's Reginald?" I called to the men and women working on number three. Four and five were behind them, or at least their chassis were. They were longer, lower than the others. I wondered why Morris would make changes to the design. I shuddered as I thought about them being turned into weapons.

A man flipped his welding mask up. He was a big man with a narrow face and a small patch of beard underneath his bottom lip he called a soul patch.

"What about Yuda?" I said.

"Haven't seen them."

"That's strange," I said. They were supposed to come back at the same time they left, thereby avoiding missing any moments in the past. That's why there were protocols.

I sighed and stared at the builder bots. There were three of them now. One had a small welder and a rivet gun for arms and was circling some kind of metal structure. I thought of the posters of Rosie and laughed a little. In the future, Rosie was a machine. Or maybe she was a he.

The cabin lights in number three flickered to life, and people cheered. Thomas picked up a woman and spun her around before they kissed.

Morris appeared at my side. "Number three," he said.

I smiled, unsure of how to fulfill my great-great-great-grandfatherly role.

"Number two took too long. Four and five shouldn't take any longer despite the modifications."

"What changes have you made?" I said.

Morris's smile broadened. "They'll travel farther, faster. What brings you to the pit?"

"I need to talk to Reginald."

Morris's smile turned into a scowl.

"Well, where is he?" I said.

"Don't know," Morris said, walking toward numbers four and five. "But Thomas just took him on number one a while ago."

"How long do you need?" Thomas said. In the future, he was some kind of a writer. Today, he was my conductor.

"Probably three hours," I said, taking in the needle-like points of the New York skyline rising beyond the abandoned warehouses, disappearing into the low clouds. "Are you sure you dropped him off here?"

Thomas nodded. "We'll make it four. Always better to take more time than you need. Last thing I want to do is go looking for ya in that city. I hate that city."

I jumped off the train. Gravel crunched beneath my feet. It always felt the same, jumping off a train, no matter how old I got.

"When did he say to pick him up?" I said.

"He didn't," Thomas said, hanging his head out the door of number one. "I've been checking back every day for two weeks. I'll see you in a minute."

To Thomas, it was entirely accurate; he'd punch the time into the machine and it would take him there.

The dust-coated gravel gnawed at my feet with every step as I walked away from the tracks. Lightning spiked a dull gray sky as the train roared to speed. There was no leaving a train behind while you went exploring, like Reginald used to do. It was too dangerous. Better to have an extraction planned. It was Yuda's idea. And now we'd lost Reginald. I was the only one willing to search for him.

A kicked stone skittered out in front of me and

I stopped, the endless windows like blocks of empty eyes staring out at the world. Rain fell on my face. I approached a large steel door. A broken lock lay on the ground in front of it, the rusty loop sheared silver. I bent and picked it up, ran my hand over the sharp edge formed by the bolt cutters.

The door groaned as I slid it open. Flakes of rusted metal fell from the frame as it shrieked. Birds darted into the rafters and through a large opening where the wall had rusted open. Water dripped within the shadows. Feathers and bird shit lined the walls below each window.

I stepped inside. Something gripped the back of my shirt and swung me around. I crashed into the wall. A cold blade pressed against my throat. I thought it was his staff. I would have been relieved if it were, but his elbow was pressed against my chin, in a way that reminded me of my training before the war. No one was supposed to escape from this hold alive.

"What are you doing here?" Reginald said.

"I'm looking for you," I said.

He pushed his elbow into the back of my neck. The blade of the knife sank deeper, causing me to gag. If he pulled the blade free, my life would go with it in a spray of blood.

Reginald began to shout, a furious roar like he was staring down a locomotive in a tunnel, before pushing me hard into the wall and letting the knife fall away.

He was already receding into the darkness, boots

wrapped in rags, when I got my breath under control, stomping through a puddle as a jagged triangle of light pierced his back.

My voice echoed back cold when I hollered after him. The click of my shoes on the concrete sounded more like a nuisance than a concerned friend.

I followed him up metal stairs that ascended beside a large silo. He stopped at a railing three stories high, overlooking the warehouse. I stood some distance away from him, oddly uneasy that he didn't have his cane.

"What do you want?" he said.

The lines in his face were etched deeper than usual. He'd lost weight. He'd been out of the diner—out of time, in a way—for two weeks. I cast about looking for signs of inhabitance and saw a few white buckets in a far corner next to a mattress.

From his perch he could view the front door—through which I'd come—and the vast expanse of the parking lot and the train tracks. He'd seen us coming.

"Why this place?" I said.

He glanced at me without moving his head. "So you're not just a dumb farm boy after all."

"Hard to stay one."

One side of his mouth perked up in a smile.

A vehicle, something sleek with a tall black windshield, pulled into the parking lot.

Reginald held a finger to his lips. "Not a word," he said, pulling me into the darkness.

We crouched beside the old silo as the metal doors screeched open. The vehicle drove in. Car doors slammed. Footsteps echoed, seeming to fall from the steel rafters. The rear hatch lifted. Reginald took my wrist and shook his head in warning; his dark brown irises gave way to a halo of gold surrounding black pupils.

I peeked over the railing and saw someone pushing a gurney away from us, a dark cloth bag occupying the bed. Whistling. The beard, the muscular body, it was all familiar.

I knew what was happening as soon as I heard the muffled screams and saw the body bag twitch, the feet pumping and head shaking as they disappeared into another chamber.

"You shouldn't be here," Reginald said.

Metal shrieked; the sound of another slamming door reverberated.

"What is that?" I said.

Reginald didn't say anything. His fingers were twitching on his thigh.

"Give me the knife," I said.

"Where would you like it?"

I took a moment to remind myself that he wasn't my friend, that I actually hated him. That he'd manipulated me since I was a child and nearly ruined my life before it ever began.

He sighed and leaned his forehead against the metal rail, stood, and walked down the gangway toward an opening in the far wall, overlooking where the man with the gurney had gone.

He turned after a few soft steps and whispered, "Are you coming?"

I stood. He pointed at my shoes and then held his fingers to his lips. I took off my shoes. As usual, he'd planned it. The rags affixed over his boots, he knew he was going to have to sneak.

The metal grating felt cold and awkward to walk on.

Reginald stopped at the wall and looked down.

I peeked around him. A spotlight hanging from a pole created an oblong circle of light on the floor. A naked man was tied to a chair in its center, a white gag in his mouth.

The man approached him holding a small knife or a scalpel. I knew it was Reginald.

"What are you doing to that man?" I said, my voice barely a whisper.

Reginald didn't explain. The man with the knife reached between his captive's legs, made a quick movement, and the man screamed. He reached in again, then stood back as a pool of blood formed between the man's legs, and walked away. The door slid open. The man drove away, the whine of the engine little more than a buzz.

The screams of the man in the chair got quieter, until his head lolled forward.

Reginald looked at him, almost sadly, and didn't move as I backed away. I ran down the steps and approached the man in the chair, ignoring the glass that cut my feet.

A dark red hole had replaced the captive's manhood. A long cut had been made on his abdomen where bits of intestine hung free. With each shudder of his breath, they slid out a little further. I moved in quickly, my training as a soldier taking over, applying pressure to the wound. Warm, sticky blood coated my hands, and he screamed as I pushed to staunch the bleeding.

His wide eyes found mine.

"It'll be okay," I said, even though I knew it wouldn't be.

I removed my hands, saw the tip of his manhood protruding from the wound in his stomach, and stepped back.

"You can't help him," Reginald said. With shoes wrapped in rags, he stood at the edge of the cone of light. "What I've done to him he'll never live with. Isn't that right, Marcel?"

Marcel was covered in sweat and had long, greasy hair and stubble. He shook his head slowly as Reginald approached, walked behind him, leaned over, and whispered, "I think I'd continue torturing you if he wasn't here." He gripped the tip of Marcel's chin and the back of his head. With one twist it was over.

"Last time I left him for dead. This is an improvement."

I didn't feel my feet move as I backed away.

"They find him, you know. He convalesces for a while in hospital, then takes a flying leap. Six stories."

I ran outside, all the way back to the train tracks, and fell to my knees. I leaned my head back, prayed to God for someone to take Reginald from my life, to kill him, to remove the evil from the world.

His boots crunched gravel behind me. I wondered if it was a test, if killing him was something I had to do. Or maybe the test was to love him, to be the only one who could put up with him for long enough to see through that mess of scar tissue to a soul that was hurting.

"I know it's hard for you to comprehend, but that outcome was an improvement."

Gravel crunched as he sat. Rain slowly washed Marcel's blood from my hands.

"I came here, festering with anger, unsure if I was going to do battle with myself or . . . continue what I'd started."

"Why'd you kill him?"

"Why do you think?"

"He had your Evelyn," I said.

"Yes. He had my Evelyn."

I faced him, watching as the rain made rivers and streams out of his hair, plastering strands to his forehead. He gave me a wan smile.

"You can't get her back."

He nodded slowly. "That may be."

The blood was almost washed away by the time Thomas showed up. He did his best to hide a scowl when he saw Reginald. I thought, if he were white, his face would have flushed with embarrassment.

We climbed aboard and Reginald looked down at his pocket watch, a gold thing I'd seen before. "Wait a few minutes," Reginald said.

It was almost four in the afternoon.

"Why?" I said.

"You'll see."

Thomas huffed. "This is ridiculous."

"We have an easier time making up five minutes than hiding scowls," Reginald said.

Thomas's lips bunched, and he turned away quickly.

The lightning grew more intense, bolts snapping overhead, the thunder so loud nearly every rivet of the train rattled. Darkness settled.

Thomas peered up at the sky through the windshield. "What the hell?"

The big ship, the one they called The Wedge, had appeared in the sky, blocking the clouds and rain, so low I could see the grid-like metal veins on its surface.

Thomas got the train moving, mumbling something to himself about five minutes.

As the rainbow masses of lights swirled across the windscreen, Reginald leaned over to me and shouted, "If I'd stayed five more minutes, I'd have been dead. I figured if I kept torturing him, I deserved to die. I wasn't sure what I was going to do."

The train slowed down as I realized it had been a test, set by him.

In a dark way, he'd passed.

Thomas turned in his seat and faced Reginald. "Where the hell did The Wedge come from?"

"They traveled light-years to reach us," Reginald said. "You didn't think they could travel back in time?"

Thomas's jaw opened, snapped closed, opened again. "How—?"

"Were you really dumb enough to think they wouldn't exploit the resources of this earth over and over again, working backward one year, one day at a time?" Reginald said, and let himself off the train.

Chapter 11

Angela

I wanted adventures. I wanted to stir more than a cappuccino in a mug. I wanted to take what was left of me and do something extraordinary; to that end, I was a success. No one had seen this sky. No one had looked upon the purple and red suns as more than a dot on a crowded telescope.

I didn't want to wait around for a broken bot to determine what was safe to eat out of an orange jungle. The leaves of every tree were thick like the skin of a pumpkin, coated with heavy, fibrous hairs, their smell foul, a mix of ammonia and compost. Insects the size of Coke cans crawled up gnarly trunks of canopy trees, their segmented bodies covered in long antennae, and attacked the builder bots that were attempting to cut down trees to build a shelter, gnawing through their wires and circuit boards.

We were still sleeping on the train, what was left of number four. Number five arrived but the math was off by a fraction of a decimal, or the new earth had been traveling several feet faster per second than originally thought. The wheels and the bottom of the cabin arrived in a blazing fireball that landed below the surface of the new earth. The wheels are sunken and misshapen beneath a curved pool of glass.

Morris told me not to look, told me not to go in. After a while I couldn't help myself. I needed to see what everyone else had turned away from.

They had already begun to smell. It was like that restaurant, the steak house, I'd walked past in Florida on a hot day. They'd just emptied the Dumpster and the smell of rotten food was thick enough to make me lose my appetite. My father complained to the manager—it was his restaurant—and they moved the Dumpsters far away from the parking lot. It didn't matter, because there was no getting rid of the odor inside. The sand melted when they landed and swirled inside the car like magma. Their feet were frozen beneath the surface, clothes and shoes perfectly preserved, melted skin puddled above. The inside of the car was a blackened oven filled with an image grisly enough to surpass the moral of even the darkest fairy tales.

Half of us, half our supplies, were already gone.

The other train wasn't in any better shape. Several wheels had fallen off, and the nose of the chassis was ripped open like a tin can. Even if it had been intact, it still would have been useless. There were no rails, no civilization that we knew of—pray, pray there wasn't—

and no way to get the train to travel fast enough to break the time barrier.

We were marooned and smart enough to know that we should be very, very afraid. Every potential pathogen was completely new to our systems; every insect bite could have new and deadly consequences.

The suns burned my eyes as I stared out at the sea. It is teeming with life, creatures large enough to swallow buildings writhing beneath its blue surface. I thought that maybe our bodies were wired to see darkness once a day, that they needed the respite, but with twin suns, there is no darkness. I sleep whenever I want to. I feel like a dog or a cat, taking naps at will.

My skin has darkened with the constant exposure. I was at my darkest in a matter of days. The sunlight seems to pierce the thin clothing I wear, because I have no tan lines. It makes me feel violated, in a way, to take off my clothes at night in front of Morris and see us, both in our aboriginal skin, come together as one.

I am pregnant.

There is something wrong with it.

The builder bots finally made a shelter. It is without a roof. Morris said there is no way to fix it anymore. They used all the wire and all the circuits from the train to help fix it over and over again, so we have to build our own roof. My belly is showing, but I still work with the others on the edge of the forest, using an axe with a stone head to cut down trees that bleed a bluish sap.

Morris says we need to find metal. We need to burn peat or start mining. The others just kind of look at him. They are so tired. So dirty. All of us have the hangry eyes of models, starved and sinewy.

Morris's grandfather, Albert, says that we need to find food to grow. He's right. Agriculture is the first way.

I'm too tired to move, so I've been writing things I remember about our history on the side of the train with a red ink made from a tree Morris calls Rosa, on account of his creativity. Everything is the same name; we have new maples and oaks, garter snakes—which have the most beautiful purple skin I've ever seen—and many other species. It's like learning another language.

I'm trying to remember how early earth became populated. I remember the Paleolithic era and early agriculture. We cleared a field, planted a kind of orange grass that doesn't have too bad a flavor if it is baked and dried.

My stomach is full with the baby. I have no idea how it has come to be so full, given that the rest of me is so thin, the spaces between the bones of my forearms shallow depressions.

We moved our camp to a place where there is fresh water. It is dangerous to go in, because the rocks are covered with tiny living things that are shaped like tubes and sting like jellyfish. I've seen small fish—more like eels—get caught by a group of them. Their gills work slower and slower as blank eyes twitch at the sun. The little things, I'm calling them tubers despite whatever taxonomical name Morris gave them, dissolve the fish and then lunge repeatedly at the water thick with its nutrients. At first, we thought the rocks were alive. I watched them for an hour, or several hours. It's so hard to tell time here.

I named her Eve. She has red eyes and her skin is as bright as the sun, a silvery layer of cells in the subdermal tissue reminds me of trout, or some other fish without scales. She does not cry. When I smile at her, I'm not sure if she sees me or not.

Other things besides fish live in the water. I wish I could go for a swim. I found a small animal with long legs like a frog's and the slimy body of a newt. I threw it in the water, and a large beetle dragged it beneath the surface. We boil the water but filter it before we boil it. Sometimes I see small black worms left in the filter cloth. The other day I ground them up and fed them to Eve. She didn't seem to mind.

I wish we hadn't left earth. Even if we'd had only a small amount of time there, it would have been better than this. Would have been better than listening to Morris endlessly prattle on about each new species he documents, each new discovery. He's made so many, he's like a kid in a playground. Meanwhile, I stay at the camp and wait for someone to discover yeast so I can have something real to drink. I think, sometimes, there must be some form of marijuana on this planet; there must be many forms of psychoactive plants. It's just a matter of time before we find them.

I'm not sure Eve can hear me. I pinched her, and she didn't scrunch up her face. I clap over her while she's asleep, and she wakes. She doesn't cry, just looks about angrily. I think maybe she hates me.

The water is turning our skin darker, I think. Morris claims it may be the sun or our diet. It's probably high in beta-carotene. That's only a guess.

He found a kind of plastic, something that's rubbery at least. He's trying to build wheels and turnstiles. I'm not sure why.

Eve is crawling. She seems so much faster than the other babies I remember. Millie has a full belly now, too. I wonder what her baby will look like, if she will have Eve's shiny skin. There's no way to know. I'd like there to be night. I feel like there is never time for me to be alone. I had a dream about racial tensions in the future. Eve will be the sparkly one, the leader, and whatever color child Millie has will be the subjugated. I think history will repeat itself, even here. I can see how Morris treats people who aren't scientists; they just do the hard work, help him build his plans.

Thomas brought home an animal today, big as a large dog. Its body has scales, its wings are covered in feathers, and it has hook-shaped claws. He said he'd been watching it for weeks in the orange jungle. He determined what it ate, a kind of fruit that grows high in the canopy, which it flies and jumps to. He started to build up a stash—the fruit is very good. It has a thick yellow skin that is bitter. The bloodred juice is very sweet. He thinks there is a chance we can make wine. I am thrilled. When Morris asked what he wanted to call the animal, he smiled and said, "Cattle."

The animal has rectangular pupils and a stoic demeanor. It made a low, moaning sound all night long, and the other animals called to it from the jungle. I got up a few minutes after Morris to check on it and followed his flashlight beam to the tent where the animal was thrashing around. Thomas and some of the other men were trying to hold it down. There was blood on the feathers of the animal's back, and it became clear Thomas was bleeding from his stomach. The animal kicked again and split his thigh down the middle. For a black man, he grew very pale. Very woozy. Or maybe that was me.

I stepped outside the tent, and the branches of the trees were alive with the other cattle, rattling leaves and calling loudly in their low, slow voices. They sound like the ghosts of whales, the rhythmic thrum of something slowly turning.

We were surrounded. Each one had to weigh several hundred pounds with those claws.

I am pregnant again. I am breeding stock. And although I understood that when I left, when Reginald and Amos and Yuda and all the others were talking about their different plans, I sat there and thought to myself how it might be kind of fun to take several men at once. I had no idea it would be like this. My feet are swollen, and I am pretty sure by the amount of water I need to drink that I have diabetes. There is no insulin. We were all deemed healthy when we left. It was all very scientific and exciting and edge-of-the-world kind of stuff. I wasn't going to be sitting by a pool forever, I would be raising children, but I'd be the center of every man's affections, and as the mother of a new humanity I could expect to be spoiled. And Morris . . . Morris made me feel like a queen. Took hold of my hand and held it until all the nerves were gone and said we'll be like Adam and Eve.

Except our child is named Eve. And I can already see men looking at her, paying special attention to her, even though she can barely crawl.

Morris raised a stone and struck the animal on its head. Its protestations were angry and frantic before. Now they were furious. It kicked Marquise, one of the men who came with us, and Thomas flew back, creating a new flap in the side of the tent. The animal charged through Morris. If I hadn't been watching, it would have run me over. It flapped several times and left the ground, its four feet still running in the air. It dropped precipitously near the river, and its feet dragged through the water, leaving white striations on its surface before something snared its foot and sucked it underwater.

I gasped. All the animals in the trees fell silent.

I'm naming the next baby Sarah, hoping that it is a girl. I'd hate to give Eve a brother and see her marry him one day. That should never happen.

Morris found a kind of rubber that insulates electricity. He's creating tubes and trying to make them watertight. He keeps eyeing the builder bots.

The roof on the main shelter has been made, but it's not very good. There are cracks of sunlight, just enough to make it seem like stars at night. It is very damp and mildewy inside. This is the frontier, Morris keeps telling people. And no, we can't go back.

Chapter 12

Amos

It was around midnight when she heard something outside, a beeping, she called it. I recognized the sound, pretended not to hear it. When Walter stood at the doorway rubbing his fist in his eye and crying, I knew it was over. Lights swirled in the field, and there was shouting.

"What on earth is going on?" Rosaline said.

It had rained hard for the last three days. We'd known it was dangerous with the ground being so soft. There were plenty of pumps and the water was being taken care of, but the earth was so soft that a cave-in was almost inevitable.

"Roz, I need to tell you something," I said.

She turned on the light and brought Walter to her and held him, like she was protecting him from me. "It's Reginald, isn't it?"

I was glad she said it. I didn't think I could. I told myself it would be easier this way, if she guessed. It wasn't. It felt much worse.

Rosaline's mouth fell open like she'd been struck. "Amos, what have you done?"

Lights swirled at the far end of the field, not making a full revolution.

"There's something I need to tell you."

It was the tunnel that led to the tracks, only a partial cave-in, like the roof of a mouth had crumbled.

Yuda met me at the opening as he crawled over debris: chunks of rock, muddy clods of dirt larger than my chest, and steel beams. "Everyone's all right—" He bit off his words as he saw Rosaline.

"Rosaline, this is Yuda. He's from the future."

She was looking past him into the hole. "How many people are down there?"

Yuda and I shared a nod before he answered. "We're approaching one and a half thousand."

Rosaline gasped.

"The future is a very, very dangerous place, ma'am. We're saving people."

"How come you didn't tell me?"

"I . . . I thought it would distress you."

"You're damn right it distresses me!" She started back toward the house.

I called after her, but she wouldn't have it.

I started after her. Yuda stopped me. "Amos, let her cool. We need to get everyone out. It's not safe."

"I should have seen this coming. If I'd been Reginald, I'd have seen it coming."

"Yeah, but Reginald wouldn't have cared if he hurt her. You do," Yuda said.

Later, I found her in the drawing room, sitting in the dark, the flashing lights of builder bots repeatedly sweeping the room as they worked outside in the field.

"Why didn't you tell me?" she said.

"I thought I had more time. I'm helping to save the future."

"What about *him*?"

"He's . . . he's trying to be good," I said.

And at that moment, I believed it. Even though I'd seen him murder people, an entire family in cold blood, I had no doubt that he was trying to save his soul by saving the world.

The people outside were getting close to the house. We didn't have much time. The parlor would be a triage center soon.

"He has my trust until he loses it."

I touched her hand where it rested on her thigh. She pulled away.

There were footsteps on the porch, a knock at the door, the sound of someone coughing.

"Who are they, Amos?"

"Good people. They're just trying to live."

Even nodding her head, she was stone. "He's not allowed in my house. Or around our son."

"Amos!" Yuda called at the door.

I moved to answer it.

"Amos?"

I stopped.

"Tell me all of this—the house, the money—it would exist without Reginald."

I couldn't answer her, so I answered the door.

She hasn't said a word to me since.

Later that night, I sat on the porch drinking whiskey with Yuda. I couldn't believe Morris had tried to travel to another planet. I didn't think we'd ever see him again.

"It's not going to work," Yuda said. "Someone has to go forward and stop them."

"Like who?"

Yuda took a long sip of his whiskey. Crickets chirped, and lightning bugs glowed over the field, glistening with dew in the moonlight. It was hard to reconcile the peace before me with the heartache of disappointing Rosaline.

"I've already been putting it off," he said. "Telling myself I could do it anytime."

"That's what I thought with Rosaline," I said.

He raised his glass. We each took a long drink.

Chapter 13

Angela

They made a dam with turning parts. Morris used the rubber material that insulates electricity and made a bodysuit so that he could enter the water. The little animals that live on the side of every rock can't grip the surface. Their electrochemical shocks don't work on it. The dam creates electricity. The first time it turned, something wasn't quite right with the wiring, and it created a great big burst of electricity that was grounded by the water. Morris was insulated in his suit. He still got shocked, just not very badly. He was talking and fell silent, his chin dipping into the water, and Marquise threw a rope around his neck and gently tugged him over to the side.

I didn't have to perform mouth-to-mouth, but I would have. I leaned over Morris, removed the noose, turned him onto his side in a recovery position. He coughed up some water, and his eyes were all red. I leaned back and noticed Marquise's hand was on my lower back. He's been very helpful lately. I think he wants me.

There are only two other women, and I am fairly certain one will die in childbirth.

Eve took her first steps.

The cattle in the woods watch us. I can hear them talking to each other. They watch us during the day and spy on us at night.

The dam creates electricity, and one of the builder bots is functioning. We have electricity. It's hard to believe. The first thing Morris did was set up the drill we'd bought and bore into the earth to make a well. He went only forty feet down before water welled up. There seem to be no organisms in the water, and it has a sweet taste to it, aqua vitae. I've been using the water to wash Eve. I think it is making her skin brighter. Those red eyes of hers are magnificently striking. If they'd had those on the runway in New York, it would have been all the rage. They are the color of liquid lava, and just as bright. She has long arms, not a lot of baby fat. I wonder if the diet we've been eating has something to do with the way she came out. I started to wonder if maybe I was pregnant during time travel, if somehow radiation or some such nonsense played a role in her not unpleasant deformities. Her skin will draw men like a shiny lure draws fish. If she needs to hunt, it may draw prey, too.

Morris and his father are playing with the rocks. They are coated with electrical filaments, they say. They want to turn the living things into wires.

Eve spoke her first word today, part of her first

sentence. I'd never heard of a child doing that before. She said, "What is Daddy doing?"

I told her he was trying to get the most out of life. She went over and had a full conversation with Morris about the biofilaments. Marquise was behind me splitting wood and said, "She's going to be a smart kid."

"She already is."

The next one is a kicker. I can feel the legs squirming, like it is fighting with sheets, trying to strangle itself with the umbilical cord. I lie in bed at night staring at the stars, wondering which one is earth and remembering the time in Morris's bed at the observatory when I was so drunk the stars spun and he pointed out all the constellations he knew. He hasn't spent much time looking up lately. He spends all his time looking down at the ground trying to fix things, trying to make this world more like home. Someday, there will be television here. I'm quite certain of it. Morris already made glass. A lightbulb won't be far off. He has something called an eidetic memory, putting him just a few spots below pure genius. His grandfather, the one who helped him solve the mathematical problem for space-and-time travel, has a better mind. The sheer number of blackboards and computers they had hooked up in the den was mind-boggling. I remember finding myself next to Reginald as he watched. He leaned over and asked if I understood any of it.

I didn't respond.

"I suppose I understand enough," he said. Yuda

joined us, and we watched for a few silent moments. "It's been proven that The Wedge can be destroyed," Reginald said. He waved a hand at their computations. "This—this is madness."

None of them tried to stop us. No one was in charge. It wasn't a dictatorship. The chances of survival were better if we all tried to do something. Time was literally running out, with the aliens moving backward in time.

I've grown rather fond of the silence, of the sounds of the cattle in the trees, watching us. I think if we messed up, if we didn't keep the fires burning at night, they might sweep in and destroy us all. We're lucky there are no Indians. We're lucky there are no indigenous people that are smart enough to go Roanoke on our asses. If the cattle were smarter, they would take us over, they would attack us every night and pick apart our bones until there was nothing left.

The other women have had children. A boy and a girl each. They both have red eyes and a silvery luminescence in their skin like Eve's. Even Maya's child, who has Maya's dark skin, appears . . . shiny.

The filaments from the rocks are working. There are electric lights, and the cords lift themselves off the ground in contraction when the power from the dam is flowing through them. They become incredibly rigid, harder than steel, Morris said. If they were back home, this would be Nobel Prize territory. Here, it is just good science.

I gave birth again. My child is just like the others,

with fiery eyes and dazzling skin. This one is a boy. I think he will love his sisters. I think he will be the father of this new earth. I named him Odin. He doesn't cry, and he suckles my breasts, and I like the feeling of him near me. I'm not afraid of him like I was Eve. And he still needs me. Eve does not. She goes wherever Morris goes. The other day, she suggested he create a device so that they could fly over the land and see what was there. He was so impressed by the idea that they will actually try it.

The builder bots are all repaired. They are tunneling into a cliff near the ocean several miles away looking for iron ore and other strong metals. If they find strong metals, they are to build another one, just like them. Robots building robots, just like back home. I told Morris if they find oil, he better never, ever use it.

The airplane has smooth wings and is not entirely symmetrical. The other children suggested that Morris not be the one to ride in it first. He is "too important," Hidalgo said, "for now." It will run off electricity. There is plenty of metal here. Part of my job is to make charcoal, so I tend fires that smolder and smoke all day and night long. They can't smelt the metal without enough heat. I am dirty at times, but Marquise still smiles at me when he brings more fuel for the fire.

Morris may sow his own just reward after being so honest with the children. They understand everything he says. He treats them like adults. I'm not so sure they have feelings, though. They never cried, after all, and they don't fight with each other. They are too busy learning from each other and from him.

Marquise and I took a walk in the forest today. I asked Morris if I could go. He said I could when Eve offered to watch Odin. We picked some of the fruit the cattle like—that name stuck—and found a flock with purple and teal feathers grazing on the side of a hill covered by vines with little blue berries on them. We each ate one of the berries and gathered several pints. We joked and said if we don't die after eating one, we'll eat two tomorrow and three the next day, so that even if they are poisonous we will have built up a tolerance and we won't even know they were poisonous. One of the cattle came close to us, sniffing. I tossed a berry lightly in its direction. He ate it quickly, gave me a sideways look.

"I think it's looking at me with its good eye," I said.

Marquise laughed.

We fed them berries until it came so close we could touch its back. I've never felt feathers so soft. Once, when I was a child, I went to the Brooklyn Zoo while my father was on business in Manhattan. They allowed us to touch small birds, titmouse, I believe. They were so small it felt like I was touching nothing, or a cotton ball. This creature, this half-bird quadruped, as Morris called it, was big enough so that I could feel the softness of its feathers. Its nostrils, or maybe its gills, were on its slender neck, just below round tympanic membranes. They flared in between swallowing gestures.

"It's hard to believe they killed Thomas," Marquise said.

"He was too rough with them," I said. "They seem to be gentle things."

A feather fell from the cattle's back, a turquoise one with filaments of plum. Marquise took it and inserted it gently into my hair.

"Now I'm a pirate?" I said.

"I forgot all about pirates." He lay back in the grass and squinted at the two suns. "Our kids won't know what stars are if they grow up here."

Marquise laid his hand on my leg, and I knew him to be a gentle man.

The trip had to last several days. Even Morris was not prepared for how long we traveled in space, cocooned in a maddening array of lightning and color. The systems, the batteries of the train, we weren't sure they would be able to sustain our life long enough to reach our destination. In a way, it was suicide to go to a planet we were only marginally sure would be able to support life. The trains were fitted with structures that would make them float if we arrived in water, but there were no guarantees if we did arrive in water. And there were no guarantees it would be a friendly planet. If we had landed in a place like the United States, it was a virtual certainty that we would be lab rats for the rest of our lives.

The planet had a letter and a number; it wasn't really

named until we arrived there. The muscles in our legs are stronger, because it has positive .01 gravity as compared to earth, so the first few days it felt like everything was heavier. I laughed and said I didn't want to step on a scale. The truth of it was we didn't have a scale, nor did we have cameras or cell phones or anything like that. Morris, though, is determined to make the new world old. Or the old, undeveloped world that was unspoiled by humans, spoiled.

Eve and Odin returned from the plane trip with Morris. They were very excited. There are buildings, they said. There are buildings made by bipeds. I'm not sure what they meant.

"Primitive, very primitive," Morris said, rushing around.

When I first met you, space was swirling all around us, I said. I never knew we were already caught up in it.

His head tilted, and he laughed before going back to whatever preparations he was making. He slid open a drawer made of orange wood and pulled out a familiar shape of metal from the old earth.

Do you think this little bump is anything to worry about? I said.

Morris pulled back the slide on the pistol, checked the barrel, and put the gun in his waistband.

You're not going to interrupt them, are you? They're a new tribe or something.

"All the more reason to make contact. We're sharing their planet."

Isn't it big enough for us both?

He kissed me on the forehead, the same kind of kiss he gave the children—who seemed bewildered by it. Of course the planet wasn't big enough for the both of us. Look what had happened on the last planet.

It was thrilling and mundane at the same time to make those kinds of statements. We were a part of two different planets.

I wonder how they're getting on back home.

"This is our home, darling," Morris said and left.

I heard the whoosh of propellers and listened to the drone slowly vanish into the sounds of the jungle like it belonged there.

The light is different on this planet. The suns aren't quite as bright. You can see the solar flares on their surface without sunglasses, although I'm glad I brought mine. There are crisscrossing shadows everywhere when both suns are up, like the many different points of shadow formed while walking on a city street at night with the streetlamps all around you. All the shadows converge at one point, your feet. The rest are split and fractured.

The wine is finally ready. We gave some to a small animal that has been mostly domesticated, a kind of scaly thing with a beak and long, ruddy-brown, rat terrier–like fur covering its back. After it took a few laps with its forked blue tongue, Marquise and I laughed at the way its balance appeared off. We waited for several hours. It slept, then returned to normal.

"Here goes nothing," Marquise said and took a sip.

He dropped the glass and grabbed his throat.

"Marq," I shouted. I hit him on the back, and his eyes were wide as he appeared to choke himself; then the son of a bitch started laughing.

You bastard. I stormed off.

"It's good, it's good," he called after me.

He entered the chamber Morris and I share and stood at the doorway, two wooden cups of the wine he'd made in his hands. He didn't plan on leaving the room anytime soon.

"Here," he said, handing me a cup. I smelled it. It had melon, citrus—clean-bathroom smell.

Everything hurt. My body, my mind. Just thinking of a clean bathroom hurt. I'd never smell another one again. Or I may, but I'd be too old to enjoy it. Morris was hurrying as fast as he could to make everything work, to make everything here more like it was back home. It would never be the same, never have as many people, as many easy forms of entertainment, and I was almost certain to never have another strawberry ice cream. There was no such thing as a strawberry on this planet. There may be an analog, as Morris was fond of saying, but that didn't make much of a difference.

Marquise clinked his wooden cup against mine.

"It's like Robinson Crusoe, in a way," he said.

In a way.

"Cheers."

I drank. It had a definite alcoholic bite and something else, a kind of sensation that made it tingle. Morris had examined it and said it was probably safe. He didn't really pay much attention to it and said we shouldn't bring alcohol into society just yet. I reminded him that all the slaves in Egypt were paid in beer, so it was no wonder we wanted alcohol now. Morris scoffed. "If you accomplish half of what they did in Egypt it will be worth it," he said. "Have a drink for me."

I coughed. It's good, I said.

"It is good." Marquise took a deep breath, making his wide chest expand to its limit, and looked around the log-cabin-like room. There were metal instruments of all sorts on a workbench—soldering irons and wires and a tube full of biofilaments. "Do you think Morris will mind if I'm in his room?"

I'm breeding stock, I said. I don't see how he can get too upset.

"Don't put it so bluntly. It sounds rude when you say it that way."

How should I put it?

He took another sip and I joined him. Was I already feeling a buzz? My head felt like a stone atop my shoulders, constantly bouncing from one fulcrum point to the next.

"Maybe say, we're lucky he's a generous man, and we should get to breeding," he said with a sly smile. He reached for my hand. Even in his grasp, my limb felt heavy.

I'm not his property. I'm not ever going to even be his.

"You don't love him. No one said you did," Marquise said, kissing my neck. His curly hair was getting long and tickled the side of my face. I wrapped my fingers in his hair and pulled him, gentle-hard, between my legs.

Be obedient, I said and arched my back for him. Maybe it was the alcohol, but there was no stopping our bodies coming together.

He stopped a moment later, pressing a finger into the side of my hip like he didn't want to lose something. "What's this?"

What's what?

His eyes were big when he looked up at me, like he'd just seen a ghost. There was a marble under my skin, deep in the muscle tissue. Another one.

◷

How long do you think we traveled? It was one of the first nights on the planet. It lasted probably no more than an hour. We were gathered around a fire, and my belly was swollen with promises of love and happiness and a new world. Every time the wind shifted we moved our blankets, fearing the smoke would somehow be toxic to us. We were afraid of everything in those days.

I lay in the crook of Morris's arm. We had a sliver of stars above in a hazy blue sky between the rising and setting suns. I wanted to see earth, even as it is seen from the moon. I knew I'd never even be able to pick out our sun or any constellation that it was a part of, because we'd never seen it from so far away before. If there was a constellation, local people had yet to name it.

The planet was pretty far away, Morris said.

How long was the trip? I said.

Maybe a few years.

I sat up. A few years?

Time dilation, he said easily. He tapped his arm.

I lay back down. Time dilation. That sounds like something that happens when you're drunk, I said, snuggling up comfortably next to him. I knew he liked having to explain things to me. He liked teaching me. It made him feel smart, and it didn't annoy him so long as I was a quick study, which I was. I may have been blonde and worldly and superficial, but I never wanted to be. I had a brain and remembered more than most people forgot about college—although I wondered now if that was just something I told myself.

It might as well be, he said. It has to do with gravitational pull and the lack thereof. While we were in space, without gravity, clocks ran slightly slower than they did on earth.

So we're actually older.

Not really, no. We experience time the same way. It's subjective.

So we were really only on the train, the space train, sorry, for a few hours?

Morris didn't say anything for a while. He pointed at the sky, where a ribbon of cloud was being dipped in the purple and gold dyes of the rising sun. That's beautiful, he said.

Morris?

A few hours. That's the way it felt to us, he said.

I didn't think to ask if we'd traveled through time. I didn't even think about Eve.

I lay in the bed next to Marquise, his fingers massaging me, guiding me into a dark and blissful state of non-awareness when gunshots drove all the little flying creatures to take flight from the orange jungle.

I sat up. What was that?

Marquise didn't say anything, just dressed and left the cabin.

He pointed when I came outside. It came from that direction.

I told Odin to be ready in case he needed to do something awful.

Like what? Odin said.

I followed Marquise toward the jungle with Hidalgo and a few others. The children stayed with the other women.

Protect them, I said to Odin.

His red eyes were piercing. I thought that I named him right and that I was also wrong about Eve being a model on a runway if we lived in the old world. With eyes like those, they would be pariahs. They would be outcasts, singled out by racist threats their entire lives.

Odin looked around and made everyone go into the cabin with the open roof.

The jungle was full of competing shadows, dense with vines. We walked for what felt like hours until we met a bend in the river I'd never seen before, a deep pool where the water was clear and devoid of life. Bubbles occasionally rose to the surface. When they did, the bottom shifted like a lens sliding to one side, then the other.

I'm not going through there, Hidalgo said, scratching the side of his big nose. I wondered if he was Puerto Rican, then decided it didn't matter. We were all alien now.

No, there was something unnerving about the water, the way it looked shallow one moment, then fathomlessly deep the next.

We heard the whine of the engine long before we saw the plane streaking over the tops of the orange trees. I screamed up at them and waved my arms—there was a pinch between my shoulder blades that hurt.

Morris didn't see me.

Wind began to toss the tops of the trees, and without even realizing it, Hidalgo and Marquise and I had backed away from the river.

I took Marquise's hand as another belch of gas rose from the pool. In the obfuscation, I saw the inverted sky on the water's surface. Something emerged out of the far side of the jungle.

They had black skin with thinly spread, thick hairs protruding from it, almost like feathers without the side follicles, and heavily shaded eyes hiding under large brows. They carried sticks with stones attached to the tops, uprooted young trees with root balls sharpened into maces. Their gazes followed the sky, tracing after Morris's plane, and fell to earth where they saw us. They loosed a war cry from their stout, thick beaks and charged into the clear water, fracturing its perfect symmetry.

Run, Marquise shouted.

We made our way through the jungle as fast as we could and didn't see them gaining behind us. We heard their shouts, like angry ravens, calling to each other, dozens of them, using their raptor feet to jump into tree branches and swinging from vine to trunk and crashing back to earth.

When we emerged back to our clearing, Morris and the children stood ready, Morris with his pistol and the children holding long, thin black rods.

I ran past them and huddled inside the cabin, watching through the cracks.

Morris shot the first two before they came out of the jungle, giant plumes of smoke rising from his pistol. It didn't stop them.

The children swung their long poles and when they connected with them, there were sparks and quick puffs of smoke where hairless spots had formed on their bodies.

One of them fell atop Morris and lunged forward, attacking his back. Its head twisted to one side and then the other as it wedged its beak into the soft flesh of his back. Marquise ran toward him and picked up the gun.

The beast on top of Morris flexed its back muscles,

claws digging into the dirt on either side of Morris's body. It pulled its beak free with a chunk of sinewy muscle. Marquise shot it in the head.

The ravens let out a renewed war cry.

Odin had the pump hose and was spraying all of them. He yelled to Marquise to pull Morris free as the other children formed a half circle around them. When the dirt was wet, they touched the ends of their long black poles to it and lightning struck.

The ground turned to glass. The attackers sank to their knees in superheated plasma. They tried to escape, arms flailing wildly, and fell forward, sinking their arms into the hot sand.

No one knew what to do; it was over so quickly. I went to Morris and knelt beside him. Marquise was pressing a blood-soaked bandage to Morris's back.

Are you okay? I said.

Morris laughed and coughed. There was blood in his mouth. I hoped he'd bitten his tongue.

I motioned for Marquise to move the bandage. The flesh below was shredded, and I saw his ribs.

I've never heard birds cry before. They were making such pitiful moaning sounds behind me. I wished one of the children would shoot them to put them out of their misery, but they just stood there, staring at them as if fascinated. I wondered that they didn't have any religion, any respect for life. We were raising them wrong.

Marquise replaced the bandage.

"We should go back home." Morris coughed.

I told him to be quiet.

"But I don't think we'd survive it."

I stood and watched the things sunk in the hardened glass, frozen there, eyes bleeding a purple fluid in pain. One of the children reached a long black pole to their sides and shocked them.

"Don't do that," I shouted. "Kill them, but don't torture them. Can't you see they're in pain?"

That's when I realized I'd never heard any of them cry before. Never seen them tear up the way normal toddlers did when they fell and scraped their knee. Hell, I'd never seen them fall. I wondered if they felt pain.

The world felt as though it were about to shake, or my knees were going to give way. I knew we were going to have to move camp. We couldn't go on having a pool of glass reminding us of this massacre. Not passing it every day and peering into its misshapen depths.

Marquise, I said, why are there three suns?

He looked at me, then at the sky.

There aren't three suns, he said, and the world tilted and rose to meet me very suddenly.

Odin wasn't an easy birth. I shouldn't have named him first. I felt like he'd be a crow, but he was more tiger than anything. Ripping and stretching. Jessica, the only person who had medical experience, kept telling me to breathe and to relax and to push, and it was the first time I saw a light that wasn't there. I didn't notice it, because it was one of those times when there was only one sun in the sky, the orange one. When I saw the other burst of light, I thought it was normal. I never thought it was me. I thought it was the pain, and when I first held Odin, I knew that he must have been ten pounds, maybe more. The first words I whispered in his ear were, "Jesus, child. You nearly killed me."

The children are using the glass that trapped those things—they're calling them birdmen. They're using the glass to create lenses and the lenses to create microscopes. Already I can hear them chattering on about the little filaments that live on the rocks, the flesh of Morris's back. They have a sample of it.

He's in a lot of pain. I saw his ribs, and I'm not sure if I saw his heart beating, moving behind that pale, purple curtain of flesh. Everything shifts when he breathes.

The lumps are bigger. There is one on my hip that Marquise found, buried in the soft flesh of my gluteus, and one on my neck that I tried to get Morris to inspect, which is shaped like an egg. I feel something between my third and fourth ribs, beneath my right breast. I'm fairly certain there's one in my head.

Three suns are too many. I don't need more than one. The third one isn't really like a sun; it's more like a blob of light that flashes when I think too hard. I suspect that if I were home, Daddy would have me taking the best medicine and talking to all the doctors who are really important in the big hospitals in the cities. Daddy would own them if they failed me, so they wouldn't fail me.

We have Jessica. She keeps saying the word *palliative.* I don't know what that means. If I had a dictionary or my phone, I could look it up and know immediately. I told Morris about it, and he said not to worry.

His back doesn't look right. The children have a chunk of his flesh, and it is starting to rot. They keep putting things on it, little things that are supposed to either clean the wound or help with him.

He says they'll be doctors someday, all of them with their shiny flesh and special minds. He said if they had IQs, they'd be in the two hundreds. I asked him what his was. He said one fifty-nine.

I smiled at him. Once I took an IQ test, and I was one sixty-one.

He kissed me on the forehead.

I lied, I said.

I know. My IQ is one fifty-nine.

His ribs have a little layer of yellow flesh growing over them. It hurts when he coughs, and his face is pale despite all of us having such great tans from the double suns. I don't even notice the light anymore. I think if it was dark, I wouldn't be able to sleep. I wouldn't be able to lie outside and doze off.

They don't let me burn my skin.

Sometimes I feel like there is a place inside my head

that is keeping thoughts from me. Secrets. Pieces of me, somehow sacred, from myself. There was a word for that sacred place I used to know. I can't remember it.

Marquise doesn't want to have sex with me, even though he says I'm full of number four, and I'm so horny that it actually hurts. I can feel the blood rush between my legs when he gets near. I have to pee all the time. Sometimes I think this next baby might be one of the balls—I don't want to use the *C* word—growing inside my stomach at a rate faster than all the others. It could be, except it kicks. I could be growing a whole new race. Every time I look at the children, I think I already have.

They don't need us.

I asked Marquise to take me down to the river. There is a bridge on the top of the dam. They have fashioned security fences with those black rods they used to make the sand turn to glass.

I saw someone else turn sand to glass once. It doesn't matter anymore.

The water is full of things that swim, and there is a beetle, a giant one with long flippers like a whale, that zooms out and attacks everything we drop in the water.

He's aggressive, I said. I wished someone else was.

Marquise touched my back, careful to avoid the bumps above the ridges of my hips, the two behind my shoulder blade that make it hard to lift heavy things.

I touched his shoulder and drove my thumb into the knot there.

It still doesn't hurt, he said.

I kind of wished it did.

The children appeared at the end of the bridge and waited for us to notice them.

It's Morris, Odin said. He's bigger than all of them. I try to remember how old he might be. I can't mark years. I can't even remember what year we arrived or how long we've been here. I think it must be a long time, though, because when I look at everyone else, they have aged. I decide to keep track of the time by how big the lumps grow. They might be as big as I am by the end of it.

Are you coming? Odin asks.

I want to feel you inside of me, I tell Marquise. There's so much inside of me that I don't want. I want there to be something I choose inside.

The baby kicked, and I almost doubled over. The sun appeared on Marquise's face, covering half his eye and most of one side of his forehead. I think maybe that means he's the one. Of course that means he's the one.

Morris had something black attached to his back when I entered the room. It was dark, and when the children touched it, it started to move, like it was breathing, like it was doing exactly what they said.

What is that? I said.

I am with them, in the room, right now. I don't feel floaty, like I have for days and days. I feel like the block in my mind is actually helping, for a change, pinning me down here, in the moment.

It's a patch, Eve says. It will help hold him together.

Morris blinked himself awake, saw us standing around him, said, What have they done?

He grabbed for me. Angela, what have they done?

I reached for the black thing on his back, and somehow it bit me. My hand was red, where it had gotten me, somehow.

It feeds off his electricity, Odin said.

We found them in the dam, gumming up the turnstile when the lights started to fail.

I looked closer at it. It was black, and its skin was gelatinous.

Angela, Morris pleaded. His eyes trailed down my hips, to my waist. You've made another one, he said.

When I looked down, my feet were soaked, in the middle of a jagged-edged puddle.

I didn't even feel my water break.

Marquise and Jessica led me to another room where I gave birth to a fish that swam right out of me. Another child with perfectly reflective skin. With red eyes.

Odin came in and looked at the child. He's beautiful.

Do you really think that?

Morris told me to say it, Odin said. I'm leaving, you know. I'm taking the plane and circumnavigating the globe, like Magellan.

Amerigo, I said.

Not him.

I know.

What you put on his back, you should take off.

We can't do that, Odin said.

Will you anyway?

He touched the side of my face and smiled. It was a cold smile, though. He was a fish.

He won't be able to take it off, I said. Not there between his shoulder blades.

He was dead without it, Odin said.

I stared after him for a long time as he walked into the third sun. I tried to tell him something, something important, something I was afraid I couldn't teach him and wouldn't be able to, not if he left and maybe never came back.

I said, Be kind, and stared into the third sun until it blinded me.

Sometimes I expect to wake up. I'm not sure when, or who will be there. I know where I hope I will be—in Morris's bed, under the skylights, and all of this will be a dream that lasted no more than a passing second, before Reginald, before The Den, before all of it turned my life on end. I'm not even sure how time passes now. It feels different. I don't know what happened yesterday from what's happening now. I tell myself it's the suns.

Morris comes and talks to me. The light is so bright, sometimes I think I can see him, moving like a shadow, or maybe we're all just ghosts, unsure if we've passed.

I know that's not the case when he tells me about the children. They are so, so very smart, he says. All of them. They've taken apart the train and they have studied the electronics. They made machines from machines and have struck an uneasy truce with the birdmen. We are, apparently, on an island. They get half, we get half.

The rest of this world is covered in water.

It makes sense, Morris says, that the world is covered in water. Given the depth and breadth of aquatic life in the river.

You always were given to puns, I say. How's your back?

This old thing? He sits on the side of my bed. I wish I could remember his face. Sometimes, when I hear him speak, I think of Marquise, how he was so gentle, how he made me feel when he touched me and took pleasure in my pleasure. Sometimes I think I'm still talking to Marquise.

I can feel it pressing deeper. Like it's growing. It's hard as rock now, on the back. It's kind of like Oobleck. If you just touch it, you can feel it tingle your skin, like it's sensing your electricity. You know, you really should let the children see you more. They think they can help.

I don't want their help, I said. Over and over I said it.

Well, just one more time, for old time's sake. I don't even feel him, just the sensation of movement against the grainy white sun, a rocking motion.

Are you done? I said.

I felt him nodding, felt him silently apologizing.

You slipped out for a minute there. I was talking to you, then you just stopped answering.

The children.

They're not children anymore.

How many did I have?

Seven. Minus the one that didn't survive. Odin is their leader. They want to help you. They really, really want to help you.

I can't see. And now I slip off, in my mind. Going places.

The medical patches—

Are living things.

They traveled under the water, yesterday. To the depths of the ocean, they claim. They took photos. Some of the things down there, they are like us. Slippery humans. I saw it in their eyes, and I wouldn't be surprised if someday one of them washes up on shore, just to see how it's treated. They're very nice, you know.

I swung my hand around, chasing the light with a broom. Get that thing away from me.

It's just a washcloth.

I know what it is. It's one of those things that Morris has on his back, wrapped around his heart and feeding off the electricity.

That's not what it is.

Mother, why don't you listen to us? You already have one. Don't you feel it?

I dropped the broom, sent my fingers crawling all over my skin, feeling for something hard if you push on it, with an electric tingle, a pulse.

You won't find it. I recognize the voice. It's Odin.

It's inside you.

In my womb, I feel it. Suddenly aware that it is coiled in my uterus, that its tentacles are wrapped around my spinal cord.

How did you think you lived so long? Haven't you felt your skin tingle when we touch you?

I thought it was you. I thought it was. How long has it been—like this?

Years, Mother. Years and years. Thirty earth years, at least.

Where is Marquise?

There is silence. I know he's dead.

All of it is happening all at once. Each year of my life. Dark, light, it doesn't matter, all I can see are memories. I wish I could wake up in any of them. For all of our hubris, for all of our managing and striving and manipulating time, I wish I could just once nail it down and stop it.

Do you want it?

Want what?

Let us show you.

No.

Hold still.

Chapter 14

Angela

I'm a mother of fish.

Chapter 15

Angela

I don't like the things they show me.

I'm floating above a city, covered in metal, with tubes and chutes for water wrapping around like neurons, firing little electric pulses over and over again like fiber optics except, in these chutes, people travel, their thoughts, their minds, all connecting as one. They give me sight.

I see the sun. All of them. Sometimes, I press its light into their minds so bright and so hard, hoping they may disconnect me from whatever they've put me in.

They never do.

I'm not sure where I am anymore. I see so much, of the people, I'm not sure if it's me they place things in front of. Sometimes I feel like a child or wonder if somehow I've died and this is hell and I've just been here so long I forgot I was ever alive.

It was nice being alive, back on earth, back in a place that had rules.

I see things from so many perspectives. I don't want to

see. I don't want to see the birds with the black things on their shoulders, talking through their beaks like people, their claws holding hands with a red-eyed child.

Odin talks to me. I reach for him, holding my hand out, hoping he will take it. I never see what he sees. I think he's too smart for that. I think every time he comes to talk to me it's out of some sick hedge bet to gather information about what we were.

The ground rumbles. At night, I hear it like the planet is snoring. They whisper about the red eye in the ground. I know what that is. It's a volcano. There's no way to stop it.

This damned watery world only has one plot of land. I saw it, looking down, from a thought I stole. It's massive. Nearly a third of the island. They've created something huge and metal that floats offshore. I don't think it is big enough.

Where is your home?

Odin, I don't know.

Who does?

Only Morris. Where is Morris?

Footsteps. Silence.

We've done a terrible thing.

We've done a terrible thing, Odin.

Even the third sun has died. There is no light. Just a gray emptiness until some old woman with a heavy black tire around her waist stumbles out, arms outstretched as if she might run into something.

I run toward the old woman and take her hand.

She's on top of me, strong old bony hands around

my neck, squeezing. I think maybe if I just close my eyes, she'll go away. Maybe if I just stop showing her what I see, she might leave me alone. It works. The pressure on my neck weakens and goes slack, the hands sliding forward onto the smooth ground. I open my eyes, and Odin has the old woman, a long spear in her back, pushed up under the ribs.

I touch her hand. Her mouth is dry. Cracked lips burn. She shows me the gray. I don't want it. Don't like the emptiness of it. The way it fades when I pull the spear out, I feel happy.

The hole from the spear heals on its own.

I don't know how I could make it more menacing. I've lived blindly, for several hundred years longer than I should have as something else pumped blood through my veins, something wrapped and coiled so tightly along my spine I don't know where it ends and I begin. I don't know where I end and everyone else begins.

You really don't know, Odin says.

And I'm nodding, turning my attention to the firehole and thinking Earth, Mars, Venus, Sun, Uranus, Pluto, Milky Way. Milky Way. That's what Morris hears. He's in there, too. I can feel him.

We've done something terribly wrong, I say to him.

"I know," Morris says. "We'll fix it. They're listening. For my neutrinos. They know it's an endless resource. One year at a time they can work their way back, to the beginning of time. Then they will set us free. They can't be here."

We can't be here, I say. We've already ruined it.

Chapter 16

Yuda

Trying to find a hazmat is easy. Take a look at someone's eyes. There are bags below them, like they've packed everything they ever had for one trip that was a month long. It was so good they couldn't let themselves sleep through any of it. I almost forgot how strung out everyone looked. Even though they had more weight on their bodies than almost everyone after the collapse, they were sickly, no tans on any of the white people, like they'd never seen the sun, and either a wasted nodding posture or paranoid, glancing eyes, always trying to take everything in like they were compensating for the stupid they'd worn the night before. There was a popular theory about how we were all enslaved, how we were all held captive to society in one way or another, through unfulfilling jobs, not enough chips, a lack of hope, that it was almost impossible to not take some haze. By itself, haze was never addictive. You could do it once, again the next night, and then wait a month until the next time you used it, or never use it again. Sure, people said they did it once and lost control, but the truth was haze was better than anything they had in their own life. If humanity was full of lab rats, haze would be the lever in the cage, and there would be nothing else in the cage. Of course, humans would pull the lever over and over again. After a while it's as habitual as looking in the fridge when you're hungry. There's no place else to look to fill that need.

We had a big need. I figured I would need at least seventeen foggers. More if I could get them, and at least as many gas masks, although I was fairly certain this was a one-way trip.

It was strange being back in the outlet town, walking through streets knowing I might bump into myself. I had Thomas and Zach with me. We were all dressed appropriately—it was amazing how the ragged poor and the refugee from the future dressed just the same—but it still felt like we stood out. I found myself comparing how I used to behave with how I might behave now.

We stepped into a bar. In the darkness my mind immediately double-checked for the weight of the gun against my hip as I passed the bouncer. I used to know his name. He squinted at me as if he recognized me, didn't know what was different, like I'd gotten a new tattoo or a new haircut but he couldn't quite put his finger on it. I didn't come here often in the past. When I did, I always had my gear, the gas mask, a canister, all of it.

We sat at the bar. A woman in a tank top with a

long snake tattoo draped over her shoulders eyed us as she wiped down the bar.

"I'm looking for Mica," I said.

I didn't know what I would say when I saw her. I was afraid I'd just drift away into the past, remembering bits of things buried beneath the surface, little tensions, things she may or may not have done yet. For all the ways we were manipulating time, Amos playing Chiron the ferry man, there was no way to know what would happen next. And *next* was a relative term. This was the future compared to some other time. It was also the past compared to every other me. It was mind-boggling to think that although I may have already failed or succeeded at bringing down The Wedge I wouldn't know until this next moment.

"You always stare like that?" the bartender said.

"What?"

"How do you know Mica?"

"She was, she is, my girlfriend."

The bartender laughed. "Sure she is. Listen, you want to sit at the bar, you order a drink."

"Whiskey," we all said.

We glanced at each other. Yeah, whiskey.

The bartender placed three glasses on the counter and ran a bottle over them.

We downed them quickly. "That'll be seventeen chips," the bartender said.

I laid fifty dollars on the bar. "That's the same thing, plus tip."

She snatched the folded paper. “What’d you do, knock over an antique store?”

“We walked out of one,” Zach said.

“Where is Mica?” I said.

“She’s not going to talk to you.”

“Humor me.”

She caught the bouncer’s eye and tossed her head to the side at a set of stairs.

I started for the stairs before the bouncer even moved.

Halfway up, the bouncer put his hand on Zach’s shoulder. Zach’s got a bit of a gut, but I’ve seen him lift a steel I beam on his own and drag it a few feet. Before the collapse, he was one of the few people power lifting in a gym, not just there to meet women or for show. Zach bent the bouncer’s finger back, clutched him by the throat, carried him to the nearest table, and forced him into a chair.

“We don’t want trouble,” Zach said.

The bouncer reached for his chest. Zach pinned his hand. There was a muffled pop, like a champagne cork under a rag. A puff of smoke rose from the bouncer’s chest.

“What the fuck?” the bartender shouted. She hit something under the bar, and the lights came on: big, bright floods that made me squint. She held an old-style tactical shotgun on us. “Back off him.”

A man in a T-shirt that said Tito’s ran to the bouncer and squatted beside him, kissed him on the side of the head, tried helping him to his feet.

The bouncer waved him off. He reached for the gun again.

"Yuda? What are you doing here?" Mica was at the top of the stairs.

"Get out of the way." The bouncer motioned with his pistol for her to move out from behind me.

Zach and Thomas moved toward the bar.

"Jesus, Hank, you're bleeding. Did you shoot yourself? Put that thing away."

"Mica?" the bartender said.

"You too," Mica shouted. "Put it away. Call an ambulance, fucking moron." She looked at me. "What happened to you?" She touched my face. She smelled like haze and cheap perfume. I had forgotten that her hands were rough, calloused.

The smell of the haze made me wish for it again. I'd thought about doing it, about getting some and bringing it back, then thought about the consequences of returning with some back-alley chemist who knew the formula, and what that would do to history, to have it present all those years, to have it working its nasty little fingers into the fabric of society when the war on drugs was actually fought with human lives, not just casualties of the end user. I leaned into her hands.

She smiled coyly and pulled away. "Do you usually wear makeup?"

"No," I said, remembering that she used to call me Maybelline, a name I never quite understood.

"Why do you look so old? And this scar . . ." She touched the side of my forehead gently, like a mother.

I'd fallen while running. I think it may have happened

in the explosion or when I was falling into the water in the chasm. It was tough to know.

"And why are you here?" she said, looking around.

"I need a few more foggers."

The look she gave me was one of distrust.

"Why?"

I nodded at the upstairs and wondered about her as I walked behind her. She went to jail. For twelve long years, she was supposed to pay the price for gassing those parties because I ratted her out. And when *The Kind* came, those prisons were easy pickings, tentacles flying through cages, ripping people's skin off if they didn't fit through the bars.

Zach and Thomas stood by the door.

Mica leaned against a desk. "How many canisters do you need?"

"Seventeen." I didn't stutter or mumble; I just came out and said it. I got a little kick at being so honest and demanding. I used to be intimidated by her. I used to wonder why I would rather share her than not have her at all.

Her eyes grew round. "Seventeen . . ." She walked behind her desk, pulled a pistol out of a drawer.

"Take off your clothes. All of you."

"Mica."

"I don't know you that well. Now."

We stripped down to our underwear.

"Who the hell wears tighty-whities?" she said.

I didn't feel the need to explain to her how happy I was to have clean drawers when we first arrived at the den. It was the little things. That Amos or someone had only had tighty-whities didn't matter. Clean underwear felt like sex.

"And a black man, too," she said, looking at Thomas's underwear. "You two, take your clothes and wait outside."

Thomas and Zach did as told.

"Take his clothes with you."

When they closed the door, she eyed me up and down, a bit of a smile on her face. "Do I need you to take off the underwear, too?"

"Would you like that?"

Without hesitating, I dropped them.

She held eye contact for a moment before looking down, appraising my manhood, then the underwear themselves.

"At least you don't have skid marks. Sit on the couch. You don't need those."

The leather was surprisingly cold on my skin. I pretended not to notice. "Seventeen," I said.

She bit her lower lip. "Seventeen. Must be some party."

"Like the end of the world."

"Well, I can't swing that many. Not even with your wood. You always get like that?"

"Only when I'm around pretty ladies." It was the pride, the pride of knowing I still had it, that if I could do it over again, I would do things differently, that I'd have the courage to make my life different. I might not be able to change everything, or anything, about the past, but at least I knew I was a different person than I was then.

"How many can you get?"

"Twelve by the end of the week."

"Tomorrow."

"In a hurry?"

I didn't want my old self to screw everything up if she saw me between now and then.

"Tomorrow, then." She typed something into her phone. "That's going to be ninety-six large. You got those kinds of circuits?"

"About that," I said.

She laughed.

"Would you accept cash?"

"Balls," she said with a smile. "Get your clothes on."

I picked up my drawers and stepped forward quickly, pushed her pistol aside, and kissed her. She resisted at first; then the gun dropped to the floor and she mashed her lips against mine. Her fingernails raked my back as I lifted her, spinning around the room with one eye open, looking for something to pin her against. We fell against the door.

I always knew she didn't love me before. I never knew she could love the man I would become.

It was strange being back where it all began, strange looking over our shoulders in the cave. Being underground was almost normal. Being underground there—knowing what happens with Reginald and that the train, *the train* that started it all, was sitting a few hundred feet away—was mad. The craziness of the idea was starting to set in. To think that I might be able to take down The Wedge.

"I know what you're thinking," Zach said, removing his sweat-stained red hat to wipe his brow.

"I doubt that," I groaned as I lifted one of the foggers off the train.

The foggers weighed about fifty-five pounds each and were essentially old propane tanks fixed with the same kind of diffusing nozzles ski resorts used to make artificial snow.

"You're thinking you can take her with you." I stopped loading and looked down the dark tunnel where spirals of psychedelic blue light woven of imagination dwelled. I tried to remember the last time I saw one of *The Kind* up close, the tentacles, the way they rolled to get around. The beaks or rows of teeth.

I felt the staff Reginald had given me in my pocket, told myself it could pierce their midnight skin.

"Can I?" I said.

"Probably not," Zach said.

"Then why would I be thinking it?"

"I heard how you went at it. I'd be thinking about it."

I hefted another fogger out of the train. "So I'm thinking about it. But I can't do it."

"What with all Amos and Reginald are doing, maybe you can."

Ever since I walked out of her office, I had been thinking about how I could change everything. How with just a few words I could make her see what I really am. And then she'd slap me and call me crazy and I'd have to drag her to the train and show her the future. By the end of it, she would crumple into my arms, nuzzle up to my neck, and say thank you.

Then a few hours later she'd be fiending for haze and demanding I take her back.

"Let's finish this up," I said.

Zach groaned.

"What, you're not a power lifter anymore?" I teased.

"No, and I'm not a real estate agent anymore, either. How the hell do you suppose we're going to get these heavy-ass cans up onto The Wedge?"

"That, my friend, is the million-dollar question."

The next day as we walked through the woods, one eye on the sky for the emergence of The Wedge, he said, "A better question that needs answering is how do you think we're going to hump those canisters all the way out here?"

"I've been thinking about that. So, I told you about the garage with all the weed-eaters, right?"

"Course."

"I told you about the ship that was just sitting there, waiting."

"We're going to steal that ship? That very ship?"

"Well, that's probably like trying to find a single nanosecond on the anthropological twenty-four-hour clock."

"Just say needle in a haystack. You sound like Reginald."

"True. You know it's nice being back in New Hampshire. The way the wind moves through the trees, even if it does get bitching cold in the winter." We approached a ridge. I could see the hint of a view forming between the limbs of the trees ahead of us.

"Quit stalling."

"I ever tell you I was a coward?" I said.

"You act like that would be news."

"Asshole," I said, without heat.

We stopped at the ridge, sipped the view in silence.

"Even though I ran that day, I don't think there's time enough to bring all those canisters on board."

"So, you're groping in the dark."

I pointed at the ravine, the shadow of the cave a flat circle in the middle. "They invade down there, at some point. We're going to invade up here, when they invade down there."

"Huh," he said. "That's pretty good."

"I thought you'd like it. Zach?"

"Yeah?"

"You okay dying for this?"

"Not really."

"Me neither. Just think about the view from up there, though."

Zach didn't say anything.

The irony of it was thick. Imagine, when Reginald

takes over, leading by default because he was smart enough to take the train when I wasn't, if I'm just a few hours in the future, taking down the whole damn Wedge and ending the war.

That night I lay on my back by the stream, staring up as The Wedge passed over and thought, it'd be easy to just hook the foggers up inside the cave. That would be the easy thing to do. Easier than taking seven days to haul them up the side of the mountain in hopes that one of *The Kind*'s spacecrafts would be near. I wondered if Mica ever would have been with me if it weren't for the way I'd handled her in the office. If I hadn't shown her a flash of what I am now.

I took out the staff and held it. It should have been heavier. The surface was cold, tingly almost. I wondered if that was in my head, if that was fear. I spun it, touched the tip of it to the ground and pushed; it didn't turn into a stool. I gave up. Where were the instructions?

The cold of the cave at night became frigid, and the susurration of the water was unrelenting. We were going to die on one of those ships or crash to earth in a fireball riding The Wedge.

Every time we climbed to the top of the mountains hauling those godforsaken canisters up the hill, we stopped and stared at the view, the endless treetops and sloping valleys, the shale sides of a mountain whose name

I would never know, and stared at the pit we were slowly filling with canisters. We were running out of days.

"You know, we could wait after this. Go back to the past, live a few years. With the train—"

"We'll lose our nerve. I'll lose my nerve."

"But the canisters won't age anymore. We can come back on the same day even if fifty years have passed in our lives."

"No, when they're all up here, it's time."

On the night we bought the canisters, Mica asked me where I got paper money.

"It's a one-time deal," I explained. "I'm just a middleman."

We were standing on a dock that ran alongside the pier that floated up and down with the tides. The tide was out. The pier towered beside us. Small waves sloshed against the thick timbers covered in barnacles.

"Well, here are the keys," she said, handing them to me.

A tarp covered the canisters in the back of the boat.

"Mica, let's not talk about this again. Tomorrow—"

"Whatever," she said and turned on her heel.

I ran after her, took her hand, spun her around, and kissed her so hard I thought I'd fall inside her. "Call me tomorrow, but let's not talk about this."

She smiled, touched a manicured nail to my nose. "I already don't know what you're talking about."

"Are you ready?" Zach said on the ridge.

I looked at my watch. We had a few more hours

before The Wedge crested the horizon. We would need every second to get down the mountain. "Yeah," I said.

Every second.

We slept in the cave again. I woke to water dripping on my forehead, tapping me awake, playing a staccato percussion rhythm on the remaining sleeping bags and tents. We left everything behind when we migrated to Amos's. Something scurried along the edge of the cave. I remembered the first time it rained inside. All the rats climbed the walls looking for high ground, perching on tarps and railings like birds and squealing at anyone nearby. We tried to kill as many as we could, but there were too many.

Zach screamed and sat up, threw a squealing rat at the wall. "Damn thing bit me," he said, holding his hand. He stood. "You know, we could do it all in one day, if we just timed it right. We have the train."

He was right. I knew it.

I lay back and ignored the sounds of the rats, the water dripping on my pillow. "I thought we had a gentleman's agreement not to discuss the fact that I'm stalling."

"You didn't say anything about carnivorous rats and sleeping in a hole."

"I was thinking, all the times I was ever bored or had nothing to do before the collapse. How I used to want to fast-forward everything. Problem with fast-forwarding is pretty soon it takes you to the end."

"Yeah, but. Rats."

I sat up. "All right, let's go."

The next day was just as rainy. We slipped and crawled up the muddy slope hauling the damn canisters. "You know, we could do this before the collapse," Zach said as he stepped over a fallen log, swung the second leg over, and sat down.

"And get caught with fifteen canisters of haze by a park ranger? That's not just a fine, you know."

"Right."

"Two more after this. One more climb."

I walked on, soaked. The muscles in my back were knotted where the canister rested to one side of my spine, fingers numb where I gripped the stock of the rifle. I had gotten it in my mind that after this trip we might go back for a while, maybe take a week of R & R back in the den before going on our final trip. The top of the hill was in view. I thought there might be a crack of blue hidden behind all the tree branches.

"Yuda, you hear that?"

I tried to still my breathing enough so I could hear anything other than the pounding of my heart, the tapping of water on leaves.

"Is that an airplane?" Zach said.

A buzzing, getting louder. Fast. A single engine streaked over the tops of the mountains.

"Who the hell would be flying a plane with them up there?" Zach said.

A shadow, like a large fish stalking its prey in a

shallow pond, followed the plane. I could only imagine the pilot inside, looking over his shoulder as the wings dipped to one side, then the other. They knew they were being followed. They must have been pretty desperate to even attempt flying, because the Air Force was the first thing to go.

A bolt shot out from the spacecraft; sparks flew from aft the wings. The nose of the plane angled down.

I didn't have time to say run. I didn't have to. What I should have said, though, was watch your step. I stepped on a loose rock, slipped, and tumbled forward. I tried to brace myself, rolled, heard a pop as my arm bent pitifully back on itself. There wasn't any pain until I skidded to a stop on top of the canister; then it felt like someone had tried to pry my arm off.

The airplane was blurred by tears as it swooped low overhead, wheels clipping the top of a pine tree and sending a spray of needles spiraling down. Branches snapped.

I couldn't move my arm.

The earth shook as the plane struck the mountain a hundred yards away. A fiery breath rose into the air, causing the tree limbs to shiver. More pine needles drizzled down.

I smelled haze. They'd struck the stockpile.

The breath of the spacecraft was hot as it passed over. Limbs shook nervously as if even the plant life were afraid of them. It hovered over the crash for a few moments, then turned and came back toward me.

I rolled onto my side, tried to stand, struggled to get enough leverage to lift the canister.

Zach was a ways down the hill, watching me, a terrified look on his face. He shook his head and kept running. I didn't blame him.

I heard hissing coming from behind me. Down the hill, Zach had only moved a few steps. The leaves swung slowly, even though I knew the motion should have been frantic as the propulsion bent each limb nearly in half. A storm of debris fell from the canopy.

I got scared when I realized I was no longer in pain. I was hazed.

There was a big lump on the top of my shoulder and my hand was on the ground, palm toward the sky, twisted backward.

I hyperventilated the steam coming out of the canister.

I couldn't lift my arm to shrug off the strap and couldn't reach my hand to move it.

I pulled my feet under me, tried to stand, fell back onto the canister. The trees swayed and bent.

Maybe if I just lay there and didn't move, *The Kind* wouldn't see me. I reached for the staff; it was a few feet away, a mere foot long hunk of gold, and stretched—just like the long mechanical arm that was descending through the trees, coming down like a viper about to drop to a jungle floor. I wriggled and managed to grab the staff.

The canister seemed heavier when the claws gripped

me, the straps digging into my shoulders. I was happy it was still spraying its toxic fumes as I spiraled upward through the trees.

It felt like what I imagined dying must be like, if there's a heaven. Just. Rising.

My breathing woke me. It felt like there was something inside my chest, filling up all the parts I needed.

It was complete dark, the blackness I'd known only inside the cave and so silent my thoughts echoed. I tasted blood.

The canister still pushed into my spine.

The pain returned instantly, like hot acid deep inside the shoulder joint. I grabbed the wrist of the bad arm and gave it a savage yank. Bursts of color, white and yellow and red, painted the darkness as the bone scraped its way back into the socket. It hurt too much to scream, too much to breathe.

I tried to calm myself. All I could think was that my broken body was no good and all the haze, the entire impetus of our plan, was ruined.

I'd always thought that we couldn't fail. We were destined to succeed. In the future, The Wedge is down. It has to go down.

It just didn't have to be me that took it down. It could have been the people in the plane. Or whoever they were trying to lead *The Kind* away from.

That had to be it. There was one man inside the plane.

He was leading them away from his family. Maybe they were in an airplane hangar and he knew they were coming.

Something slow and heavy moved across my leg. I kicked it off. The motion sent more colors of pain dancing in the darkness. It was the haze that made the pain a thing. It was the same thing it did with sex, why everyone couldn't help falling into orgiastic carnal pleasure when they were on it. The orgasm, the pumping, all of it became a pulsing blue psychic line you could feel in your entire body, like you were dancing with the sensation as much as driving in and out of your partner.

Mica's face surfaced from the darkness, hovering over me. I reached for her. She vanished, my fingers stirring and dispersing the smoke her mirage was made of.

A line of white light traced diagonally across the darkness, and hot pain seared my leg where the thing had touched me.

This was it. I was in the experiment. I was the witness in the abduction. A million torturous ideas flooded my brain, being stretched, shocked, injected, my intestines being slowly coiled on a spit as I watched.

The screaming didn't come from inside me. It was everywhere, radiating from every inch of my body. My throat was raw. I couldn't hear anything. Not my breathing, not the scratch of my clothing or the hiss of the canister. Nothing. My eyes felt dry and itchy. When I scratched, bits of sand stuck to my hand.

I knew what was happening. I was overdosed on

haze. I'd been inhaling everything from one fogger in an airtight room. Of course this room was airtight. It was a spacecraft. Everyone knew that after five minutes, you absolutely had to ventilate the space after a fogger. That's why the sitter wore a gas mask.

Something heavy was on my face, and the sound of my breathing returned. As I exhaled, the dark was driven back by a curious fog.

I reached up and ripped the mask off.

This isn't real.

The mask was heavy, dark green. The little round stamp on the inside right cheek was still there, my thumb clearly able to read *R.P.P.* like braille.

I set it aside, tried again to move.

The pain in my leg was real, like I'd been cut open and cauterized. I wasn't sure I could move it.

I flexed both hands, thinking I should start small. In the darkness, I'd need to orient myself by touch, even if it was only crawling.

The ship pitched to one side, and I slid off the canister and into a wall, my chest slamming against a sharp angle. I didn't think I could do it.

I prayed. I didn't know why.

I slipped the strap off my shoulder and rolled off the canister.

The roar of the engines filled my ears, and I realized I'd gotten exactly what I wanted, at least for the moment. I was inside a ship, probably heading toward The Wedge.

I was naive to think it would go perfectly. I wondered how the engines worked and what kind of propulsion system they used. The staff. I'd forgotten about the staff. I felt around with my hands, moved my legs back and forth like a kid creating a snow angel. I reasoned that it had to be near me because the ship just pitched to one side. I stretched. Crawling was nearly impossible with an arm that wouldn't bear weight. I pulled my knees up underneath me and shuffled forward. Eventually, I'd try walking. I'd put my foot down, and if nothing else, I'd swing my fist at the damn beasts when I saw them. Or I'd sneak around and find the propulsion system. I bet that just by turning dials and knobs and hitting buttons, the whole ship could come down. And there would have to be one button, perhaps under glass, that no one should ever touch. I'd touch that one, push it a hundred times, and hopefully lights would swirl and disco music would play as confetti made little tumbling spirals, and I'd ride that damn ship into the ground.

Careful, I thought. I knew what this was. This was the speedy part of the haze. This was when your mind wouldn't turn off and everything was intense and steady and more real than it should be; people had tried running marathons on it. People had tried, but their hearts exploded, so steady, stay calm, take a moment, and breathe. Just be.

I was looking for the staff, that little stumpy lump of gold that somehow allowed Reginald to do whatever he wanted. I shuffled again, almost tumbled as the ship rolled slightly to one side, then the other, not nearly as violently as before. Something clinked.

There. I slid toward it on my knees, trying to ignore the fact that I felt like a kid. At school, the teacher forced us to go outside even when there was snow on the ground. She helped me with my boots and once, out in the snow, me and this girl, we made tracks in the snow by doing this, sliding around on our knees, and I accidentally hit a rock, rammed it right into the soft flesh beneath the kneecap. She watched me as I cried. Watched as whatever good grace I'd been building up with her—Sam, that was her name—turned to fear and suspicion.

I shook the memory loose. I wasn't getting lost in the past. I'd done that before on haze, lying in bed. It was so easy to go back because everything was real on it, because everything materialized like Mica's face. I'd wasted an entire day watching that man take a leap off the building, seeing his face in every painful second as he disappeared inside a smoke ring and the blood rose out of the concrete around his body.

Careful, I warned, seeing him again. You're doing it. I took a deep breath, leaned back, intending to take the weight off my cramped knees, forgot that my right arm couldn't bear any weight. It crumbled and I fell hard backward, my quads hyperextended. A fiery burst of pain shot through my knees as I leaned to one side to unfold one leg, then the other—there. Right against my nose, the cold metal staff, shaped like an oval brick with smooth edges. I laughed.

It was a desperate laugh, the kind that jumps up and down on a tottering scale, begging a feather's weight to descend fully into hysteria. In the darkness, I had no idea if it was the staff or not. It could have been anything—a stray piece of pipe, whatever.

I pulled up my knees, rubbed the staff over them, felt a prickly cold seep into my bones from it, and wished like hell it would be the staff.

If there was a God, I didn't know what he'd look like. I tried to imagine him, at first as an old Confucian with a beard, a scroll stretched out before him, then wiped that wisp of smoke away. I tried a white man, also bearded, wearing an Arab robe, and wiped him away and made him the short green man with pointed ears carrying a staff as tall as he—a walking staff.

I reached forward into the smoke mirage and felt the block of golden staff grow thinner, longer. I tapped the tapered edge against the floor, and it made a hollow sound, like when Sergeant Brillow knocked on the fuselage of an S-33 fighter drone. I smiled. I was in the Air Force, after all. I might even be the last of my kind. The last fighting *Kind.*

I pictured the staff in Reginald's hands, dripping like candle wax into his famous golden stool, his pauper's throne, and felt the staff shift in my hands to form a hard, flat surface. I felt for the three feet and found them all in place. I picked up the stool by the leg and decided

I needed to walk. The staff's mass became centralized, long, thin, balanced. So that's how he controlled it. It was all about will, about telling it what he needed.

On my feet, it felt like liquid sloshed inside my skull so that if I tilted it too much one way or the other, its momentum threatened to pull me down. I took one easy step, placed the staff on the ground, and shuffled my weight forward. The ship pitched to one side. I staggered, used the staff to make myself into a tripod. The canister of haze rolled across the floor, making a sound like a giant marble, and crashed against the side of the ship.

The noise was so loud I froze. Doubts came over me; I had no idea where I was going, if they were watching me on infrared cameras, knowing my every move, laughing in whatever weird language they spoke.

The hull jostled again, and metal struck metal as the ship settled. A slit of light appeared at the end of the ship. It took me a moment to realize the hold of the spacecraft was opening. Behind me was a flat wall, a metal tentacle coiled in place on its surface, a large door in the corner that must have opened to a cockpit. The pilot would be coming out soon.

I ran and jumped onto the hangar floor. It was like being inside an aircraft carrier. All the ships were lined up. The air was frigid. I began to shiver. Behind me, an expanse of dazzlingly clear blue sky stretched to infinity. I almost lost my balance.

One of *The Kind* rolled out of the ship slowly, its tentacles whipping the ground with each revolution. Its skin wasn't black, as I'd always thought. It was brown, scaly, and dry. A tentacle shot out toward me, wrapped around my legs, and dragged me screaming across the floor.

It loomed over me, a hundred black eyes hidden within each scaly fold of skin. Part of the skin peeled back. A short, rounded beak snapped open and closed slowly, like it was trying to talk to me. I shoved the staff at the thing's mouth. The beak snapped closed with a terrible noise. One of its tentacles coiled around my wrist while another reached for the staff. I needed a sword.

The Kind made a shriek like a wounded crow and withdrew its tentacle from around the staff, now flat and serrated. Its eyes grew wide and it leaned forward, pinning my arm down while its beak loosed a terrible screech, its breath like rotten seaweed.

Don't hurt me, I thought. The beak closed slowly, its thousand eyes focused on the center of my nose, darting around my periphery. It moved back, lifting itself on its tentacles. Its eyes focused on the hand holding the staff, and slowly a long, snakelike tentacle curled around it like an Asclepius.

I inhaled deeply as my hand contracted, all the muscles inside my arm and shoulder going rigid as electricity flowed through the staff into me. I tried to scream. My mouth was sealed shut, teeth grinding.

I saw darkness littered with veiny orange autumnal structures; then *The Kind* released me, its eyes inspecting me. It moved backward quickly and did the best it could to prostrate itself, its tentacles lying flat and its eyes fixed on the ground in front of it.

"You can communicate through this, can't you?" I said, holding up the staff.

Its many eyes looked up at me, something sad within them like a dog. I followed its gaze to my leg.

My pants were torn. The flesh was black. Something hard had adhered itself to my leg.

"What is it?" I said.

I took a step forward. The thing got lower to the ground, like a cowering animal. I moved forward, holding the staff out before me, until it was less than an inch away from the thing's eyes.

It swelled briefly, its round body inhaling, then exhaled and shrank as all its eyes closed.

I drove the staff home.

The tentacles flailed, striking the floor with rapid staccato drumbeats. None of them struck me. I pushed harder and twisted the staff. It slid off whatever final resistance held it from slipping deeper, and the thing burst and sank so deep that I almost lost the staff inside.

The Kind fell limp, its tentacles ceasing to move as its body continued to shrink, pothole indentations forming on its head.

I pulled the staff free. Shock ran up my arm again, only it didn't stop at my chest; it ran down my injured leg, the fingers of electricity cramping my leg so hard I fell to the ground.

It felt like it was wrapping around my bone. The black thing on my leg, it was inside me, filaments moving and growing. I struck my leg with the staff, but it still didn't relent, the contraction so intense my bowels shifted. I touched the tip of the staff to the black area and screamed.

A bolt of electricity jumped from the tip of the staff and struck the black spot. Immediately the pressure on my bowels relented and I felt it withdrawing, pulling its tendrils, its bone-fine fingers out from my leg, stopping just above my knee. I touched the tip of the staff to it again. In my mind my scream was me pulling the trigger on a static gun. The shock went off, bright even behind my eyelids. The needle threads of the black thing pulled out completely.

The black thing rolled off my leg and onto the floor. I backed away. The thing had small, villi-like tentacles that shook and contracted like it was having a seizure, pulsing uncontrollably like a dysrhythmic heart. The villi shrank, withered, curled in on itself until it was like a dead spider.

I hit it with the staff, and it didn't move.

My leg hurt. A long laceration ran the length of my shin, deep enough to see stark-white bone.

I exhaled slowly. I'd made it safely aboard the ship. I'd killed one. Maybe one and a baby.

I didn't even look when I heard the sound of another ship approaching the landing bay; I just ran for the nearest door and touched the staff to the control beside it.

The door shot out of the way, disappearing into the wall, opening onto a huge compartment where metal tubes and ducts ran in a seemingly endless maze behind a metal latticework. Several stories above me, a platform led to another door.

The spacecraft touched down behind me with a metallic rumble. I decided that I wouldn't be able to climb with my shoulder, so I tucked the staff into my belt and went down.

I forced myself to hold on with the bad hand even though it was excruciating. I had no other choice. I kept the arm close to my body and stepped down, knowing that if I extended it, it would probably pop out of joint again. I wouldn't be able to stand the pain.

The rungs were round and rough, like the surfaces of barbells. I was maybe a few floors down when the doors opened above me. One of *The Kind*, this one's skin black, rubbery, not at all scaly like the other, flew across the chasm between walls, its tentacles catching the metal latticework before its body ever touched the wall and propelled itself up toward the next platform. I waited until the door closed behind it, and dropped down, finding a platform below me.

I touched the staff to the control. Nothing happened. I touched the tip to it again. Still nothing. The door above me opened, and I shoved the tip against the controls. "Open, damn it."

The staff sparked, and the door retracted into the

wall. I dashed inside.

A long hallway with a low ceiling was lined with flat metal beds on either side. My stomach curled and flipped. Bile rose in my throat. The skin sagged off the people in the beds, dripping almost, the melting remains of a skeletal system protruding beneath their blackening skin. Their teeth were encased by clear lips, dripping with a thick, viscous saliva. I could see their organs, contorted and shrinking beneath that slick, slimy exterior. Their limbs long, the bones of their arms separated. I placed the staff near one that looked vaguely feminine. It reached out and tried to grab it, the weakened bones of its arm flopping over it. Musculature was starting to form, however. It slowly tightened its grip on the staff. I expected it to communicate, as the one in the hangar had. Crackling sparks of electricity moved like an electron cloud from the remains of its head, into the trunk, down the arm, flickering until it disappeared into the staff. The charge didn't shock me; it reached my ears as a scream, a flash of recognition, a stretched syllable: *Help.*

I pulled the staff out and backed into the center of the room.

The door opened. Without thinking, I dashed underneath a bed. Tentacles, still endowed with all the bones of toes and hands, flopped onto both sides like curtains as two of *The Kind* came into the room, their tentacles easily propelling them over the beds. They stopped down the row and quickly retreated back the way they'd come. One of the tentacles draped over the side of the bed touched the staff. I was standing again, in front of a mirror, reaching toward a melting face as images flashed in my brain of a brutal war with sharp beaks and claws, tearing chunks from flesh, and then a boiling volcano spewing lava and ash high into the air. Then I was underwater, swimming after a fish, capturing it with my tentacles, and inserting something: a strangely sexual proboscis. Then I was the fish, darting and swimming faster than I had before.

The Kind retreated. The door closed, and I pulled the staff free of the tentacles. All four of them had wrapped around it. Both legs, the arms. The teeth chattered at me, the jaw unhinged, floating inside the strange, blackened, translucent body. All of them had been human. All of them were *The Kind.*

At the end of the row, I stopped at Zach's bed. I would have been able to tell it was his big, power lifter's body even if he hadn't been holding his crumpled red hat in his hands. His eyes were closed. Still. The back of his head was covered in the same kind of black thing that had been inside my leg. Half his skull was missing. I didn't need to touch the staff to him to find out what had happened. That he knew they were coming for him, that he decided he'd rather eat a bullet.

I moved on. There was nothing I could do but cry. He wouldn't have wanted me to do that.

I touched the staff to the door at the end of the room

and came to another tall shaft lined with rungs. There was another platform, maybe two stories up. I started climbing, my shoulder complaining with a grinding noise every time it bore weight. Twice the pain was so shocking I nearly let go. On the platform, my breath caught. I doubled over, clutching my shoulder to my body. It hadn't hurt with them inside me. It hadn't hurt at all. I tried to sort through the images, the memories it gave me. I realized it was an organism, all *The Kind* were a single organism, some deep-sea monster that had climbed from species to species until it had encountered something big. Something smart. Something almost human.

The next room was nowhere near as big. A central ring of red light glowed in the center around a long, rectangular shape in the middle, at least thirty feet long and fifteen feet tall. The shape struck me as a giant altar. I wondered if it was a sanctuary, a chapel of some sort. It hadn't even occurred to me that they might have religious beliefs, their own strange gods. Flashes of a congregation of *The Kind*, gathered around its slick steel surface ran through my mind. Maybe if I couldn't destroy The Wedge, I could destroy the pillar of their faith.

I walked around the glowing ring, daring not to cross it. There was something familiar about the size and shape of the altar; fifty feet long, ten feet high. I waved the tip of the staff over the ring of light, eyeing the walls, the ceilings, expecting a trap.

Nothing.

I stepped over the ring toward the altar. It was in a depression in the floor. I pictured *The Kind* rolling toward it, downhill. The surface was incredibly smooth, made of black metal. I walked around it and shuddered when I realized where I recognized the shape from. I reached my hand out, allowed my fingers to slide along the rough surface as I came to the back. It was built into the floor, rising as if a sheet had been draped over something on a table. If it had wheels, it could be a bus.

I touched the tip of the staff to the side, and it let out a steel gasp as a metal gill appeared on the side and slid back out of the way. I hesitated before the entrance, hefting the weight of the staff in my hand to keep me grounded, then stepped inside.

There was a control panel, made out of glass surfaces. Words scrolled across the surface, as did numbers. I got closer.

Time To Departure: 1:126:18:46

The *46* turned to *45,* then *44.*

It was a countdown. I stepped back. My heart hammered. I looked over the cabin, measuring it against memory. It had the dimensions of a train. All it needed was wheels. It didn't need wheels. It was affixed to the spacecraft. The spacecraft was the wheels.

I went back to the control panel, unnerved at how I reached for the monitor that read *Destination*: *-1 year. Earth.*

I snatched my hand back. It was in English. Everything was in English.

I touched the destination screen, selecting a positive

number a thousand years in advance, changed the departure time to ten minutes.

The door retracted with a loud metal shriek as I hit the button. I heard the rush of *The Kind*'s tentacles flailing at the floor as they moved into the room outside the train.

I peered through the door. They were waiting for me, their hundreds of eyes focused on me. The red ring of light pulsed beneath their tentacles, making them look like demons.

I stepped out of the train. "I know you understand me," I said, waving the staff as a warning.

A tentacle slithered toward me, and I touched the tip of the staff to it. A burst of electricity sent a spark, and the thing withdrew behind a wisp of smoke.

I pointed the staff at a wall and willed it again. A crooked bolt of electricity shot out and struck the wall, superheating the steel as the electricity moved through it, melting a hole into the next chamber, but not without consequences. The shock radiated through the floors and the ceiling. Every muscle of my body contracted. I bit off the tip of my tongue. When the electrical pulse passed, I fell to my knees.

The Kind was affected, too. Their tentacles writhed and slapped and curled into themselves, turning each one into giant, spiderlike balls.

As they regained their consciousness, I pushed myself to my feet and ran for the hole in the wall I'd created. There were different varieties of them; some had smooth black or brown skin, a row of clearly defined teeth, and only two eyes; others were scaly and brown, black or gray with beaks, like the one I'd killed above in the hangar.

I moved a glowing red stalactite of melting metal out of the way with the staff, then jumped through.

I couldn't hear anything over the rushing wind and electrical storm. The chamber had a huge, conical shape in the middle ascending toward the ceiling where an electrical coil snapped and hummed, bolts of static electricity flashing within its core. Huge conductors ran to smaller towers on the sides, creating a constant downdraft and the hum of machinery. It reminded me of being inside the Hoover Dam, the turbines whining.

The Kind attempted to push through the small hole I'd made in the wall and shrieked as they retreated, too large to squeeze through without touching the hot metal edges. Tentacles shot toward me through the hole as I ran around the cylinder. There were five ahead of me. The air was thick and potent. These are the engines, I thought. The reactor above was the core that powered them.

A caution sign warned of radiation high on the walls, and I suddenly remembered that I was still on haze. My vision was blurry. I prayed I wasn't imagining all of this.

I came to a curve in the wall, where another door was recessed. I touched the tip of the staff to the control. It opened quickly. Tentacles shot through, gripping the inside of the doorway and propelling their bulbous bodies forward.

I backed up and gave what must have been a bloody

smile as an endless stream of them poured through the entrance, climbing the walls, clinging to it. I watched as they surrounded me, even climbing above me onto the cylindrical turbines. I spit blood on the floor. It reminded me of being in the cave, when Reginald first returned on the train, all of them clinging to the walls, waiting.

Something flashed behind me in the flickering way of an arc welder. The hole I'd seared in the side of the room with the train in it was a mesh of electricity. Even though I couldn't see outside, I knew none of them had checked the train; we were traveling through time. Maybe through space.

The tentacles of *The Kind* were restless, twitching like a predatory cat's tail. I wondered if they knew it was over.

"Study hard." I touched the tip of the staff to the wall of the central turbine behind me, willed a final burst of electricity from it.

In the all-consuming white light, Mica reached for me.

Chapter 17

Amos

A minute can be a long time. A minute standing in the sun while sweat drips down your neck, as horseflies dart at your head, testing your reflexes, your patience, can be a very long time. The sun glistened on the rails where the rusted iron had been sheared to silver from use.

Thomas tapped his watch. Even from where I stood, I could see the seconds ticking by. It had been more than a minute. The sun beat down. A car rolled toward us, trailing dust swirls. The driver waved as it passed. We shielded ourselves from the dust.

"Something must have happened," Thomas said.

Yuda didn't want us to go after them. He said, "We'll come back in a minute, in a few weeks, with a great story to tell," and we waited through a minute that felt like a week. They were gone. They didn't even tell us the time or location they were going to so we could go and stop them from dying.

"Where's number one?"

"Reginald has it."

"Three?"

"In the station."

I wanted to be alone. Rosaline was in the house, and she still wasn't talking to me. I couldn't blame her. The entire world had been snatched out from beneath her feet.

I went into the den, climbed aboard, and got the train moving, enjoying the way it felt, the way a normal train feels, before the fingers of God brought me to another time.

The bowl of grass was as I remembered, a shimmering oasis tucked away in the mountains, the long, lush grass swaying in the breeze. If there was a heaven, this might be it.

Number one, the original train, was in the middle of the pasture. Reginald was here.

I checked the train. He wasn't inside. The sky was clear, the sun warm. No spacecraft darted on the horizon. In the distance, where the vinous pedestal had risen out of the earth, was nothing.

I didn't want to be afraid anymore. I didn't want to fear the future. I climbed to the edge of the bowl, where the tracks stopped, and looked down and saw The Wedge half-buried in the wasteland. Dust devils swirled down the side of the desert mountain, drawing my gaze to a trail of depressions in the gravelly sand leading down the hill.

I set out, half-aware that I was probably going to get myself killed, that whatever I might find inside, Reginald or otherwise, might be too much to handle. Even though The Wedge was down, it didn't mean *The Kind* that remained weren't still using it the way we used the den.

I picked up a rock. That was a stupid idea, just like it was stupid to try to keep everything from Rosaline. I knew that I could go back, that I should, but it felt dirty. Like, God forgive me, something Reginald would do.

Small landslides preceded me as I slid down the hill. Pebbles worked their way into my shoes. My heel caught something, a rock buried beneath the surface, sending shooting pain up my leg. My momentum lifted my body away from the surface of the mountain. I might as well have pole-vaulted. I tumbled forward, and red earth and sky alternated in a cloud of dust.

I lay on the ground a while, spitting dirt, wiping it from my eyes, before getting up. I lifted each leg, shaking off my pant legs, and thanked God I hadn't broken anything. It was going to be a long climb. I was thirsty. I hadn't even brought water.

The Wedge was taller than any building in New York, wider than the largest warehouse I'd ever laid eyes on. Some of the metal was streaked black on the underside where there had been an explosion. I shuddered, remembering my time overseas, all those men climbing Omaha Beach, sacrificing their lives so the man behind them could take a few steps farther.

Nice job, Yuda, I thought.

I hadn't liked his plan. He said it didn't matter.

The night we sat watching the fireflies and drinking whiskey, he said, "I could just wait, hoping someone else will come along and do it at some point."

He wasn't wired like that. I knew that the moment I met him.

"I used to think everyone had something like that. That maybe there was one great thing we could achieve. Most people can't tell the difference," Yuda said. "God, is talk cheap."

There was a hole in the side of The Wedge a few feet off the ground. The removed panel lay submerged in red sand. There were claw marks around the edges of the hole. The corner of the panel was turned up as though something had tried to pry its way inside.

I lifted myself and stared into the darkness. It was surprisingly spacious, a single shaft running at a forty-five-degree rise with ladderlike rungs. I climbed, cursing myself for being so stupid, for even trying this. I should have stayed home. I should have made up with Rosaline. I should have gone back and changed that. I was a country boy. I had no business being anywhere thousands of years in the future.

I stopped at the first platform I came to, a tilted hunk of metal with doors half retracted into the wall, to catch my breath. A drop of sweat fell sideways, onto the wall. Suddenly I felt very dizzy and clung to the rungs. I was in an alien ship hundreds of years in the future. I had no business. I could have lived out my years blissfully unaware of all of it.

"What fresh hell is this?"

I straightened, swallowing hard.

Reginald stepped from the darkness into a ray of light created by a crater in the ceiling or perhaps what used to be a wall.

"I came to find you."

"It isn't safe here, Amos." Reginald was wearing a heavy leather coat. His spectacles were red until he took another step forward and the light caught his face, at which time they turned clear and I briefly saw his eyes, squinting at me, before they became dark and tinted, shielding the light. It smelled like burnt diesel fuel. "You should know that. You've been here before." His staff struck the floor as he came forward.

I motioned to it with a hand that felt weak, powerless. "I thought you gave that to Yuda."

Reginald held the staff to the side, inspecting it as if he hadn't realized he'd been holding it. "Yes, well, I knew where to find it," he said, waving the staff in an arc at his surroundings.

"So it was Yuda."

"Yes, it was Yuda. Careful."

I stepped to the side, right into what he'd warned me about. Tentacles quickly wrapped around my leg and pulled me down. My head hit the floor, and the ceiling rushed by as I was dragged to a corner of the room and lifted off my feet.

Reginald rushed up the sloping floor toward me where I hung upside down.

"Let him go," Reginald said, poking the staff into *The Kind*.

It let out a hissing sound, and I smelled its breath: stale tire air and rotting flesh.

I gagged.

"Let him go," Reginald commanded, stabbing it with the staff.

I fell, and Reginald nearly caught me, or at least he stopped my head from being the first thing to hit the ground.

He helped me to my feet. I pushed him away, backing into the center of the room, where the light was. I wiped at my face.

The Kind was in a corner, partially hidden by the bars of a cage made out of the ladder rungs I'd climbed to reach the room, the edges of which had been soldered together.

I glanced at Reginald. Suddenly the jacket, exhaust smell, and spectacles made sense. He'd been welding.

"What is that?"

Reginald extended the staff at an angle. "Would you like to speak to him?"

"Him, who?"

"Well, you'll just have to find out, won't you?"

I took the staff. It vibrated in my hands, making the muscles in my forearm contract. I couldn't have dropped it if I'd wanted to.

"Go on," Reginald said.

I stepped forward. The thing looked very sad, its black eyes wary. Two of its tentacles were wrapped around the bars; the other two dangled near the front of the cage like feet. I took a few more steps, and they stretched out straight, reaching for me, not aggressively but curiously, like a circus elephant's trunk. I extended the tip of the staff slowly, until just the point of its tentacle could connect with the handle.

I was no longer in the room next to Reginald. I was alone, next to a giant metal surface generating electricity, surrounded by *The Kind*. I touched the edge of the staff to the metal and was blown off my feet, through the arms of a waiting woman and into one of *The Kind*, which wrapped its tentacles around me, shielding me from the blast. I woke, alone, without the staff, with something black affixed to the bottom half of my charred legs, my buttocks, and my back, consuming it. Consuming me. I was crying.

Then I was alone, floating above an orange plain, two suns hanging in the air, the insistent whispers of an old lady flowing through me, shouting a warning as a golden baton tumbled out of oblivion toward me. Then Morris was on his side in some sort of infirmary, a gaping wound on his back filled with darkness.

The thing removed its tentacle, and I snapped back to the present, staring at what used to be Yuda in the cage. Its tentacles dropped to the floor, like it had used the last of its energy.

Reginald snatched the staff from me. "Interesting, isn't it? How one person can undergo such a dramatic change."

"Why is he locked up?"

The thing in the cage hissed.

"Would you let him out? Look at him. He's clearly not human anymore. He's like the rest of them. Maybe not as many tentacles as the ones that came from space, but he's not the same."

I backed away from him.

"Rrmmm," a voice tried to speak.

I turned, facing the darkness. I couldn't see anything in its depths beyond the single slice of sunshine. "Who's there?"

"Might as well take the tour," Reginald said. "Go on."

I stepped into the light, through it, waited as my eyes adjusted. Someone was in a corner. At first, I thought it was another one of those things like Yuda; then I saw that it was still human, secured firmly with ropes that were tied to rungs above, below, and beside it at angles that made them look like tentacles.

She shook her head wildly, moaning something unintelligible through the gag, begging me not to come near. Her hair was matted, and dirt streaked her face. She wasn't clothed. The ropes were cutting red swaths into the flesh on her wrists, her upper thighs. I knelt and tried to pull the gag out of her mouth. It was so tight I couldn't move it without untying it, and when I did, she spit the filthy rag out.

"Behind you," she shouted.

Not for the first time, Reginald knocked me unconscious.

I woke with my wrists tied, arms straight out to the sides, with a splitting headache fueled by the bright sun streaming through the hole in the hull of The Wedge. A wet rag was crammed in my mouth.

I struggled, testing the ropes.

"Ah, nice to see you're awake. I must admit I've become a fan of not rushing. Not hurrying things along. Taking the seconds, waiting, reflecting. Meditating like a smooth lake at dawn. Would you like to speak?"

I nodded.

"No yelling," Reginald said before removing the gag. "Shouts echo in this tin can."

I spit the gag out and tried to still my racing heart with a few deep breaths.

Reginald's eyebrows rose. He waited, taking the moment.

"Evelyn," I said.

"How do you know my name?" she said from the corner.

"Volume," Reginald shouted, striking the floor with his staff. The metal reverberated with the impact and left a dent in the floor.

"He's obsessed with you," I whispered. "I was there, the thing with his sister."

"The intervention," Reginald said, looking out at the landscape.

I twisted my arms, trying the ropes again. They were securely fastened.

"Reginald, I have to use the bathroom," I said.

"Piss yourself," he said.

I looked at the corner where the thing that used to be Yuda was. His tentacles were stretched out straight toward the ropes fastened to the walls, still nearly a foot away.

"I haven't seen Charles in a while, come to think of it," I said.

Reginald looked over his shoulder at me, the light slanting in across his nose behind the spectacles.

"When exactly did you try to kill me?" I said.

Reginald laughed. "Which time? There were so many. Some I didn't even tell you about. It was a bit of a pastime, I must admit. You and that family. Never seemed to get old."

"Monster," Evelyn said.

"Me? Look at that thing in the corner! That's a monster I could just as easily turn you into." Reginald hurried toward a corner and slid a small flap of metal aside. He pulled a black, writhing mass from a hole in the wall and held it in front of Evelyn's face. "Would you like that?" he said, pushing it toward her. The tentacles stretched and reached for her, like Yuda's still stretching toward the ropes. His body was beginning to contort, pressing through the bars of his cage.

Reginald lowered the writhing black mass. "We could be together. We could read each other's thoughts with a touch. I could finally understand you."

"Get it away from me!"

Reginald slapped her with the staff and, in the same motion, wheeled and threw the little black thing at the wall. It struck the hull with a dull thump, then came scurrying back, skittering faster than a shadow, a demon, across the floor toward her.

Evelyn screamed so loud it hurt my ears.

Yuda was inches from the rope.

Reginald bent and screamed at her, matching her fury, his spectacles glowing red. That's when I knew there was no going back for him. All the times he'd taken me with him, to Russia, to save his sister, were just an act. He was never going to change.

He stood and jammed the staff into the ground, spearing the black alien thing at the last second before it leapt onto Evelyn. Its tentacles writhed, and its body trembled and convulsed, its sides massaging the air with its fury. Reginald stooped, picked it up, and walked back to where he'd been keeping it. He threw it inside and slammed the metal flap shut.

The tension on my left arm slackened. I didn't look.

"Quit torturing her, Reginald," I said.

He ambled over to me, hands behind his back.

"Can't you see you're torturing yourself?" I said.

"Me? I'm torturing myself?" Reginald laughed. "Sure, try to play mind games with me. I'll bite."

"You love her, don't you?"

Reginald's face went blank. "Yes."

"More than anything. You'd move mountains for her."

"Yes."

"And yet, you still don't get that hurting her is making you into a monster."

Reginald stepped forward suddenly, getting right in my face. "I was made a monster long before she stopped loving me!"

"Reggie," Evelyn said. She was crying. I could hear it in that one word. "I do love you. Just not like this. I can't love you like this. Why don't you let me go? We can go back, to when we first met." Her voice was choked with grief.

"You don't have to do this," I said.

Reginald walked over to her, held her chin by thumb and forefinger. "Oh, you'd like that, wouldn't you?"

She nodded. "I would."

"Don't insult me like that," Reginald said, dropping her chin. "Don't you think I've tried? Don't you think, maybe, the first thing that occurred to me was to go back and try it again? To go back and try everything again?" He raised the staff at her, and she cowered.

"Reginald," I called. "Reginald, why didn't that little alien thing attack you?"

He turned to me. "An intelligent question. I'm impressed, Amos." The staff morphed into a stool, and he sat in front of me. "I'm very impressed." He took out a small knife from his coat's hip pocket. "Let me show you," he said, unfolding the blade and sinking it into his forearm.

I gasped. Evelyn screamed—which made Reginald smile.

He removed the knife. The wound didn't bleed as he dug his fingers in, peeling back the skin like plastic. "It's inside of me already." There was no blood inside of him, no human tissue, just a semitranslucent gelatinous material through which sparks of electricity jumped and traveled as he flexed his hand.

"I don't understand," I said.

"Well, allow me to explain." He folded the flap of skin back and rolled out the sleeve. "I'm too much for it," he said simply.

"What?"

"I'm too much for it."

"You're too much for an alien race that's completely taken over your body?"

"My will," Reginald said. "Too strong, too potent to be subjugated. Look at that heap in the corner, either corner. Do you think an invasive species would have any trouble breaking their spirits on a molecular level?"

I glanced at Yuda. His tentacles were coiling over themselves, his body puffed up, ready to attack.

"He's more of a man than you'll ever be. Even like that."

Reginald stood. "What did you say?"

"He's more of a man than you are. You know what he did? He sacrificed himself. Don't believe me? Go touch your damn cane to him and see what he shows you. He had a woman, too," I said, not even aware I knew the words until they toppled out of my mouth. "He could have gone back, could have spent an eternity of extra seconds trying to make her love him, and instead . . ."

Reginald was inches from my face.

I sighed. "I'm wasting my breath."

He wound up and punched. I pulled my head to the side at the last second and yanked the end of the rope free. I grabbed Reginald, wrapped the rope around his neck as Yuda's tentacles grabbed the far end of the rope and pulled it tight, stretching it tight between us. Yuda's other tentacles reached forward, wrapped around Reginald's neck, and let the rope go slack as he pulled Reginald toward him.

I grabbed the knife out of Reginald's hip pocket and cut myself free.

Reginald continued to struggle even as his skin turned ashen. He nearly had his fingers under Yuda's tentacles.

I picked up the chair and thought, I want to kill Reginald. The cold molten gold dripped around and through my hand, lengthening into a lance. I charged, focusing on Reginald's red eyes.

The lance slipped deep within Reginald and fired a pulse. White light filled the cavernous space.

I woke when the sun was far lower on the horizon.

Reginald sat below the cage, Yuda's limp coil of tentacles draped around him, his body sagging, pressing through the bottom rungs of the cage, unmoving, deflated.

Evelyn cried in the corner.

The staff was still inside Reginald. I pushed on the end of it, half expecting his eyes to open, for him to grab me, but he didn't move. When I pulled the staff out, his shoulders slumped and he fell to one side.

I untied Evelyn, and she threw her arms around me. She was smaller than Rosaline. I found her pants and gave her my shirt. "Come on," I said, and together we climbed the mountain and went back to the train.

A spacecraft hovered over the mountains, its red eye watching us.

"We need to hurry," I said as it drew near.

It stopped at the edge of the meadow and the vinous platform I'd seen as a child rose to cradle it.

I knew then that we would never defeat them. Whatever organism had taken over Reginald and deformed Yuda, it lived inside the earth. It wouldn't give it back.

I helped Evelyn board the train and looked down at the controls. I'm still there, I thought. I could go back, an hour, even less, and Reginald would still be there in The Wedge, fighting us. Maybe even winning.

"What are you doing?" Evelyn said.

"You're going to have to trust me," I said and set our destination.

Chapter 18

Amos

We arrived back exactly where we started. I came around the front of number one to familiar voices.

"Perhaps we should start again," Reginald said. "I'm Sir Reginald of Raleigh, descendant of President Walter Hindsley and currently the only emissary to *The Kind*. Please, sit and introduce yourselves."

"You're more than just an emissary," I called. "Hi, Charles. Children, don't bother sitting." It was hard to believe I was ever so small. And Rosaline, she was just as beautiful as I remember her being, cheeks on fire, indignant.

"Who are you?" Reginald snapped. He held his staff like a club.

"I'm Amos. A little bit older." I winked at myself. "And I believe you know this woman," I said as Evelyn rounded the corner.

"Evelyn," Reginald gasped.

Evelyn didn't say anything. She walked up to

Reginald and slapped him in the face. The staff flew out of his hands. "You have no right," she growled.

I stopped next to Charles. "Have we met yet?" I said.

"Just now," Charles said. "You know me?"

"You teach science to kids. I'm a little further along than you. Can I have the red bottle?"

Charles got sheepish.

"Evelyn, how are you here right now? I thought, during the collapse . . ." Reginald stammered.

"You brought me here, you piece of shit."

"I . . . brought you?"

"You murderous, evil man. I wish I'd never met you." Evelyn spit on the ground at his feet.

I held my hand out to Charles. He reached into his pocket without saying a word and placed the red bottle in my hands. I unstoppered it and drank it all.

Sitting in the grass, my past self looked down at the bottle as it drained before him. I hated the memory of it just as much as the taste as it slid down my throat.

"I'm sorry, Charles," I said and struck him with Reginald's staff.

His hips twisted to one side, his knees buckled and fell to the ground. His mouth hung open, a few blades of grass bending around his mouth.

Reginald pushed Evelyn aside and came toward me.

"After all you did to bring her here, you're just going to push her aside?" I said. "Temper, temper."

Reginald looked at the staff in my hand. "What have you done?" he gasped, looking around for his staff.

"Looking for this?" Evelyn said, holding the staff from the future.

"What is this? Whatever it is you think I've done, I haven't done it yet."

"You know," I said to Reginald, "that's just the thing. It's all happening at once. That's the only way to explain me standing here, talking as an adult in front of my future wife. And you can't really save anyone. You can't even save yourself."

The children looked at each other.

In the distance, the spaceship hovered over the vinous landing pad as it grew out of the ground to cradle it.

"And you," I said to Reginald. "You already have it inside you, don't you?"

"Have what?" he growled.

"Reginald," Evelyn said.

Reginald turned as Evelyn drove the staff into his belly.

"I hate you," she said, and whatever toxic energy had bound them together for so long fractured inside the staff. A burst of electric light threw them apart, and the staff in my hand crumbled to dust, a breeze scattering the particles into the grass.

"Children, your ride is here," I said, taking Charles's knife off his hip and tucking it into my pocket.

They looked from me to each other, turned, saw the spacecraft. Rosaline screamed and tried to run. I grabbed her, glad that my senses were dulled as I bruised the skin of her arm.

Amos attacked me, telling me to let her go. I grabbed

him by the hair and dragged him across the field toward the ship.

The children were heavy. I had to push Amos to the ground and put my knee in his back, tell him he would be fine, until he nodded and said "Uncle" three times before he finally walked on his own.

I was tenacious but no match for my adult self with the red liquid coursing through my veins, making me strong. I couldn't have done it without it. I would have doubted the choice. I would have doubted everything. I never would have been able to drag Rosaline by the soft flesh of her arm through the reedy grass, soiling her dress. I missed her, wondered if I'd ever be able to hold her again, and I knew if I ever saw her again she'd remember me as this, a monster accosting her in the most traumatic event of her life.

The vinous structure was made out of some kind of dark green hardwood, knotty in spots, with oval leaves growing on the handrails and a net of vine forming walls up the spiral staircase. I threw them onto the steps and pulled Charles's knife.

"Walk," I said.

Rosaline had tears in her eyes. Amos's cheeks were hot with anger, striped with scratches from the grass. There were claw marks on his forehead, but I didn't remember scratching him.

"You're not me," he said. "I would never do this."

At that moment I understood Reginald and his

twin ambitions completely, to save the world and endear himself to Evelyn, how those desires could conspire to drag him down. He could have been a great man, if only saving the world hadn't been about making her love him.

"Walk," I said.

They cried as they climbed.

"You don't have to do this," Amos said, tears in both our eyes.

"I don't have a choice."

"That's not true," Amos said, facing me. "It's all about choice. That's what it's all about! That's what my father said."

And it was true. My father had said that. But my father had carved an idiot. He didn't know anything.

"Today it's about sacrifice. Now walk," I said.

It wasn't about Jesus. It wasn't about God. It was about Me.

Rosaline took Amos's hand, and together they turned and ascended the stairs. The mountains appeared to circle us as we climbed higher and higher. The air became crisp and cool. The clouds grew closer, more expansive. The shadow of *The Kind* loomed.

We rounded the final turn in the stairs. The children stepped forward, confronted by their vague reflection in the icy steel side of the spacecraft. They huddled together as the side slid open, revealing darkness.

"Give us a chance," Amos said.

"You've already failed," I said.

Tentacles shot out from the spacecraft.

Chapter 19

Amos

"You're too young to be a hobo," the man in the chair said, his voice surprisingly girlish.

I sat in the office just next to the station platform, three men surrounding me.

"Listen," the man in the chair said, "this is a hard life. Why don't you go home?"

"Can't rightly say," I said. I knew I should be nervous, worried they were going to hurt me, but I wasn't. "Are you fellas going to rough me up or cut me loose?"

He sighed and gathered up my things spread on the desk: my father's silver pocket watch, the matches and twine I used to start fires, a drawing of my mother one of her friends had done, and motioned for me to take them.

"Don't let me catch you in New York again, you hear?" he said in a high, nasally voice.

"Thank you, sir. You won't, sir."

I stopped at the door, one foot out. A train whistle blew, and I could hear the slow chugging of the pistons beginning to fire as it began to pull away. "I'll be sure to catch the first train out of the city," I said, slammed the door behind me, and bolted.

I saw her on the train platform, her gaze following me as I ran through the crowd, the bulls not too far behind. I cut across the platform, weaving through the people like I was cutting out after church, heading for the river to fish, and jumped on the last car of the train as it left the station.

I laughed at the bulls, all out of breath and bent over on the platform, and blew the young lady a kiss. I watched till she was no more than a speck on the horizon. I couldn't explain how I knew that if I could have talked to her, I would have married her. I dreamed about her for years after. Even when I found work in Cincinnati and settled down with a girl named Marilyn, it felt like she was still there on the platform, watching as the train raced ahead, separating us by unfathomable distances, and no matter how much time passed, it always felt as if we were just a second away from knowing each other.

Acknowledgments

There are so many people I must thank, but none more than Megan, who gives me the time, space, and encouragement needed to create, and my muse, Scruffy, who listens diligently to every word and keystroke.

Thanks to my parents for believing in my artistic goals even when it pained them.

To Laurie Ellis for nurturing a seed of creativity I had nearly forgotten about in my late teens.

To everyone who has helped me hone my writing over the years, including all my friends and mentors at Stonecoast, and especially Michael Kimball.

To my editor, Emily Steele, for believing in this book from the beginning and helping make it the best it can be. To Arturo Delgado, for the fantastic cover art, and everyone else at Medallion.

To G, for giving me not only the dream that inspired the book but the drive and ability to write it.

And, finally, to my readers. Thanks for making it this far.